Affair

700818

Amanda Quick

Affair

Large Type

c. 1

WHEELER
PUBLISHING, INC.
ROCKLAND, MA

★ AN AMERICAN COMPANY ★

Published in Large Print by arrangement with Bantam Books, a division of Bantam Doubleday Dell Publishing Group, Inc. in the United States and Canada.

Wheeler Large Print Book Series.

Set in 16 pt Plantin.

Library of Congress Cataloging-in-Publication Data

Quick, Amanda.
    Affair / Amanda Quick.
      p. (large print) cm.(Wheeler large print book series)
    ISBN 1-56895-475-1 (hardcover)
    1. Large type books.
I. Title. II. Series
[PS3561.R44A69 1997b]
813'.54—dc21   97-29621
                                                      CIP

For Irwin Applebaum,
with great respect and admiration.

Your commitment to publishing popular fiction has altered the landscape of the book world. You have brought new writers with fresh, new voices and a legion of enthusiastic new readers into mainstream publishing. But, then, you always understood that telling a good story was what it was all about.

My thanks.

Affair

Prologue ❧

Midnight
London

Charlotte never knew what it was that awakened her in the early hours before dawn. Perhaps her sleeping brain had registered the squeak of a floor tread or a man's muffled voice. Whatever the cause, she opened her eyes abruptly and sat straight up in bed. She was consumed with a sense of overwhelming urgency. A cold foreboding permeated her entire body.

It was the housekeeper's night off. Her stepfather, Winterbourne, never came home before dawn these days. Charlotte knew that she and her sister, Ariel, should have been alone in the house.

But someone had just climbed the staircase and walked down the hall.

She tossed aside the covers and stood, shivering, on the cold floor. For a moment she had not the least notion of what to do next.

Another floorboard groaned.

She went to the door, opened it a few inches, and gazed out into the darkened corridor. Two figures shrouded in voluminous greatcoats hovered in the dense shadows at the end of the hall. They stood in front of Ariel's door.

One of the men held a candle. The light revealed Winterbourne's thick, dissipated features.

"Be quick about it," Winterbourne said in a slurred growl. "And then be on your way. It's almost dawn."

"But I wish to enjoy this rare pleasure. It is so seldom that one has the opportunity to savor a genuine virgin descended from such excellent bloodlines. Fourteen, did you say? A good age. I intend to take my time, Winterbourne."

Charlotte bit back a scream of rage and fear. The second man's voice was a darkly played musical instrument, a thing of grace and power even when pitched at a whisper. It was a voice that could have soothed wild animals or sung hymns but it was the most terrifying sound she had ever heard.

"Are you insane?" Winterbourne hissed. "Hurry and be done with it."

"You do owe me a great deal of money, Winterbourne. Surely you do not expect to settle the debt by allowing me only a few minutes with my very expensive little innocent. I want an hour at the very least."

"Impossible," Winterbourne muttered. "The older girl's just down the hall. She's a bitch. Absolutely ungovernable. If you wake her, there's no telling what she'll do."

"That is your problem, not mine. You are the master in this household, are you not? I shall leave it to you to deal with her."

"What the devil do you expect me to do if she awakens?"

"Lock her in her room. Bind her. Put a gag in her mouth. Beat her senseless. I care not how you manage the matter, just see to it that she does not interfere with my pleasures."

Charlotte eased her bedroom door closed and whirled around to gaze wildly about her moonlit bedchamber. She took a deep breath, collected her panic-stricken senses, and hurried across the carpet to a chest that stood near the window.

She fumbled with the lock of the chest, got it open, and yanked aside the two blankets on top. The case that contained her father's pistol lay at the bottom of the chest.

Charlotte grabbed the case, opened it with trembling fingers, and removed the heavy weapon. It was unloaded. There was nothing she could do about that. She lacked the necessary powder and ball as well as the time to figure out how it all went into the pistol.

She went to the door, flung it open, and stepped out into the hall. She knew intuitively that the stranger who intended to rape Ariel was the more dangerous of the two men. She sensed that he would be emboldened by any show of anxiousness or uncertainty, let alone a glimpse of the raw panic that was coursing through her.

"Stop at once or I will shoot," Charlotte said quietly.

Winterbourne lurched about in surprise. The

3

flame of his candle revealed his gaping mouth. "Hell's teeth. Charlotte."

The second man turned more slowly. His greatcoat swirled around him with a soft, rustling sound. The weak flame of Winterbourne's candle did not cast any light on his features. He had not removed his hat. The wide brim, together with the high collar of his coat, obscured his face in deep shadows.

"Ah," he murmured. "The older sister, I presume?"

Charlotte realized that she was standing in a stream of moonlight that poured from her window through the open door. The stranger could likely see the outline of her body silhouetted through her white linen nightgown.

She wished with all her heart that the pistol she held was filled with a ball and a strong charge. She had never hated anyone as much as she hated this creature. Nor had she ever been so frightened.

In that moment her imagination threatened to run roughshod over her intelligence. Some elemental part of her was convinced that it was not a mere man she faced, but a monster.

Guided only by instinct, Charlotte said nothing. She wrapped both hands around the pistol, raised it with deliberate precision, just as though it were fully loaded, and cocked it. The unmistakable sound was very loud in the quiet hall.

"Damnation, girl, are you mad?" Winterbourne surged forward and then came to a shambling halt a few feet away. "Put down the pistol."

"Get out." Charlotte did not allow the weapon to waver. She kept her whole attention focused on the monster in the black greatcoat. "Both of you. Get out now."

"I do believe she means to pull the trigger, Winterbourne." The monster's mellifluous voice oozed honey and venom and a terrifying degree of amusement.

"She would not dare." But Winterbourne took a pace back. "Charlotte, listen to me. You cannot be so foolish as to think that you can simply shoot a man in cold blood. You will hang."

"So be it." Charlotte held the pistol steady.

"Come, Winterbourne," the monster said softly. "Let us be off. The chit means to lodge a bullet in one of us and I rather think she intends to make me her victim. No virgin is worth this much trouble."

"But what about my vouchers?" Winterbourne asked in a quivering voice. "You promised you would give them back to me if I let you have the younger girl."

"It would appear that you must find some other way to pay your debts."

"But I have no other resource, sir." Winterbourne sounded desperate. "There is nothing left to sell that will fetch enough to cover my losses to you. My wife's jewelry is gone. Only a bit of the silver remains. And I do not own this house. I am merely renting it."

"I'm sure you will come up with some

5

means of repaying me." The monster walked slowly toward the staircase. He did not take his attention off Charlotte. "But make certain that whatever it is, it does not require me to get past an avenging angel armed with a pistol in order to secure my payment."

Charlotte kept the pistol trained on the stranger as he went down the stairs. By avoiding Winterbourne's candle, he managed to keep himself cloaked in shadow the entire time. She leaned over the banister and watched as he opened the front door.

To her horror, he paused and looked up at her. "Do you believe in destiny, Miss Arkendale?" His voice floated up to her from out of the night.

"I do not concern myself with such matters."

"Pity. Given that you have just demonstrated that you are one of those rare persons with the power to shape it, you really ought to pay more attention to the subject."

"Leave this house."

"Farewell, Miss Arkendale. It has been amusing, to say the least." With a last swirl of his greatcoat, the monster was gone.

Charlotte was able to breathe again. She turned back to Winterbourne.

"You, too, sir. Begone, or I shall pull this trigger."

His heavy features worked furiously. "Do you know what you have done, you stupid bitch? I owe him a bloody fortune."

"I do not care how much you have lost to him. He is a monster. And you are a man

6

who would feed an innocent child to a beast. That makes you a monster, too. Get out of here."

"You cannot throw me out of my own house."

"That is just what I intend to do. Leave, or I shall pull this trigger. Do not doubt me, Winterbourne."

"I'm your stepfather, by God."

"You are a wretched, contemptible liar. You are also a thief. You stole the inheritance that my father left for Ariel and me and you have squandered it in the gaming hells. Do you think I feel any loyalty to you after what you have done? If so, you are quite mad."

Winterbourne was incensed. "That money became mine when I married your mother."

"*Leave this house.*"

"Charlotte, wait, you do not comprehend the situation. That man who just left is not to be trifled with. He has demanded that I repay my gaming debt tonight. I must settle my affairs with him. I do not know what he will do to me if I fail."

"Leave."

Winterbourne opened his mouth and then closed it abruptly. He stared helplessly at the pistol and then, with an anguished groan, he hastened toward the staircase. Clutching the banister rail for support, he went down the steps, then crossed the hall and let himself out.

Charlotte stood very still in the shadows at the top of the stairs until the door closed behind Winterbourne. She took several deep breaths and slowly lowered the pistol.

For a moment the world seemed to waver and shift around her. The sound of carriages rattling past in the street was distant and unreal. The familiar shape of the hall and the staircase took on the quality of an eerie illusion.

Ariel's door opened at the end of the corridor. "Charlotte? I heard voices. Are you all right?"

"Yes." Charlotte held the empty pistol against her thigh so that her sister would not see it. She turned slowly and summoned a shaky smile. "Yes, I am fine, Ariel. Winterbourne came home drunk, as usual. We argued a bit. But he has left the house now. He will not be back tonight."

Ariel was very quiet for a moment. "I wish Mama was still here. Sometimes I am very frightened in this house."

Charlotte felt tears sting her eyes. "Sometimes I am frightened, too, Ariel. But we shall soon be free. In fact, we shall take the stage to Yorkshire tomorrow."

She hurried toward her sister and put one arm around her. She pushed the pistol deeper into the folds of her nightgown. The cold iron burned against her thigh.

"You have finished selling the silver and what was left of Mama's jewels?" Ariel asked.

"Yes. I pawned the tea tray yesterday. There is nothing left."

In the year since their mother's untimely

death in a riding accident, Winterbourne had sold off the best pieces of the Arkendale jewels and most of the larger silver items in order to pay his mounting gaming debts.

But when she had realized what was happening, Charlotte had stealthily hidden a number of small rings, brooches, and a pendant. She had also tucked away bits of the silver tea service. During the past few months she had surreptitiously pawned them.

Winterbourne spent so much of the time in an inebriated state that he did not even realize how many of the household valuables had disappeared. When he did, on occasion, notice that something had gone missing, Charlotte informed him that he, himself, had pawned it while drunk.

Ariel looked up. "Do you think that we shall enjoy Yorkshire?"

"It will be lovely. We shall find a little cottage to rent."

"But how will we live?" Even at the tender age of fourteen, Ariel displayed an amazingly practical streak. "The money you got for Mama's things will not last long."

Charlotte hugged her. "Do not fret. I shall think of a way to make a living for us."

Ariel frowned. "You will not be obliged to become a governess, will you? You know how terrible things are for ladies in that career. No one pays them very much and they are often treated very shabbily. And I shall likely not be able to stay with you if you go into service in someone else's house."

"You may be certain that I shall find some other way to support us," Charlotte vowed.

Everyone knew that a governess's lot was not a pleasant one. In addition to the low wages and the humiliating treatment, there were risks from the men of the household who considered the governess fair game.

There had to be another way to support herself and Ariel, Charlotte thought.

But in the morning, everything changed.

Lord Winterbourne was found floating facedown in the Thames, his throat slit. It was assumed that he had been the victim of a footpad.

There was no longer any reason to escape to Yorkshire but there was still a need for Charlotte to invent a career for herself.

She received the news of Winterbourne's death with vast relief. But she knew that she would never forget the monster with the compellingly beautiful voice that she had encountered in the hall.

Midnight

The coast of Italy, two years later

"So, in the end you chose to betray me." Morgan Judd spoke from the doorway of the ancient stone chamber that served as his laboratory. "A pity. You and I have much in common, St. Ives. Together we could have forged an alliance that would have brought us both undreamed of wealth and power. A great waste of a grand destiny. But, then, you don't believe in destiny, do you?"

Baxter St. Ives clenched his fingers fiercely around the damning notebook that he had just discovered. He turned to face Morgan.

Women considered Judd to be endowed with the countenance of a fallen angel. His black hair curled naturally in the carelessly stylish manner of the Romantic poets. It framed a high, intelligent brow and eyes the impossible blue of glacial ice.

Morgan's voice could have belonged to Lucifer himself. It was the voice of a man who had sung in the choir at Oxford, read poetry aloud to enthralled listeners, and charmed high-ranking ladies into bed. It was a rich, dark, compelling voice, a voice shaded with subtle meanings and unspoken promises. It was a voice of power and passion and Morgan used it, as he did everything and everyone, to achieve his own ends.

His bloodlines were as blue as the ice in his eyes. They flowed from one of England's most noble families. But his elegant, aristocratic mien belied the true circumstances of his birth.

Morgan Judd was a bastard. It was one of the two things that Baxter could say they truly had in common. The other was a fascination with chemistry. It was the latter that had brought about this midnight confrontation.

"Destiny is for romantic poets and writers of novels." Baxter pushed his gold wire spectacles more firmly in place on his nose. "I'm a man of science. I have no interest in such metaphysical nonsense. But I do know that it is possible for a man to sell his soul to the devil. Why did you do it, Morgan?"

"You speak of the compact that I have made with Napoleon, I presume." Morgan's sensual mouth curved faintly in cold amusement.

He took two steps into the shadowy chamber and halted. The folds of his black cloak swirled around the tops of his gleaming boots in a manner that reminded Baxter of the wings of a large bird of prey.

"Yes," Baxter said. "I refer to your bargain."

"There is no great mystery about my decision. I do what must be done to fulfill my destiny."

"You would betray your country to fulfill this mad notion of a grand destiny?"

"I owe nothing to England and neither do you. It is a land governed by laws and unwritten social rules that combine to prohibit superior men such as you and I from taking our rightful place in the natural order." Morgan's eyes glittered in the candlelight. His voice crackled with bitter rage. "It is not too late, Baxter. Join me in this endeavor."

Baxter held up the notebook. "You want me to help you finish formulating these terrible chemical concoctions so that Napoleon can use them as weapons against your own countrymen? You truly are crazed."

"I'm not mad, but you are most definitely

a fool." Morgan produced a pistol from the enveloping folds of the black cloak. "And blind in spite of your eyeglasses, if you cannot see that Napoleon is the future."

Baxter shook his head. "He has tried to grab too much power. It will destroy him."

"He is a man who comprehends that great destinies are crafted by those who have the will and the intellect to fashion them. What is more, he is a man who believes in progress. He is the only ruler in all of Europe who truly comprehends the potential value of science."

"I'm aware that he has given large sums of money to those who conduct experiments in chemistry and physics and the like." Baxter watched the pistol in Morgan's hand. "But he will use what you are creating here in this laboratory to help him win the war. Englishmen will die cruel deaths if you are successful in producing quantities of lethal vapors. Does that mean nothing to you?"

Morgan laughed. The sound had the low, deep resonance of a great bell rung very softly. "Nothing at all."

"Have you consigned your own honor as well as your native land to hell?"

"St. Ives, you amaze me. When will you learn that honor is a sport designed to amuse men who are born on the right side of the blanket?"

"I disagree." Tucking the notebook under one arm, Baxter removed his spectacles and began to polish the lenses with his handkerchief. "Honor is a quality that any man can acquire and shape for himself." He smiled

13

slightly. "Not unlike your own notion of destiny, when you consider it closely."

Morgan's eyes hardened with scorn and a chilling fury. "Honor is for men who inherit power and wealth in the cradle simply because their mothers had the good sense to secure a marriage license before they spread their thighs. It is for men such as our noble fathers who bequeath titles and estates to their legitimate sons and leave their bastards with nothing. It is not for the likes of us."

"Do you know what your greatest flaw is, Morgan?" Baxter carefully replaced his spectacles. "You allow yourself to become much too impassioned about certain subjects. Strong emotion is not a sound trait in a chemist."

"Damn you, St. Ives." Morgan's hand tightened around the grip of the pistol. "I've had enough of your exceedingly dull, excessively boring lectures. *Your* greatest flaw is that you lack the fortitude and the daring nature to alter the course of your own fate."

Baxter shrugged. "If there is such a thing as destiny, then I expect mine is to be a crashing bore until the day I expire."

"I fear that day has arrived. You may not believe this, but I regret the necessity of killing you. You are one of the few men in all of Europe who could have appreciated the brilliance of my accomplishments. It is a pity that you will not be alive to watch my destiny unfold."

"Destiny, indeed. What utter rubbish. I must tell you, this obsession with the metaphysical and the occult is another poor characteristic in a man of science. It was once merely an amusing pastime for you. When did you start to actually put credence into such nonsense?"

"Fool." Morgan aimed carefully and cocked the pistol.

Time had run out. There was nothing left to lose. In desperation, Baxter seized the heavy candle stand. He hurled it, together with the flaring taper, toward the nearest cluttered workbench.

The iron stand and its candle crashed into a glass flask, shattering it instantly. The pale green fluid inside splashed out across the workbench and lapped at the still-burning flame.

The spilled liquid ignited with a deadly rush.

"No," Morgan screamed. "Damn you, St. Ives."

He pulled the trigger but his attention was on the spreading fire, not his aim. The bullet slammed into the window behind Baxter. One of the small panes exploded.

Baxter ran toward the door, the notebook in his hand.

"How dare you attempt to interfere with my plans?" Morgan scooped a green glass bottle off a nearby shelf and spun around to block Baxter's path. "You bloody fool. You cannot stop me."

"The fire is spreading quickly. Run, for God's sake."

But Morgan ignored the warning. Features

15

twisted in rage, he dashed the contents of the green bottle straight at Baxter.

Acting on instinct, Baxter covered his eyes with his arm and turned away.

The acid struck his shoulder and back. For a second he felt nothing except a curiously cold sensation. It was as if he had been doused with water. But in the next instant, the chemicals finished eating through his linen shirt and seared his bare skin.

Pain lanced through him, a scorching agony that threatened to destroy his concentration. He forced himself to focus only on the need to escape.

Fire blossomed quickly in the stone chamber. A thick, foul smoke was beginning to form as more flasks shattered and released their contents to the flames.

Morgan lunged for a drawer, opened it, and produced a second pistol. He whirled toward Baxter, squinting to aim the weapon through the growing pall of vapors.

Baxter felt as if his skin were being peeled off in strips. Through a growing haze of smoke and pain he saw that the path to the door was already blocked by towering flames. There would be no escape in that direction.

He lashed out with one booted foot and kicked over the heavy air pump. It toppled against Morgan's left leg.

"God damn you." Morgan staggered to the side as the device struck him. He fell to his knees. The pistol clattered on the stones.

Baxter ran for the window. The pieces of his

ruined shirt flapped wildly. He gained the wide, stone sill and glanced down.

Below lay a roiling, churning sea. In the thin, silver moonlight he could see the foaming surf as it crashed against the rocks that formed the foundation of the ancient castle.

The pistol thundered.

Baxter flung himself toward the dark waters. A series of fiery explosions echoed in the night as he plummeted downward.

He managed to miss the rocks but the impact tore Morgan Judd's notebook from his grasp. It vanished forever into the depths.

When he surfaced a moment later amid the pounding waves, Baxter realized that his eye-glasses were also gone. But he did not need them to see that the laboratory in the castle tower had turned into an inferno. Terrible smoke billowed forth into the night.

No one could live through such a confla-gration. Morgan Judd was dead.

Baxter considered the fact that he had brought about the death of the man who had once been his closest friend and colleague.

It was almost enough to make a man believe in the notion of destiny.

One

London, three years later

"You leave me no option but to be blunt, Mr. St. Ives. Unfortunately, the truth of the matter is that you are not quite what I had in mind in the way of a man-of-affairs." Charlotte Arkendale clasped her hands together on top of the wide mahogany desk and regarded Baxter with a critical eye. "I am sorry for the waste of your time."

The interview was not going well. Baxter adjusted the gold-framed eyeglasses on the bridge of his nose and silently vowed that he would not give in to the impulse to grind his back teeth.

"Forgive me, Miss Arkendale, but I was under the impression that you wished to employ a person who appeared completely innocuous and uninteresting."

"Quite true."

"I believe your exact description of the ideal candidate for the position was, and I quote, *a person who is as bland as a potato pudding*."

Charlotte blinked wide, disconcertingly intelligent, green eyes. "You do not comprehend me properly, sir."

"I rarely make mistakes, Miss Arkendale. I

am nothing if not precise, methodical, and deliberate in my ways. Mistakes are made by those who are impulsive or inclined toward excessive passions. I assure you, I am not of that temperament."

"I could not agree with you more on the risks of a passionate nature," she said quickly. "Indeed, that is one of the problems"

"Allow me to read to you precisely what you wrote in your letter to your recently retired man-of-affairs."

"There is no need. I am perfectly aware of what I wrote to Mr. Marcle."

Baxter ignored her. He reached into the inside pocket of his slightly rumpled coat and removed the letter he had stored there. He had read the damn thing so many times that he almost had it memorized, but he made a show of glancing down at the flamboyant handwriting.

" 'As you know, Mr. Marcle, I require a man-of-affairs to take your place. He must be a person who presents an ordinary, unassuming appearance. I want a man who can go about his business unnoticed; a gentleman with whom I can meet frequently without attracting undue attention or comment.

" 'In addition to the customary duties of a man-of-affairs, duties which you have fulfilled so very admirably during the past five years, sir, I must ask that the gentleman whom you recommend possess certain other skills.

" 'I shall not trouble you with the details of the situation in which I find myself. Suffice it to say that due to recent events I am in need of a stout, keenly alert individual who can be depended upon to protect my person. In short, I wish to employ a bodyguard as well as a man-of-affairs.

" 'Expense, as always, must be a consideration. Therefore, rather than undertake the cost of engaging two men to fill two posts, I have concluded that it will prove more economical to employ one man who can carry out the responsibilities of both positions—' "

"Yes, yes, I recall my own words quite clearly," Charlotte interrupted testily. "But that is not the point."
Baxter doggedly continued:

" 'I therefore request that you send me a respectable gentleman who meets the above requirements and who presents an appearance that is as bland as a potato pudding.' "

"I fail to see why you must repeat aloud everything on the page, Mr. St. Ives."
Baxter pressed on:

" "He must be endowed with a high degree of intelligence as I shall require him to make the usual delicate inquiries for me. But in his capacity as a bodyguard, he must also be skilled in the use of a pistol in case events take a nasty turn. Above all, Mr. Marcle, as you well know, he must be discreet.' "

"Enough, Mr. St. Ives." Charlotte picked up a small volume bound in red leather and slapped it smartly against the desktop to get his attention.

Baxter glanced up from the letter. "I believe I meet most of your requirements, Miss Arkendale."

"I am certain that you do meet a few of them." She favored him with a frosty smile. "Mr. Marcle would never have recommended you to me if that were not the case. Unfortunately, there is one very important qualification that you lack."

Baxter deliberately refolded the letter and slipped it back inside his coat. "Time is of the essence, according to Marcle."

"Quite correct." An anxious expression came and went in her brilliant eyes. "I need someone to fill the post immediately."

"Then perhaps you should not be too choosy, Miss Arkendale."

She flushed. "But the thing is, Mr. St. Ives, I wish to employ a man who meets *all* of my requirements, not just some of them."

"I must insist that I do meet all of them, Miss Arkendale." He paused. "Or very nearly all. I am intelligent, alert, and amazingly discreet. I confess that I have little interest in pistols. I find them to be generally inaccurate and unreliable."

"Ah-ha." She brightened at that news. "There you are. Another requirement that you do not meet, sir."

"But I have some skill in chemistry."

"Chemistry?" She frowned. "What good will that do?"

"One never knows, Miss Arkendale. Occasionally I find it quite useful."

"I see. Well, that is all very interesting, of course. Unfortunately, I have no need of a chemist."

"You insisted upon a man who would draw little attention. A staid, unremarkable man-of-affairs."

"Yes, but—"

"Allow me to tell you that I am often described in those very terms. Bland as a potato pudding in every way."

Irritation began to simmer in Charlotte's eyes. She leaped to her feet and stalked around the corner of her desk. "I find that extremely difficult to believe, sir."

"I cannot imagine why." Baxter removed his spectacles as she began to pace the small study. "Even my own aunt informs me that I am capable of inducing a state of acute boredom in anyone within a radius of twenty paces in less than ten minutes. Miss Arkendale, I can assure you that I not only look dull, I am dull."

"Perhaps weak eyesight runs in your family, sir. I recommend that your aunt obtain a pair of eyeglasses such as those that you wear."

"My aunt would not be seen dead in a pair of spectacles." Baxter reflected briefly on the outrageously stylish Rosalind, Lady Trengloss, as he polished the lenses of his eyeglasses. "She wears hers only when she knows herself to be entirely alone. I doubt that her own maid has seen her in them."

"Which only confirms my suspicion that she has not taken a close look at you in some time, sir. Perhaps not since you were a babe in arms."

"I beg your pardon?"

Charlotte spun around to face him. "Mr. St. Ives, the matter of eyesight bears very much on the point I am attempting to make here."

Baxter replaced his spectacles with cautious deliberation. He was definitely losing the thread of the conversation. Not a good sign. He forced himself to study Charlotte with his customary analytical detachment.

She bore little resemblance to most of the ladies of his acquaintance. In truth, the longer he was in her presence, the more Baxter was convinced that she was entirely unique.

To his amazement, he found himself reluctantly fascinated in spite of what he knew about her. She was somewhat older than he had expected. Five-and-twenty, he had learned in passing.

Expressions came and went across her face with the rapidity of a chemical reaction in a flask positioned over an intense flame. Strong brows and long lashes framed her eyes. An assertive nose, high cheekbones, and an elo-

24

quent mouth conveyed spirited determination and an indomitable will.

In other words, Baxter thought, *this is one bloody-minded female.*

Her glossy auburn hair was parted in the center above a high, intelligent forehead. The tresses were drawn up in a neat knot and arranged so that a few corkscrew curls bounced around her temples.

In the midst of a Season that featured a plethora of low-cut bodices and gossamer fabrics designed to reveal a maximum amount of the female form, Charlotte wore a surprisingly modest gown. It was fashioned of yellow muslin, high-waisted and trimmed with long sleeves and a white ruff. A pair of yellow kid slippers peeked out from beneath the severely restrained flounce that decorated the hem. He could not help but notice that she had very pretty feet. Nicely shaped with dainty ankles.

Appalled at the direction of his thoughts, Baxter looked away. "Forgive me, Miss Arkendale, but I seem to have missed your point."

"You will simply not do as my man-of-affairs."

"Because I wear spectacles?" He frowned. "I would have thought that they rather enhanced the impression of potato-pudding blandness."

"Your spectacles are not the problem." She sounded thoroughly exasperated now.

"I thought you just said they were the problem."

25

"Haven't you been listening? I begin to believe that you are deliberately misunderstanding me, sir. I repeat, you are not qualified for this post."

"I am perfectly suited to it. May I remind you that your own man-of-affairs has recommended me for this position?"

Charlotte dismissed that with a wave of her hand. "Mr. Marcle is no longer my man-of-affairs. He is even now on his way to a cottage in Devon."

"I believe he did say something to the effect that he felt he had earned a long and peaceful retirement. I gained the impression that you were a somewhat demanding employer, Miss Arkendale."

She stiffened. "I beg your pardon?"

"Never mind. Marcle's retirement is not the issue. What is of importance here is that you called upon him one last time and gave him instructions to find his replacement. He has selected me to take over his responsibilities."

"I make the final decision in this matter and I say that you will not do, sir."

"I assure you that Marcle thought me eminently qualified for the post. He was pleased to write the letter of recommendation that I showed to you."

The silver-haired, dapper John Marcle had been in the midst of packing up his household when he had received his last instructions from his soon-to-be former employer. Baxter's timing had been perfect. Or so he had thought until he tried to persuade the dubious Marcle that he wished to apply for the position.

Rather than relief at the prospect of solving his last "Arkendale problem," as he termed it, the conscientious Marcle had felt compelled to discourage Baxter from the outset.

"Miss Arkendale is, ah, somewhat unusual," Marcle said as he toyed with his pen. "Are you quite certain you wish to apply for the post?"

"Quite certain," Baxter said.

Marcle peered at him from beneath a solid line of thick, white brows. "Forgive me, sir, but I do not comprehend precisely why you wish to engage yourself to Miss Arkendale in this capacity."

"The usual reasons. I'm in need of employment."

"Yes, yes, I understand. But there must be other positions available."

Baxter decided to embroider his story a bit. He assumed what he hoped was a confidential air. "We both know how mundane most such posts are. Instructions to solicitors and various agents. Arrangements for the buying and selling of properties. Banking matters. All very uninspiring."

"After five years as Miss Arkendale's man-of-affairs, I can assure you that there is much to be said for the routine and the uninspiring."

"I am eager for something a bit different," Baxter said earnestly. "This post sounds as if it will be somewhat out of the ordinary.

Indeed, I sense that it will offer me a certain challenge."

"Challenge?" Marcle closed his eyes. "I doubt that you know the meaning of the word yet, sir."

"I have been told that I am in a rut. It has been suggested that I add an element of excitement to my life, sir. I am hoping that this post will afford me the opportunity to do that."

Marcle's eyes snapped open in alarm. "You say you seek excitement?"

"Indeed, sir. A man of my nature gets very little of that commodity in the normal course of events." Baxter hoped he was not overdoing it. "I have always lived a quiet life."

And what was more, he much preferred his peaceful existence, he thought glumly. This damnable mission that his aunt had begged him to undertake was an unwelcome interruption in his placid routine.

The only reason he had allowed himself to be talked into it was because he knew Rosalind well. She had a flair for the dramatic—her greatest regret was that she had never gone on the stage—but she was not given to foolish fancies and feverish imaginings.

Rosalind was genuinely concerned about the circumstances surrounding the murder of her friend, Drusilla Heskett. The authorities had declared that the woman had been shot by a housebreaker. Rosalind suspected that the killer was none other than Charlotte Arkendale.

Baxter had agreed to look into the situation on his aunt's behalf.

A discreet inquiry had turned up the information that the mysterious Miss Arkendale happened to be in need of a new man-of-affairs. Baxter had seized the opportunity to apply for the post.

He reasoned that if he could talk his way into the position he would be ideally situated to conduct his investigation. With any luck he would resolve the matter in short order and be able to return to the calm refuge of his laboratory.

Marcle exhaled heavily. "It's true that working for Miss Arkendale can sometimes produce an element of excitement, but I am not altogether certain it is the type of adventure you would enjoy, Mr. St. Ives."

"I shall be the judge of that."

"Believe me, sir, if it's excitement you crave, you would do better to take yourself off to a gaming hell."

"I don't enjoy games of chance."

Marcle grimaced. "I assure you, a lively hell would be infinitely less maddening than embroiling yourself in Miss Arkendale's affairs."

Baxter had not considered the possibility that Charlotte Arkendale was a candidate for Bedlam. "You believe her to be mad?"

"How many ladies of your acquaintance require a man-of-affairs who can also undertake the duties of a bodyguard, sir?"

An excellent question, Baxter thought ruefully. The entire matter sounded more bizarre by the moment. "Nevertheless, I wish to apply for the post. It is obvious why she needs a new man-of-affairs. You are retiring, after all, and she must replace you. But perhaps you would be good enough to explain why Miss Arkendale is in need of a bodyguard?"

"How the devil should I know the answer to that?" Marcle tossed aside his pen. "Miss Arkendale is a most peculiar female. I have served as her man-of-affairs since the death of her stepfather, Lord Winterbourne. I can assure you, these past five years have been the longest years of my life."

Baxter eyed him curiously. "If you disliked your post, why did you continue in it?"

Marcle sighed. "She pays extraordinarily well."

"I see."

"But I must confess that whenever I received a letter of instruction from her, I trembled in my shoes. I never knew what strange demand she would make next. And that was before she took a notion to add the duties of a bodyguard to the post."

"What sort of demands does she make in the normal course of affairs?"

Marcle groaned. "She has sent me to make inquiries of the oddest people. I have gone haring off to the North in order to obtain information on a certain gentleman. I have interviewed the managers of the most appalling hells and brothels on her behalf. I have inquired into the financial affairs of any number of men who would be shocked to learn of her interest."

"Odd, indeed."

"And most unladylike. Upon my oath, sir, if she did not pay so handsomely, I would have quit my position after the first month of service. But at least I was never required to act as a bodyguard. I am grateful for that much."

"You have no notion of why she feels herself to be in danger?"

"None whatsoever." Marcle's chair squeaked as he leaned back in it. "Miss Arkendale has not seen fit to confide in me on that score. In truth, there is a great deal Miss Arkendale has never seen fit to confide in me. I am extremely vague about the actual source of her income, for example."

Baxter was very good at controlling his expressions. A bastard, even one who was the by-blow of a wealthy earl, learned the skill early on in life. The talent served him well at that moment. He managed to convey only casual interest in Marcle's last statement.

"I was under the impression that Miss Arkendale's mother, Lady Winterbourne, had a substantial income from her first marriage," Baxter said carefully. "I assumed the inheritance was passed on to Miss Arkendale and her sister."

Marcle's brows rose. "That is what Miss Charlotte would have you believe. But I can tell you that Winterbourne squandered nearly every penny of the Arkendale inheritance before he had the grace to get himself murdered by a footpad five years ago."

Baxter removed his spectacles and began to

polish them with his handkerchief. "Just what do you suspect is the real source of Miss Arkendale's money?"

Marcle examined his nails. "I will be truthful, sir. Although I have assisted in the investment and management of her income for five years, to this day I have no notion of where the money originates. I recommend that if you take this post, you follow my example. Sometimes it's best not to know all of the facts."

Baxter slowly replaced his eyeglasses. "Fascinating. I expect some distant relative died and left an inheritance that has made up for the one that Winterbourne frittered away."

"I do not believe that to be the case," Marcle said slowly. "I succumbed to curiosity a couple of years ago and made some discreet inquiries. There was no such wealthy Arkendale relative. I fear the source of her funds is simply one more peculiar mystery surrounding Miss Arkendale."

It was no mystery at all if Rosalind was correct in her conclusions, Baxter thought. The lady was a blackmailer.

A distinct tapping sound brought his thoughts back to the present. He glanced at Charlotte, who had come to a halt near the fireplace. She was drumming her fingers on the marble mantel.

"I do not see how Marcle could possibly have imagined you to be qualified for this post," she said.

Baxter had had enough of arguing the point. "It is not as if there are a great many men about who can meet your absurd requirements, Miss Arkendale."

She glowered. "But surely Mr. Marcle can find me a gentleman who is more suited to the position than yourself."

"Have you forgotten? Marcle is halfway to Devon. Would you mind telling me precisely what it is about me that is so unsuitable?"

"Other than your lack of skill with a pistol?" she asked much too sweetly.

"Yes, other than that failing."

"You force me to be rude, sir. The problem is your appearance."

"What the devil is wrong with my appearance? No one could be more unprepossessing than myself."

Charlotte scowled. "Do not feed me that Banbury tale. You most certainly are not a potato pudding. Just the opposite, in fact."

He stared at her. "I beg your pardon?"

"You must know very well, sir, that your spectacles are a poor disguise."

"Disguise?" He wondered if he had got the wrong address and the wrong Charlotte Arkendale. Perhaps he had got the wrong town. "What in the name of the devil do you believe me to be concealing?"

"Surely you are not suffering from the illusion that those spectacles mask your true nature."

"My true nature?" Baxter lost his grip on his patience. "Bloody hell, just what am I, if not innocuous and unprepossessing?"

She spread her hands wide. "You have the

look of a man of strong passions who has mastered his temperament with even stronger powers of self-control."

"I beg your pardon?"

Her eyes narrowed with grim determination. "Such a man cannot hope to go about unnoticed. You are bound to attract attention when you conduct business on my behalf. I cannot have that in my man-of-affairs. I require someone who can disappear into a crowd. Someone whose face no one recalls very clearly. Don't you understand, sir? You give the appearance of being rather, well, to be quite blunt, *dangerous*."

Baxter was bereft of words.

Charlotte clasped her hands behind her back and resumed her pacing. "It is quite obvious you will never be able to pass for a dull, ordinary man-of-affairs. Therefore, you must see that you would not do at all for my purposes."

Baxter realized his mouth was hanging open. He managed to get it closed. He had been called many things, bastard, ill-mannered, and a great bore being among the more common epithets. But no one had ever labeled him a man of strong passions. No one had ever claimed that he looked dangerous.

He was a man of science. He prided himself on his detached, unemotional approach to problems, people, and situations. It was a trait he had honed to perfection years ago when he discovered that, as the bastard son of the Earl of Esherton and the notorious Emma, Lady Sultenham, he would be forever excluded from his rightful heritage.

He had been a subject of speculation and gossip since the day he was born. He had learned early to seek refuge amid his books and scientific apparatus.

Although some women initially found the notion of an affair with the bastard son of an earl somewhat exciting, especially when they learned that he was a very wealthy bastard son, the sentiment did not last long. The weak flames generated in the course of his infrequent liaisons burned for only a very short time before sputtering out.

His affairs had become even shorter in duration since his return from Italy three years ago. The acid burns on his back and shoulders had healed but he was marked for life.

Women reacted to the raw, ugly scars with shock and disgust. Baxter did not entirely blame them. He had never been handsome and the acid lacerations had done nothing to improve his looks. Fortunately, his face had been spared. He was, however, fed up with the inconvenience of having to make certain that the candles were snuffed and the fire banked before he got undressed and climbed into bed with a lady.

On the last such occasion, some six months ago, he had nearly brained himself on the bedpost when he had tripped over his own boot in the inky darkness of the widow's unlit bedchamber. The incident had put a distinct damper on the remainder of the evening.

For the most part, he sought his satisfactions and pleasures in his laboratory. There, surrounded by his gleaming beakers, flasks, retorts, and blowpipes, he could avoid the empty conversations and frivolous pursuits of the Polite World. It was a world he had never enjoyed. A world that did not begin to comprehend him. A world that he found excruciatingly superficial and insipid. A world in which he had never felt at home.

Baxter schooled his thoughts and forced himself to reason swiftly. Charlotte had plainly dismissed him as a possible man-of-affairs. A new approach was required if he was to convince her to employ him.

"Miss Arkendale, there seems to be some discrepancy between your view of my nature and the views of virtually everyone else in the world. May I suggest we resolve the matter by conducting an experiment?"

She went very still. "What sort of experiment?"

"I recommend that you summon the members of your household and ask them for their opinions. If the consensus is that I can successfully go about my duties unnoticed and unremarked, you will employ me. If they concur with your views, I shall take my leave and look elsewhere for a post."

She hesitated, clearly dubious. Then she gave a quick, decisive nod. "Very well, sir. That seems quite logical. We shall conduct the experiment at once. I shall summon my sister and housekeeper. They are both extremely observant."

She reached for the velvet bell pull that

hung beside the fireplace and gave it a strong tug.

"You agree to abide by the results of this test?" he asked warily.

"You have my word on it, sir." She smiled with ill-concealed triumph. "We shall settle the matter at once."

Footsteps sounded in the hall. Baxter adjusted his eyeglasses and sat back in his chair to await the outcome of the experiment.

He was certain that he could safely predict the results. He knew his strong points better than anyone else. No one could top him when it came to appearing as bland and uninteresting as a potato pudding.

❧

Twenty minutes later, Baxter went down the steps of the Arkendale town house with a sense of quiet exultation. He noted that the crisp March breeze, which had been decidedly chilly an hour earlier, now felt fresh and invigorating.

There was nothing quite like a properly conducted scientific experiment to settle things, he thought as he hailed a passing hackney. It had not been easy but he had finally secured his new post. As he had anticipated, Charlotte Arkendale was the only person in the small household, indeed, very likely the only person in the whole of London, who would ever notice him in a crowd.

He was not sure what her peculiar notions

concerning his nature said about her except that they definitely verified John Marcle's opinion. Charlotte was a very unique sort of female.

Not at all what one would expect in the way of a blackmailer and murderess, Baxter thought.

Two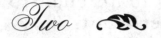

"I do not know why you are fretting so, Charlotte." Ariel paused to examine a tray of eggs arranged on the sideboard. "Mr. St. Ives appears to be just what you wanted. A man-of-affairs who will not draw attention to himself when he goes about his duties. He also seems to be in excellent physical condition. Not so tall as one might wish, but quite broad and solid looking about the shoulders. I think that he will serve nicely as a bodyguard should such a necessity arise."

"I thought him sufficiently tall." Charlotte wondered morosely why she felt compelled to defend Baxter's stature. Why did she care if her sister thought him less than perfect in height? "I had to look up to meet his eyes."

Ariel grinned. "That is because you are a trifle short. In a most attractive fashion, of course."

Charlotte grimaced. "Of course."

"In truth, Mr. St. Ives is not more than an inch above my own height."

"You are very tall for a woman." *And grace-*

ful and willowy and very, very lovely, Charlotte thought with a rush of sisterly pride. Perhaps it was more in the nature of maternal pride. After all, she reminded herself, she had been responsible for Ariel since the death of their mother.

And Ariel had turned out wonderfully well, Charlotte decided. She was a beautiful young lady of nineteen. Fair haired, blue eyed, and blessed with classical features and, yes, striking stature, she was the living image of their mother.

Charlotte had had many regrets and doubts in the course of the past few years. She had been all too well aware that she could never make up for what had been lost. Ariel had been only eleven when their tall, handsome, affectionate father had died. She had been barely thirteen when they had lost their beautiful, vivacious mother. Then Winterbourne had destroyed the inheritance that would have allowed Ariel freedom of choice in so many things, including marriage.

One of Charlotte's greatest regrets was that she had been unable to give her sister a Season. With her looks and poise and the education she had received first from their beautiful bluestocking mother and that Charlotte had continued, Ariel would have been a smashing success. What's more, she thought, her sister would have thoroughly enjoyed the opera and the theater and the excitement of the balls and soirees. She had inherited their parents' love of art and entertainment. She should have had a chance to meet the people who should have been her social equals. She should have had an opportunity to dance the waltz with a handsome young man.

So many things that should have been Ariel's had been lost.

Charlotte pulled herself back to the problem at hand. She forced herself to do what she always did when thoughts of the past threatened to lower her spirits. She concentrated on the future. And right now that future included Baxter St. Ives.

"I wish I could feel as certain about Mr. St. Ives as you do." Charlotte propped her elbow on the morning room table and rested her chin on the heel of one hand.

"He is a perfect man-of-affairs," Ariel declared.

Charlotte sighed. It was now quite clear that she was the only one in the household who sensed that there was a great deal more to Baxter St. Ives than met the eye. Yesterday Ariel and Mrs. Witty, the housekeeper, had both pronounced themselves well satisfied with Marcle's replacement. The two were so convinced of their impressions that Charlotte had almost begun to doubt her own instinctive wariness.

Almost, but not quite. She had had a great deal of experience assessing gentlemen, after all, and her intuition in such matters rarely failed her. She could not dismiss it out of hand.

But she was baffled by the fact that the others could not see past the lenses of Baxter's spectacles to the truth that blazed there.

He claimed to have an interest in chemistry

but in her opinion, he was no modern man of science. The man had the eyes of an alchemist, one of those legendary seekers obsessed with the search for the mystical secrets of the Philosopher's Stone. She could easily envision him hunched over a fiery crucible, concocting experiments that would enable him to transmute lead into gold.

Intense intelligence, unrelenting determination, and a will of iron burned in the amber depths of his eyes. The same qualities were etched into his blunt, strong face. She had sensed something else in him, too, something that she could not quite define. A hint of melancholia perhaps. Which, now that she considered it, was not unexpected.

There was a long artistic tradition of depicting that dark, wistful emotion with the emblems of alchemy. Those who engaged in an endless quest for nature's arcane secrets were no doubt doomed to experience episodes of despair and disappointment.

Baxter St. Ives was far and away the most interesting man she had ever met, Charlotte admitted to herself. But the same qualities that made him intriguing could also make a man dangerous. At the very least, they made him less than pliable.

She required a man-of-affairs who would take instructions without argument, not one who would demand constant explanations and justifications. She did not think that Baxter would be easily ordered about. At best, he was likely to prove difficult.

"Perhaps now that Mr. St. Ives has a new post, he will be able to afford a new tailor." Ariel chuckled as she carried her plate back to the table. "His coat certainly did not fit him very well and his waistcoat was quite plain. Did you notice that he was wearing breeches instead of trousers?"

"I noticed."

She would have been blind had she failed to observe the manner in which the snug breeches had revealed the sleekly muscled outline of his thighs, she thought. She summoned up the memory of Baxter as he sat across from her attired in a rumpled blue coat, unpleated linen shirt, and the conservative breeches and unpolished boots. She frowned slightly. "His clothes were of excellent quality."

"Yes, but sadly unfashionable, even for a gentleman in his position." Ariel took a bite of sausage. "And his neckcloth was tied in a very mundane manner. I fear our Mr. St. Ives has no sense of style at all."

"One does not look for style in a man-of-affairs."

"Precisely." Ariel winked. "Which only goes to prove that he is just what he appears to be, a gentleman badly in need of a position. Probably a second son from the country. You know how that is."

Charlotte fiddled with her coffee cup. "I suppose so." It was common knowledge that many second and third sons of the country gentry who were not in line for the family farm were obliged to make their livings as men-of-affairs.

"Cheer up," Ariel said. "I'm quite sure stodgy old Marcle would not have sent St. Ives to you unless he was suitably qualified."

Charlotte watched as her sister attacked the eggs and sausages on her plate. Her own appetite was normally quite sharp in the mornings but today she was barely able to contemplate the cup of coffee in front of her.

"I don't know, Ariel. I just don't know."

"Really, Charlotte, this mood of gloom is quite unlike you. You are usually so much more enthusiastic in the mornings."

"I did not sleep well last night."

That was not the half of it, Charlotte thought. In truth she had barely slept at all. She had tossed and turned for hours, caught in the grip of a deeply troubling sense of unease. Ariel was right, her mood was indeed dark this morning.

"Have you told Mr. St. Ives precisely why you are in need of a bodyguard?" Ariel asked.

"Not yet. I instructed him to return this afternoon so that I could explain the exact nature of his duties."

Ariel's eyes widened. "You mean he has no notion of why you have employed him?"

"No."

The truth was, she had needed time to think about the situation. Time to be certain that taking on the enigmatic St. Ives was the right course of action. There was a great deal at stake. But the more contemplation she gave to the matter, the fewer alternatives Charlotte perceived.

She was, in fact, quite desperate.

Ariel put down her fork and gave Charlotte a direct look. "Perhaps he will not want the position once he learns the details."

Charlotte pondered that. She did not know whether to be cheered or alarmed by the prospect. "Things might be a good deal simpler if Mr. St. Ives takes to his heels when he learns the true nature of his responsibilities."

Mrs. Witty hove to in the doorway of the morning room, a fresh pot of coffee in one broad, work-worn fist. "You'd best hope he doesn't run off when he learns what ye want him to do for ye, Miss Charlotte. It's not as if there's any number of gentlemen running about London who would be willing to help ye investigate a murder."

"I'm aware of that." Charlotte scowled. "I've agreed to hire St. Ives, have I not?"

"Aye, and thank the good Lord. I don't mind tellin' ye, I don't much like this situation. Making inquiries into a bloody murder ain't in our usual line around here."

"I'm aware of that as well." Charlotte watched Mrs. Witty pour fresh coffee.

The housekeeper was an imposing woman whose monumental proportions would have done credit to an ancient goddess. In the three years since she had joined the household, Charlotte had had cause to be grateful for her steady nerves. Not many housekeepers would have tolerated an employer engaged in a career such as the one Charlotte had carved out for herself. Fewer still would have been willing to provide valuable assistance.

Then again, there were not many housekeepers as well dressed as Mrs. Witty, Charlotte thought. When one required unusual services from one's staff, one naturally paid very well.

"She's right." Ariel's expression grew more serious. "What you are proposing to do could prove dangerous, Charlotte."

"I have no choice," Charlotte said quietly. "I must discover who killed Drusilla Heskett."

❧

Baxter was in his laboratory unpacking a new shipment of glassware that had been designed to his exacting specifications when the knock came on the door.

"What is it, Lambert?" He removed a gleaming new retort from the box and held it up to the light to admire it. "I am occupied at the moment."

The door opened.

"Lady Trengloss, sir," Lambert announced in his tomblike accents.

Baxter reluctantly put down the retort and looked at Lambert. His butler had a pained expression on his pinched face but that was nothing new. Lambert always looked pained. He was sixty-six years of age, well past the time when most men in his position retired with their pensions.

The years had taken their toll. He suffered greatly from painful joints. His hands were gnarled and swollen and his movements had grown noticeably slower in the past year.

"I suppose my aunt wants a full report on my new career as a man-of-affairs," Baxter said, resigned to the inevitable interview.

"Lady Trengloss appears to be somewhat agitated, sir."

"Show her in here, Lambert."

"Aye, sir." Lambert made to remove himself and then paused. "There is something else I should mention, sir. The new housekeeper departed an hour ago."

"Bloody hell." Baxter scowled at a small flaw in a glass flask. "Not another one. That makes three in the past five months."

"Aye, sir."

"What did this one have to complain of? There have been no explosions of any significance in the laboratory in weeks and I have taken care to make certain that noxious odors did not permeate the hall."

"Mrs. Hardy apparently concluded that you were attempting to poison her, sir," Lambert said.

"Poison her?" Baxter was outraged. "Why in God's name would she think that? Bloody damn difficult to keep housekeepers as it is. The last thing I would do is poison one."

Lambert cleared his throat. "Something about the bottles of chemicals that she found in the kitchen last evening, I believe."

"Devil take it, I only put them in there because I was preparing an experiment that required a very large pneumatic trough. You

46

know I always use the kitchen sink for that purpose."

"Apparently the sight of the bottles disturbed her, sir."

"Damnation. Well, there is nothing for it. Take yourself off to the agency and find us another housekeeper. God only knows what we'll have to pay this time. Each one seems to be more expensive than the last."

"Aye, sir." Lambert shuffled backward a pace and winced. He pressed his hand to his lower back.

Baxter frowned. "Rheumatism bad today, I take it?"

"Aye, sir."

"Sorry to hear that. Any luck with those new treatments you're undergoing?"

"I believe I do feel some improvement for a time after each session with Dr. Flatt but unfortunately the relief is quite temporary. The doctor assures me that with more treatments, the pains will steadily decrease in severity, however."

"Hmm." Baxter did not ask any more questions.

He had absolutely no faith in Dr. Flatt's treatments, which involved the use of animal magnetism or mesmerism, as it was often called. It was all quackery, so far as scientists such as himself were concerned. Distinguished authorities such as Benjamin Franklin from America and the French chemist Antoine Lavoisier had denounced Mesmer's work several years ago. Their opinions, however, had done nothing to stem the rising tide of practitioners who claimed to achieve amazing results using variations on Dr. Mesmer's methods.

"Lady Trengloss, sir," Lambert reminded him.

"Yes, yes, send her in. I may as well get this over with as quickly as possible." Baxter glanced at the tall clock. "I have an appointment with my new employer in an hour."

"Employer? Is that what you call her?" Rosalind, Lady Trengloss, swept past Lambert and sailed into Baxter's laboratory. "What an odd description of the creature."

"But, unfortunately, an accurate one." Baxter nodded brusquely at his aunt. "Thanks to you, madam, I seem to have secured gainful employment at last, whether I like it or not."

"Do not blame me for your scheme." Rosalind removed her black and white silk bonnet and sank into a chair with theatrical grace. Her striking black and silver hair was elegantly styled to enhance her noble features. Her dark eyes glittered with determination.

Baxter eyed her with a combination of gruff affection and acute impatience. Rosalind was his late mother's younger sister. He had known her all of his life. She was sixty now but she retained the innate sense of elegance and dashing style that had graced both women from the cradle.

Emma and Rosalind Claremont had taken London by storm in their younger days. Both had made brilliant matches. Both had found themselves widowed in their early twenties.

Neither had ever remarried. They had reveled instead in the enormous power they had wielded as wealthy, beautiful, titled widows. Their status and charm had enabled them to survive scandals and gossip that would have ruined other women.

Baxter smiled grimly as Lambert removed himself soundlessly from the laboratory. "You must admit that I am uniquely qualified to be a man-of-affairs."

Rosalind tipped her head slightly and considered that. "In an odd way, you may be right. You have had a great deal of experience managing finances, have you not?"

"Indeed."

"Tell me what you discovered when you went to see Charlotte Arkendale yesterday."

"Actually, I learned very little. I am to be told the details of my new position this afternoon. In less than an hour's time, as a matter of fact."

Baxter sat down at the writing table he used to record his notes. Something crunched under his thigh. He saw that he had just crumpled a page of observations that he had made on a recent experiment.

"Bloody hell." He picked up the foolscap and smoothed it carefully.

Rosalind glanced dismissively at the mangled notes and then peered intently at Baxter. "Do not keep me in suspense. What are your first impressions of Miss Arkendale?"

"I found her to be..." Baxter hesitated, searching for the correct word. "Formidable."

"Fiendishly clever, would you say?"

"Possibly."

"A deceiving, coldhearted villainess?"

Baxter hesitated. "I must point out, madam, that you really do not have any proof of your accusations."

"Bah. You will find the evidence we need soon enough."

"Do not be too certain of that. I can envision Miss Arkendale in many roles." *Including that of a paramour.* The images came out of nowhere, searing and intense. His body reacted as though he had been plunged into a recently tumbled bed that smelled of passion and desire. Perhaps it had been a bit too long since his last liaison, he thought glumly. "But it's difficult to see her as a blackmailing murderess."

Rosalind glared at him. "Are you entertaining doubts about this project we have embarked upon?"

"We? I seem to find myself alone in this endeavor."

"Do not mince words with me. You know very well what I mean."

"I have told you from the start that I have doubts," Baxter said. "Grave doubts. For starters, you have absolutely no proof that Charlotte Arkendale was blackmailing Drusilla Heskett, let alone that she murdered her."

"Drusilla herself confided to me one night after we had gone through a bottle of port, that she had paid Miss Arkendale a considerable sum. When I inquired as to why she had done such a thing, she suddenly changed the topic. I did not think much about it until after she was killed. Then I recalled how mysterious she had been about the matter. It is all too much of a coincidence, Baxter."

"Mrs. Heskett was a close friend of yours. Surely she would have told you if she was being blackmailed," Baxter said.

"Not necessarily. By its very nature, blackmail must touch on some extremely intimate and personal secret. It must threaten to reveal something the victim would not want anyone, perhaps most especially her closest friends, to know."

"If Mrs. Heskett was willing to pay, why would the blackmailer murder her? Rather defeats the purpose, don't you think?"

"Who knows how a blackmailer thinks?" Rosalind got to her feet with regal grace and started toward the door. "Perhaps Drusilla stopped the payments. I expect you to discover the truth about her death, Baxter. I have made it my goal to see that justice is done. Keep me informed."

"Hmm."

"By the bye." Rosalind paused in the doorway and lowered her voice. "I really do think that you are going to have to pension off poor old Lambert. It takes him forever to answer the door these days. I vow, I waited on your front step for nearly ten minutes."

"I consider his slowness in opening the door to be one of his greatest assets. Most people who come to call give up and go away without ever discovering that I am at home. Saves me a great deal of trouble."

He waited until Rosalind had left the laboratory. Then he walked slowly to the window and examined the three pots that sat on the sill.

The pots were part of an ongoing experiment in agricultural chemistry. Each contained some sweet pea seeds buried in barren soil that had been laced with his most recent blend of minerals and chemicals.

So far there was no sign of life.

❧

The ticking of the study clock seemed inordinately loud. Charlotte composed herself and gazed across her desk at Baxter with what she hoped was an air of professional competence. She had been dreading this meeting all day.

Dreading it and yet anticipating it with an inexplicable sense of what could only be termed morbid excitement.

"Before I give you instructions regarding your initial duties, Mr. St. Ives, I shall have to tell you something that I never found it necessary to reveal to Mr. Marcle."

Baxter studied her with an expression of polite inquiry. "Indeed."

"I must tell you precisely how I make my living."

Baxter took off his spectacles and began to

52

polish the lenses with a large white handkerchief. "That would certainly be of some interest to your man-of-affairs, Miss Arkendale."

"Yes, I suppose so. But it is a little difficult to explain."

"I see."

"Some would say my career borders on the scandalous but I feel it is more in the nature of a calling."

"Rather like becoming a nun, would you say?" Baxter held his eyeglasses up to the light, apparently checking for smudges.

"Yes." Charlotte cheered slightly. "That is an excellent analogy. You see, Mr. St. Ives, I operate a very exclusive service. I cater solely to women who have come into a bit of money. An inheritance, perhaps, or an unusually large pension from a grateful employer."

"I see."

"Respectable ladies of a certain age who find themselves alone in the world, possessed of an income and who are considering marriage."

Baxter placed his spectacles on his nose with grave precision. His alchemist's eyes gleamed. "And just what sort of services do you provide for these ladies?"

"I conduct inquiries for them. Very discreet inquiries."

"Inquiries into what?"

She cleared her throat. "Into the backgrounds of the gentlemen who wish to marry them."

He gazed at her for a long moment. "Their backgrounds?"

"It is my task, sir, indeed, my calling, to assist such ladies in ascertaining that the men who express a desire to marry them are not fortune hunters, opportunists, or rakehells. I help them avoid the perils and pitfalls such women inevitably face."

An acute silence fell on the study. Baxter stared at her.

"Good God," he said eventually.

Charlotte bristled. So much for hoping that he would be favorably impressed by her unique career. "I perform a valuable service, sir."

"What on earth are you playing at? Surely you do not imagine yourself to be some sort of female Bow Street Runner."

"Not at all. I make the sort of extremely delicate inquiries that no Runner could possibly conduct. And I am proud to say that I have been personally responsible for saving several ladies from forming disastrous connections with men who would have ruined their finances."

"Bloody hell. I begin to see why you might require the services of a bodyguard, Miss Arkendale. You must have acquired any number of enemies in your time."

"Nonsense. I conduct my business affairs with complete confidentiality. My clients are cautioned to discuss my services only with other ladies who might be in need of them."

"This is astounding, Miss Arkendale. How the devil do you proceed with your work?"

"In addition to dispatching my man-of-affairs to collect certain types of information, I also have the assistance of my sister and my housekeeper."

Baxter gazed at her, bemused. "Your housekeeper?"

"Mrs. Witty is very helpful when it comes to making inquiries among servants and staff. Such people often know more about their employers than anyone else. It has all worked very well until now." Charlotte got to her feet and went to stand at the window. She contemplated the small garden. "But something dreadful has happened."

"Something that makes you think that you need a bodyguard as well as a new man-of-affairs?" Baxter asked bluntly.

"Yes. Until recently, my clients have all been women of a certain station in life. Respectable but not wealthy. Governesses, spinsters, and widows from the gentry. But two months ago, I acquired a new client, one who moved in Polite Circles. I was extremely excited because it meant that I might be able to extend my business to a wealthier clientele."

"Bloody hell," Baxter said very softly.

She pretended not to have heard him. There was no turning back now. She had already said too much. She must press on and hope for the best. "Her name was Mrs. Drusilla Heskett. I conducted the inquiries she requested and gave her my report. She paid me and I assumed that was the end of the matter. I hoped she would recommend me to some of her friends."

"What happened?"

"Last week she was found murdered in her own bedchamber. Shot dead by a house-breaker, the authorities said. All of her servants had been dismissed for the evening. I have some cause to believe that the person who killed her was one of the men whom I had investigated on her behalf."

"Good God."

She turned to face him. "I must learn the truth, sir."

"Why? What business is it of yours?"

"Don't you see? If the man who murdered her was one of those whom I had investigated and perhaps recommended as honest and sincere, then, in a sense, I bear part of the responsibility for her murder. I must determine the truth of the situation."

"Just what is it that makes you think the killer was one of her suitors?" Baxter asked swiftly.

"I received a note from Mrs. Heskett on the very day of her death. In it she stated that she had been nearly run down twice in recent days, once on the street and once in a park. In both instances, the vehicle was a black phaeton. She feared that the incidents were not mere accidents, but actual attempts on her life."

"Bloody hell."

"She did not see the driver's face but she came to the logical conclusion that one of her reject-ed suitors was so enraged by her refusal to wed, he was trying to murder her. The next morning I learned of her death. Hardly a coincidence, sir. I must discover the truth."

"And you expect me to assist you in this crazed quest?"

"Yes, I most certainly do." She was beginning to grow annoyed. "You agreed to accept the post and I am paying you an excellent salary, sir. I expect you to fulfill your duties as my man-of-affairs and as a bodyguard. It all seems quite simple and straightforward to me."

"About as simple and straightforward as the phlogiston theory of combustion," Baxter retorted.

"I beg your pardon?"

"Nothing, Miss Arkendale. I merely made a passing reference to that old nonsense the Germans came up with concerning the substance phlogiston. The theory was said to explain the combustion of materials. It relates to chemistry. I doubt that you are familiar with it."

She raised her brows. "On the contrary, Mr. St. Ives, I am well aware that a few years ago Lavoisier conducted several exceedingly clever experiments that disproved the old theory of phlogiston."

It took Baxter a moment to digest that. "You have an interest in chemistry, Miss Arkendale?"

"No." She made a face. "But I was required to read Mr. Basil Valentine's *Conversations on Chemistry* in the schoolroom, just as is virtu-

57

ally every other young person in England. Some of the information managed to stick in my brain."

"I see." Baxter's gaze was inscrutable. "I take it you found Valentine's book exceedingly dull?"

"Chemistry is not a favorite subject of mine." She gave him an apologetic smile. "I have other interests."

"I can well believe that."

"Perhaps we should return to the subject of Mrs. Heskett's murder," Charlotte said grimly.

"Indeed. Tell me, Miss Arkendale, just how do you propose to go about finding the killer?"

"Mrs. Heskett rejected four men during the past month. One, a Mr. Charles Dill, died of a heart seizure two weeks ago, so he can be discounted as a suspect. The other three are Lords Lennox, Randeleigh, and Esly. I intend to interview all of them. But first we must start with an examination of the scene of the crime."

Baxter blinked owlishly. "An examination?"

"I intend to search Drusilla Heskett's town house for clues."

"You intend to do *what*?"

"Really, Mr. St. Ives, you must try to pay closer attention. You cannot expect me to repeat everything. I wish to search the premises of Mrs. Heskett's town house. I have ascertained that the place is vacant. You will accompany me and make yourself useful."

Baxter gazed at her as if she were a creature from some supernatural realm. "Bloody hell."

Three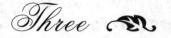

She had read *Conversations on Chemistry* and was familiar with the discredited theory of phlogiston. She could drop Lavoisier's name into casual conversation. There were a number of excellent books in her study on a variety of other subjects that she presumably had read as well. What of it? Baxter thought. The evidence of an intellectual bent did not prove that she was not a blackmailer and a murderess.

Any number of well-educated upper-class villains could spout scientific facts, he reminded himself. A good education did not indicate a pure heart and an honest soul. Morgan Judd, for example, had been one of the most intelligent, well-read men he had ever met.

Baxter surveyed the fog-shrouded street with a sense of foreboding. The neighborhood was quiet and sedate. Eminently respectable. There were no great mansions but the houses obviously belonged to those possessed of comfortable incomes.

He still could not believe that he had allowed himself to be dragged out on such a miserable night to search for clues relating to a case of murder.

Charlotte was either quite sincere or quite mad, or she was using him to assist her and protect her person while she advanced her own schemes. A lady involved in blackmail and murder would certainly have need of a man-of-affairs-cum-bodyguard.

Baxter stifled a sigh. He really was not cut out for this sort of thing. Life was so much simpler, so much more logical and orderly back in his laboratory.

"We are fortunate to have the fog tonight, are we not, Mr. St. Ives?" Charlotte's voice was muffled by the hood of her cloak and a thick, woolen scarf. "It will serve to conceal our presence in this neighborhood. Even if someone were to notice us, he would not be able to see us clearly enough to make out our identities."

Baxter was annoyed by her optimistic spirits. He glanced at her as she stood beside him in front of the darkened Heskett house. Her cloak rendered her anonymous. He knew himself to be equally well covered. He had turned up the wide collar of his greatcoat and pulled down the brim of his hat to ensure that his features were drenched in dense shadows.

The weak gas lights that had recently been installed in this part of town could not penetrate far into the fog. So long as he and Charlotte stayed out of the short range of the lamplight, they would be reasonably safe from detection. Nevertheless, Baxter thought it best to make one more stab at discouraging his new employer from her risky activities.

"You would do well to have some concerns on the subject, Miss Arkendale. As I have already advised you, this little adventure of yours is fraught with danger. It is not too late to turn back. The carriage I hired is waiting just a short distance away in the park."

"Not another word, if you please, St. Ives," she said crisply. "You have been attempting to dissuade me from this project ever since we first discussed it. It grows wearying. I did not employ you to be the voice of gloom."

"I feel an obligation to advise you."

"I do not employ you for advice, either, sir. Enough. We don't have time for any more of your warnings and dire predictions. The time has come to get on with it."

"As you say, Miss Arkendale."

He watched as she unfastened the low iron gate to the side of the main entrance and started down the stone steps that led to the kitchen.

The front area of the town house, designed to provide access for servants and tradesmen, was situated below street level. Tendrils of fog swirled out of the black pit at the bottom of the steps. Charlotte's cloaked figure wafted, ghostlike, down into the stygian darkness before Baxter could think of any more warnings or arguments.

He moved swiftly to overtake Charlotte. He caught up with her as she came to a halt in the shadows near the kitchen door.

"Allow me, Miss Arkendale."

"Very well, sir, but I pray you will not delay us any further."

"I would not dream of it. Stand back."

"Whatever for, sir?"

"Miss Arkendale, it is my turn to warn you not to delay us with idle questions. Now that we are committed to this piece of idiocy, speed is of the essence."

"Of course, Mr. St. Ives." Charlotte's shoes scraped lightly on the stone as she stepped back. "Please proceed."

Baxter could not see a thing in the thick darkness there below the street. He needed some light but he dared not use the lantern until they were inside the house.

He reached into the pocket of his greatcoat and withdrew one of three small glass vials he had stored there. He snapped the vial in half. There was a flash of bright, intense light. He used his body to shield the glow. The glare revealed the kitchen door and its lock.

Charlotte gave a startled exclamation. "What in heaven's name is that, Mr. St. Ives?"

"I have devoted some time recently to working on a new method of producing instantaneous lights." Baxter fished a set of steel needles out of his pocket. "I am attempting to develop one that will last for more than a few seconds."

"I see." Charlotte's soft voice was imbued with admiration. "How very clever of you, sir. Where did you get those little tools?"

"We men-of-affairs must acquire a variety of skills in order to stay employable." He had learned to use the lock picks before the venture to Italy, knowing full well that he would be obliged to get through several locked doors in Morgan Judd's castle.

The light was already fading. Baxter selected a needle and slid it into the lock.

He closed his eyes and applied the lock pick gently. There was a faint click. The lock gave just as the last of the flaring light created by his new phosphorous compound sputtered out of existence.

"Excellent work, Mr. St. Ives."

"It depends entirely on one's point of view." Baxter pushed open the door and moved cautiously into the kitchen. "The new owner of this house, for example, may not be so happily impressed. In fact, he might well have a serious objection to this little act of housebreaking. I certainly would if I were in his shoes."

"I told you, I made inquiries. The house is empty and likely to remain so until Mrs. Heskett's heir arrives to deal with the estate. By all accounts he is a distant relative who lives somewhere in Scotland and is quite infirm. No one expects him anytime soon."

"What of the servants?"

"They all left shortly after the murder. There was no one around to pay their wages. We have the place to ourselves."

"As you are determined to go through with this business of searching for clues, we had best move quickly." Baxter closed the kitchen door and lit the lantern. "I instructed the coachman to come in search of us if we did not reappear in the park within half an hour's time."

"Half an hour?" Charlotte's disapproving

frown was plainly revealed by the dim, golden glow of the lantern. "I do not know if that will be long enough to go through this entire house."

Baxter glanced quickly around the empty kitchen. "The sooner we're finished, the better."

"Need I remind you, sir, that you are not the one in charge of this affair? You are employed by me and I will give the instructions."

Baxter brushed past her into the hall. He opened another door and saw an empty sitting room that had no doubt been the province of the housekeeper. "We may as well start with the bedchambers upstairs and work our way back down through the house."

"Now see here, Mr. St. Ives—"

"Don't dawdle, Miss Arkendale." Baxter took the stairs two at a time. "The first rule of housebreaking is to be quick and efficient. Now, then, as I have the lantern, I propose that we work together."

"Wait for me." Charlotte's footsteps sounded lightly on the stairs. "Really, sir, when this is finished, you and I are going to have a serious discussion regarding the precise nature of your duties."

"Whatever you say, Miss Arkendale." He turned the corner on the landing and started up the next flight of stairs. "It might save some time if you were to tell me just what we are looking for here tonight."

"I only wish I knew." She sounded slightly breathless as she hurried to catch up with him. "I'm hoping something useful will come to light."

"I was afraid of that." He paused at the top of the stairs and gazed down the length of the darkened corridor. "The bedchambers, I believe. Shall we start at the end of the hall?"

Charlotte came to a halt beside him and peered into the shadows. "That sounds logical."

"I am nothing if not logical, Miss Arkendale."

"Nor am I, Mr. St. Ives." She lifted her chin and led the way to the door at the end of the corridor.

Baxter followed her into the first bedchamber and set the lantern down on a table. He watched Charlotte swiftly open and close drawers. Her expression was serious and intent. Whatever this was, it was no game to her, he realized.

"May I ask how long you have been pursuing your rather bizarre career, Miss Arkendale?" Baxter halted in front of a wardrobe and opened the door.

"Since shortly after my stepfather was murdered a few years ago." Charlotte peered into the depths of a dressing table drawer. "My sister and I were left with very little in the way of funds. There are not a great many careers open to ladies. It was either become a governess, which does not provide sufficient income for two, or invent an alternative."

Baxter pushed aside a row of gowns to check the back of the wardrobe. "Where did you get the inspiration for this particular alternative?"

"My stepfather," Charlotte said coldly. "Lord Winterbourne. He was a greedy opportunist who took advantage of my mother after she was widowed. He convinced her that he wished to take care of her as well as my sister and myself, but in truth he only wanted to get his hands on her money."

"I see."

"My poor mother died within months after Winterbourne married her. I do not think she ever realized what a truly dreadful man he was. But in truth he was a selfish, cruel, unfeeling creature. Neither my sister nor I could mourn him."

"It does sound as though you are far better off without him," Baxter said as he tried another wardrobe drawer.

"Infinitely so." Charlotte went down on her knees beside the bed. "Society is riddled with such despicable liars, Mr. St. Ives. And for the most part women in my mother's situation are extremely vulnerable. They have very few means by which to ascertain the true facts about a suitor's background and financial status."

"So you offer them your services." Baxter went to the window and probed behind the heavy curtains. "Was your stepfather's killer found?"

"No." Charlotte rose to her feet and gazed around the room, searching for another likely hiding place. "Some nameless footpad did the deed."

How very convenient, Baxter thought. "This business of having one of your clients die on you makes for your second brush with murder in a relatively short span of years. Many people live out their entire lives without ever coming so close to that particular crime even once, let alone twice."

Charlotte swung around to face him. "Just what are you implying, sir?"

"Merely an observation. Those of us who are interested in science cannot resist noting odd bits of logic and unusual connections." He was about to let the curtain fall back into place when he saw a slight movement on the other side of the street.

Baxter narrowed his eyes slightly. There was just enough glare reflected from the gas lamp to make out the shadowy figure that slipped through the swirling fog. A servant returning after an evening off from his duties perhaps, Baxter thought.

Or was it someone who had no more business being in this neighborhood than he and Charlotte?

"Is something wrong, Mr. St. Ives? Why are you staring out the window?"

"I was merely examining the street." The shadowy figure had disappeared. Baxter let the curtains fall back into place. "I believe we have done a sufficiently thorough job on this bedchamber. Let's move on to the next one."

"Yes, of course. I wish to find Mrs. Heskett's chamber." Charlotte scooped up the lantern and hurried toward the door.

She gave him a sharp, reproving glance as she went past him. Her cloak billowed out behind her in a seething, roiling movement that seemed to reflect its owner's irritation.

Baxter followed slowly.

A few minutes later, in the midst of searching the last bedchamber, Baxter heard Charlotte give a soft gasp of surprise.

"Find something?" Baxter turned to look at her.

She was down on her knees again, bent at the waist, tugging on some object she had discovered beneath a large, mirrored wardrobe.

"What do you make of this, Mr. St. Ives?" She hauled out a large leather-bound volume and flipped it open.

"What is it?" He walked across the carpet to join her. "A journal?"

"No, it's a watercolor sketchbook." Charlotte turned a few pages to reveal a series of delicate pastel drawings. "Very likely it belonged to Mrs. Heskett." She paused abruptly and stared at one of the sketches. "Good heavens."

Baxter raised his brows as he surveyed the watercolors. "Mrs. Heskett appears to have had a great interest in classical statuary."

"Indeed," Charlotte said dryly. "Greek and Roman gods for the most part, I believe. They are, uh, exceptionally well-endowed figures."

"Indeed."

Together they both gazed silently at the pictures of nude male statues that filled the sketchbook.

Charlotte cleared her throat. "I have seen a few of these statues myself in the British

Museum. I think it's safe to say that Mrs. Heskett has taken some artistic liberties with certain portions of the anatomies."

"One could certainly say that."

Charlotte closed the book with a snap. "Well, her choice of subject is not of interest to us. The important thing is that I found this sketchbook shoved out of sight beneath the cabinet."

"What's so odd about that? Many ladies enjoy painting with watercolors."

"Quite true. My sister, Ariel, enjoys watercolors also." Charlotte raised her head, her eyes gleaming. "But she does not hide her sketchbook under a cabinet."

He suddenly understood where her deductions had led her. "Hold on a moment, Miss Arkendale. I would advise you not to leap to baseless conclusions. It's highly unlikely that Drusilla Heskett deliberately hid her book of watercolors. It was no doubt accidentally kicked under there by one of the servants when they packed up after her death."

"I disagree, sir. I think it was deliberately concealed there."

"If so, it may well have been because of the subject matter. Perhaps Mrs. Heskett did not want her staff to know that she enjoyed drawing pictures of oversized phalluses."

Charlotte blinked. She looked away and suddenly became very busy attempting to tuck the large sketchbook inside her cloak. "Nevertheless, I shall want to examine it. I'm going to take it with me." She gave up trying to stuff the book inside her cloak and clutched it very firmly in front of her.

Baxter frowned at her sudden agitation. It took him a few seconds to realize that he had embarrassed her. The notion of the formidable Miss Arkendale being disconcerted by the use of the word *phallus* amused him.

"Miss Arkendale, I feel compelled to point out that if you take that volume out of this house you will have committed what some would call an act of theft."

"Nonsense. I'm merely going to borrow it for a while."

"Borrow it?"

"I am involved in an inquiry into the circumstances of my client's death, after all," she reminded him brusquely. "I need as much information as I can get."

"What sort of information do you expect to find in a sketchbook full of pictures of nude statuary?" Baxter demanded.

"Who can say?" She whirled about and marched determinedly past him. "Come. We still have the downstairs rooms left to search."

Baxter swore softly and started to follow her. But curiosity and an uneasy stirring at the back of his neck caused him to hesitate.

He went back to the window, moved the curtain aside an inch or so, and looked down into the street. The view from this bedchamber was similar to that of the first room he and Charlotte had searched.

The fog had thickened. The gas lamp across the way was only a pinpoint of glare now. It did nothing to illuminate the scene. Baxter waited for a long moment, searching for shadows amid the shadows, but he could not detect any movement.

"Come along, Mr. St. Ives," Charlotte called softly from the hall. "We must hurry."

Baxter released the curtain and turned toward the door. He had seen no evidence of anyone lurking in the fog but for some reason he did not feel any sense of relief.

He followed Charlotte downstairs.

A short time later, he closed the last drawer in a desk and pulled his watch from his waistcoat pocket. "We must be off, Miss Arkendale."

"Just a few more minutes." Charlotte stood on tiptoe to replace some volumes she had removed from a bookshelf. "I am almost finished."

"We cannot linger any longer." Baxter picked up the lantern.

She scanned the bookshelves with a quick, anxious eye. "But what if we have overlooked something of importance?"

"You do not even know what you are searching for, so how will you know if you have overlooked anything?" He took her arm and led her swiftly toward the hall. "Move, Miss Arkendale."

She glanced at him with sudden alarm. "Is there something wrong, sir?"

"Need you ask?" He drew her down the stairs toward the kitchen. "It is past midnight and we are entertaining ourselves by searching the house of a lady who was recently murdered. You are even now preparing to take an item that once belonged to the previous occupant of these premises. Many people might well feel that there is some cause for concern in this situation."

"There is no call for sarcasm, sir. When I asked if there was something wrong, I meant something other than your earlier fears concerning our project. You seem more uneasy of a sudden."

He glanced at her, startled by her perceptiveness. She was right. He had been growing increasingly restless and ill at ease ever since he had spotted the man in the shadows across the street.

It had been a long time since he had experienced this particular very unpleasant, very cold frisson. Three years, to be precise.

He was a man of science and as such he refused to label the feeling as a premonition. But the last time the sensation had struck had been memorable, to say the least. He had the scars to prove how close he had come to getting himself killed.

"Be careful, sir, or we shall both trip on these stairs," Charlotte whispered. "It will be difficult to get out of here if we are sporting broken legs."

"We're almost back to the kitchen," Baxter said as they went past the housekeeper's room. "I'm going to put out the lantern now. We will be nearly blind until we get back outside. Do not let go of my arm."

"Why don't we wait until we are back on the street before we put out the lantern?"

"Because I don't want to take the chance of having anyone notice our departure."

"But no one will be able to see us in the fog," Charlotte protested.

"The glow of the lantern will be visible, even if our faces are not. Are you ready?"

She gave him an odd, searching look. He thought she was going to continue to argue about the lantern. But something she must have seen in his face apparently convinced her to let the subject drop. She tightened her grip on the sketchbook and nodded once, very quickly.

Baxter put out the light. The darkness of the kitchen enclosed them in an instant.

Relying on his memory of the room, Baxter led the way back to the door. It opened easily, with only a small, betraying squeak. The dim glare of fog-reflected lamplight beckoned from the street above the front area.

Charlotte put a foot on the first of the stone steps. Baxter seized her arm again and held her still. She obediently came to a halt, waiting for him to signal her that it was safe to continue on up to the street.

Mercifully, she did not ask any more questions. He was grateful for her continued silence. He stood listening intently for a moment. The rattle of carriage wheels on the paving stones sounded from somewhere in the distance but there was no indication that anyone waited nearby.

Baxter nudged Charlotte gently. She hastened up the steps. He followed swiftly. When they reached the street he turned and drew her toward the park, where the carriage waited.

The shadows in front of them shifted without warning.

A massive figure loomed out of the mist. The heavily built man was garbed in a bulky coachman's coat and a low-crowned hat. The glare of the nearby gas lamp glinted dully on the large, long-barreled pistol in his beefy fist.

"Well, now, what 'ave we 'ere?" the man asked in a rasping voice. "Looks like a couple of gentry coves nosin' around in my business."

Baxter heard Charlotte draw a sharp, alarmed breath, but she did not cry out.

"Stand aside," Baxter ordered.

"Not so fast." There was enough light to see several large, dark holes in places where the villain's teeth should have been. "You just came out of my house and I ain't lettin' you leave with anything that belongs to me."

"Your house?" Charlotte stared at him in amazement. "How dare you? I happen to know that particular house was recently owned by someone else."

"Uh, Miss Arkendale," Baxter said softly. "This may not be a good time—"

"It's my house, I tell ye," the big man snarled at Charlotte. "I spotted it three nights back and I been watchin' it real close ever since."

"Watching it for what reason?" Charlotte demanded.

"Making sure the owner was gone for a

good long while and weren't planning to come back unexpected-like in the middle of the night, of course."

"Good heavens, you're a professional house-breaker."

"I am that, right enough. Real professional." The man grinned with pride. "Never been caught on account of I'm real careful. Always make sure the owners are out of town before I go in and help meself. I was getting ready to make my move tonight and what do I see? A couple of the fancy trying to beat me out of my profits."

Baxter softened his voice. "I said, stand aside. I will not tell you again."

"Glad to hear that. Ain't got time for any dull lectures tonight." The man dismissed Baxter with one last, mocking glance and turned his toothless grin back on Charlotte. "Now, then, Madam Busybody, just what did ye make off with? A bit of the silver, perhaps? A few trinkets from the jewelry drawer? Whatever it is, it belongs to me. Hand it over."

"We took no valuables from that house," Charlotte declared.

"Must have taken something." The man scowled at the sketchbook. "What's that?"

"Just a book. It's nothing to do with you."

"I ain't interested in no book, but I'll have a look at whatever ye got inside that cloak. I'll wager ye tucked a few nice candlesticks and maybe a necklace or two in there. Open that cloak."

"I will do no such thing," Charlotte said with icy disdain.

"Mouthy bitch, aren't ye? Well, here's a little illustration of what'll 'appen if ye don't give me my rightful earnings."

The man whipped around with surprising speed. He brought the pistol up high as if it were a club and swung it in a short, savage arc aimed at Baxter's head.

"No," Charlotte gasped. "Wait, don't hurt him. He merely works for me."

Baxter was already moving, ducking swiftly to avoid the slashing pistol. He yanked one of the glass vials out of the small box in his pocket, snapped it open, and hurled it straight into his assailant's face.

The special phosphorous compound flashed into a harsh, startling light on contact with air. The villain roared in shock and rage and awkwardly leaped back, clawing at his eyes. The pistol clattered on the paving.

Baxter stepped forward and slammed a fist into the man's jaw. Still partially blinded by the instantaneous light that had exploded in his face, the villain reeled.

"Ye've blinded me, ye bloody bastard. I'm *blind*."

Baxter saw no reason to assure him that the effect was only temporary. He seized Charlotte's arm. "Come. I hear the carriage."

"It ain't fair," the villain whined. "I'm the one what spotted that vacant house. It's mine. Go find yer own house."

Charlotte glanced back at the outraged villain. "We're going to inform the magistrate that you're skulking about in this neighborhood. You'd better leave at once."

"That's enough." Baxter saw the carriage lamps in the distance. He hauled Charlotte forward. "We've got our own problems."

"I don't want that villain to think that he can go into Mrs. Heskett's house and steal whatever he likes."

"Why not? We just did exactly that."

"Taking this sketchbook is a different matter entirely," she protested breathlessly.

"Hmm." The carriage was almost upon them.

"I must tell you, I was most impressed with the way you handled that situation, Mr. St. Ives. Very clever of you to think of using your instantaneous lights in that fashion. Very clever, indeed."

Baxter ignored the admiration in her words. He was too intent on watching the dark carriage materialize out of the fog.

The horses appeared first, a pair of gray phantoms coalescing out of the mist. The bulk of the vehicle took shape behind them. The coachman, hired from Severedges Stables along with the carriage and team, had driven for Baxter many times. He was accustomed to the eccentricities of his client.

Baxter had patronized the large livery stable for years. He found it more efficient and economical to send around to Severedges's whenever he required a carriage than to maintain his own stable. In exchange for his long-standing business and prompt payment of accounts, he was assured of service and discretion.

"Anything wrong, sir?" the coachman inquired as he wheeled the horses to a halt.

"Nothing that my companion and I could not handle." Baxter yanked the carriage door open. He caught Charlotte around the waist and tossed her lightly into the cab. "Take us back to Miss Arkendale's house."

"Aye, sir."

Baxter vaulted into the carriage, closed the door, and sank down on the seat across from Charlotte. The vehicle rumbled into motion.

He checked to make certain that the curtains were still drawn across the windows. Then he turned back to Charlotte. In the pale glow of the interior lamps, her eyes were very brilliant.

"Mr. St. Ives, I cannot thank you enough for your actions tonight," she said. "You were truly noble and heroic and terribly quick-witted in the crisis. All of my doubts concerning your employment have been resolved. Mr. Marcle was quite right to send you to me."

Anger surged through him without warning. She could have gotten herself killed tonight, he thought. And there she sat, glowing with enthusiasm and praising him as if he were a servant who had performed his duties particularly well. It was enough to make any reasonable man want to lose his temper.

"I am delighted that you are satisfied with my services, Miss Arkendale."

"Oh, I am, sir. Most delighted. You will, indeed, make me an excellent man-of-affairs."

"But in my *professional* opinion," he continued very softly, "your reckless actions this evening were intolerable. There is no excuse for such foolishness. I must have been out of my mind to allow you to search Drusilla Heskett's house."

"I do not recall asking your permission, sir."

"You could have been hurt, perhaps even killed by that man who accosted us."

"I was in no danger, thanks to you, sir. Indeed, I do not know what I would have done without you this evening." Her eyes glowed. "No man has ever come to my rescue, Mr. St. Ives. It was quite thrilling, actually. Just the sort of thing one reads about in Gothic novels or in one of Byron's poems."

"Bloody hell, Miss Arkendale—"

"You were wonderful, sir." Without warning, she launched herself across the short distance that separated them. She threw her arms around his neck and gave him a quick, exuberant hug.

The folds of her cloak settled lightly around him. Baxter was suddenly enveloped by a warm, tantalizing, indescribable fragrance. It was composed of the light flowery perfume Charlotte wore, the herbal essence of the soap she used, and the incredibly unique, utterly feminine scent of her body.

He felt as though he had been thrust into one of his own bell jars. Some unseen air pump seemed to have sucked all of the oxygen out of the atmosphere. All that was left to breathe was the essence of Charlotte.

A searing awareness flashed through him with the speed of an electrical charge. It created a truly alchemical reaction. The ancients had believed that, with the aid of fire, it was possible to transmute base lead into glorious gold. Baxter knew now that it was possible for the heat in his blood to change his anger into intense sexual desire.

He wanted her. Now. Tonight. He had never wanted a woman so badly in the whole of his life.

He caught her face between his palms as she started to pull away from him. He gazed down at her, baffled by the force of his own need.

"Forgive me, Mr. St. Ives." Charlotte looked flustered. Her smile was tremulous. Her eyes went to his mouth. "I did not mean to embarrass you. The excitement of the moment must have overcome my senses."

Baxter did not respond. He could not think of a damn thing to say.

He did the only thing he could do. He kissed her.

Four

For an instant, Charlotte did not understand what had happened. She knew only that Baxter's mouth was on hers and that he was kissing her. And then it dawned on her. He was making love to her. Right there in the carriage.

The flames of the fierce, vital passion that

she had seen in his eyes at their first meeting had exploded. They dazzled her senses the way instantaneous lights dazzled one's vision.

It was as though she had walked into a strange, bewildering room that glittered with too many mirrors and sparkled with an unnatural number of massed candles. It was both thrilling and confusing and a little frightening. She could not see the door. She was not certain how she would escape should escape prove necessary.

Baxter's mouth moved on hers, deepening the kiss. He gave a husky groan. His hands tightened gently on her face until she was acutely aware of the strength in him. She could feel the muscles in his thighs. They were taut and hard and unyielding against her leg.

A startling warmth invaded her. It pooled in her lower body and caused her to shiver from head to foot. She had never reacted to anything or anyone in such an odd manner.

"Charlotte." Baxter's voice was low and infinitely compelling. It contained need and insistent demand and an aching sense of longing. *"Charlotte."*

She gripped his shoulders. Her lips parted of their own accord.

He tore his mouth free for a moment, raised his head slightly, and stared down at her with an intensity that should have terrified her. The lamplight glittered on the gold frames of his eyeglasses. Fire burned in his amber eyes.

The eyes of an alchemist, she thought.

With an abrupt, impatient movement,

Baxter jerked off his spectacles and tossed them onto the opposite seat. "Bloody hell. What have you done to me?"

She shook her head, unable to look away. She realized she was clinging to his shoulders as though afraid she might fall into a bottomless sea if she let go of him. "I was about to ask you the same question."

"Bloody hell." He lowered his mouth to hers once more.

She felt his hand slip inside the hood of her cloak to cup the nape of her neck. His fingers were strong and warm. The intimacy of the caress sent another wave of excitement through her.

He shifted his hold on her so that she was draped across his thighs. He cradled her in the curve of one arm and bent his head to kiss her throat. He pushed aside the folds of her cloak.

Charlotte heard her own soft gasp as Baxter's hand closed over her breast. She could feel the heat of his palm straight through the thin wool of her gown. But she could not bring herself to pull away. A stunning sense of urgency infused her entire body. She tugged at the lapels of his greatcoat.

"Mr. St. Ives—"

His hand moved slowly down over the curve of her breast and tightened on her hip. He squeezed carefully.

"Dear heaven," she whispered, shaken.

The solid, heavy length of his manhood pressed against her thigh. She closed her eyes as she sank beneath another wave of sensation. She felt as if she had slipped into a delicious trance. Perhaps this was how it felt to undergo a session of mesmerism.

She put her hands inside Baxter's coat, desperate for the feel of him. She was enthralled by what she found. Through the fabric of his linen shirt she could distinguish the sleek, powerful muscles of his chest. The heat and scent of him were intoxicating. She wanted more, so much more.

He gathered up her tumbled skirts and the flowing folds of the cloak. He lifted them above her knees. Charlotte shivered again when he touched the inside of her thigh. He stroked her bare skin above her neatly tied garter. A shock went through her.

The carriage slowed to a halt.

Charlotte froze. Reality returned in a rush.

"Bloody hell." Baxter straightened quickly. He leaned across Charlotte and snatched his spectacles off the cushion. Then he moved a carriage curtain aside. "We have arrived at your house. How the devil did we get here so quickly? I had several things I wished to say to you tonight."

"And I had much to discuss with you." Charlotte struggled to collect herself. She felt awkward and off balance. She also felt flushed and breathless and filled with a strange sense of anticipation. "We did not even begin to discuss the events of the evening."

"No, we did not." He watched her with

grim, narrowed eyes as she scooted back to the opposite seat and composed herself. "I shall call upon you tomorrow."

His curt manner had the effect of lowering her spirits. The man had just been kissing her with great passion, she thought, and now he was speaking to her as if she had offended him. Then it struck her that he was no doubt deeply shaken by the emotions that had briefly overcome both of them.

In truth, she was just as disturbed by the tumultuous embrace. But as Baxter's employer, it was her responsibility to take charge of the situation. Baxter was no doubt castigating himself quite savagely for having succumbed to the more passionate elements of his nature.

She leaned forward to touch his hand in what she hoped was a reassuring fashion. "Do not concern yourself, sir. You are in no way to blame for what just occurred. That sort of intense emotion is often precipitated by excitement and danger. Our encounter with that dreadful man outside Mrs. Heskett's house was the cause of our heightened emotions."

Baxter gazed at her very steadily. "Do you think so?"

"Yes, of course. It is the only explanation. The threat of violence can open a floodgate of intense passions."

"You have had a great deal of experience with this type of thing?"

"Well, no, not exactly," she admitted. "But

I have read enough Byron to know that what happened to us just now was not unusual. When one faces danger, all of one's senses are aroused and...and stimulated."

"Good God. You are basing your conclusions on the work of a bloody poet?"

She was a little hurt by his obvious disdain. "Byron writes very convincingly of the darker passions. He appears to have a sound comprehension of their effects. I feel that one can learn a great deal from his work and the work of the other romantic poets."

"That would be laughable were it not so ludicrous."

"I am attempting to give you a logical explanation for an event that has clearly troubled you, Mr. St. Ives."

He glanced down at her hand, where it rested on his. When he looked up there was a dangerous gleam in his eyes. "Thank you, Miss Arkendale, but I believe I will survive the experience without having to resort to your odd logic. The day I seek explanations and illumination from a damned poet will be the day that I commit myself to Bedlam."

She hastily removed her hand from his thigh. Baxter was in a foul mood. There was no point attempting to soothe him tonight.

"Very well, sir," she said, determined to sound cheerful and unruffled. "I'm sure that by morning we shall both have forgotten all about the entire affair."

He said nothing for the space of several

seconds. A couple of thuds outside announced that the coachman had jumped down from the box.

"That remains to be seen," Baxter said finally.

Charlotte drew a steadying breath. "Tomorrow when you call, we shall compare our observations of Mrs. Heskett's house."

"Yes."

"I will have had a chance to look through her watercolor sketchbook. Perhaps I shall discover something useful in it."

"I doubt that." Baxter leaned forward and caught her chin on the edge of his hand. "Listen to me and listen well. I shall see you safely inside your house tonight. You will make certain that every window is locked and the doors securely bolted before you retire to bed."

She blinked. "Of course, Mr. St. Ives. I always check the locks before I retire. It is a very old habit, I assure you. But I doubt that there is any cause for particular alarm tonight. That villain who accosted us was in no condition to have followed this carriage through the fog."

"You may be correct, but you will do exactly as I tell you, nevertheless. Is that clear?"

Charlotte sensed intuitively that it would not be a sound notion to allow Baxter to gain the upper hand in their association. She must stay in command. "I appreciate your concern, but I am your employer. While I am willing to listen to your advice, you must comprehend that I form my own opinions and make my own decisions."

"You will do more than listen to my advice, Charlotte," Baxter said with an infuriating calm. "You will heed it."

The carriage door opened at that moment. Very much aware of the coachman standing politely in the shadows, Charlotte contented herself with a raised brow. "You proved yourself an excellent assistant tonight, sir, but there are no doubt other qualified persons available who could replace you. If you wish to retain your post, you will do well to exhibit at least a modicum of deference to your employer."

Amusement glittered briefly in his eyes. "Are you threatening to dismiss me, Charlotte? After all we have been through tonight? I am crushed."

His silent laughter was so infuriating that she did not trust herself to respond in front of the coachman. Without a word, Charlotte collected her skirts and prepared to descend from the carriage.

The coachman handed her down with grave politeness. In the weak glow of the carriage lamps she could not be certain of the expression on his carefully blank features but Charlotte could have sworn that she saw a flicker of amused sympathy on his face.

Baxter followed her out of the carriage, took her arm, and walked her up the front steps to her door. He took the key from her hand and inserted it into the lock.

"Good night, Mr. St. Ives." Charlotte

stepped into the hall and turned to face him. She summoned the sort of cool, authoritative smile that was proper for an employer to bestow upon a person in her service who had done a good night's work. "I must tell you again how very pleased I am with the dramatic demonstration of your professional skills that I witnessed this evening."

"Thank you." Baxter planted a broad hand on the door frame and regarded her with a considering expression. "There is just one thing."

"What is that, sir?"

"Perhaps you should consider calling me by my given name. I see no point in attempting to maintain a great deal of formality between us under the circumstances."

She stared at him, speechless.

Apparently satisfied with her reaction, he reached out and gently pulled the door closed in her face.

Twenty minutes later Baxter was still seething as he strode through the door of his library. He could not believe his stunning loss of self-control.

"Bloody hell."

He crossed the room to the small table near the fireplace and picked up the crystal decanter that sat there. He was the master of his own emotions, he told himself savagely. He was a man of science. He had worshiped at the altar of logic and reason and control all of his life.

He splashed brandy into a glass. He could not even remember when he had learned to keep all of his feelings under a strict rein. It was something he had always understood, something he had always known how to do. Even in the midst of his brief sexual liaisons he never allowed passion to overwhelm common sense. He had seen firsthand the damage that could result.

He took a deep swallow of the potent brandy and savored the fire.

To make matters worse, Charlotte had had the unmitigated nerve to inform him that the explanation for his behavior could be found in Byron's overheated, melodramatic poetry.

It was enough to make a man lock himself in the sanctuary of his laboratory and never emerge.

He threw himself down into his favorite reading chair and contemplated the flames on the hearth. They reminded him of Charlotte. Both produced extremely volatile chemical reactions of the sort that could burn an unwary man.

He closed his eyes but the threat of the fire did not vanish. In his mind he saw again the flames that glowed red in Charlotte's lantern-lit hair. He wanted to sink his fingers deep into their dangerous warmth. His hand tightened violently around the brandy glass.

He had not been the only one who had lost control in the carriage, he reminded himself. Charlotte's response to him had been unmistakable. If the coachman had not halted the vehicle, the evening would have had a different ending.

He had a vivid image of Charlotte's soft thighs wrapped around his waist, her small nails pressed deep into his back.

He took another swallow of brandy, aware that he could still taste Charlotte. His head was filled with her scent. His palm remembered the shape of one exquisitely rigid nipple.

It was going to be a long night.

Logic and sound reasoning would do him little good this evening. He knew he would not be able to banish the memory of Charlotte in his arms. It was too riveting, too compelling.

But the next time he saw her, he would be in command of himself. He would not allow his self-control to slip again.

He glanced at his glass and saw that he had already emptied it. He made to set it down on the table beside the chair. A folded and sealed sheet of foolscap was in the way. He recognized it immediately. It was a note that had been delivered earlier, shortly before he had left the house to meet Charlotte.

It was from his father's widow, Maryann, Lady Esherton. It was the third message she had sent this week.

"Bloody hell." With a sense of resignation, Baxter picked up the letter and broke the seal.

The message was almost identical to the other two notes Maryann had dispatched to him during the past few days. It was very short and to the point.

Dear Baxter:

I wish to speak with you. The matter is most urgent. I request that you call upon me at your earliest convenience.

Yours very truly,
Lady E.

Baxter crumpled the note and tossed it onto the fire just as he had the earlier notes from Maryann. Her notion of a crisis did not equate with his own. Maryann's gravest problems tended to revolve around money, specifically the Esherton fortune. Baxter's father had left him in charge of the inheritance until Maryann's son, Hamilton, reached the age of twenty-five. Maryann was not pleased with the arrangement. Nor was Hamilton, for that matter.

Baxter had a few more years of the thankless task to endure before he could dump the entire responsibility into his half brother's lap.

Impatiently, he pushed aside his old problems and considered the new set he had acquired. He propped his elbows on the leather arms of the chair, steepled his fingers, and gazed into the fire.

Whatever else could be said about the night's events, one thing was clear. There was danger afoot and Charlotte was in the midst of it.

In the black and crimson chamber the coals on the brazier burned low. The rich, spicy vapors of the incense had opened his senses. His mind was attuned to the forces of the metaphysical plane. He was ready.

"Read the cards, my love," he whispered.

The fortune-teller turned over the first card. "The golden griffin."

"A man."

"Always." The fortune-teller looked at him across the low table. "Beware. The griffin would stand in your way."

"Will he be able to alter my plans?"

She turned over another card, hesitated. "The phoenix." She reached for the next card, placed it faceup. "The red ring."

"Well?"

"No. The golden griffin may prove difficult but ultimately you will prevail."

He smiled. "Yes. Now tell me about the woman."

The fortune-teller turned over another card. "The lady with the crystal eyes. She searches."

"But she will not find."

The fortune-teller shook her head. "No. She will not find what she seeks."

"She's only a woman, after all. She will not be a problem."

And neither would the fortune-teller be a problem when this was finished, he thought.

He would dispose of her when the time came. She was useful at the moment, however, and it was a simple matter to hold her in thrall with the bonds of her own passions.

❧

What do you make of this curious design, Ariel?" Charlotte pushed Drusilla Heskett's watercolor sketchbook across her desk. "You are more conversant with current fashion than I. Have you ever seen anything similar?"

Ariel paused in the act of pouring another cup of tea. She glanced at the sketchbook, which was open to a page near the middle. Her eyes widened as she gazed at the picture of a nude statue that decorated the left side of the paper.

"Uh, no," Ariel said dryly. "I do not believe that I have ever encountered anything similar to that particular design."

Charlotte gave her a reproving glare. "Not the picture of the statue. The little drawing in the corner. It appears to be a circle with a triangle inside. And there are little tiny figures around the edges and in the center of the triangle."

"Yes, I see." Ariel shook her head. "It bears no resemblance to any of the fashionable motifs I have seen in *La Belle Assemblée* or *Ackermann's Repository of the Arts*. Perhaps one of the other ladies' magazines contains such a design."

"Perhaps it is Egyptian or Roman."

"I do not believe so." With the tip of one finger, Ariel traced the poorly drawn pattern. "Heaven knows there are any number of decorative designs that have been copied from Egyptian and Roman antiquities. Every modiste and decorator in London uses them. And since ancient Zamar has come into fashion we have seen a great many dolphins and shells. But this design is not familiar to me. Why is it of interest?"

"For some reason Drusilla Heskett saw fit to copy it onto this page in her watercolor sketchbook. A sketchbook she appears to have devoted entirely to pictures of nude statues."

Ariel glanced up with an inquiring look. "But this is not a watercolor picture. It is a drawing made with pen and ink."

"Yes. And it is completely unlike all of the other scenes in the sketchbook."

"Indeed." Ariel smiled faintly. "I wonder if Mrs. Heskett is typical of the sort of client you hope to attract from the fashionable circles. She appears to have had a lively interest in the male figure."

"Yes, well, I suppose her tastes are no longer very important. What bothers me is that I cannot help but wonder why she chose to add this extremely strange design to her book."

"What is that reddish brown stain on the binding?" Ariel asked. "Spilled watercolor paint?"

"Perhaps." Charlotte touched the stain with her fingertips. "But what if it is dried blood?"

"Dear heaven."

"What if Mrs. Heskett lived long enough after she was shot to shove this sketchbook under the wardrobe?" Charlotte whispered.

"You will likely never know for certain."

"No, I suppose not." Charlotte nibbled on her lower lip, thinking of the possibilities.

Ariel picked up her teacup and regarded Charlotte over the rim. "You have many questions to answer, but I have some of my own."

"Such as?"

"What, exactly, happened last night when you went out to search Drusilla Heskett's house?"

Charlotte sat back in her chair. "I gave you the entire tale last night. Mr. St. Ives and I discovered the sketchbook and then were accosted by a housebreaker as we left the house. That is all there was to it."

"Do you know, it is your description of St. Ives's role in the affair that sticks in my mind this morning."

Charlotte smiled with deep satisfaction. "As I said, Mr. St. Ives was magnificent."

"Magnificent is not a word that you are accustomed to use, especially not when you are describing a member of the opposite sex."

Charlotte cleared her throat. "Well, there really is no other word that suits in this particular situation. Mr. St. Ives was clever, resourceful, quick-thinking, and astonishingly brave. I shudder to think what might have happened had he not accompanied me."

"All in all, quite the perfect man-of-affairs, would you say?"

"Perfect. Mr. Marcle was absolutely correct to recommend him for the position."

"He kissed you, did he not?" Ariel asked softly.

"Good lord, what a strange thing to say. Why on earth would I kiss John Marcle?" Charlotte reached for her tea. "He's a very nice man, but he's at least thirty years older than I am and I do not think that he's particularly interested in females."

"You know very well I meant Mr. St. Ives, not Mr. Marcle."

Charlotte felt the warmth rise furiously into her cheeks. "You believe that Mr. St. Ives kissed me? Wherever did you get such a crazed notion?"

"When I came to your bedchamber last night to inquire into your adventures you looked..." Ariel hesitated, clearly searching for the right word. "Different."

"Different?"

"Overheated. Very bright. Practically glowing." Ariel waved one hand in a vague gesture. "A little disheveled, too. There was an odd look in your eyes."

"Really, Ariel, this is too much. I had just had a very disturbing encounter with an extremely violent villain. How the devil is one supposed to look after such an occasion?"

"I don't know how the average lady looks after she has had a near miss with a villain but I know how you look."

"What on earth do you mean? I have not had any other direct encounters with villains."

"You have had one that I recall quite distinctly." Ariel put her cup down gently on its saucer. "Five years ago. The night before Winterbourne got his throat slit by a footpad. I heard you in the hall that night. You used Papa's pistol to drive Winterbourne and one of his gaming cronies from the house."

Charlotte stared at her. "I did not realize that you understood what had happened that night."

"I did not comprehend matters entirely until I was much older. But even then I understood that you had dealt with a very dangerous situation. And I saw the expression in your eyes afterward. It was not the same look I saw there last night."

"I'm sorry. I did not mean for you to ever learn just how evil Winterbourne was."

"His companion was infinitely worse, was he not?"

Charlotte shuddered at the memory. "He was a monster. But that was a long time ago, Ariel. And we both came through it safely."

"The point is, I recall your demeanor on that night quite clearly. You were cold to the touch. Your eyes were stark."

Charlotte rubbed her temples. "I do not know what to say. I was terrified. I do not recall anything else about my emotional state."

"Last night you had a scare, too. But you were not cold. Your eyes were anything but bleak. Indeed, you were excited and animated and almost exuberant."

"Get to the point, Ariel."

"The point is, I believe that Mr. St. Ives kissed you."

Charlotte groaned and threw up her hands. "Very well, he kissed me. We were both overwrought and somewhat overstimulated by the night's events. Danger sometimes has that effect on the senses, you know."

"It does?"

"Yes," Charlotte said very firmly. "The poets are always writing about the problem. Even the senses of a person who is cool and clearheaded and not inclined toward strong passions can be overcome by a thrilling experience."

"Even a person such as Mr. St. Ives?"

"Actually, I was referring to myself." Charlotte smiled ruefully. "Mr. St. Ives is cool and clearheaded also, of course, but it is obvious that he must employ a fine degree of self-discipline in order to achieve that serene state."

Ariel's lips parted in astonishment. "I beg your pardon?"

"Underneath that stern, steady exterior, he is a man of dangerously strong passions."

"Strong passions? Mr. St. Ives?"

"I know that I expressed some concerns in the beginning but I no longer believe his temperament will present any great difficulties for us," Charlotte said with a false heartiness. "I am convinced he will do very well in his position."

"I'm glad you're satisfied, but I'm beginning to have a few qualms. Charlotte, if Mr. St. Ives has kissed you, things have taken on a whole new aspect. How much do you really know about him?"

"What do you mean?" Charlotte gave her a searching look. "Mr. Marcle sent a glowing letter of reference."

"Yes, but we have not done any research on St. Ives ourselves. We have not even made the sort of inquiries that we would have made if we were examining him on behalf of a client."

"Don't be ridiculous. My instincts are perfectly sound in such matters. You know that."

"My instincts are very sound, too. And I'm beginning to wonder about St. Ives."

"There is absolutely no need to be concerned."

"Charlotte, you allowed him to kiss you."

"Well, what of it?" Charlotte clasped her hands together on her desk. "It was merely a kiss."

"You are not given to entertaining yourself with gentlemen's kisses," Ariel retorted.

Charlotte knew she could not argue with that observation. Her mother's experience with Lord Winterbourne and a career spent looking into the murky pasts of several callous gentlemen with so-called honorable intentions had left her with few illusions about men.

That did not mean that she did not have a few lingering romantic inclinations and the perfectly natural curiosity of a healthy young woman. Her memories of her parents' marriage were good ones, after all, and there were times when she would have given a great deal to know the same kind of intimate happiness her mother had shared with her father.

But she was all too well aware that the risks of marriage were very great for a woman. She had no interest in the wedded state, which was just as well, given her age and circumstances, but she had toyed with the notion of a discreet affair.

Unfortunately, such things were easier to contemplate than they were to carry out. For one thing, it was difficult for a woman in her situation to find a suitable man.

She did not move in social circles. She did not receive invitations and introductions. The handful of respectable gentlemen who had entered her life over the years had failed to inspire any strong emotions in her. Many, such as Marcle, had been much too old. Others had simply been uninspiring.

It seemed rather pointless to have an affair unless one was infused with a truly grand passion, she thought. Why bother with the risks unless one expected to experience the stimulating emotions and exciting metaphysical feelings that the poets related?

The sort of feelings, for example, that had swept over her last night when Baxter had kissed her.

The thought stopped Charlotte cold. Was she actually considering the possibility of having an affair with Baxter St. Ives?

She looked at the strange design that Drusilla Heskett had drawn in the watercolor sketchbook. The pattern was an enigma. Not unlike her feelings for Baxter.

Five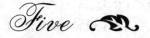

"A lady in your position cannot be too careful, Miss Patterson." Charlotte smiled at the woman seated across from her. She had a theory that it was good business to compliment a client's foresight and caution. "You were wise to verify the impression Mr. Adams made."

"I told myself I must be careful."

"Indeed. But I am happy to inform you that our inquiries produced no reason to doubt either Mr. Adams's credibility or the security of his financial situation."

"I do not mind telling you that I am enormously relieved to hear that. I do not know how to thank you." Honoria Patterson, a pleasantly rounded woman with a pretty face and warm eyes, visibly relaxed her fierce grip on the reticule that rested on her lap.

There was an air of sweet, soft femininity, almost a maternal quality about Honoria, which made her appear a trifle fragile. Charlotte was not deceived. She knew full well that any woman who had kept her spirits strong and optimistic after nearly ten years as a governess was no delicate flower.

Honoria was typical of many of the clients whom Charlotte assisted. She was nearing thirty and had never been married. After struggling to support herself since the age of seventeen, she had come into a small, respectable, and completely unexpected inheritance.

Predictably, a handful of suitors had materialized in the wake of the news of Honoria's good fortune. She had dismissed most of them without hesitation. A governess learned early to be wary of a gentleman's intentions. But one, William Adams, a widower in his early thirties with two children, had captivated her interest and, apparently, her heart.

As she had explained to Charlotte, the years she had spent instilling the principles of logic and sound reasoning into her young charges had given her a measure of hard-won wisdom and a healthy sense of caution. A friend who operated an agency for governesses had referred her to Charlotte.

"I'm delighted to have been of service," Charlotte said. "Especially so in a case such as this where the results of our inquiries are positive."

"I am so very fond of Mr. Adams." Honoria blushed. "And the children are delightful. But you know how it is. Ladies of our advanced years must question a man's intentions. After all, the world considers us well and truly on the shelf."

On the shelf.

Charlotte sighed. She was already twenty-five. Where had the time gone? she wondered. It seemed only yesterday that she had been desperate to create a career that would allow her to support herself and her sister. She had devoted all of her energy and passion to the task and somehow five years had gone by in the blink of an eye.

She did not regret having passed beyond what Society considered a marriageable age for a lady. Business had improved noticeably, in fact, after she began to look as though she were no longer fresh out of the schoolroom. But she could not help wondering now just what she had missed never having known the thrill of passion.

The sense of wistfulness startled her. She was not lonely. She took great satisfaction in her work. She had her independence. What more could she truly want? Perhaps she had, indeed, been reading too much poetry lately, she thought.

Nevertheless, she did not want Ariel to follow precisely the same path. The business was important and Ariel was keenly interested in it. But Charlotte did not want her sister to sacrifice everything to it, as she had done. There was no longer such a pressing need. They had sufficient income to keep them in comfortable, if not luxurious, circumstances. If her plans to attract clients from the Polite World proved successful, a bit of luxury would even be possible.

She would give a great deal to ensure that Ariel had an opportunity to experience some of the innocent pleasures of young womanhood. Such pleasures should have been part of her inheritance. Those advanced years that Honoria had mentioned came all too quickly.

With the ease of long habit, Charlotte

pushed aside the intrusive thoughts. She forced herself to concentrate on her client.

"A sensible, intelligent woman must be cautious in a situation such as this, Miss Patterson," she said briskly.

"After all, it is not as though I am a beauty," Honoria said in the practical tone of a woman who has long since accepted the facts of life.

Nor am I, Charlotte thought with a fresh twinge of unease. Last night Baxter's passion had clearly been induced by the excitement they had shared. She had to be prepared for the possibility that he would no longer find her so alluring now that the stimulating effects of danger had dissipated.

"And what with this recent inheritance from my cousin," Honoria continued, "well, I'm sure you comprehend why I felt the need to make inquiries into Mr. Adams's background."

"I understand."

"I never expected to marry. Indeed, I had convinced myself that I was quite content with my life now that I am financially independent. But Mr. Adams came along and suddenly I saw other possibilities. We share a great many interests."

"I'm delighted for you."

This was not the first time that one of Charlotte's clients had become excessively talkative after receiving good news. Initially, the ladies who sought out her services tended to be tight-lipped and extremely reticent. They were invariably stiff with tension when they first sat down in the chair on the other side of the desk. Teacups rattled against saucers. Gloved hands fluttered anxiously. Expressions were solemn.

When the news was bad, tears usually flowed. Charlotte kept a pile of linen handkerchiefs in one of her desk drawers for such unhappy occasions.

A favorable report, however, frequently induced a mild euphoria. It made some clients want to chatter endlessly about the recently verified virtues of their suitors.

Generally speaking, Charlotte simply listened and made encouraging noises. Satisfied clients made excellent, very discreet references. She could afford to be generous with her time during the final interview.

But this afternoon, Charlotte had an inexplicable urge to do the talking. "I am happy for you, Miss Patterson. And pleased that I was able to confirm your good opinion of Mr. Adams. But you must realize that there is always some risk for a lady when it comes to marriage."

Honoria gave her a quizzical look. "Risk?"

"I have done my best to make certain that Mr. Adams is not a drunkard. He is not given to outrageous wagers. He does not frequent brothels. He has a reliable income and he appears to possess a stable, calm temperament."

Honoria glowed. "All in all, a wonderful gentleman."

"Yes. But you do realize that I cannot

absolutely guarantee that Mr. Adams will remain such a model of masculine perfection after the wedding."

"I beg your pardon?"

Charlotte leaned forward impulsively. "He could decide to abandon you and his children next year in order to go off in search of adventure in the South Seas. Or he might grow bored with his new life as a husband and take to drinking too much wine. He may suffer a siege of melancholy that will cause him to become extremely unpleasant. There are any number of things that can go wrong in a marriage."

"Well, yes, I suppose that is true." Honoria shifted uneasily in her chair. Her gaze became wary. "I realize that there can be no guarantees in a situation such as this."

"Precisely. Yet you choose to go forth along the path that leads toward marriage."

Honoria frowned. "You seem a bit agitated of a sudden, Miss Arkendale. Is something wrong?"

"I am merely wondering why you are so set on marrying Mr. Adams. It is not as if there is no alternative."

"I told you, none of the other gentlemen interested me in the least."

"That is not what I meant by alternative. Miss Patterson, may I ask you a question that is of a somewhat personal nature?"

Honoria glanced at the door, as if gauging the distance. "What is it you wish to know, Miss Arkendale?"

"Forgive me, but I cannot help wondering why you do not consider the possibility of a discreet liaison with Mr. Adams. Why hazard the dangers of marriage?"

Honoria stared at her. For an instant Charlotte was afraid that she had offended her in an unforgivable fashion. Silently she cursed her impulsiveness. Business was business, after all. She could not afford to go about horrifying her clients.

"Have an affair, do you mean?" Honoria asked with a refreshing candor.

Charlotte flushed. "It would seem to be an obvious solution. Granted, a young lady could not engage in a romantic liaison without bringing scandal down on her head, but a woman of, ah, our mature years has more freedom. So long as she exercises discretion, of course."

Honoria regarded Charlotte with a thoughtful expression. Then an odd little smile curved her mouth. "Perhaps you have been engaged in your present career a trifle too long, Miss Arkendale."

"What do you mean?"

"It strikes me that the business of making inquiries into gentlemen's backgrounds may have given you a rather cynical view of the world and of gentlemen, in particular. Perhaps you have lost sight of the reason why a lady would choose to make such inquiries in the first place."

"I beg your pardon?"

"An affair may do very well for some people." Honoria adjusted the strings of her bonnet and got to her feet. "But Mr. Adams and I are both looking for a good deal more."

"I do not understand."

"It is difficult to put into words, Miss Arkendale. If you do not intuitively comprehend the answer to your own question, I doubt that I can explain it to you. Suffice it to say that one enters marriage with hope."

"Hope?"

"And trust. And a vision of the future." Honoria gave her a pitying glance. "An affair cannot offer any of that, can it? By its very nature it is an extremely limited connection. If you will excuse me, I must be on my way. I thank you again for your services."

Charlotte jumped to her feet, driven by the questions bubbling forth inside her. She suddenly wanted to know what Honoria Patterson sought in marriage that could possibly make it worth the dreadful risk of finding oneself shackled to a man such as Winterbourne.

There were even worse possibilities, she reminded herself. Possibilities that sprang straight from the heart of a nightmare. What could make it worth the risk of binding oneself to a monster such as the creature who had slithered in the shadows of the hall outside Ariel's bedchamber five years ago?

Charlotte realized that Honoria had paused at the door. Her expression was one of grave concern.

"Are you feeling ill, Miss Arkendale?"

"No, not at all." Charlotte drew a deep, steadying breath. What on earth was the matter with her? she wondered. She reached out and braced herself by planting both of her hands flat on her desk. With an act of will she produced what she hoped was a businesslike smile. "My apologies. I shall summon my housekeeper to see you out."

A sharp knock interrupted Charlotte just as she reached for the velvet bell pull. The door of the study opened.

Mrs. Witty's majestic form loomed grandly. "Mr. St. Ives is here to see you, ma'am. Says he has an appointment."

Charlotte's morbid thoughts and unanswered questions vanished in a heartbeat. Baxter was there. She tried and failed to suppress the little burst of delight that flowered inside her.

"Thank you, Mrs. Witty. Miss Patterson was just leaving. Will you see her out, please?"

Mrs. Witty stood back and looked expectantly at Honoria. "Yes, ma'am."

Honoria went out into the hall with a cheerful spring in her step that had not been present when she had arrived a short while earlier.

It occurred to Charlotte that she had just been presented with a golden opportunity to conduct another experiment on Baxter.

"Oh, Miss Patterson, a moment if you please." Charlotte hurried around the corner of her desk and went to the doorway of the study. She peered out into the hall.

Baxter stood there, enveloped in the unshakable aura of limitless calm that Charlotte found both intriguing and disturbing. Others might interpret his self-possessed air as the patience of a naturally staid, rather boring individual, but she knew it was something else entirely. It was a manifestation of his inner strength and self-mastery.

She drew in a little breath at the sight of him. He was dressed in a severely cut dark blue coat that, although a bit wrinkled, nevertheless revealed the powerful line of his shoulders. His plainly tied cravat, conservative breeches, and boots suited him, she thought. Fashion was clearly unimportant to him. He was a man of deeper sensibilities.

His gaze met hers at that moment. His eyes glinted behind the lenses of his spectacles. She had the uncomfortable impression that he knew precisely what she was thinking. She felt the rush of warmth into her cheeks and was thoroughly annoyed. She was a lady of *advanced years* and far too much a woman of the world to blush, she told herself.

"Was there something else, Miss Arkendale?" Honoria asked politely.

Charlotte took a single step out into the hall. "Before you leave, Miss Patterson, may I present Mr. St. Ives?" She paused as Honoria turned toward Baxter. "He is my man-of-affairs."

"Mr. St. Ives," Honoria murmured.

"Miss Patterson." Baxter inclined his head in a short, brusque manner.

Charlotte watched Honoria's face very carefully. There was no trace of surprise or curiosity or anything else to indicate that she suspected Baxter of being something other than what he was supposed to be, an ordinary man of business.

Amazing, Charlotte thought. She caught herself just as she was about to shake her head and smiled at Honoria instead. "Mr. St. Ives is of great assistance to me. I do not know what I would do without him."

Baxter's eyes glinted. "You flatter me, Miss Arkendale."

"Not in the least, Mr. St. Ives. You are invaluable."

"I'm delighted to hear you say so."

Honoria gave both of them a vague smile. "If you will excuse me, I have a number of calls to make." She turned and went out the front door without a backward glance.

Charlotte waited until Mrs. Witty had closed the door. Then she stepped back into her study and waved Baxter into her sanctum. "Do come in, Mr. St. Ives. We have much to discuss."

Baxter walked across the hall to join her. "You do not yet know the half of it, Miss Arkendale."

She ignored the remark to glance at the housekeeper. "Would you please bring us a fresh tea tray, Mrs. Witty?"

"Yes, ma'am." Mrs. Witty went down the hall to the kitchen.

Charlotte closed the door and whirled around to face Baxter. "Miss Patterson did not even hesitate at the introduction. She obviously accepted you as my man-of-affairs without so much as a qualm."

"I told you that I would have no difficulty

playing the role." His mouth twisted slightly. "You are the only one who has ever questioned my striking ability to masquerade as a potato pudding."

The grim tone of his voice brought her up short. "What on earth is the matter, sir?"

He went to stand at the window. "Last night after I left you, I did a great deal of thinking."

"So did I."

"I doubt that we came to similar conclusions."

"Mr. St. Ives, I do not understand what this is all about."

"There are some things I must explain to you."

"What things?" A coil of unease began to untwist within her. Perhaps he already regretted last night's brief bout of passion. "Sir, you are behaving in a rather mysterious fashion today. Is something wrong?"

"Bloody hell. We are engaged in a hunt for a murderer. Of course something is wrong. For your information, Charlotte, this sort of venture is not a common occupation for ladies. Nor is it considered a gentleman's sport, for that matter."

"I see." She took refuge in pride. "If you are having second thoughts, you may, of course, resign your position in my service."

"I fear that I can no longer play the part of your man-of-affairs, regardless of how well suited I am to the role."

It is finished. So soon. Before I have even got-

ten to know him. Baxter was going to walk out the door. The intense sense of loss that surged through her alarmed Charlotte. This was ridiculous. She barely knew the man. She must get a grip on her emotions.

"Perhaps you would be good enough to explain, sir?" she said crisply.

"It would be best to begin at the start of this affair, I suppose." Baxter turned to face her at last. His eyes were unreadable. "It was no coincidence that I applied for the position you offered. I had already tracked down John Marcle with the intention of discovering everything I could about your finances."

"Good heavens." Charlotte felt a cold, prickling sensation on her skin. Slowly she sank down into her chair. "Why?"

"My aunt was a close friend of Drusilla Heskett's. She asked me to make inquiries into the murder. The trail led immediately to you. In fact, it started with you."

"My God."

"She believed that you were responsible for Mrs. Heskett's murder, you see."

"Bloody hell." Whatever it was she had braced herself to hear, this was certainly not it. For a moment Charlotte was bereft of speech.

"Yes, I know," Baxter muttered. "I warned you this would be a little difficult to explain."

"Let me be sure I have this clear. Your aunt believes that I killed poor Mrs. Heskett? But what could possibly have given her such a notion?"

"The fact that Mrs. Heskett had recently paid you a large sum of money."

Charlotte was outraged. "But that was for my services. I told you, I made inquiries on Drusilla Heskett's behalf into the background of some of the gentlemen who wished to marry her."

Baxter shoved his hand through his hair. "I'm aware of that now. But my aunt did not know it. Apparently Mrs. Heskett honored your desire for confidentiality. She never told my aunt the nature of her business with you. After the murder, Rosalind assumed the worst."

"I see. What exactly did your aunt make of the fact that Mrs. Heskett had paid me a large sum of money?"

"She assumed that you had blackmailed Drusilla."

"*Blackmail.*" Charlotte groaned and dropped her head into her hands. Visions of her hard-won career in ruins due to ghastly rumors that she might be a villainess danced wildly in her brain. "This grows worse by the minute. We have moved from the incredible to the truly bizarre."

"Indeed." Baxter walked slowly across the carpet to stand behind the chair in front of the desk.

Charlotte raised her head and watched warily as he gripped the polished mahogany chair. For some reason she found herself transfixed by his big, capable hands.

"Go on, sir. I have the feeling there is more to come."

"Having decided that you were a black-mailer, it was no great leap for my aunt to arrive at the conclusion that you had also murdered Mrs. Heskett."

"No, I suppose not. I can see how one false assumption would lead to the next."

"You and my aunt will no doubt get along famously. The two of you obviously think in the same erratic manner."

"Carry on, Mr. St. Ives. Finish the business."

"As I said, logic led me to Marcle, your man-of-affairs."

"How is that?"

He shrugged. "I reasoned that if blackmail was involved, it made sense to start with the financial end of things."

Silently she acknowledged the brilliance of that line of reasoning. "How did you discover that I employed John Marcle?"

"It was not difficult. I have my own man-of-affairs."

She winced. "Yes, of course."

"I instructed him to consult with my bankers, who made inquiries of your bankers. I not only learned about Marcle, I also discovered that he was searching for someone to replace him."

"So you applied for the position." She exhaled slowly. "How bloody clever of you, sir."

He hesitated and then added in a strangely neutral tone, "I have had some experience in this sort of thing."

"Which sort of thing? Acting as a man-of-affairs or spying?"

"Both, actually." He glanced down at his hands, which were clenched on the chair back. When he looked up again, his eyes were bleak. "As far as the business part is concerned, I have managed a sizable fortune for several years."

"A fortune?" It was to be one shock after another today, she thought, dazed.

"Two, actually. My own and that of my half brother."

"I see." She swallowed. "And the spying bit?"

Baxter looked pained. "I prefer not to use the word *spy*."

She narrowed her eyes. "Spies do have a rather unpleasant reputation, do they not? An unsavory, disreputable lot, completely lacking in honor."

"Indeed." The strong line of his jaw grew even more rigid. "The profession may be a necessary one, but it is not considered honorable."

Charlotte felt terrible. He had deserved the cruel insult but for some reason she wished that she had not succumbed to the urge to level it at him.

"My apologies," she said brusquely. "Gentlemen do not engage in spying."

"No, they do not." He did not even attempt to defend himself.

"A man of honor, however," she added very delicately, "might make himself available to the proper authorities for a clandestine mission."

"I assure you, I did not volunteer," Baxter said dryly. "My knowledge of chemistry was what caught the interest of the authorities. A highly placed gentleman approached my father and asked if I would be willing to aid in the inquiries. My father came to me and I agreed to look into the matter."

"Who, exactly, is your father?"

"The fourth Earl of Esherton." Baxter's hands flexed on the chair back. "He died two years ago."

"Esherton." Charlotte was dumbfounded. "Surely you are not about to tell me that you are the fifth Earl of Esherton? That would really be too much, sir."

"No. I'm a bastard, Charlotte, not an earl."

"Well, thank God for that much, at least."

Baxter looked briefly startled by her reaction. "My half brother, Hamilton, is the current Earl of Esherton."

"I'm relieved to hear that."

Baxter's brows rose above the rims of his eyeglasses. "Are you, indeed?"

"Most definitely. It would have made things ever so much more complicated, you see. The last thing I need is an earl running about the place." A thought struck her. "What is your aunt's name?"

"Rosalind, Lady Trengloss."

"Good lord, another title." Charlotte frowned. "Trengloss. I believe Drusilla Heskett mentioned her in passing."

"As I said, Mrs. Heskett was a good friend of my aunt's."

Charlotte nodded wearily. "Quite natural that you would look into the matter of the murder on behalf of your aunt. I would have done the same in your place."

Baxter smiled humorlessly. "Very understanding of you."

"May I assume that you are telling me all of this because you have concluded that I am not a murdering blackmailer after all?"

"I was never convinced that you were a villainess in the first place."

"Thank you for that much, at least."

"But certain issues had been raised. My approach to such matters is to pursue the most logical line of inquiry until I discover evidence to the contrary."

"It must be the scientist in you." Charlotte studied the nib of her pen with great attention. "And what proof did you uncover that convinced you I was innocent, Mr. St. Ives?"

"For one thing, you did not seem to know your way around Drusilla Heskett's house."

Charlotte looked up sharply. "I beg your pardon?"

"Mrs. Heskett was murdered in her own home. Her bedchamber, to be precise."

"Yes, I know."

"When we reached the top of the stairs last night, you hesitated. You did not know which bedchamber was hers until we discovered the one that contained her personal possessions."

"I see." Charlotte swallowed. "Very logical."

"Also, you did not appear to know what you hoped to find in the house. You stumbled across the watercolor sketchbook but other than that, you seemed uncertain about what constituted a clue. You were obviously not there to retrieve specific evidence that you knew might implicate you."

No doubt she should have been pleased that his powers of logic had brought him to the conclusion that she was innocent of the crimes. But for some reason her spirits were still depressed. What had she expected to hear? That Baxter had taken one look at her and trusted her on sight? Ridiculous.

"So," she said with what she privately thought was commendable aplomb under the circumstances, "having resolved the issue of my guilt in the matter, you naturally wish to resign your post and go about your own affairs."

"Not exactly."

"Perfectly reasonable, under the circumstances. After all, there is no need for you to continue your inquiries in my direction. You may as well—" She broke off as his words penetrated. "What do you mean, *not exactly*?"

Baxter released his grip on the chair and turned to walk across the room. He halted in front of the bookcase and stood with his back to her. "I wish to continue working with you on this matter, Charlotte."

Her flagging spirits abruptly rallied. "You do?"

"The problem that brought us together still remains," he pointed out. "There is still the matter of Mrs. Heskett's murder to resolve. You and my aunt both want answers."

"Yes." She was suddenly feeling much more

cheerful. "Yes, we do, indeed, sir. And there is certainly truth in the old saying that two heads are better than one."

"But there will have to be a small change in our association."

A frisson of wariness went down her spine. "A change?"

He turned around and clasped his hands behind his back. "I fear that I cannot continue to pass myself off as your man-of-affairs."

"I admit I had my doubts about that, even after my sister and my housekeeper claimed that there was no cause for concern. But I think Miss Patterson's reaction to you proves that you will, indeed, be able to continue on in that role quite successfully."

"The problem," Baxter said carefully, "is that our inquiries will likely take us into Drusilla Heskett's circle of acquaintances."

"Yes, of course. What of it?"

"Mrs. Heskett's circle of acquaintances overlaps my aunt's. And people in that circle know me." His mouth curved coldly. "Those who don't, know *of* me. I am Esherton's bastard, after all. In the Polite World, it will be impossible for me to go about unnoticed."

"I see." Charlotte's mind raced. "We must come up with another excuse for being seen frequently in each other's company."

"I spent most of the night considering the problem." Baxter paused. "I believe that I examined all of the possibilities."

She gave him an expectant smile. "And?"

"And I have come to the inescapable conclusion that there is really only one socially acceptable reason for the two of us to spend an inordinate amount of time together."

"I am eager to hear it."

"An engagement."

She suddenly could not breathe for a few dazed seconds.

"I beg your pardon?" she finally managed to say very carefully.

"You and I shall announce that we are engaged to be married." He gave her a wry, fleeting smile. "And in light of that situation, I really must insist that you start calling me Baxter."

Six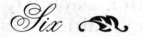

Baxter braced himself for the explosion. But even with his extensive knowledge of volatile substances, he could not have predicted Charlotte's initial reaction.

She went utterly still. Her eyes widened and then narrowed. Her mouth opened and closed twice.

And then she exploded.

"An *engagement*?" Charlotte erupted from her chair with more force than the legendary Vesuvius. She gazed at him in wild disbelief from behind the barricade of her desk. "Have you gone mad, sir?"

"Very likely." Baxter wondered briefly why

he was feeling so chagrined by her reaction. It was only to be expected. Why the devil should she be excited by the prospect of playing the part of his fiancée?

Nevertheless, given that he had spent most of the night in a state of semi-arousal, it would have been pleasant to see a little less shock and dismay in her eyes. He was not the only one who had succumbed to a burst of passion last night.

"That is a crazed suggestion." Charlotte made a visible effort to compose herself. "Whatever put it into your head?"

"I thought I made that clear." He'd worked hard on the logic of the thing. She was an intelligent female. She should have been able to see the problem and its solution as clearly as he did. "If we are to pursue our inquiries into my aunt's circle of acquaintances, you cannot continue to pass me off as your man-of-affairs. It won't work. We need a believable reason to explain our connection."

"A believable reason," she repeated numbly.

"Yes." Baxter was suddenly aware of a driving need to pace back and forth across the study. Annoyed, he forced himself to remain bolted to the floor. Pacing was a clear sign of an unsettled emotional state. His emotions were never unsettled.

"You think this reason is believable?"

"If you can think of a better excuse, I shall be happy to hear it."

"There must be a more reasonable excuse."

Charlotte drummed her fingers on the desk. "Give me a moment to think."

"Take your time." The sensation of restlessness grew stronger. To ease it, Baxter picked up the book that was lying on a nearby table. Absently he glanced at the words inscribed on the leather binding. When he saw Byron's name he swore softly and put down the volume as if it had become red-hot in his hand.

"We could pretend to have become acquainted through a mutual interest in chemistry," Charlotte said slowly. "We shall say that we met at a meeting of one of the scientific societies."

"That would account for our initial meeting and for an occasional conversation in public but not much more than that."

"There is another possibility."

She was certainly eager to find an alternative, he thought grimly. Obviously the notion of an engagement, even a false one, was anathema to her. "Very well, what is that?"

She slanted him a quick, searching glance and then gazed fixedly at a globe positioned near the window. "We could allow your aunt and her circle of acquaintances to assume that you and I had formed a...a romantic attachment."

"I would have thought that was the essence of my plan."

"I meant an illicit sort of romantic attachment." She turned a bright shade of pink and continued to focus steadily on the globe. "That we are involved in a liaison."

"Bloody hell. You wish people to think that we're having an *affair*? That's the most idiotic notion I've ever heard."

Her chin lifted slightly. "It seems a perfectly reasonable notion to me."

"Not in my case."

"What on earth do you mean by that?" She turned her head quickly and then her flush deepened. "Oh, dear. Surely you do not mean to imply that you are not interested in females in that way? I always knew that Mr. Marcle had no inclinations of that sort but after last night, I, uh, gained the distinct impression that you did. Have inclinations. Of that sort."

"I most definitely possess inclinations," Baxter said very evenly. "But I do not take them into Society."

"I beg your pardon?"

Baxter sighed. This interview was faring much worse than he had envisioned. "I'm not the sort who conducts his affairs in the full view of the Polite World. To put it bluntly, I'm not my father."

"I see." But she looked bemused.

"Charlotte, the people who know me, know very well that I would never flaunt a paramour, especially a relatively young woman who has never been married, in Society. It would be completely out of character, if you see what I mean."

"I think I'm beginning to comprehend the situation. You are, at heart, a gentleman, sir. It is very noble of you to worry about my

124

reputation, but I can assure you that I am not at all concerned with gossip."

"You'd bloody well better be concerned with gossip if you hope to continue in your career after this matter is finished." It was a shot in the dark, but it was all he could think of at the moment.

Her eyes widened. "Good heavens. I had not considered that aspect of the thing. Do you really believe that gossip about a romantic liaison between the two of us could hurt my business?"

Baxter saw his opening and bore down ruthlessly. "Society can be very fickle and extremely hypocritical about such things. You must be aware that the ladies of the ton whom you hope to attract as clients are known to demand higher standards of those they employ than they do of themselves."

"I see what you mean." Charlotte studied her hands. "My housekeeper, Mrs. Witty, has told me tales of elegant ladies who have any number of affairs but who would not hesitate to dismiss a maid who got pregnant by the footman."

"Just so. Such ladies would certainly be reluctant to do business with a woman who has had a highly visible affair with a man in my position."

"Your position?"

"As I keep reminding you, I'm a bastard."

"A bastard who appears to be obsessed with not becoming an object of gossip."

"Perhaps I wish to avoid it because I have lived with it since the day I was born."

"Yes, of course." Slowly she sank back down in her chair. "My apologies, sir. I had not considered your feelings in the matter. It must have been difficult for you at times."

"Let us just say that scandal broth is not my favorite beverage." He did not like the sympathy he saw in her eyes. He finally gave in to the restlessness that threatened to consume him. He walked deliberately toward the window. "I have had my fill of it for the past thirty-two years."

"No doubt."

He braced a hand on the windowsill. "What I told you about myself during our first interview was nothing less than the truth. I am as bland as potato pudding. What is more, I prefer it that way. I have worked hard to achieve a calm, orderly existence that does not require me to go into Society. I have made it a practice to avoid situations that are likely to produce titillation and rumor. I cherish my privacy above all else."

"Perfectly understandable."

He looked out into the rain-drenched garden and saw scenes from his own past. "I do not conduct scandalous affairs with dashing widows. I do not allow passion to create chaos in my life. I do not become involved in liaisons that may oblige me to defend my paramour's honor at dawn. I do not conduct outrageous rows with my lover in the center of a crowded ballroom while my five-year-old son watches from the balcony."

"I can well believe that."

Baxter's hand tightened on the windowsill. "I do not sire illegitimate children who must answer the taunts of their companions with their fists. I do not produce offspring who, because they are born on the wrong side of the blanket, are forever denied the lands and the heritage that should have been theirs."

"In short, Mr. St. Ives, you do not conduct your personal affairs in the same manner in which your parents conducted theirs. Is that what you are telling me?"

"Yes." What in bloody hell had come over him? Baxter wondered. He gave himself a small mental shake to dispatch the old images. He had never intended to say such things to Charlotte. He never discussed his most personal memories with anyone.

"I congratulate you, sir," Charlotte said very quietly. "And I admire you."

He turned so swiftly that he caught the globe with his elbow. The world spun away and plummeted toward the floor. Furious with his uncharacteristic clumsiness and all that it implied about his lack of control, he made a quick grab for the globe. He barely caught it before it struck the carpet.

"Damnation." Feeling a complete idiot, he concentrated on righting the world and setting it back in place on the sill. Then he looked at Charlotte, who was watching him very intently. "For God's sake, why do you say that you admire me?"

"You are obviously a man of strong will and great fortitude. You have created your own rules. Although you do not possess the title that should have been yours by right of blood, you do possess honor and courage."

The sincerity of her words stunned him. To conceal his sense of disorientation, he folded his arms across his chest and propped one shoulder against the wall. He took refuge in cool amusement. "Kind of you to say so."

"We do have something in common on this score." Charlotte touched the ornate silver inkstand on her desk. "It is not only illegitimate offspring who must sometimes stand by and watch as their inheritance is stolen. My sister and I lost most of what should have been ours to my mother's second husband."

"Winterbourne."

"Yes." Charlotte's mouth tightened. "Whenever I think of all the things that Ariel has missed because of him, of all the things I could never give her, I...well, I'm sure you understand."

He watched her closely. "So long as we are being completely honest with each other, I should confess that I have a great deal of admiration for you, also."

She looked up quickly. "You do?"

"I'm aware that there are not many options available to a lady who finds herself cast adrift with a young sister to support. I'm impressed by what you have accomplished."

She gave him a small, surprised smile. "Thank you, Mr. St. Ives. Coming from you, such a compliment is gratifying, indeed."

"And given my deep admiration," he continued deliberately, "I'm certain you can comprehend why I do not intend to allow you to destroy your reputation in this venture."

The moment of mutual understanding that had flashed between them vanished with the speed of a magician's illusion.

Charlotte glared. "You are attempting to manipulate me, sir."

"I'm trying to convince you with logic and reason. If you are correct in your belief that Drusilla Heskett was murdered by one of her suitors, then that man may well be someone who moves in the Polite World. Correct?"

"Yes, all but one of Mrs. Heskett's recent suitors were members of the ton," she said impatiently. "Mr. Charles Dill was the only one who did not move in Society, and as I told you, he died of a heart seizure nearly two weeks before Mrs. Heskett was murdered."

"Indeed. Then one of those whose suspicions might well be aroused by uncharacteristic behavior on my part could well be her killer."

Charlotte opened her mouth and then closed it quickly. She grimaced. "You may be correct."

"Therefore, given my personal inclination to avoid scandal and gossip and your desire not to ruin the chance of future business, we are left with only the one alternative. We shall announce our engagement. It will give us the perfect excuse for going about in Society while we conduct our inquiries."

A short, tense silence gripped the room.

"We?" Charlotte repeated very politely.

"You are still determined to track down Drusilla Heskett's killer, are you not?"

"She was a client who may have been killed because I failed to uncover certain crucial information." Charlotte drew a deep breath. "I owe her some justice."

"I disagree. You do not owe her anything of the sort. But I realize that I cannot dissuade you from your goal."

"No, you cannot stop me."

"As I have explained, I am committed to the same goal because of the promise that I made to my aunt." Baxter met her eyes. "It seems we must cooperate to achieve our mutual ends."

Charlotte shook her head slowly in a gesture of mingled resignation and disbelief. "Everything I sensed about you at our first meeting has proven to be true, Mr. St. Ives."

He frowned. "What do you mean?"

"You are, indeed, a very dangerous man."

❧

"Engaged? To Charlotte Arkendale?" Rosalind crashed her dainty teacup down into its saucer. "I do not believe it. You cannot have gone and engaged yourself to such a creature. You must be mad."

"It's a possibility that I have considered closely," Baxter admitted.

"Are you joking with me?" Rosalind gave him a reproving frown. "You know very well that I have never entirely comprehended your decidedly odd sense of humor. Tell me precisely what is going on here."

"I thought I had explained. It's the logical course of action, assuming you wish me to pursue my inquiries."

He walked across the drawing room to examine the new chimneypiece that had just been installed above the fireplace. The elaborately carved design was in the new Zamarian style, as was virtually everything else in the chamber. Rosalind had recently redecorated. The Egyptian-style drawing room with its hieroglyph-covered wallpaper, palm trees, strange statues, and artificial columns had been converted into a Zamarian courtyard scene.

It was the latest in a long line of such alterations for the large town house. Growing up here with his mother and his aunt, Baxter had played in an Etruscan cottage, studied in a Chinese garden, practiced fencing in a Greek temple, and, mercifully, moved out of a Roman sepulchral monument.

From the day he had taken his own lodgings Baxter had established one cardinal rule for his household. No changes in the interior design were made solely for the purpose of accommodating a new fashion.

It occurred to him as he surveyed the gilded chimneypiece that he had always resisted change and the turmoil it brought.

As a child, the major upheavals in his life had always seemed to follow on the heels of some strong, emotional outburst between his parents. The pair had been experts in the fine art of conducting flamboyant lovers' quarrels and passionate reunions. Indeed, they had thrived on such scenes and had shone particularly well in front of an audience. They had not cared if that audience sometimes consisted of only one small boy.

Baxter had dreaded the inevitable battles, waited anxiously for the reunions, and in between endured the cruelty of his peers.

From his earliest years, he had set out to suppress any trace of his parents' tumultuous natures that he might have inherited. He had fashioned a life for himself that was designed to be hermetically sealed against strong emotion in the same way that he sealed a bell jar against contaminating vapors.

He told himself that the only excitement that intrigued him was that which took place in his laboratory. But now Charlotte had entered his self-contained, well-ordered world and he feared that he would not be able to resist conducting a few risky experiments.

If he was not very careful things would explode in his face.

"Are you completely convinced that this Miss Arkendale is truly innocent?" Rosalind asked.

"Yes." Baxter turned away from the fireplace frieze. "I no longer have any doubts at all on that point. When you meet her, you will understand."

"If you're quite certain," Rosalind said hesitantly.

"There is little choice in the matter. She is as determined to track down Drusilla Heskett's murderer as you are. I cannot talk her out of the business so I am obliged to work with her."

"You intend to use this fictitious engagement as an excuse for the two of you to go about together."

"It is the only way."

Rosalind looked unconvinced. She rested one arm on the elegantly curved arm of the Zamarian green sofa and examined Baxter closely. "I do not know what to say."

"As it happens, I don't want you to say anything at all. Not even to your closest friends. No one must know that this engagement is a fraud, do you understand? Absolutely no one."

"This is to be a conspiracy? Really, Baxter, you can hardly expect me to go along with such an outlandish scheme."

"On the contrary, I know you very well, Rosalind. I suspect you will enjoy the whole thing very much. It's just the sort of play-acting that should appeal to your taste for the melodramatic."

Rosalind managed to look affronted. "What a thing to say to your own aunt."

"Think of it this way: a gentleman in your circle of acquaintances may be a murderer."

Rosalind shuddered. "Are you even sure that you are searching for a man? The killer could have been a woman."

Baxter shrugged. "Mrs. Heskett sent Charlotte a note saying that she believed someone was trying to kill her. She was concerned that one of her recent suitors might had become enraged when she rejected him."

"I see. This could be quite a fascinating endeavor, Baxter."

"I thought you'd come to that opinion. Charlotte and I must start somewhere, so we intend to begin our inquiries with Mrs. Heskett's suitors. The last one to be rejected was Lord Lennox."

"Lennox." Rosalind frowned. "Drusilla was quite fond of him for a time. Claimed the man had stamina."

"Stamina?"

Rosalind looked amused. "Drusilla liked stamina in a gentleman. She also liked it in a footman or a coachman or a groom. To be quite blunt, Drusilla was fond of any man who could keep up with her in bed."

"I see." Baxter removed his eyeglasses and pulled his handkerchief from his pocket. "Assuming that it was one of her lovers who killed her, we could be looking at a very long list of potential murderers."

"I doubt it. Few of her conquests would have had a motive for murder. Perhaps I could be of some assistance, Baxter."

"I do have a favor to ask of you."

"What is that?"

Baxter replaced his spectacles. "I would very much appreciate it if you would take my fiancée shopping."

"*Shopping.*"

"And her sister as well. You may send the bills to me."

Rosalind's eyes gleamed. "Good God, Baxter, I'm stunned. This is so unlike you. I do believe you are beginning to sound a bit like your father."

"Thank you for the warning. I shall be on my guard."

Three days later Charlotte stood at the edge of a crowded ballroom and smiled with unconcealed pleasure. "I must tell you, Mr. St. Ives, whatever the result of our venture, I shall be forever indebted to your aunt."

Baxter glanced at her as he took a sip from his champagne glass. "My aunt?"

"Lady Trengloss has made my sister a spectacular success. I know that was not the point of the evening, but I am delighted, nonetheless. I vow, Ariel has had a partner for nearly every dance. Just look at her out there on the floor. She is a diamond of the first water, is she not?"

Baxter frowned as he searched the dancers for Ariel. It was not difficult to spot her. She was taller than most of the other women on the floor. He saw that she was whirling about in an exuberant waltz with a young man who wore a distinctly dazzled expression.

"She appears to be enjoying herself," he said.

"Yes. My parents would have been so proud. Lady Trengloss was correct when she declared that Ariel must wear only blue and gold. The colors are perfect for her."

It dawned on Baxter that Charlotte looked

very good in the canary yellow satin gown that she wore. It set off the dark flames in her hair and emphasized the green of her eyes. The bodice was low and square-cut, revealing her creamy shoulders and a decorous hint of the gentle swell of her breasts. There was a dashing little confection of a cap trimmed with a yellow plume perched on her head.

This was the first time he had seen her in anything other than a high-necked, long-sleeved day gown, he realized. He was no expert on fashion but in his opinion she was the most attractive woman in the room.

He took a swallow of champagne. "Blue and gold are all very well. I prefer yellow."

"Yellow would have been quite atrocious on Ariel."

He slid her a sidelong glance. "I was referring to your gown."

"Oh." Charlotte gave him a brilliant smile. "Thank you. You look very nice in black and white, Mr. St. Ives. It suits you."

He did not know whether that was a compliment or not. He suddenly felt compelled to explain his limited selection of evening attire. "As I told you, I don't go into Society very often."

"You did mention that you try to avoid the Polite World."

"No logical reason to order a great many evening coats when one has a limited social life."

"Very practical of you to stick with black."

"Haven't paid much attention to the latest fancy cravat knots."

"I see."

"Damned silly for a man to tie his neckcloth in such a tricky way that he can't even turn his head."

"There is a lot to be said for simplicity," Charlotte agreed politely.

He was sinking deeper by the second. Baxter glanced around, searching for inspiration, and was, for once, inordinately relieved to see his aunt on the horizon. Rosalind had Lord Lennox in tow.

"Time to go to work," Baxter said softly. "That man coming toward us with Rosalind was Drusilla Heskett's last suitor."

"That gentleman with the bald head and the bushy whiskers is Lennox?"

"Yes. Would have thought you'd recognize him on sight."

She frowned. "I never actually saw him, you know. It's not generally necessary to know what a gentleman looks like in the flesh in order to discover whether or not he is a rakehell or a gamester."

"No, I suppose not."

Charlotte pursed her lips. "Nevertheless, I had imagined him to be a younger man."

"Whatever gave you that notion?"

"Mrs. Heskett's description of him, I imagine."

"What did she say about him?" Baxter asked.

"Something to the effect that Lennox resembled a stallion in the bedchamber. She said he had stamina."

Baxter coughed on his last swallow of champagne. "I see. Why did she reject him?"

"She felt he was too old for her. She was uncertain how long his stamina would last."

"He's no youngster. Lennox has got two married daughters. His heir, who is the youngest of the brood, is twenty-one or so. I saw him a short while ago at the buffet table."

"Lennox's heir?"

"Yes. Norris is his name, I believe. He was talking to Hamilton. They're close friends."

"Who is Hamilton?"

"I beg your pardon." Baxter deliberately set his empty glass down on a passing tray. "I should have said the fifth Earl of Esherton."

"Oh, yes. Your brother."

"My *half* brother."

"Whatever." Charlotte turned to greet Rosalind with a warm smile. "Good evening, Lady Trengloss."

Rosalind beamed as she came to a halt. She caught Baxter's eye and winked. He stifled a groan. As he had anticipated, his aunt was thoroughly enjoying herself.

Rosalind dangled Lennox triumphantly in front of Charlotte as though awarding her a prize.

"My dear, allow me to present an acquaintance of mine, Lord Lennox."

"My lord," Charlotte murmured.

Baxter barely managed to conceal his surprise as he watched her sink into an elegant little curtsy. The graceful dip was accented with an equally gracious inclination of her head.

It all spoke volumes about her past and her upbringing. She had, indeed, been bred for a much higher position in the social hierarchy than the one in which she moved.

"Well, well, well, this is a pleasure, indeed, m'dear." Lennox bent his gleaming head over Charlotte's gloved hand. "Allow me to tell you that you look lovely. A vision, indeed. As bright as Spring itself."

"Thank you, my lord," Charlotte murmured.

Lennox shot Baxter a knowing look from beneath his bushy brows. "It's about time you found yourself a wife, St. Ives. A man your age should have more interesting things to do than spend his time mucking around with a bunch of chemicals in a laboratory, eh?"

"Indeed." Baxter avoided Charlotte's eye.

"Volatile things, chemicals." Lennox leaned close to Baxter and lowered his voice so that Charlotte and Rosalind could not hear. "If I were you, I'd avoid 'em entirely now that you're about to get married. Never know when you might damage something vital in an explosion. Be a shame to crawl into bed on your wedding night and discover you'd accidentally blown off your ballocks in some damn experiment."

"I'll keep your advice in mind," Baxter said.

"That's the spirit, St. Ives." Lennox clapped Baxter on the shoulder. "I say, any objections to my having a spin around the floor with your lovely fiancée?"

Now that he thought about it, Baxter realized that he did have a few objections. The notion of Charlotte in another man's arms, even the arms of a man who was old enough to be her grandfather, was an astonishingly unpleasant one. But he saw the gleam in Charlotte's eye and knew he had better keep his opinions to himself.

"I have a feeling my fiancée would enjoy a little exercise." Baxter adjusted his spectacles. "Is that correct, Charlotte?"

"I would be very pleased to dance with you, Lord Lennox." Charlotte placed her hand delicately on his sleeve.

"Excellent." Lennox led her gallantly toward the dance floor. "Let's be off, shall we?"

Baxter watched as the pair was absorbed into the crowd of dancers.

"Do stop scowling so, Baxter," Rosalind murmured. "People will think that you're preparing to call out poor Lennox."

"The day I challenge any man to a duel over a woman will be the day I cease studying chemistry and take up alchemy."

"Sometimes I quite despair of you. Where is your passion? Your sensibilities? Your emotions? No, do not bother to answer that question." Rosalind peered intently at the crowd. "Do you really believe that Lennox could have murdered poor Drusilla?"

"I doubt it. He does not have a financial motive, for one thing. And in my opinion, he lacks the temperament for murder."

Rosalind glanced at him in surprise. "Then

why are we wasting time with this little drama tonight?"

"I explained that Charlotte is convinced that Drusilla Heskett's note implicated one of her most recently rejected suitors. Lennox was one of those men. We must proceed in a logical manner."

"I suppose that makes sense. Well, Lennox is all we have to work with for the moment. I discovered that Randeleigh and Esly are in the country for several days. They are not expected back until the end of the month."

"I shall have my man-of-affairs make some inquiries in that direction."

"I cannot picture either of them as murderers, either."

"Neither can I," Baxter admitted.

Rosalind gave him a considering look. "You know, speaking of logic, it would appear perfectly reasonable if you were to dance with your own fiancée."

"I haven't danced in years. Never was much good at it."

"That is not the point, Baxter, I merely—" Rosalind broke off to gaze at someone coming up behind him. She smiled coolly. "Speaking of people who believe that they have a motive for murder, here comes Lady Esherton."

He glanced around and saw Maryann coming toward them. He abruptly recalled the three notes he had tossed into the fire during the previous fortnight. "Bloody hell."

"She cannot have any reason to speak to me," Rosalind said, "so it must be you she wishes to corner. If you will excuse me, I believe I see a dear friend on the other side of the room." She turned and swept off into the crowd.

"Coward."

He was left to face his father's widow alone.

Maryann was fifty-two years of age. She had been eighteen when she had married Baxter's father. The earl had been forty-three. It was his second marriage. His first had been childless and he was desperate for an heir.

The reigning belle of her Season, Maryann had had her pick of the eligible men of the ton but, at the prodding of her ambitious parents, she had set her cap for Esherton. He, in turn, had needed a virgin wife with an unblemished reputation and an impeccable family background. Their wedding had been the match of the Season. Everyone, including the earl's long-standing mistress, Emma, Lady Sultenham, had attended the festivities.

With her petite figure, gray eyes, and honey-colored hair, Maryann was Emma's opposite in almost every way. Baxter sometimes wondered if his father had selected her to be his countess because she did not resemble his dashing dark-haired, dark-eyed mistress or simply because he liked the variety.

Two years after the marriage, Emma, who was thirty-seven and considered herself safely past childbearing age, gave birth to the earl's first son. Esherton had been very pleased with Baxter. He had thrown a huge party to celebrate the event. Unfortunately, nothing could alter the fact that Baxter was a bastard and therefore unable to inherit the title.

Another ten years had passed before Maryann had finally managed to produce an heir for her lord. Baxter was well aware that those years had not been easy for her. The earl had never bothered to conceal his affection for his illegitimate son or his intense passion for Emma.

Baxter did not like the grim determination in Maryann's expression tonight. It did not bode well. As always when he was obliged to meet with her, he recalled the deathbed vows that had ensured that they could never ignore each other no matter how fervently each wished to do so.

His father had bound them together until Hamilton turned twenty-five. The scene was as vivid in his mind tonight as if the events had transpired yesterday. He had stood on one side of the massive four-poster bed. Maryann and Hamilton had stood on the opposite side.

"The time has come for me to say farewell to my two fine sons." Arthur, the fourth Earl of Esherton, had gripped both Baxter's and Hamilton's hands. "I'm proud of both of you. You're as different as night and day but you each carry my blood in your veins. Do you hear me, Hamilton?"

"Yes, Father." Hamilton looked at Baxter, his eyes simmering with resentment.

The earl's eyes switched to Baxter. "You're Hamilton's older brother. Never forget that."

"I'm not likely to forget the fact that I'm related to him, sir." Baxter was overcome by a strange sense of unreality. It was impossible to believe that the big, vital, larger-than-life man who had sired him was dying.

Esherton's trembling hand tightened briefly on Baxter's. "You've got a responsibility to him and his mother."

"I doubt they'll need anything from me." Baxter felt the weakness in his father's once-powerful fingers and had to blink back the dampness that threatened to film his eyes.

"You're wrong," Arthur whispered hoarsely. "Set it out in my will. You've got the sort of steady temperament it takes to handle money, Baxter. Damnation, son, you were born steady and reliable. Hamilton's too young to handle the estates. You'll have to deal with things until he's twenty-five."

"No." Maryann was the first to realize the full significance of what her husband had said. Her hand went to her throat. "My lord, what have you done?"

Arthur turned his head on the pillow to look up at her. In spite of his weakened state he managed to produce a shadow of the wicked Esherton grin. "You're prettier now than the day I married you, m'dear."

"Esherton, please. What have you done?"

"No need to fret, Maryann. I've put Baxter in charge of the family finances until Hamilton gets a bit older."

Maryann's shocked gaze met Baxter's. "There is no need for such an arrangement."

"Afraid there is. Hamilton's got my hot blood in him, my sweet. He needs time to learn how to control it. Don't know how my two sons

144

turned out so damned different, but there you are." Esherton broke off on a racking cough.

Baxter felt his father slip a little further away into the waiting darkness. "Sir—"

Arthur recovered from the coughing fit and fell back, exhausted, against the pillows. "I know what I'm doing. Hamilton's going to need your guidance and advice for a few years, Baxter."

"Father, please," Hamilton whispered. "I don't need Baxter to handle my money and make decisions for me. I'm old enough to take care of the Esherton lands."

"Just for a few more years." Arthur gave a hoarse chuckle. "Give yourself a chance to sow your wild oats. Who better to keep an eye on you than your older brother, eh?"

"But he's not really my brother," Hamilton insisted. "He's just my half brother."

"You're brothers, by God." For a moment a measure of the earl's old strength burned in his amber eyes. He looked fiercely at Baxter. "Do you understand me, son? You're Hamilton's brother. You have a responsibility to look after him. I want your oath on it."

Baxter gripped his father's hand. "I understand. Please, calm yourself, sir."

"Your oath, by God."

"You have it," Baxter said quietly.

The earl relaxed. "Steady and clearheaded. Reliable as the sunrise." He closed his eyes. "Knew I could depend on you to look after the family."

Baxter shook himself free of the memories as Maryann came to a halt in front of him.

"Good evening, Baxter."

"Maryann."

"You have not responded to my requests for a meeting. I have sent three notes."

"I've been occupied with other matters," Baxter said with the icy politeness he had cultivated years ago for just such occasions. "If this is about money, you know I gave the bankers instructions to honor any reasonable request for funds."

"This has nothing to do with money. If you don't mind, I would prefer to discuss the matter in private. Shall we go out into the gardens?"

"Some other time, perhaps. I intend to dance the next waltz with my fiancée."

Maryann frowned. "It's true that you are engaged, then?"

"Yes." Baxter caught sight of Charlotte in Lennox's arms. They were both moving very briskly around the floor. Stamina.

"I see. I suppose I should congratulate you."

"There's no need for you to go out of your way."

Maryann's lips tightened. "Baxter, please, I must speak with you about Hamilton. I am extremely concerned. You know very well that your father told me that if I ever needed your help, you would assist me."

Baxter turned his head slowly to meet Maryann's desperate eyes and knew that he had no choice in the matter. He had given his father his oath.

He inclined his head a bare half inch in acceptance of the inevitable. "I believe you are correct, madam. It would no doubt be best if we held this conversation out in the gardens."

Seven

"I have heard that you were well acquainted with poor Mrs. Heskett." Charlotte realized to her chagrin that she sounded a trifle breathless. It was not easy keeping up with Lord Lennox. He set a demanding pace on the dance floor and she was definitely out of practice. "Dreadful thing, her murder. Makes one wonder what the world is coming to, does it not?"

"It certainly does. A shocking incident." Lennox whipped Charlotte around in a grand, gliding turn that took them halfway across the floor. "You knew her also, did you?"

"We were not terribly close, but we had several conversations. She, uh, mentioned you, my lord."

"Very fond of her, I was. Wanted to marry her, doncha know. But, alas, she turned down my offer. Couldn't believe it when I heard she'd been felled by a damned villain. Quite chilling."

"Indeed. You said you were fond of her?"

"Drusilla? Lord, yes. Enjoyed her company immensely. A real goer, Drusilla was. That woman had stamina, if y'know what I mean."

"She used to say much the same about you, my lord."

"Did she now?" Lennox looked briefly pleased. "Glad to hear it. I'm going to miss the lady, even if she did reject my offer of marriage." He winked. "Dru made it clear that she wouldn't be averse to the occasional bounce in bed after she settled on the business of a husband, doncha know."

"I see."

"I was to call on her that very night, you know."

Charlotte looked up quickly. "You went to see her the night she was killed?"

"No, no. I was supposed to pay a visit that evening. Got a message at the last minute informing me that she was ill and would not be able to receive me. Often wondered what would have happened if I'd gone to her house that evening."

"Indeed." Charlotte saw that Lennox had her on a collision course with an elderly man in a blue coat and a woman gowned in pale lavender silk. "Lord Lennox, perhaps we should—"

"Dru had a head on her shoulders." Lennox executed a nimble move that narrowly avoided the other dancers. "Understood that marriage didn't have to interfere with a spot of fun now and again."

"Indeed." Charlotte caught a flash of lavender silk out of the corner of her eye. She gave

Lennox a smile of relief and tried to think of how best to pursue her inquiries.

The problem was that Lennox gave every appearance of being exactly what her earlier investigations had indicated, good-natured and financially stable. She could not envision him as a murderer. Yet Drusilla had specifically mentioned his name in her last note.

"I see your fiancé headed toward the gardens with Lady Esherton," Lennox announced as he swung Charlotte into another galloping turn. "Don't envy him. The old man left St. Ives in a devil of a fix when he put him in charge of the family purse strings."

Charlotte recalled what Baxter had said about managing his half brother's income as well as his own. She had assumed the situation existed simply because Baxter was good at finances. "You mean the old earl actually stipulated in his will that Mr. St. Ives was to control the fortune?"

"It's no great secret that old Esherton made Baxter his executor until Hamilton is five-and-twenty. Sound thinking on Esherton's part, if you ask me. Anyone can see that young Hamilton needs some time to settle. Takes after his father, he does. The old earl was a neck-or-nothing rakehell in his youth." Lennox paused. "Come to think of it, he didn't change much over the years. He was a rakehell until the day he died."

"I see."

"But he wasn't foolish when it came to the fortune," Lennox continued. "By the time he inherited it, he was nearly thirty and he managed the estates nicely, indeed. Baxter's got his father's head for that sort of thing and the old man knew it. But it does put St. Ives into an uncomfortable spot. Bound to be a lot of resentment in a situation such as that."

"Indeed."

Lennox's expression grew unexpectedly troubled. "Hamilton ain't the only young man who's runnin' a bit wild these days. Seems as if the whole lot of the young bloods are feeling their oats. Don't mind telling you that my own son, Norris, has given me a few shudders of late. He and Hamilton are friends, doncha know."

"I suppose they're both into the usual bloody-minded occupations of young males," Charlotte said carefully. "Driving too fast, drinking too much, risking their necks in silly dares?"

"Wish that were the whole of it," Lennox said. "Mind you, I'm all in favor of a young man sowing his wild oats early in life. The devil knows, I got into my share of trouble when I was that age. Nearly got myself killed in a duel over a little high-flyer of an opera dancer on one occasion. Went a few rounds with a bruiser named Bull Keeley. Smuggled a bit of French brandy. That sort of thing."

"I see."

"Just the old-fashioned, innocent pleasures of youth." Lennox sent them whirling into another turn. "But these days becoming a man seems to be a riskier business than it was when I was a lad."

"What do you mean?"

"The gaming hells are more dangerous for one thing," Lennox said very seriously. "Friend of Norris's lost his estates in a place called The Green Table the other night. Young Crossmore went home and put a bullet in his head."

"How terrible."

"Warned Norris that if he didn't watch his step, I'd send him on an extended tour of the Continent."

"Has your threat worked?"

"Norris knows I won't tolerate any nonsense. Unfortunately for young Hamilton, his father ain't around to pull in the reins. Left the job to St. Ives along with the responsibility for the fortune."

With a final flourish, the music stopped. Charlotte was panting. She gave Lennox another curtsy and a bright smile. "Thank you, my lord, I needed the exercise."

"Builds stamina," he assured her as he led her off the floor. "Can I fetch you a glass of lemonade or champagne?"

"No, thank you, I believe I'll go find Lady Trengloss."

"Ah, yes, the lovely Rosalind. Charming woman." Lennox looked briefly wistful. "Imagine she misses her sister."

"Mr. St. Ives's mother?"

"Yes. Emma died four years ago. In their younger days, she and Rosalind kept things lively in Society. Never a dull moment. Emma was always the wilder of the two, though. Her affair with Esherton lasted until the day she died. I tell you, it's damned hard to believe that St. Ives is the offspring of that pair."

"Why do you say that?"

"Young Baxter's temperament is the complete opposite of his parents'. Oh, he takes after Esherton in some ways. No mistaking those eyes, of course. And he got his mother's dark hair. But he lacks Emma's sense of humor and dash and he didn't get even a modicum of the St. Ives style, sad to say."

"The St. Ives style?"

"You know what they say about the men of the St. Ives line. They do everything with style. Hamilton's living up to the family heritage but, I vow, Baxter looks as if he makes his livin' as someone's man-of-affairs."

"Looks can be deceiving, sir. Please excuse me."

"Of course, of course. Enjoyed the dance."

Charlotte turned and walked toward the French doors, which stood open to admit the evening air into the overheated ballroom.

Outside she found the wide terrace lit with colorful lanterns. Here and there couples murmured and laughed discreetly in the shadows. Beyond lay the night-darkened expanse of the gardens.

There was no sign of Baxter in the immediate vicinity but Charlotte was almost certain that he had not come back into the ballroom.

There was just enough moonlight to make out the looming shapes of clipped hedges and thickly clustered bushes. Baxter was out there somewhere. He had no taste for Society. It would be just like him to retreat to the solitude of the gardens until it was time to leave.

She went down the stone steps and started along the path that wound into the heart of the gardens. Her soft kid slippers made no sound on the old bricks. The night was crisp. She folded her arms and hugged herself a little to ward off the chill. She would not be able to stay out there long without her cloak.

A woman's low, anxious voice brought Charlotte to a halt. There was another couple on the far side of the high hedge on her left. She was about to continue on her way when she heard Baxter's characteristically brusque response.

"I do not know what the devil you expect me to do about the matter, madam. Hamilton is two-and-twenty." Baxter hesitated briefly before adding very dryly, "And he *is* the Earl of Esherton, after all."

"He is still a boy in so many ways." The woman's words were laced with desperation. "And so like his father. You must do something, Baxter. Ever since his lordship died, Hamilton has grown increasingly headstrong. I thought it was a stage that would pass when he recovered from his grief. But lately he and his closest friend, Norris—"

"Lennox's heir?"

"Yes. The two of them have taken up with new associates and I fear the worst. They no longer go off to their old clubs in the evenings. Hamilton tells me they prefer a new one they have discovered. A place called The Green Table."

"A lot of young men prefer the clubs that cater to them, rather than to the men of their fathers' generation."

"Yes, but I believe that this place is nothing more than a gaming hell."

"Calm yourself, Maryann. Hamilton cannot lose the Esherton fortune in a night of deep play. I have control of the funds for another three years, if you will recall."

"I never thought I'd live to thank God for his lordship's foresight in that matter, but I must admit it is a good thing that Hamilton does not yet have access to his fortune. Nevertheless, there are so many risks awaiting a young man of his temperament."

"Such as?"

"I do not know." Maryann's voice rose. "That is the worst of it, Baxter. I do not know the extent of the risks he takes. One hears things, dreadful things about the activities that take place in some of those hells."

"You are overwrought, Maryann."

"I am not overwrought, I am terrified. There are stories involving depravity and debauchery among the young bloods of the ton these days that would alarm any mother. I have heard tales of people who deliberately partake of too much opium in order to induce dreamlike trances, for example."

"A few poets may choose to amuse themselves in that fashion, perhaps, but I believe it's a fairly limited number."

"Who knows what is really going on at Hamilton's new club? I tell you, my son is not himself these days. He will not listen to me. You must speak to him."

"What makes you think he will listen to me?"

"You are my only hope, Baxter. Your father charged you with the responsibility of guiding Hamilton until he has gained maturity. Do not deny it. We all heard his lordship's dying instructions."

"It is astonishing, is it not?" Baxter said in an oddly reflective tone of voice. "Even from beyond the grave, my father is still capable of creating turmoil in all our lives. I wonder if he is enjoying himself as he watches the little dramas he continues to stage."

"Do not speak of his lordship with such disrespect. Baxter, I am depending upon you. You must stop Hamilton before he gets into serious trouble."

Charlotte heard what sounded like a muffled sob. There was a rush of silk skirts and the soft thud of slippers on the grass. She stepped hastily back into the shadows as Maryann emerged from behind the far end of the hedge. Charlotte watched the other woman walk swiftly back toward the lantern-lit terrace.

There was a short pause and then Baxter spoke from the opposite end of the hedge. "Did you hear enough or do you want me to summarize the pertinent details of the conversation for you?"

"Mr. St. Ives." Charlotte whirled around.

For a moment she could not make him out in the darkness. Then she saw him detach himself from the deep shadows of the high hedge and walk toward her. When he moved through a swath of weak moonlight she caught a glimpse of his harsh, unyielding expression.

"One of these days you really must start calling me by my given name, Charlotte."

"My apologies, sir. I did not mean to eavesdrop."

"But you do it so well."

"I could not help but overhear the last of your conversation with Lady Esherton."

"Do not concern yourself." He came to a halt in front of her. "We are partners, are we not?"

"Well, yes, but that does not give me the right to intrude on your private family business."

"Intrude all you wish. Society has been entertained by my family's business for years. Have you finished your interrogation of poor Lennox?"

Charlotte sighed. "I think I have got all the information I am going to get this evening. I did learn that he had an invitation to visit Mrs. Heskett the night she died but he received a note telling him that she was ill and would not be able to receive him."

"Hmm. I doubt he would have admitted that much if he was guilty."

"True. I cannot envision him as a killer."

"I agree. If you are satisfied, let's be on our way." Baxter took her arm and started back toward the big house. "I have had enough of

156

the social whirl. If I indulge in any more of this sort of excitement, I am likely to expire from boredom."

"I understand, but Ariel is enjoying herself so much. I hate to ask her to leave. It's only midnight."

"True, and for the ton the evening has just begun. Don't worry about your sister. I have a plan. We shall pack her off with my aunt, who will keep her out until dawn."

Charlotte glanced at him. "Do you think Lady Trengloss will mind?"

"Not in the least. Between announcing our engagement and introducing Ariel to the Polite World, she is enjoying herself immensely." He drew Charlotte up the terrace steps and back into the brilliantly lit ballroom. "Give me a moment to locate Rosalind and make the arrangements."

"I shall find Ariel and tell her that she is free to go with your aunt. She is no doubt out on the dance floor again. I vow, she has spent the entire evening there." Charlotte stood on tiptoe to search the crowd.

"I see her," Baxter said.

"Oh, yes, there she is." Charlotte smiled at the sight of Ariel moving elegantly to the notes of a waltz. "Dancing with that very handsome young man who is wearing the impossibly complicated cravat. I wonder who he is."

"His name is Hamilton," Baxter said dryly. "The Earl of Esherton. My half brother."

Half an hour later, the carriage shuddered to a halt in front of the Arkendale town house. Baxter roused himself from the moody thoughts that had overtaken him during the short journey. He looked at Charlotte, who was seated on the opposite cushion, and wondered what had possessed him to suggest that they end the evening so soon.

True, he'd had no wish to remain at the ball, especially after the unpleasant discussion with Maryann, but he certainly did not want to bid Charlotte good night.

Now they were at her house. The evening was concluded and there was no more time for conversation or anything else.

He had done a fine job of wasting the past half hour, he thought. For a man who prided himself on his powers of logic and intellect, he could be a bloody idiot at times.

Charlotte glanced out the window. "It would seem we have arrived, Mr. St. Ives."

Baxter heard the coachman descend from the carriage box. "Bloody hell."

Charlotte raised her brows but she offered no comment. He wondered exactly what it was that she was thinking. At times such as this, he was acutely aware of his poor understanding of the opposite sex. The only thing he knew for certain was that he did not want to say good night.

"Uh, Charlotte..."

The carriage door opened. Baxter could not think of an excuse to delay the inevitable.

With a soft rustle of her skirts, Charlotte descended from the carriage. Baxter followed reluctantly. He took her arm to guide her up the steps to her front door.

Fool. Bloody damn idiot. A whole half hour wasted. He could have passed the time in the carriage with Charlotte in his arms. Instead he had spent it contemplating morose thoughts of the past and the present. It was Maryann's fault. She had ruined his mood and his evening. Typical.

Charlotte took her key out of her beaded reticule. "Would you care to come in for a brandy, Mr. St. Ives?"

Baxter, fixated on his own gloomy thoughts, was certain that he had not heard correctly. He realized that she was watching him with a quizzical expression.

"A brandy?" He took the key from her hand and opened the door with fingers that had suddenly become clumsy.

"I realize it is late but we have a great deal to discuss." She stepped briskly into the darkened hall and turned to face him. "What with the rush of preparations to enter Society, I have not yet had an opportunity to show you the small picture I discovered in Mrs. Heskett's sketchbook."

She wanted to discuss business with him.

"Is something wrong, Mr. St. Ives?"

He realized he was still standing on her front steps. "Whatever gave you that notion?"

"Oh, dear, I've outraged your sense of propriety, haven't I?" She gave him an apologetic look. "I assure you that you need have no qualms about your reputation. Absolutely no one except your coachman will know if you come in for a few minutes. Mrs. Witty has gone to visit her cousin for the night. She will not be home until tomorrow."

"I see."

She gave him a laughing smile. "And we are supposed to be engaged, if you will recall. In short, Mr. St. Ives, your virtue is quite safe with me."

She was laughing at him.

"I believe I could use a brandy. A large one." He stalked into the tiled hall and closed the front door very deliberately.

There was enough moonlight pouring in through the windows that surrounded the door for Baxter to see Charlotte slip out of her evening cloak. She hung it on a wall hook.

He watched as she reached up to light a wall sconce. He could not take his eyes off the curves of her breasts as they rose gently in response to her movements. A moment later light flared warmly, spilling across her smooth skin. With alchemical magic the lamp revealed the fire buried in her dark hair and transmuted her yellow satin gown to gold. When she turned to look at him, her eyes were fathomless jewels.

"Shall we go into my study, Mr. St. Ives? I will show you Mrs. Heskett's little picture."

"By all means," Baxter heard himself say.

A great longing gripped him as he watched her walk toward the darkened room. The graceful sway of her hips beneath the golden skirts heated the blood in his veins.

"The brandy is on the table near the window," Charlotte called from inside the study. Light flared again as she lit another lamp inside the small room.

The glow from the doorway of the study beckoned Baxter with the compelling power of a sorcerer's spell. He hesitated a moment longer.

Entering the study was probably not a sound notion.

Definitely not a sensible, logical act.

"Bloody hell." He yanked savagely at the knot of his cravat and crossed the hall to enter the dream world that lay on the other side of the study door.

"What did you say?" Charlotte asked as he entered the room.

"Nothing of any importance." He went to light the fire. Then he straightened and headed for the brandy table.

Charlotte walked around behind her desk and bent down to open a bottom drawer. "I tore the page that contained the little picture out of the sketchbook. As far as I can tell, none of the other watercolor drawings in the book have anything to do with the small sketch and they were very distracting."

"Indeed." Baxter eyed Charlotte's nicely rounded bottom as she stooped to fumble in the low drawer. "Very distracting."

"Every time I tried to discuss the picture with

Ariel, her attention kept straying to the nude figures. And Mrs. Witty was no better."

"What of your own attention, Charlotte? Were you distracted by the nude figures, too?"

"I have a talent for keeping my mind on business." Charlotte straightened and put a sheet of neatly torn paper on the desk.

"Indeed." He concentrated hard on pouring two glasses of brandy. "It is one of my own great skills."

He turned, brandy glasses in hand, and looked at her. She was seated behind her desk. He wondered if she had any notion of how the lamplight warmed the curves of her breasts and deepened the mystery of her eyes.

"I was disappointed in the results of my questioning of Lennox." Charlotte frowned. "He seemed more concerned with the risks awaiting the younger generation of gentlemen these days than he did with Drusilla Heskett's death."

Baxter put one glass down in front of her. He ignored the page from the sketchbook. "Sounds as if Lennox and Maryann have something in common."

"I suspect that parents of every generation have worried about the dangers that their offspring must face."

"No doubt." He realized that if he stood there drinking in the sight of Charlotte's bare shoulders and gently swelling breasts for one more minute he would not be able to keep his hands off her.

He made himself walk to the window, hoping that the sight of the moonlit garden would lower the temperature of his overheated blood. But all he saw when he looked into the glass was Charlotte's reflection.

"Speaking of Lady Esherton," she said gently, "what will you do about your brother, Hamilton?"

He stilled. "That is the last thing I wish to discuss tonight."

"I see. I only brought up the subject because it appeared to be preying upon your mind during the ride home in the carriage."

"Do not concern yourself with my personal problems, Charlotte. I shall deal with them."

"Yes, of course." Charlotte hesitated and then, as if she could not help herself, she added softly, "They are right, you know."

He watched her reflection as she picked up the brandy glass and took a swallow. "Who?"

"Lennox and Lady Esherton." She set the glass down very slowly. "The younger generation faces many dangers."

"No offense, Charlotte, but you are in no position to talk when it comes to the subject of danger. May I remind you that you are the one who felt it necessary to hire a man-of-affairs who could also function as a bodyguard."

"I am a mature woman who knows very well what she is about. It is different for a much younger person."

Something in her voice caught Baxter's

attention. "You do not sound as if you are speaking generally."

She was quiet for a long moment. "The night before my stepfather was killed, he brought a monster to our house."

Baxter turned slowly to face her. "A monster?"

"Winterbourne had lost a great deal of money to the creature." Charlotte gazed at the brandy glass as though she saw the past in it. "My stepfather intended to pay his debts by feeding my sister to the beast."

"God's blood, Charlotte. What happened?"

"I used my father's pistol to force Winterbourne and the monster out of the house." The glass in her hand trembled a little. "They did not return."

He had a vision of her facing down the two men with only a pistol. A jolt of rage and fear went through him. "You are a very brave woman."

She did not appear to have heard him. "The next morning Winterbourne was found dead. His throat was cut by a footpad, they said. I do not know what really happened after the two left the house that night but I know that my stepfather was afraid of the beast. I have sometimes wondered if the monster murdered him in retaliation for failing to pay his gaming debts."

"Any man who would deliver a young woman into the hands of a monster in order to satisfy his vouchers deserves to die."

"Yes." Charlotte raised her eyes to meet his.

"Do not think for a moment that I mourn Winterbourne or that I feel some guilt because I forced him out into the night where he was killed. That is not what troubles me."

A jarring flash of intuition swept through Baxter. He sensed the secret dread that lay beneath the determined, independent spirit that animated Charlotte. The knowing was not unlike the moments of intense understanding that came upon him once in a while when an experiment allowed him a glimpse of a great scientific truth. This knowledge, however, was of a far more intimate nature than anything that he had ever discovered in his laboratory.

"I understand," he said quietly. "What truly troubles you is that even after all these years you cannot forget that the monster is still out there somewhere."

"No. I cannot forget. Sometimes the memory comes back in the guise of a dream. It wakes me in the middle of the night at the same hour that I was awakened on that night when the events occurred. In the dream I see myself in the dark hall outside my sister's bedroom. I have the pistol in my hand, just as I did then. But this time the monster is aware that it is not loaded."

"Christ." Baxter felt his insides go cold. "Are you telling me that the pistol you used that night was unloaded?"

"It had been stored in a chest for years. I had no ball or powder for it. It was very dark in the hall and neither Winterbourne nor the monster knew that I held an empty pistol. But in

165

my dream, the monster laughs because he knows the truth. He knows I cannot stop him this time."

Baxter took a step forward. "Charlotte—"

"And in my dream, I know that I will fail to protect my sister."

"It's only a dream, Charlotte." Baxter hesitated. "I have one of my own that recurs from time to time and is unpleasant enough to awaken me in the middle of the night."

She searched his face. "Dreams can be troublesome things."

"Yes." Baxter set his glass down on a nearby table. "Let us talk of other things."

"Of course. Our inquiries."

"No, not our inquiries. Did you enjoy your waltz?"

"With Lennox?" Charlotte grimaced. "I believe I know why Drusilla Heskett was in the habit of comparing him to a stallion."

Baxter raised his brows.

Charlotte chuckled. "His lordship does, indeed, possess a great deal of stamina. When the music stopped, I felt as though I had just finished a brisk morning ride on a sturdy jumper."

Baxter gazed thoughtfully at her for a moment. "Did I tell you that you looked very lovely this evening?"

She blinked. "I beg your pardon?"

"I rather thought that I had neglected to pay you any compliments. My apologies."

"Do not concern yourself, Mr. St. Ives." She folded her hands on her desk and gave him a blinding smile. "We are business associates, not intimate friends."

"There is something else I neglected to do." He walked behind the desk and reached down to close his hands around Charlotte's bare shoulders. Her skin was warm and impossibly soft.

"What was that?"

"I did not ask you to dance with me." He hauled her lightly to her feet. "Do you think that if we had danced the waltz together earlier this evening, you would now be able to call me by my first name?"

Her eyes were very green in the lamplight. She smiled as she put her arms slowly around his neck. "I don't know. Why don't you ask me and we shall see?"

"Dance with me, Charlotte."

"I would be very pleased to dance with you, Baxter."

This was what he had been waiting for all evening, he thought. This was what he needed.

He bent his head and took her mouth.

Eight ❧

Baxter was conducting some sort of experiment. Charlotte knew it with absolute certainty as soon as his lips touched hers. This kiss was different from the one they had shared in the carriage the other night. Even as he pulled her close against him and tightened his arms around her, she could feel him holding back something of himself.

It was as though he thought to observe and control the results of the embrace. She wondered if he believed that he could regulate his own desire the way he did the flames he used to heat volatile chemicals.

With understanding came a shock of anger. She was not some curious mixture to be tested and examined in a laboratory. Charlotte tightened her arms around his neck and pressed herself against him. She was suddenly determined to show Baxter that he could not remain an aloof observer of his own passion.

If this was an experiment, she decided, he was as much a part of it as she.

"Charlotte." Baxter's mouth moved on hers, tasting, probing, exploring. His hands moved up to cradle her head. He shoved his fingers into her hair, loosening the pins. "Say my name again."

"Baxter." Excitement flowed through her, so bright and hot that she could not believe that he did not feel it also.

"Again." He slid his thumbs along the line of her jaw.

"*Baxter.*"

"Open your mouth for me."

She obeyed. And then gave a soft, muffled gasp of surprise when his teeth sank gently into her lower lip.

"I won't hurt you," he whispered.

"I know." She clutched at him, inviting him to deepen the kiss.

He sifted his fingers through her hair. Pins pinged on the polished surface of the desk. And then he slid his hands downward, pausing briefly on her bare shoulders.

"You are so soft." He stroked the curve of her throat and moved his mouth to the place just below her ear. "Everything about you is smooth and soft."

She flattened her hands on his chest, savoring the feel of the sleek muscles beneath his crisp, white linen shirt. "And everything about you is very strong and very hard."

Baxter lifted his head. He removed his spectacles and set them down on the desk beside the fallen hairpins.

She looked into his eyes and caught her breath. Without the veil of his eyeglasses the alchemist's fires that burned in his gaze flared more intensely than molten gold. She could see the danger, but the flames fascinated and enthralled her.

"I want to feel your breasts in my hands." Baxter tugged gently at the tiny sleeves of her gown.

The bodice fell away, baring her to the waist. She shivered, violently aware of the lamplight that revealed her taut nipples. She ached. It was a delicious, thrilling, unbelievable sensation. She heard herself cry out softly when Baxter cupped her in his palms.

"You're beautiful." His voice was so low and husky that the words were almost inaudible.

He rasped his thumbs across the tips of her swollen breasts. She could not get any air into her lungs. It was only the driving need to inhale more of his intoxicating, utterly masculine scent that made her draw in another deep breath.

A great urgency poured through her. She crushed the fabric of his shirt in her fingers. Her head fell back. "Baxter. This is incredible."

"Yes." He bent his head and took one nipple between his teeth.

"Oh, my God." Swiftly she untied his cravat and sought the fastenings of his shirt with trembling fingers.

He froze. "No."

She ignored him. She got the shirt open and pushed her hands inside.

"Bloody hell." Baxter did not move. It was as if he awaited a blow he knew he could not avoid.

She touched him eagerly, savoring the heat and strength of his body. Her fingers moved through the crisp, curling hair of his chest and then she wrapped her arms around him and flattened her palms against his back.

She felt the roughened skin and knew it for what it was. Baxter was badly scarred.

It was her turn to go very still. She raised her head and looked at him. "You've been hurt."

"Three years ago." His eyes were grim and unwavering. "Long since healed."

"What happened?"

"Acid."

"Dear God. A laboratory accident?"

His smile was completely lacking in humor. "In a manner of speaking."

"I am so sorry. It must have been very painful."

"Not anymore. But the scars are unsightly. Give me a moment to put out the light." He made to step back from her.

"There is no need." Slowly, deliberately, she peeled the linen shirt off his shoulders and dropped it on the carpet. She could see the pale, rough patches of ruined skin scattered across his right shoulder. She closed her eyes against the pain she knew he must have experienced.

"Charlotte—"

"You cannot possibly think that the sight of your injuries would offend me. The only thing that matters is that your wounds have healed."

Very gently she touched one of the acid marks on his shoulder. Then she stood on tiptoe and kissed it. Baxter shuddered. She moved her lips up along his throat to his mouth.

"*Charlotte.*" His arms tightened fiercely around her.

For a moment there was nothing detached or remote about the embrace. She sensed the banked fires that burned within him. There was a raw, aching sensuality in his kiss that threatened to overwhelm her.

She gave herself up to the conflagration with an exultant rush of excitement.

He fitted his hands to her waist, lifted her off her feet, and kissed her breast.

She gasped when she felt his teeth on her nipple. "Baxter." She clutched at him with a strange sense of desperation.

He carried her toward the sofa. A moment later the room spun on its axis. And then Charlotte felt the cushions beneath her. The skirts of her gown fluttered around her thighs.

Before she could reorient herself, Baxter came down on top of her. He was heavy. Thrillingly so. The weight of his body crushed her deep into the velvet sofa. She could feel the fabric of his breeches against her bare skin above her gartered stockings.

And she could also feel the thickened weight of his aroused manhood. She sucked in her breath.

He raised his head and looked down into her eyes. "I want you."

She stared into the glowing crucible of his gaze and was lost in the spell of desire that swirled around them.

Surely it was impossible for any man, even one with a will as strong as Baxter's, to look at a woman with such raging need and still remain a dispassionate experimenter.

She threaded her fingers through his hair and did not bother to conceal her sense of wonder. "I have never known any emotion that was as strong as this."

"I'm glad." He kissed her deeply, hungrily.

She felt his hand glide down her leg and slide beneath the skirts of her gown. He curved his fingers around her calf.

She sank her nails into the rigid muscles of his back and shoulders.

He groaned. His hand moved up the inside of her thigh and then he was pressing against the damp, throbbing place between her legs. He dipped one finger into her, pushing gently to force his way past the small, tight muscles.

She shivered in reaction to the exotic invasion. "Please." She twisted restlessly, seeking something more. "Do not stop."

He withdrew his finger very slowly and then eased it back into her. At the same time his thumb moved higher, skimming lightly over the firm little nub at the top of her sex.

"Baxter." She could not think. She was awash in sensation. She clung to him, silently demanding an end to the exquisite torment yet unable to pull away. *"Baxter."*

He bent his head to her breast. His finger moved inside her. Instead of pushing deeper into the passage, he pressed upward. Again and again he repeated the caress.

A great tension built within her. She had never known such a coiling, restless, clenching need. She knew intuitively that the sensation could not continue to build. There had to be some release from the ever-mounting pressure.

She clutched at Baxter's shoulders.

There *had* to be a release.

She would surely shatter if something did not give. This relentless, driving force could not go on forever.

Without warning she came undone in a series of deep, convulsive shudders.

"Baxter."

She heard her own scream echo in the study as she fell from an impossibly high cliff.

Baxter held her while she floated down

through a liquid atmosphere in which he was the only solid object. She knew a dazed sense of wonder that robbed her of speech.

Gradually she once more became aware of the crackle of flames on the hearth and the feel of the sofa cushions beneath her back.

Baxter's weight still rested along the length of her body. When she finally opened her eyes she found him gazing down at her with glittering intensity.

"That was amazing," she whispered. "Quite wonderful."

He smiled and kissed her brow. "Yes, it was."

She touched his jaw. "But you did not experience the same sensation."

"Not this time." He straightened, carefully extricating himself from her tumbled skirts. "But there will be other times." He paused to touch the edge of her mouth with one blunt finger. "At least I hope that will be the case."

"Baxter, wait. Where are you going?"

"We must talk."

He got to his feet and walked across the room to where his shirt lay on the floor. The firelight flared on the acid scars that marked his back and shoulders. So much pain, Charlotte thought. Thank God the acid had not struck his eyes. He would surely have been blinded.

She watched as he picked up his shirt and shrugged into it with quick, practiced movements. Leaving it unfastened, he went to the desk, found his spectacles, and shoved them onto his nose.

Without a word he crossed to the hearth to stand in front of the fire. He stood gazing down into the flames.

Alarmed by the change in his mood, Charlotte sat up slowly. She fumbled with the bodice of her gown. "Is something wrong?"

"No." He took a poker from the stand and leaned down to stir the flames. "But I would have an understanding between us before we go any farther down this road."

She stared at him. His dark hair was tousled from where she had raked her fingers through it. The glow of the flames cast fierce shadows on the blunt planes and sharp angles of his forbidding features. She knew again the disturbing sense of wariness that she had felt the first day she met him.

"What sort of understanding?" she asked carefully.

"Will you have an affair with me, Charlotte?" The quiet words were spoken without inflection. Baxter's voice was stripped of all emotion.

"An affair?" She suddenly felt so clumsy that she could barely finish fastening the tapes of her gown. "With you?"

"It would seem that we are attracted to each other."

"Yes, but—" She broke off, not certain what to say. After all, she reminded herself, she had been considering just such a possibility.

"In my experience this sort of emotion is not unlike an illusion," Baxter said. "It seems real for a time and then it fades."

"I see." She could not deny his claim.

Passion alone was not to be trusted. She knew that better than most. She had established a career on the foundation of that simple principle. Only true love could add some element of safety and certainty to the dangerous brew. "You believe that the fires that warm us now will soon burn themselves out."

"From my observation of such matters, boredom and ennui eventually turn the hottest flames to ashes."

"Has that been the fate of your past liaisons?"

"I'm a chemist, not a poet." Baxter clasped his hands behind his back. "Over time the distinction becomes more pronounced."

"I do not understand."

"To put it more plainly, women tend to find me somewhat dull once the initial physical attraction has passed."

"Women find you dull?" That was too much. Anger flared in Charlotte, temporarily swamping the unhappiness that had been welling up inside her. "How dare you, sir. Do not try to fob me off with that sort of nonsense. If you have no great interest in a long-term connection, then at least have the decency to say so. Do not expect me to believe that your previous affairs have all ended because you bored your paramours to death."

He glanced at her, startled. "I assure you, it is the simple truth."

"Rubbish." She scrambled off the sofa and shook out her skirts. "You seek to make excuses. I expected better of you, sir."

He swung around to confront her. "I am not

making excuses. I am attempting to be practical."

"Indeed." She drew herself up proudly. "And what of your precious reputation, Mr. St. Ives?"

"It so happens that this charade of an engagement we have concocted provides us with the perfect cover for an affair."

Charlotte seethed. "This charade, as you call it, was created by you and is designed to last only as long as it takes us to find the villain who murdered Drusilla Heskett."

"There is no reason it cannot continue after we have achieved our primary goal."

"The usual engagement lasts a year, at best."

"I would not presume to estimate the lengths of your previous liaisons, but mine, on average, have lasted about two months or less."

"That is no great recommendation, sir."

"It's the bloody truth. Well?" He narrowed his gaze. "What is your answer? Are you interested in having an affair with me or not?"

She was trembling, not from passion this time, but from outrage. She lifted her chin. "Surely you do not expect an immediate response? I shall give you my decision after I have had an opportunity to study the matter more closely."

"Bloody hell." Baxter swept out a hand to indicate the sofa. "After what just took place, you tell me that you must give the matter further study?"

She smiled coolly. "As I often advise my

clients, one must not make important personal decisions in the heat of passion."

His jaw tightened. Without a word, he started toward her, his booted feet soundless on the carpet.

Charlotte braced herself. Pushing Baxter to the edge of his self-control was a risk, albeit not a physical one. She knew deep in her bones that he would never hurt her. But there was a strong element of unpredictability in this situation.

Before she could discover what he intended, one of the floorboards in the hallway outside the study gave out a groan. She froze.

Baxter halted, too. He glanced at the door and then frowned at Charlotte. "One of your staff?"

"No." She whirled around to stare at the closed door of the study. "I told you, my housekeeper is gone for the entire night. It cannot be Ariel. We would have heard your aunt's carriage arrive."

Footsteps thudded in the corridor. Charlotte realized that someone was running down the hall toward the door at the rear of the small town house.

"Bloody hell." Baxter launched himself forward. "Stay here." He yanked open the door and raced out into the front hall.

Charlotte picked up a heavy silver candlestick in one hand, grabbed her skirts with the other, and ran after him.

Darkness greeted her. Someone had extinguished the wall sconce that she had lit earlier. The only light was that which spilled from the study.

Footsteps echoed from the back of the house. Two sets. Baxter's and the intruder's.

She plunged into the inky depths of the hallway.

A cold draft told her that the back door was open. She could see the dim glow of moonlight at the end of the corridor. The intruder was already outside. He had fled into the garden.

She came to a halt in the doorway, straining to see into the shadows. There was no sign of anyone slinking through the bushes.

"Baxter? Where are you?"

There was no response.

Panic welled in Charlotte. The housebreaker had no doubt been armed. She had heard no pistol shots but many footpads preferred the silence of the blade. Visions of Baxter wounded, perhaps dying in the vicinity of the rose bushes, impelled her forward into the night.

"*Baxter*. Oh, my God, where are you? Speak to me, Baxter."

"I thought I told you to wait inside." Baxter materialized out of the intense darkness. One moment he was not there and the next he was standing directly in front of her. Moonlight glanced off the side of his face and glimmered on his spectacles.

"Are you all right?"

"Yes." He took her arm and steered her back toward the house. "But I failed to catch him. He disappeared into the alley behind the garden. He knew his way around. Must have studied the house and planned his escape route before he undertook this night's work. He seemed to know exactly where he was going."

"Thank God you did not catch him. He might have had a knife or a pistol."

"Kind of you to be concerned about my health."

"There is no call for sarcasm."

"Sorry." He urged her back through the doorway. "I occasionally resort to sarcasm when I have had too much excitement in one evening."

Charlotte chose to ignore that remark. Baxter had had a near brush with a villain. He had every right to be in a foul temper.

"Good heavens," she whispered as he closed the door. "Something has just occurred to me. We heard no sound in the hall or on the stairs earlier. That means that the intruder must have been in the house when we arrived home."

"Very likely."

"What a ghastly notion." Charlotte shuddered. "To think that he was there, listening, all the while you and I were...were..." She could not bring herself to finish the sentence.

"I suspect he was upstairs when we interrupted his plans." Baxter lit a wall sconce. "He no doubt decided to wait until he was certain that we were well occupied before he fled."

"Do you suppose he overheard us?"

Baxter lifted one shoulder in a disinterested movement. "Possibly." He bent to examine the lock on the door. "But I suspect he was far more interested in making good his escape than he was in playing the voyeur."

"I wonder if he managed to make off with anything." She frowned at Baxter, who was fiddling with the door. "What are you doing?"

"Attempting to determine precisely how he got inside. The front door was locked when we returned so he must have entered the house through this entrance." Baxter straightened, a thoughtful expression on his face. "But this lock has not been damaged and there are no broken windows. It would appear that our man knew what he was about."

"How dreadful. A professional member of the criminal class was right here in my house." Charlotte rubbed her hands over her chilled arms. "I must have a look around to see what is missing. I do hope that he did not steal the silver tea service or the ormolu clock."

"I'll walk through the house with you." Baxter strode toward the stairs. "I caught only a glimpse of his coat in the darkness but he did not appear to be carrying anything heavy enough to slow him down. With any luck we shall discover that your possessions are still here."

"Baxter?"

He glanced impatiently back over his shoulder, his whole attention clearly riveted on the matter at hand. "What is it?"

"Thank you." Charlotte smiled tremulously. "It was very brave of you to chase that villain off tonight."

"All in a day's work, Miss Arkendale."

The incense burned low in the black and crimson room. His senses were open. It was time.

"Read the cards, my love."

The fortune-teller placed the first card on the table. "The golden griffin."

"He is persistent."

She turned over the next card. "The lady with the crystal eyes."

"A nuisance."

The fortune-teller plucked another card from the deck. "The silver ring." She looked up. "The griffin and the lady have formed an alliance."

"It must be severed. I shall deal with it." He leaned forward. "What of the phoenix?"

The fortune-teller hesitated. Then she placed another card faceup on the table. "The phoenix will triumph."

"Yes." He was satisfied.

When the fortune-teller shivered with longing, he pushed her down onto the carpet. He knew the golden griffin's weaknesses well. And one of them was the lady with the crystal eyes, the woman who now belonged to the griffin.

There could be no more satisfactory way to

destroy a man of honor than to savage one whom such a man felt honor bound to protect.

❧

A housebreaker?" Ariel paused in the act of helping herself to the scrambled eggs and turned to look at Charlotte in amazement. "I do not believe it. You say he was right here in the house when you returned home with Mr. St. Ives?"

"Yes." Charlotte busied herself with her napkin while she mentally reviewed the portions of the tale that she did not intend to relate. There was no need to tell Ariel exactly what she and Baxter had been doing prior to the intruder's untimely interruption. "Mr. St. Ives and I went into the study to discuss the results of the evening's inquiries and we heard someone in the hall. You know how that floorboard near the kitchen creaks whenever it is trod upon."

"Yes, I know. What happened? Was anything taken?"

"No, thank heavens. Mr. St. Ives pursued the villain and chased him off through the garden."

Ariel tipped her head to one side. "St. Ives gave chase?"

"Yes. He is extraordinarily brave and quite fleet of foot. But the intruder had a head start and disappeared into the night."

"Fleet of foot?" Ariel looked briefly intrigued

by that observation. "I would not have thought of Mr. St. Ives as fleet of foot. Oh, well, do go on. Tell me the rest."

"There is not much else to tell. Mr. St. Ives and I walked through the entire house after the villain fled. We checked the silver and other things that a thief might have wanted to carry off but nothing seemed to be missing. Mr. St. Ives feels that we interrupted the intruder before he could complete his work."

"Thank God." Ariel sat down with a bemused expression. "This is absolutely amazing. Some footpad must have noticed that the house was empty last night and decided to take advantage of the opportunity."

"That's how it appears."

"How fortunate that you were not alone when you heard the villain in the hall."

"Yes."

"Why did you not tell me about this the instant I walked through the door?" Ariel asked.

"As no harm had been done, I concluded that there was no point in waiting up in order to tell you the story." And no reason to mention that after Baxter had left, she had lain awake for hours listening to every creak and groan of the house, Charlotte thought.

When she had not been aware of every sound, she had kept herself occupied with thoughts of Baxter. His mood had changed after the business with the intruder. His steely self-mastery had reasserted itself. There had been no further discussion of an affair.

She did not know whether to be vastly relieved or gravely disappointed.

"It was quite late when Lady Trengloss brought me home in her carriage," Ariel admitted. "I do not believe that I have ever stayed up until dawn before in my life. Her ladyship tells me that during the Season most of the ton is up until sunrise."

Charlotte spread gooseberry jam on her toast. "Did you enjoy yourself?"

A glowing warmth bloomed in Ariel's cheeks. "I had a wonderful evening. It was as if I stepped into another world."

"It is a world Mother greatly enjoyed." Charlotte felt a pang of the familiar wistfulness that she always got when she recalled the old memories of the time before Winterbourne. "Do you remember how much Mama loved the Season?"

"She looked so very beautiful when she went out in the evenings." Ariel's eyes softened. "And Father was so handsome. I remember how I loved to stand at the window and watch them drive off together in the carriage. I imagined that they were a prince and a princess in a fairy tale."

A short silence descended on the morning room. Charlotte shook off the past. She sensed Ariel doing the same. There was no point reminding each other of how the fairy tale had ended.

"I noticed that you danced with the Earl of Esherton at the Hiltson ball," Charlotte said.

Ariel blushed. "I danced with him again later in the evening at the Todd soiree. He is an excellent dancer. And his conversation is most interesting."

"He is a fine-looking man."

"Yes, he is. And a perfect gentleman. I only wish I could have danced every waltz with him. But that would have caused gossip, of course."

"Of course."

"He went off to his club around three so I did not see him after that."

The happy excitement in Ariel's eyes worried Charlotte for some reason. She was not certain what to say. She did not even know if she ought to say anything. Her sister was a sensible young woman, far more levelheaded than most her age. This experience of the Season was precisely what she had wished for Ariel. Surely there was no harm in encouraging her to enjoy herself. The adventure would end all too soon.

It occurred to Charlotte that she could give herself the same advice. A pleasant warmth suffused her whole body as memories of the passionate embrace returned. The prospect of an affair with Baxter compelled her imagination.

And then she recalled how cool and remote he had been when he had asked her to become his paramour, how he had deliberately seduced her on the sofa while holding himself in check.

She had been the subject of an experiment last night, Charlotte reminded herself. She did not care for the feeling.

Mrs. Witty stuck her head into the morning room. "A lady to see you, Miss Charlotte. Says she's here on urgent business."

"A client?" Charlotte glanced at the clock and frowned. "It's only eleven. I do not have any appointments until this afternoon."

"Could be this particular client is a bit more desperate than most." Mrs. Witty raised her brows. "She appears to be in immediate need of a husband, if you take my meaning."

Charlotte was startled. "Do you mean she's increasing?"

"Pregnant as a ewe in Spring," Mrs. Witty said cheerfully. "If I were in her shoes, I wouldn't be wastin' any time making inquiries into the background of any man who'd made an offer. I'd take him up on it before he could change his mind."

Ariel looked up. "I could interview her if you like, Charlotte."

Mrs. Witty looked at Charlotte. "She specifically asked for you, Miss Charlotte. Said she couldn't talk to anyone else."

"Show her into the study, Mrs. Witty." Charlotte rose from the table. "Tell her that I shall join her presently."

"Yes, Miss Charlotte." Mrs. Witty started to withdraw.

"One more thing," Charlotte said quickly. "I have a favor to ask of you, Mrs. Witty. We know that Mrs. Heskett's staff was out of the house on the night of the murder but I wonder if it might be worth a chat with her housekeeper.

She may be able to tell us something of her employer's plans for that evening. Do you think you could locate her?"

Mrs. Witty nodded. "I'll have a go at it."

"I shall be in here if you need me, Charlotte." Ariel went back to the sideboard to refill her plate. "Lady Trengloss says that I am to fortify myself for tonight's round of social affairs. She claims that the Season requires a lady to have stamina."

"Lady Trengloss is no doubt an authority on the subject."

Charlotte went out the door and down the hall. She paused in front of the mirror to make certain that she presented a professional, competent appearance and then she walked into the study.

The lady seated in front of the desk appeared to be about Charlotte's age. She was quite pretty, with light brown hair and soft features.

She was also quite pregnant. A blue pelisse was stretched taut over a high, rounded belly.

"Miss Arkendale?" The woman looked at Charlotte with anxious eyes much reddened from recent tears.

"Yes." Charlotte gave the woman a reassuring smile as she gently closed the study door. "I'm afraid that my housekeeper did not supply me with your name."

"Because I did not give it to her." The woman dabbed at her eyes with a damp handkerchief. "My name is Juliana Post. And I am here because I heard rumors that you were engaged to Mr. Baxter St. Ives. Is it true?"

Charlotte halted midway across the study. "Why, yes. Why do you ask?"

Juliana began to sob into her handkerchief. "Because I was his last paramour. It is his babe I carry. His bastard. Baxter has left me a ruined woman, Miss Arkendale. I thought you should know what sort of man he is."

Dumbfounded, Charlotte stared at Juliana's bent head. "What on earth are you saying?"

"He promised me marriage, Miss Arkendale." Juliana rose to her feet. "He said we would be wed. That is how he convinced me to submit to his embraces. But when he learned that I was pregnant, he cast me off. I have no family. I do not know what will become of me."

"If this is an attempt to obtain money from me—"

"No, no, it is not." Sobbing, Juliana rushed toward the door.

"Miss Post, wait, I have some questions to ask you."

"I cannot bear to talk about it." Juliana paused in the doorway and looked back at Charlotte with bitter eyes. "I came here today because I felt it was my duty to warn you that St. Ives is a bastard not only by birth, but by temperament. I am lost, Miss Arkendale. But it is not too late to save yourself. Take care or you will meet the same bad end."

Nine ❧

Charlotte heard the front door slam shut behind Juliana Post. She hurried out into the hall and peered through the window. She was in time to watch Juliana climb into a hackney carriage with an agility that was amazing in a woman who was so far advanced in her pregnancy.

Charlotte whirled around and seized a deep-brimmed straw bonnet from a wall hook. She grabbed the serviceable woolen coat that hung beside it.

Mrs. Witty emerged from the kitchens. She dried her hands on the neat white apron that covered her new bombazine gown and frowned at Charlotte. "Whatever is the matter?"

"I'm going to follow that woman who just left." Charlotte yanked open the front door and started down the steps. "I want to see where she goes."

"This is madness," Mrs. Witty called from the doorway. "She left in a carriage. You cannot hope to keep up with her on foot."

"The traffic is so slow in this part of town that I should be able to keep the carriage in sight if I hurry." Charlotte jammed her bonnet down onto her head and started to run.

"But you may have to follow her for a great distance," Mrs. Witty yelled.

Charlotte paid no attention. Several heads turned to watch as she flew along the walkway. She ignored the assortment of amused expressions and disapproving looks. She was well aware that those who knew her already thought her rather odd. Strangers would only shrug at the sight of a woman rushing through the throng of delivery carts and farmers' wagons that crowded the streets at this hour of the day.

The lumbering hackney turned the corner

at the far end of the street. Charlotte realized that if she cut through the park, she would be able to shorten the distance that separated her from the vehicle.

She turned and dashed through the iron gates that marked the entrance to the small green square. Clutching her bonnet, she emerged, breathless, at the opposite gate.

Mrs. Witty had been right. She could not go on much farther at this pace. Juliana's carriage was gaining ground.

She scanned the street with a sense of growing desperation. A flower cart driven by a youth of about fifteen stood midway down the block. She raced toward it, waving to get the boy's attention.

He glanced at her with a curious expression as she reached the cart. "Did ye want to buy some flowers, ma'am?"

"No, but I will pay you well if you will take me up and follow that hackney."

The boy frowned. "Don't know if me pa would want me doin' that, ma'am."

"I will make it worth your while." Charlotte hiked up her skirts and started to climb aboard. "I will purchase every flower on your cart if you will help me."

"Well..."

"Just think, you will be free for the rest of the day and when you return home this afternoon, your pa will be happy enough when he sees you've sold every bloom."

The boy still looked dubious. "You'll be wantin' every single flower?"

"Yes, indeed." Charlotte sat down and gave the young man an encouraging smile. "I love flowers."

The boy hesitated only a second longer. Then he shrugged. "Me pa always did say the fancy was peculiar."

He flapped the reins vigorously. Startled, the plump pony broke into a brisk trot. Charlotte strove to catch her breath as the cart jolted forward in pursuit of the hackney.

Fifteen minutes later the flower cart rounded another corner in a modest neighborhood. Charlotte watched Juliana's carriage come to a halt in front of a small house.

"This is far enough," Charlotte said. "You need not wait for me. I shall find my own way home."

" 'Ere, now, what about me flowers?"

"I have not forgotten." Charlotte collected her skirts and scrambled down from the cart. "I shall give you my direction. Take all the flowers there and inform my housekeeper that I told you she was to purchase every stem."

"All right, then." The boy eyed her. "Are ye sure ye don't want me to wait for ye?"

"No. I shall be able to find a hackney." She smiled and rattled off the information he needed to locate her town house. "It is very kind of you to be concerned, but I assure you, I can take care of myself."

"Whatever ye say." The boy clucked at the pony.

Charlotte waited until the flower cart had clattered off down the street before she walked toward the small house Juliana had entered. Mentally she composed a variety of ways to demand an explanation for the woman's actions. She finally decided that she would be obliged to wait for inspiration until she was inside.

She went up the steps and banged the knocker. There was silence and then came the sound of heavy footsteps. A moment later a stout-looking housekeeper opened the door.

"Yes, ma'am?"

"Please inform your mistress that I have come to call," Charlotte said firmly.

The housekeeper peered at her suspiciously. "Did ye have an appointment?"

An odd question, Charlotte thought. A housekeeper might inquire as to whether or not a caller was expected but the word *appointment* was used for business visits. Her own clients had appointments.

"Yes," Charlotte said smoothly. "I do have an appointment."

"Bit early," the woman grumbled as she stood back and opened the door. "Miss Post don't usually see her clients until the afternoon."

"She made an exception for me." Charlotte stepped swiftly through the opening before the housekeeper could have second thoughts. "It's rather urgent."

The housekeeper gave her a quizzical look but did not comment. She closed the door. "May I have your name?"

Charlotte seized upon the first name that sprang to mind. "Mrs. Witty."

193

"Very well. This way, then. I'll let Miss Post know that you're here, Mrs. Witty."

"Thank you."

Charlotte glanced curiously around the hall as she followed the housekeeper. The woodwork gleamed from a recent waxing. The tile floor was clean and polished. The oak and ebony cabinet on the side was handsomely inlaid with brass. Juliana Post did not appear to be wealthy, but she certainly was not impoverished. In fact, for a ruined woman, she appeared to be doing very well for herself.

The housekeeper opened a door on the far side of the hall. "Please go on in, Mrs. Witty. I'll fetch Miss Post."

Charlotte swept into the small parlor and halted, astonished.

She found herself in an exotic chamber decorated in the Eastern style. Everything was done in shades of crimson and black. The lingering scent of incense was strong although the brazier was unlit.

It was midday but in there it could have been midnight. The heavy red velvet drapes were pulled across the windows, throwing the parlor into an unnatural gloom. Great swaths of red and black ceiling hangings billowed low over the scene. The only light came from two tall lotus-flower candelabras.

There were no chairs but a number of crimson pillows trimmed with black fringe were arranged on the red and black carpet. A low, scarlet sofa was placed near the hearth.

In the center of the room a small ebony stand held a deck of cards.

"Mrs. Witty?" Juliana Post spoke from the doorway. "I'm afraid that I do not recall our appointment but I believe that I can accommodate you."

Charlotte removed her bonnet and turned slowly.

Juliana had already changed her attire. She now wore flowing scarlet robes and a great number of beads.

"I did not make an appointment," Charlotte said.

Juliana stiffened. "It's you." Something that might have been fear flickered in her eyes. "What are you doing here? How did you find me?"

"It was not difficult." Charlotte examined Juliana's newly slimmed figure and smiled grimly. "I assume that you are no longer concerned about being cast out into the streets and ruined forever?"

Juliana flushed. "It would be best if you left now, Miss Arkendale."

"I do not intend to leave here without an explanation."

"I have no explanations to give."

Charlotte said nothing for a long moment. Then she walked over to the small ebony table. "These are not the sort of cards one uses for whist."

"No."

Charlotte bent down to pick up the deck.

She examined the ornate decorations on the backs of the cards and then she glanced at the strange figures on the facing sides. She had seen such cards used once long ago at a masquerade party.

"Do you tell fortunes, Miss Post?"

Juliana watched her warily. "I read the cards in order to advise young ladies in matters of love and marriage."

"For a fee."

Juliana's smile was cold. "Naturally."

"When your housekeeper answered the door just now she assumed that I had an appointment. Did she think that I had come here to have you read the cards for me?"

"Yes."

Charlotte glanced meaningfully around the room. "I must commend you on your establishment. You have created a most intriguing atmosphere in which to practice your profession."

"Thank you."

"It would seem that your business is a profitable one."

"I manage." A bitter anger flashed across Juliana's face. "I have become quite the rage among a certain set of fashionable young ladies. Some of them find it amusing to have me read their fates in the cards. Others take it more seriously. Either way, they are prepared to pay for the entertainment I provide."

"Have you been in this career very long?"

"Since shortly after my dear guardian finished off the last of my inheritance." Cynical amusement lit Juliana's eyes. "That occurred when I was eighteen. Once the money was gone he no longer found it convenient to have me in his house."

"He sounds as if he came from the same mold as my stepfather." Charlotte set down the deck of cards. "Do you know, Miss Post, I believe we may have something in common."

"I doubt that very much."

"I, too, have a small business that caters to ladies. And I was also obliged to invent a career for reasons not unlike your own." She smiled faintly. "At least we both managed to escape the usual fate of women in our situation. Neither of us became a governess or was obliged to walk the streets."

"Please leave," Juliana whispered. "You should not have come here today."

"It is not easy for a woman to make her own way in the world, is it?"

The small bells attached to Juliana's crimson robes jangled dissonantly. She clenched her hands at her sides. "Do not think that you can cozen me into telling you what you wish to know. I will tell you nothing."

"I am prepared to pay for the information I seek."

Juliana gave a crack of mirthless laughter. "You're a fool if you think that there is any amount of money in the world that would persuade me to answer your question."

"Do you feel so much loyalty, then, to the person who hired you to play the part of a cast-off lover?"

"I made a bargain. I have kept my end of it. What happens now is none of my affair. I must insist that you leave at once."

Charlotte caught her breath as intuition struck. "You are afraid."

"That is nonsense."

"Whom do you fear? Perhaps I can assist you."

"Assist me?" Juliana gave her an incredulous look. "You can have no notion of what you are talking about."

"Do you know, Miss Post, in other circumstances, I believe we might have been friends."

"What in the name of God makes you say such a thing?"

"I would have thought it was obvious," Charlotte said quietly. "I suspect that we have many mutual interests and concerns. For instance, do you send your bills to your clients after their appointments or do you request that they pay you before you provide your services?"

Juliana frowned. "I expect reimbursement at the time of the appointments. I learned long ago that clients have a habit of letting their accounts languish if I wait to send my bills."

"I learned the same lesson early on in my career."

Juliana hesitated warily. "What, precisely, is the nature of your career?"

"You mean, you do not even know that much about me?"

"I know nothing about you, except where

you live and that you are engaged to Baxter St. Ives. I was employed to act a role and I did so. That was to be the end of it."

"I see. Well, as we are both engaged in a similar line, I do not mind telling you something about my business. Generally speaking, though, I do try to maintain a degree of confidentiality."

Juliana was clearly curious, in spite of her uneasy mood. "What services do you provide?"

"Very discreet services. Ladies who have received offers of marriage sometimes seek me out. I make inquiries into the backgrounds of the men who have expressed a desire to wed them."

"Inquiries? I do not understand."

"I attempt to verify that my clients' suitors are not rakehells, gamesters, or fortune hunters. In short, Miss Post, I endeavor to ensure that the ladies who consult with me do not make the mistake of marrying a man such as your guardian or my stepfather."

"That is astounding. You make these inquiries by yourself?"

"I have some assistants."

Juliana appeared reluctantly fascinated. "But how do you obtain your information?"

"From many sources. Servants in the household or those employed in gaming hells and brothels supply some of the answers." Charlotte smiled wryly. "No one ever notices the staff in such places."

"That is very true." Juliana shook her head

in amazement. "Inquiries into gentlemen's backgrounds. What an extraordinarily clever notion."

In spite of the situation, Charlotte was unable to resist a modest smile of pride. "Coming, as it does, from one who also understands the difficulties and rewards of inventing a singular career for herself, that is a great compliment."

Juliana's mouth thinned. "It also sounds an exceedingly dangerous business."

"On the whole I cannot say that I have had any great difficulty." *Until recently,* Charlotte added silently.

Juliana looked uncertain. She glanced over her shoulder as if she half expected to see someone materialize there. And then she took an urgent step closer to Charlotte and lowered her voice. "You say you feel that, in other circumstances, we might have been friends and colleagues."

"Yes."

"Speaking as a person who could have been your friend and colleague, I will give you this advice. I do not know what you have got yourself into that involves Baxter St. Ives, but I do know this much. You would do well to abandon whatever course you have set for yourself that is connected to him."

Charlotte stilled. "What do you mean?"

"I can say no more." Juliana flung out a hand to indicate the door. "You must leave at once. Do not return. Ever."

Charlotte was stunned by the undisguised fear that flickered in Juliana's eyes. "Very well." She turned and walked slowly toward the door. "But should you change your mind or wish my help, I pray that you will send a message to me. You have my direction." She put her hand on the knob.

"Miss Arkendale?"

Charlotte turned. "Yes?"

"You did not believe my little charade this morning, did you?" Juliana searched her face. "Not even for a moment."

"No, not even for a moment."

"May I ask why? Am I so poor an actress?"

"You are a very convincing actress," Charlotte said gently. "But I know Mr. St. Ives rather well. He is not the sort to abandon his own unborn child."

Juliana grimaced. "You are surprisingly naive, considering your choice of career. I will give you one more piece of advice, Miss Arkendale. Do not trust a man who can make you feel passion. Such men are dangerous magicians."

"I am only too well aware of the risks. I see them every day in the course of my profession. Good day, Miss Post." Charlotte let herself out of the incense-laced room and closed the door very quietly.

She did not take a deep breath until she was outside on the walk in front of Juliana Post's small house.

Baxter pondered the idiotic impulse that had prompted him to request his half brother to pay a visit this morning. He did not understand why he had succumbed to the urge to hold this unpleasant conference but he knew one thing for certain. It had been a mistake.

"Well, Baxter, I have answered your summons." Hamilton stalked back and forth across the laboratory.

It was not an easy task. He was obliged to wend a twisting path between the workbenches, the air pump, and the large stand that held the great burning lens that Baxter used when he needed to generate the most intense heat for an experiment.

Hamilton was, as usual, dressed to the nines. His pleated buff-colored trousers, cream-and-rose-striped waistcoat, elaborately tied cravat, and short, double-breasted coat identified him to all and sundry as a man of fashion.

Baxter eyed him thoughtfully. Hamilton's clothes always fitted him perfectly and he wore them with a natural, seemingly negligent ease. He was tall and lean and graceful in his movements. His tailors loved him. His gloves were perfectly shaped to his long-fingered hands. His neckcloth was always tied in a rakish manner. His boots gleamed.

Hamilton's attire was never stained with the residue of old chemicals, Baxter thought. His coat was never rumpled. He did not wear spectacles. The old earl, their father, had had the same innate, self-assured elegance and the ability to set the fashion.

Baxter was well aware that he was the one glaring exception to the commonly held view that the St. Ives men did everything with style.

"Thank you for coming so promptly," Baxter said.

Hamilton shot him a quick, searching glance. "I trust you will not waste my time. Have you finally decided to loosen the purse strings?"

Baxter lounged back against one of the workbenches and folded his arms. "Are you short of funds? One would never guess from that expensive new carriage you've got parked outside."

"Damnation, that is not the point, as you are very well aware." Hamilton whirled around, his shoulders rigid with anger. "I am the Earl of Esherton and I have a right to my inheritance. Father intended for me to have that money."

"In due course."

Hamilton narrowed his eyes. "I know that you enjoy the temporary power that you wield over my funds."

"Not particularly," Baxter said with great depth of feeling. "I would far rather Father had not burdened me with the task of managing your affairs. It is a bloody nuisance, if you want to know the truth."

"Do not expect me to believe that. We are

both well aware that controlling my inheritance gives you a measure of revenge." Hamilton came to a halt near the table that held Baxter's balance instrument. He picked up one of the small brass weights and examined it. "Gloat while you can. I already have the title. In a few years I shall have the fortune."

"Believe it or not, I expect to survive very nicely without your title or your fortune. But that is not important at the moment. Hamilton, I did not ask you here in order to discuss your financial situation."

"I should have guessed that you had not changed your mind about the handling of my inheritance." Hamilton dropped the brass weight back into the pan. He started toward the door. "I may as well be on my way, as it appears that we have nothing to say to each other."

"Your mother is concerned about you."

"My *mother*." Hamilton came to an abrupt halt. "My mother spoke to you about me?"

"Yes. She sought me out last night at one of the affairs I attended with my...fiancée."

"There is no reason why Mama would do such a thing," Hamilton exploded. "I cannot imagine her doing it. She can barely tolerate you. The very sight of you causes her pain."

"I am aware of that. The fact that she talked to me about her concerns is certainly proof of her anxious state."

Hamilton watched him warily. "What is it that concerns her?"

"Your choice of amusements."

"That is utter nonsense. She thinks I'm still in leading strings. But I'm a man now. Mother will have to accept that I have a right to enjoy myself with my friends. It's only natural that I spend more time at my club."

"About this club you have recently joined," Baxter said slowly. "What is the name of it?"

"Why do you care?"

"Merely curious."

Hamilton hesitated and then shrugged. "It's called The Green Table. But if you are thinking of applying for membership, I suggest you reconsider." He smiled thinly. "I do not believe that you would find it suitable to a man of your advanced years and unexciting temperament."

"I see. Do not concern yourself. I spend little enough time at my own club. I have no interest in joining a new one."

"I am relieved to hear it. I cannot imagine the two of us hanging about the same club. It would be damned awkward."

"No doubt."

"It's not as if we share the same interests."

"No."

Hamilton eyed him suspiciously. "You have no compelling curiosity about the nature of events on the metaphysical plane."

"You are quite correct in that assumption."

"And I cannot think you would want to discuss the latest works of the Romantic poets."

"The subject is not high on my list of dinner table conversation topics," Baxter admitted.

"And you certainly would not care to experiment with various methods of establishing the truth about the philosophy of the supernatural."

"Even lower on my list of favored topics than romantical poetry," Baxter agreed cheerfully. "Are those the sorts of discussions with which you amuse yourself at The Green Table?"

"For the most part."

"I understood it was a gaming hell, not a philosophical salon."

"My friends and I have created a club within a club. The management of The Green Table caters to our preferences in a separate portion of the establishment."

"I see. I believe I shall stick to my laboratory."

"Yes, that would be best. You would not enjoy yourself at The Green Table." Hamilton gazed at an array of glass tubes arranged on a nearby stand. "Father spent a lot of time here in your laboratory."

"He had a great interest in science. My experiments intrigued him."

"He always said you were quite brilliant." Hamilton's mouth twisted. "Called you a bloody hero because of some task you performed during the war."

Baxter was surprised by that information. "He exaggerated."

"I was sure he had. You're hardly the heroic sort."

"True. Being heroic requires a great deal of energy and strong emotion. Much too wearying for a person of my temperament."

Hamilton hesitated. "When I was fourteen, Father made me study that book you wrote under a pseudonym, *Conversations on Chemistry*."

"I'm sure you found it deadly dull."

"Yes, I did, as a matter of fact. But I followed one of the recipes for making a mild acid and somehow managed to spill the stuff all over my copy of the book." Hamilton smiled. "It quite ruined the pages."

"I see. Hamilton, I am aware that we have little in common but we do share a mutual interest in your inheritance."

Alarm lit Hamilton's eyes. "Now, see here, Baxter, if you think to steal my fortune—"

"There is no need to become agitated, I have no intention of helping myself to your money." Baxter walked to the windowsill and looked at the three sweet pea pots. There was still no sign of any green shoots. "But it has occurred to me that, as the money I now manage for you will one day be yours, you might have some interest in learning how to invest it."

"Explain yourself."

Baxter met his eyes. "I could show you how to deal with bankers and men of business. I would be happy to teach you the various ways of investing your income. How to employ the people you will require to manage your estates. That kind of thing."

"I want nothing from you except the money that is rightfully mine. I am not a child who requires a tutor in finances. There is nothing I can learn from you. Not one damned thing. Is that understood?"

"Yes."

Hamilton turned back toward the door with an angry, disgusted motion. "I have wasted enough time here today. I have better things to do."

The door opened just as he reached for the knob. Lambert loomed. He gazed impassively at Baxter. "A somewhat impetuous visitor to see you, sir."

"Baxter." Charlotte rushed into the laboratory without waiting for Lambert to finish announcing her. "I must tell you what has just happened. I have had the most amazing... Ooomph." She broke off in breathless confusion as she barely avoided a collision with Hamilton. "I beg your pardon, sir, I did not see you there."

"I do not believe that you and my half brother were introduced last night," Baxter said. "We left the ball somewhat early, if you will recall."

Charlotte glanced at Baxter. A hint of pink tinged her cheeks but he could not decide if the color was the result of her present state of high excitement or because she was remembering her passionate response to him last night.

"Yes, we did leave early," she murmured politely.

"Allow me to present the Earl of Esherton," Baxter said. "Hamilton, this is my fiancée, Miss Charlotte Arkendale."

Charlotte smiled warmly at Hamilton. "Your lordship."

Baxter watched her sink into an elegant curtsy.

"Miss Arkendale." Hamilton's scowl vanished as he took her hand. An unmistakable eagerness lit his eyes. "Lady Trengloss introduced me to your lovely sister last night. I had the very great honor of dancing with her. She is a most charming lady."

"In that we are agreed, my lord," Charlotte said.

Baxter cleared his throat. "You have not congratulated me on my engagement, Hamilton."

Hamilton's jaw clenched mutinously but the demands of civility prevailed. "My apologies. My felicitations to you both. If you will pardon me, I must be on my way."

"Of course," Charlotte said.

Hamilton nodded and hurried through the door.

Charlotte waited until they were alone. Then she favored Baxter with a bright, approving smile.

"So, you decided to take your brother in hand, after all." She removed her straw bonnet. "Lady Esherton will be greatly relieved, I'm sure."

"Not bloody likely. Hamilton does not want any advice from me." Baxter frowned at the clock. "Where the devil have you been, Charlotte? I sent a message around to your house an hour and a half ago. I got a note back from your sister informing me that you were out."

"It is a long story." She turned slowly on her

heel, examining the laboratory with an expression of great interest. "So this is where you perform your chemical experiments."

"Yes." He watched her walk to the windowsill.

"What have you got in these three pots?"

"Sweet pea seeds. I'm conducting an experiment to test the efficacy of adding certain minerals to soil that has been worn out from too many plantings."

Charlotte touched the earth in one pot with the tip of her finger. "The seeds have not sprouted."

"No," he said. "They may never sprout. That is the way of many such experiments. What is this tale that you wish to tell me?"

"It is the most amazing thing." She turned, shimmering with renewed excitement. "I may as well start at the beginning. This morning I had a visit from a lady who claimed to be pregnant with your child."

"*What?*"

"Brace yourself, Baxter. It only gets more interesting."

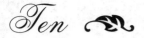 Ten

"You followed that woman back to her house?" Baxter was stunned. "Confronted her in her own hall? I don't believe this. What a crazed, idiotic, featherbrained thing to do."

"On the contrary. It was the logical thing to do under the circumstances," Charlotte said soothingly. "I had to discover what Miss Post was about. Surely you can understand that."

"Bloody hell." Beneath his anger, Baxter sensed the raw, wrenching fear. He made a futile attempt to contain the volatile mix of emotions. He knew he was not reacting in an entirely rational manner, but he could not stop himself. "How did you dare to take such a risk? Have you gone mad?"

Charlotte looked honestly baffled by his outrage. "There was no risk. I merely spoke to her."

"You should have talked to me before you undertook such a dangerous scheme." He swept out a hand. "I'm supposed to be your partner. And your bodyguard, devil take it." *And your lover,* something inside him wanted to add in a loud, clear voice. *I'm supposed to be your lover, dammit.*

"But there was no time to send a message around to you, sir. I had to act swiftly or I would have lost sight of Miss Post's carriage."

"Unbelievable. You went after her in a flower cart driven by some stranger who could well have proven to be the most dangerous sort of villain."

"I'm quite certain that he was only a boy from the country. I suspect that very few villains drive through London in flower carts."

"You went straight into the house of the woman who had just attempted to feed you a fantastic lie. Have you no common sense at all?" Baxter scowled as he passed the balance stationed on the end of one of the workbenches. Good God, he was moving about the

211

laboratory. He was pacing. He never paced.

The knowledge only served to darken his seething mood. Unfortunately, he had no choice but to continue prowling up and down the aisles between workbenches. He knew that if he paused even briefly he might succumb to the urge to seize the nearest glass retort and hurl it against the wall.

Charlotte had no business taking such risks. She would surely drive him mad before this was over. Her independent, unpredictable nature was a serious threat to his hard-won serenity. He was a chemist, not a poet. He could not deal with such surges of strong emotion.

Last night he had convinced himself that he had found a way to handle the tide of restless desire that Charlotte elicited in him. He had established to his own satisfaction that he was in command of himself and of the situation. He had concluded that it was safe to have an affair.

He had reasoned that the liaison would allow the unstable fires of passion to burn themselves out in a natural, controlled manner. The principle was not unlike his practice of using a carefully monitored flame to heat the contents of a flask full of volatile chemicals. So long as one was cautious and careful, no dangerous explosion would result.

In the end the contents of the flask would turn to ashes.

He had endured too much during the past twenty-four hours, he thought. He had assumed from her response to him that Charlotte would be amenable to his suggestion of an affair. But rather than give him a straightforward answer to his simple question, she had told him that she would consider the matter.

Consider the matter. Of all the bloody nerve. She had left him to twist in the wind while she dithered.

Then had come that nasty business with the housebreaker.

Now he was faced with this morning's crazed escapade.

And he was seething. He never seethed. Seething, like pacing, was a sign of a lack of self-mastery. It was a signal that emotion, rather than reason, ruled one's brain.

It was too much for a serious-minded, methodical, logical sort. If he had not been a modern man of science he would no doubt have been tempted to believe that some malign supernatural force had entered his life with the intention of wreaking havoc.

The knowledge that Charlotte had this sort of power over him stirred the hair on the nape of his neck and sent a chill down his spine.

"I resent the implication that I have no common sense, Mr. St. Ives." Charlotte's voice was drained of much of her earlier enthusiasm. The placating note was gone, too. She was starting to sound annoyed. "I am a mature adult, after all. I have operated my own business quite successfully for several years. I am no fool."

"I did not say that you were a fool." Damn. One wrong turn after another, Baxter thought glumly. In another moment the entire experiment would be ruined before it had even been properly begun and he would have no one to blame but himself.

"I'm delighted to hear that," Charlotte said crisply. "I would like to point out that this morning's events occurred because Miss Post heard the rumor that we were engaged to be married."

He paused near the large burning lens stand. "What has that to do with this?"

She gave him a very direct look. "It was your idea to announce this fraudulent engagement of ours and it was the engagement that brought Miss Post to my door with her wild tale. Therefore, I do not see how you can blame me for what transpired. To be perfectly blunt, it was all your fault."

Baxter began to feel hunted. He seized on the one thing that for some irrational reason irritated him the most. "Our engagement is not fraudulent."

"Indeed. What would you term it?"

He searched for words. "It is a stratagem."

"I fail to distinguish much difference between a stratagem and a fraud."

"Well, I can bloody well tell the difference," he said. "Or have you forgotten already that our engagement is designed to allow us to move in Society for the purposes of discovering a killer?"

She turned the straw bonnet absently in her hands, her expression suddenly thoughtful.

"And a very clever ruse it has proven to be. Only consider. We have got our first real clue thanks to your little stratagem, as you call it."

"What clue?"

"Don't you see?" Her eyes sparkled with renewed excitement. "When I confronted her, Miss Post as much as admitted that someone had employed her to visit me in the guise of your pregnant paramour. She would not tell me who had done so, but it was evident that her task was to destroy my faith in you."

"Obviously." Baxter got a sinking sensation in his stomach. Any number of gently bred women would have believed Miss Post's outlandish story.

"Someone went to great pains to end our so-called engagement," Charlotte continued. "We must ask ourselves why anyone would go to such lengths."

Baxter shoved his fingers through his hair. "Bloody hell."

"It would appear that someone does not want the two of us to form a close association."

"Calm yourself, Charlotte. I doubt very much that this episode with Miss Post has anything to do with our attempt to discover a murderer."

"What do you mean?"

He exhaled slowly. "I suspect that you were merely the victim of someone's notion of a malicious practical joke."

Charlotte stared at him. "But who would play such a hoax?"

"The first person who comes to mind is my bloody-minded half brother."

"Hamilton? That's ridiculous."

"A few days ago, I would have agreed with you. There is no great affection between Hamilton and myself, but I had not realized until this morning that he might be..." Baxter hesitated, still dubious of his own observations and conclusions. "Envious of me."

"Envious?"

Baxter recalled the bitter expression he had seen in Hamilton's eyes when he had described his willful destruction of his copy of *Conversations on Chemistry*. "I know it makes no sense, but I got the impression today that he harbors a personal grudge against me."

"Why is that?"

"I'm not entirely certain," Baxter admitted. "His mother would have influenced his view of me, of course. Maryann has always detested the very sight of me for obvious reasons. But I believe there may be more to Hamilton's dislike. Something beyond the perceived insult to his mother, I mean."

"What reasons?"

"His ill will toward me may have to do with the fact that my father and I spent a good deal of time together working on chemical experiments." Baxter grimaced. "Apparently Father went so far as to inform Hamilton of my small venture on behalf of England during the war. And he once forced Hamilton to read a book I wrote. Hamilton seemed to resent all that."

216

"I see." Understanding lit Charlotte's eyes. "A younger brother might be jealous of an older brother who had garnered much of their father's admiration and attention."

Another kind of emotion, the old, familiar, cold sensation, rippled through Baxter. It had an oddly calming effect. He knew this feeling well. Unlike the restless anger, this was something he understood and could control. "Hamilton got the title and the estates. What more can he want? It's not my fault that he didn't share Father's interest in science."

"No, it's not your fault, but to a very young man it could be a reason for envy." Charlotte frowned. "However, I cannot see Lord Esherton stooping to such a vicious piece of mischief as hiring a woman to ruin your engagement."

"You barely know Hamilton."

"True, but I have sound intuition. Also, Ariel seems quite taken with him and even though she is young, her perceptions about men are generally quite solid, too."

"Intuition." Baxter did not trouble to hide the sarcasm in his voice. "Allow me to tell you, Miss Arkendale, intuition is an extremely poor guide. It is based on emotion, not science. It is not to be trusted."

"Sometimes one has nothing else to go on," she said gently.

"Enough. I shall deal with the problem of Hamilton later."

"You cannot be certain that Hamilton was behind Miss Post's visit."

"It is the most logical assumption," Baxter

said. "The point here is that you had no business confronting that strange woman this morning. You had no notion of what you were walking into when you entered her house."

"Really, Mr. St. Ives."

"Yes, really." He turned and started toward her down an aisle. "There will be no more such rash actions on your part while we are engaged in this affair, is that clear?"

"I must remind you that I do not take orders from you or anyone else."

He stopped a few paces away from her. "That leaves us with a small problem, does it not?"

She put her bonnet down on the workbench with a very deliberate movement. "There will be no great difficulty so long as you play your assigned role in this business."

"You mean so long as I remember my place, do you not?"

"I would not put it in quite those terms."

"You had bloody well better not put it in such terms. I'm not your servant, Miss Arkendale."

"I did not say that you were. However, I did hire you in the beginning, if you will recall. If it will clarify the situation, I am still prepared to pay you a fee for your services."

"You dare to talk to me of a salary? After what occurred between us last night?"

She flushed and glanced uneasily toward the closed door. "There is no need to speak quite so loudly, sir. I can hear you very well."

"I never raise my voice. Speaking in a loud

218

voice is an indication that one cannot control one's temper."

She searched his face. "Yes, I suppose it is."

"Dammit, Charlotte, I will not be treated as though I were your employee." He took two swift strides forward, trapping her against a workbench. "Last night I asked you a question. You have kept me dangling long enough. I deserve the courtesy of a reply."

She frowned. "But we are discussing Miss Post."

"Devil take Miss Post. I told you, I will deal with her later. Just give me my answer. Will you have an affair with me?"

She stared at him, her unblinking gaze as brilliant as the fabled glow of the Philosopher's Stone. A dreadful silence descended on the laboratory. Baxter could almost see his own words hanging in the air, glittering with a dangerous light.

His timing could not have been worse, he thought with bleak despair. It did not take the exquisite sensibilities of a romantic poet to comprehend that one did not ask a woman to become one's lover when one was in the middle of a blazing row with her.

Charlotte shattered the crystalline silence by delicately clearing her throat. "We are discussing our business association here, Mr. St. Ives. What do personal matters have to do with this situation?"

"Nothing. Absolutely nothing."

If he had any sense at all he would step back from the blazing crucible before the explosion occurred. But he could not turn aside. The only thing that mattered now was obtaining a conclusive result to this reckless experiment.

"Nothing?" she repeated very softly.

"No, that is a damned lie. Our personal situation has everything to do with this. I need an answer, Charlotte. I shall likely go mad if you do not give me one."

Her eyes were suddenly swimming with mystery, full of unfathomable promise. But her voice was remarkably cool. "I vow, St. Ives, you are the most annoying man it has ever been my misfortune to employ. I can see nothing but complications ahead, but, yes, I shall have an affair with you. Now, then, can we please get back to business?"

For a single, unbearable instant, Baxter could not react. She had agreed to the affair.

He was aware that by some incredible good fortune the dangerously overheated crucible had not yet exploded in his hands, but he was as shaken as if his experiment had blown down the very walls.

Charlotte reached up to touch his cheek. "Baxter? Are you ill?"

"Very likely." He caught her face between his palms. "If I am, one thing is certain. You are the only one who can supply the elixir I require to cure the fever."

"Oh, *Baxter*." She stood on tiptoe and wrapped her arms very tightly around his neck. "You are the most amazing, most maddening man."

She kissed him with such fierceness that her teeth scraped against his own. Baxter staggered back a step. He caught her, steadied her, and returned the kiss with a sense of euphoric desperation.

Her undisguised desire was his final undoing. She wanted him. It was all that mattered in this moment.

He consigned his self-control to oblivion without a qualm and savored the great, ravening hunger that roared through his veins.

The world was suddenly fashioned of quicksilver. Bright, gleaming, ever-changing, endlessly fascinating. Nothing stayed in focus. It was impossible to concentrate on logic. His unquenchable need was all.

He crushed her lips beneath his own, seeking the damp heat of her mouth. He leaned into her, bending her back until she came up hard against the workbench.

"Oomph." Charlotte sounded startled but she did not pull away. Instead, her fingers clenched fiercely in his hair.

Shuddering with hunger, he kissed her cheek, her eyes, her ears, her throat.

He raised his head just long enough to yank off his spectacles. He tossed them carelessly aside. Then he shoved one booted foot between her stocking-clad legs and slid his knee upward. She cried out and clung to him when she found herself astride his upper thigh.

"I can feel your heat straight through my breeches," he muttered, awed. "You're already dampening the fabric."

She groaned and buried her face against his shirt. "You embarrass me, sir."

"On my oath, that was not my intent." He ripped several pins from her hair. "If you like, I shall study some of that bloody romantic poetry. Perhaps I can learn a more refined language to use at moments such as this."

"Do not trouble yourself." She started to jerk open the fastenings of his shirt with trembling hands. "You are doing very well without a course of study."

Her fingers splayed across his bare chest. Baxter squeezed his eyes shut and sucked in his breath. His shaft threatened to burst through the front of his breeches.

Charlotte put her lips to one of his nipples. She said something against his skin. The words were unintelligible but the meaning was unmistakable. He realized with a sense of unfurling triumph and boundless gratitude that she was as desperate for him as he was for her.

A part of him wanted to take ample time to relish this first joining. But he was powerless to halt the headlong rush so long as Charlotte was rushing in the same direction. The combined force of their desire was truly irresistible.

There would be opportunity enough later to make the lovemaking last for hours, he promised himself. This time it was too elemental, too primitive a thing.

He grasped a fistful of her fine muslin skirts and hauled them up to her waist. He lowered his knee slowly and slid his hands beneath her bare, rounded buttocks. He eased her up onto the edge of the workbench.

A ceramic flask got knocked on its side as he struggled with the foaming skirts. The jar rolled to the edge of the bench and crashed to the floor. He ignored it.

"Baxter?" Charlotte sounded disoriented, confused.

"Just hold on, my sweet." He grasped her legs and pulled them around his waist. "That's all you have to do. I'll take care of the rest."

He quickly opened the front of his breeches and guided himself to her.

"Dear God, *Baxter*." She gripped his shoulders.

The feel of her fingertips on the old scars sent shock waves through him again, just as it had last night. But this time he did not fight the sensation. It rolled through him with the force of lightning and he gloried in it.

"Tell me that you want me," he said into the curve of her throat. "Let me hear you say it."

"I want you." Feminine need throbbed in her voice.

He put one hand on her sex. She pulsed gently against him, her flesh swollen with desire. He could feel the small bud straining against the pad of his thumb. He rubbed it gently and reveled in the way her entire body quivered in response.

"Make love to me, Baxter. Please."

He almost laughed. The sound emerged

from his throat as a short, husky croak. "I could not stop now, not even for the secret of the Philosopher's Stone itself."

He braced her against the sturdy workbench and guided his shaft to the entrance of her moist passage. He felt her go very still.

He thrust heavily into her, willing himself to go as slowly as possible because he knew from last night's explorations that she was snug and tight. It had no doubt been some time since her last lover, he thought, perhaps even longer than it had been since his own last affair.

But his willpower had been weakened along with his brain, he discovered. The moment he felt the clinging grasp of her narrow channel, he forgot all about restraint. In the grip of a triumphant recklessness, he cradled her buttocks and plunged forward.

Charlotte yelped. Her body went rigid. Her nails dug into the acid marks on his shoulders.

He suddenly realized the truth. Charlotte had had no previous lovers.

"Bloody hell."

In spite of her knowledge of men, in spite of the veneer of worldly sophistication she exhibited, in spite of her age, she was a virgin.

Correction, he thought. She had been a virgin.

He stopped moving but he was already sunk deep inside her. He could feel the small muscles of her soft passage straining to encompass him.

"Why did you not tell me?" he demanded.

"You never asked." She kissed his throat. And then she smiled. "And it does not matter. I wanted this."

"God help me, so do I."

He adjusted himself carefully and began to move. He retreated slowly, aware of a sensation that was both pain and pleasure. It seemed to take forever to withdraw to the very entrance. She clung tightly to him the whole way. He finally halted when only the tip of his shaft remained inside her.

She drew in a deep, shuddering breath.

He reached between them, found the taut nubbin hidden in the soft curls of her sex, and stroked it until he felt her begin to relax.

"Yes." She kissed him frantically. Her legs tightened around his waist. "Yes. *Yes*."

She lowered her hand and gently, tentatively, cradled him. The blood roared in his veins.

Stroking gently, he pushed himself deliberately into her until he was once more sunk to the hilt.

She sighed and wriggled her hips.

"For God's sake, don't move," he muttered.

She did not appear to hear him. Perhaps she was not listening. She twisted herself with mounting eagerness. Baxter closed his eyes. His hands shook when he tried to hold her still. But he was too close to the fire now. The lure of the crucible drew him with inescapable power.

Charlotte kissed him again. He was lost.

"Next time," he heard himself promise in a hoarse whisper. He began to move more quickly within her. "Next time…"

But he did not have to make her wait until the next occasion for her release. He heard her cry out, a wonderfully triumphant scream of delight and satisfaction.

And then she turned to molten gold in his hands.

She convulsed around him, tiny spasms kneading his engorged flesh. He slammed into her one last time and spilled himself into her warm, welcoming body.

The workbench trembled and shook.

Baxter was dimly aware of the sound of breaking glass. Another flask had been knocked to the floor. Something heavy, the cast iron pneumatic trough, perhaps, toppled and fell. A metallic clang echoed through the room as two brass instruments rolled into each other.

Baxter ignored the chaos around him and lost himself in the whirlpool.

❧

Charlotte floated gently down out of a world that was composed of pure sensation and found herself sitting on the edge of one of Baxter's workbenches. She opened her eyes.

Baxter was no longer embedded within her body but he still stood between her legs. He was watching her with a shuttered, fiercely intent expression.

"You should have told me that you had never had a lover."

The eerily emotionless quality of his voice washed away the last traces of warmth.

"It was my business," she said. "I do not see that the facts of the situation need concern you in any way. You need assume no responsibility as a result of having been my first paramour. I am not a girl, I am a mature woman."

"Granted." His expression hardened. "But I do not appreciate being surprised by that kind of information."

For some ridiculous reason, she was suddenly on the verge of tears. She blinked the moisture away with an act of sheer will. She refused to cry simply because Baxter had reverted to his customary brusque nature.

This was not how things should be after such an exhilarating experience, she thought. There should be great tenderness between them now. At least for a few moments they should both be able to indulge themselves in the wonderful sense of intimacy that had enveloped them during the passionate encounter.

Perhaps her emotions were still in an unusually volatile state due to recent events. But, damnation, here she was falling in love with this exceedingly difficult man and he stood there between her thighs, scowling as if she had done something unforgivable. Had their passion meant nothing to him?

"Baxter, you are making far too much of this."

His jaw tightened. "Perhaps I am. After

all, you were as eager as I for what occurred."

"Indeed," she said stiffly.

His mouth twisted. He glanced down, apparently amazed to discover that his fingers were still curved around her upper thighs.

A wave of acute embarrassment swept over Charlotte. She was keenly aware of a disturbing scent that she knew must have resulted from the lovemaking. And there was a great deal of dampness between her legs. She shifted gingerly and fumbled with her skirts.

"Wait," Baxter muttered. "I've got a clean handkerchief here somewhere."

He fished around in his clothing until he produced a large square of neatly pressed linen. Charlotte flinched and blushed furiously when he used it to wipe away the traces of their passion. She submitted for a few seconds and then pushed his hand away.

"If you're quite finished." She managed to get her legs closed. She jerked her skirts downward and slid off the workbench.

Her knees threatened to give way. She put out a hand to catch her balance.

"Why?" Baxter asked.

She glanced at him. "I beg your pardon?"

He crushed the wet handkerchief in his fingers. His alchemist's eyes blazed. "Why did you choose me to be your first lover?"

Damn him. Two could play at this game. She dredged up what she hoped was a cool smile. "You, of all people, sir, should understand that sometimes the urge to conduct an experiment proves quite overwhelming."

Eleven

He had been nothing more than an experiment for her. A damned *experiment*.

Baxter's initial rage was now inextricably bound up with a gut-wrenching sense of frustrated despair. He fought hard to conceal both behind the veil of emotionless detachment that had worked so often and so well for him in the past.

He escorted Charlotte home with a brusque civility that clearly annoyed her but it was all that he was prepared to give. She sat across from him in the carriage, her spine elegantly straight, and refused to meet his eyes during the whole of the short ride. She kept her attention fixed on the street. There was a flush in her cheeks but Baxter concluded that it was not a result of the fact that he had just made love to her. She said not a single word.

Her lack of conversation suited him perfectly, he thought. God knew he'd had more than enough of strong emotions today. He certainly did not want to discuss them.

He followed her up the steps of her little town house in silence. It was a relief to retreat into the deep, remote place where feeling was muted, distanced, and far easier to contain.

Mrs. Witty opened the door with alacrity. "About time you got home, Miss Charlotte.

Miss Ariel and myself were starting to fret. Wondered if we ought to send word to Mr. St. Ives—" She broke off as she took in the sight of Baxter standing on the step behind Charlotte. Her face cleared. "Oh, I see you found her, sir. Well, that's a fortunate turn of events."

"That depends upon one's point of view." Baxter ignored Charlotte's glowering, sidelong glance as he stepped into the hall.

He stopped short as the overpowering fragrance of a vast quantity of massed flowers hit him in a scented wave. "What the devil is this? Have you turned the house into a bloody conservatory?"

Mrs. Witty grimaced as she followed his gaze. "They started arriving this morning. Used every vase and bowl we had in the house. Quite a sight, eh?"

Rank upon rank of vases filled with innumerable blooms were clustered in the hall. Pots of marigolds marched up the staircase. Tulips framed the mirror. Roses and orchids and lilies were massed against the walls.

Baxter was abruptly incensed. "Who the devil thinks he has the right to send you all of these damned posies, Charlotte? The only man you danced with last night was old Lennox."

"I sent some of them to myself." Charlotte untied her bonnet strings. "I made a bargain with the young boy who drove the flower cart, you see. He only agreed to help me follow Miss Post after I said I would purchase all of his wares."

"Ah, yes. The bloody flower cart boy."

Baxter scowled at Mrs. Witty. "Were you a party to that episode?"

"Don't look at me, sir." Mrs. Witty took his hat. "I'm entirely innocent. I suggested that chasing after Miss Post was not the wisest course of action, but who listens to the housekeeper? In any event, not all of these flowers are from the flower cart. A good many were sent around this morning by Miss Ariel's admirers."

Charlotte brightened. "Of course. Ariel was the toast of every young man in the ton last night. The gentlemen fell at her feet in droves."

"Charlotte, you're back." Ariel's voice sang out from the rear of the hall. Quick footsteps sounded on the tile as she hurried toward the front of the house. "I was starting to become concerned. Mrs. Witty said that you'd gone haring off after some woman who claimed that Mr. St. Ives had seduced and abandoned her—Oh, Mr. St. Ives." Ariel blushed as she emerged from the corridor. "I did not see you, sir."

"Think nothing of it." Baxter folded his arms and propped one shoulder against the door frame. "I'm accustomed to being ignored."

"Pay no attention to him." Charlotte marched briskly toward the stairs. "Mr. St. Ives is in an ill temper. Show him into my study, Mrs. Witty. I shall be down in a minute. I want to freshen myself. It has been a somewhat hectic morning."

"Hectic." Baxter watched Charlotte hurry

up the staircase. "Yes, indeed. Just another busy morning in the laboratory observing the results of one's experiments, eh, Miss Arkendale?"

She paused on the landing to give him a brittle smile. "As you say, Mr. St. Ives."

"Bear in mind that occasionally the results of certain experiments take some time to develop," he said. "As long as nine months in some instances."

He had the satisfaction of seeing her eyes widen in shock as his meaning sank home. Bleakly satisfied, he turned and walked into the study.

Another scented wave swept over him. This room, too, was filled with blooms. A particularly large bowl of pale pink roses dominated the scene.

Nine months. His own words struck him with the impact of a hammer blow. What if Charlotte was pregnant?

He made for the brandy table.

Charlotte's outraged yell sounded from the floor above just as Baxter got the top off the brandy decanter.

"It's gone." Footsteps pounded overhead. "The bastard took it."

Baxter put down the decanter with a long-suffering sigh. A man could not even take a medicinal draught in this household without being interrupted.

He made his way back to the doorway of the study. Ariel and Mrs. Witty were gazing up at the landing in open-mouthed astonishment.

Charlotte stood there looking as though she had just received a strong jolt from an electricity machine.

"What is it?" Ariel demanded. "What happened?"

Mrs. Witty stared at her. "What's wrong?"

Charlotte flung her arms wide. "I just told you. Didn't you hear me? He took it."

"Calm yourself, Charlotte," Baxter said. Everyone fell silent and turned to look at him. "Now, then, why don't you tell us precisely who took what?"

"The villain we surprised here in this house last night," she said impatiently.

"What about him?"

"I concluded that he had not managed to steal anything, but I was wrong. I only thought to check those items that I believed would appeal to a thief, the silver and such." Charlotte drew a breath. "I did not bother to check Drusilla Heskett's watercolor sketchbook. I stored it in a wardrobe drawer."

Baxter went cold. "Are you saying it's gone?"

"Yes. That was no ordinary housebreaker, Baxter. He was after that sketchbook. And he got it." She leveled an accusing finger at him. "I told you that book contained a valuable clue, St. Ives."

Baxter adjusted his spectacles absently as he considered the implications. "When you have finished refreshing yourself, come down here at once. Kindly do not dawdle."

"Damn you, St. Ives. Don't you dare give

me orders in my own house. Furthermore, I do not dawdle. I'm the one who followed Miss Post this morning, if you will but recall. When I attempted to tell you about the incident, you created a...a great distraction right there in your own laboratory. Any dawdling done this day was done by you, sir."

Baxter closed the study door very gently and went back to the brandy table.

Fifteen minutes later, feeling vastly more composed, Charlotte swept into the study. Ariel and Mrs. Witty followed on her heels. Baxter was seated in the wingback chair in front of the fire. He glanced at the women and put down the half-finished brandy.

"About time," he murmured as he got to his feet.

Charlotte ignored him. "It is extremely fortunate that I thought to tear out the page that contained Drusilla Heskett's little drawing." She went around her desk and opened a drawer. The torn sheet of sketch paper was inside, right where she had put it last night after Baxter had left. "This has got to be the clue. It was the only odd thing in the sketchbook."

"I thought there were a number of oddities in that sketchbook," Ariel said cheerfully. "Some of them quite interesting."

Charlotte scowled at her as she put the ragged page on top of the desk. "That is precisely why I removed this particular sketch."

234

Mrs. Witty peered at the pen-and-ink drawing. "Looks like so much nonsense to me. A triangle within a circle, three worms swimming about, and—" She squinted. "What's that thing in the center? A dragon?"

"Some sort of winged creature, I believe." Charlotte pursed her lips. "Difficult to be certain. Mrs. Heskett did not possess a great talent for drawing. Except for certain types of anatomical studies, that is."

Baxter crossed to the desk. "Let me see the picture."

Charlotte felt a stirring sensation on her skin as he came to a halt and stood gazing down at the sketch. She had his full attention now, she thought. The news of the theft of the sketchbook had caused him to focus his considerable intellect on the situation.

It seemed to her that the quiet power he radiated when he was this intense shimmered around him in an invisible aura. She wondered how Ariel and Mrs. Witty could fail to notice. And then she saw that both of them had moved slightly, as if to give Baxter more room. But in truth there was ample space at the desk. Neither seemed aware of the subtle change in position.

Charlotte almost smiled. Most people might not be conscious of Baxter's solid, inner strength, but that did not mean they failed to respond to it in an instinctive fashion.

He picked up the sheet of paper and looked more closely at the drawing. His brows drew together in a dark line above the rims of his spectacles. "There is something familiar about this picture."

Excitement rushed through Charlotte. "What do you mean? Have you seen such a design somewhere else?"

"Perhaps. A long time ago." Baxter glanced up from the drawing. His eyes met hers. "I shall have to do some research in my library."

"You have seen something similar in one of your books?" Ariel asked quickly.

"Possibly." He eyed the picture again. "I cannot be certain, but if memory serves, it is a very ancient thing."

"Ancient." Charlotte shuddered. "Why in heaven's name would Mrs. Heskett have copied an old design in her sketchbook and why would someone want to steal it?"

"You're assuming that whoever took the sketchbook did so because of this drawing," Baxter said.

"The villain must have been after that picture. It was the only one that was different and unusual."

"Hmm." Baxter folded the sheet of paper. "It has been my experience as a chemist that the easiest way to go about finding solutions to problems is to begin by eliminating obvious loose ends."

Mrs. Witty sighed. "Seems to me that all ye've got at this point are loose ends, sir."

"One or two can be snipped off," he said. "With luck, the situation will become clearer once I have taken care of them."

"You refer to the matter of Miss Post's

visit," Charlotte said. "What do you intend to do?"

"Assure myself that there is no connection between her and Drusilla Heskett's murder," Baxter said. "The way to eliminate that possibility is to discover whether or not my half brother sent her to you in an act of deliberate mischief."

"Hamilton?" Ariel's mouth dropped open in outrage. "You cannot mean to suggest that Lord Esherton sent Miss Post to tell that outlandish tale to Charlotte?"

"He thinks Hamilton may have done it as a sort of practical joke," Charlotte explained hastily. "I have told St. Ives that is highly unlikely."

"Unlikely? It's impossible," Ariel declared. "His lordship is a gentleman. He would never stoop to such a nasty trick."

Baxter raised his brows. "I see Hamilton has managed to make an excellent impression on this household."

Ariel gestured toward the large vase of pink roses. "He sent those magnificent flowers this morning. His taste, as you can see, is very refined. He is not the sort to play a vicious practical joke."

Baxter gave the roses a disgusted look. "It doesn't take exquisite sensibilities or a noble character to conclude that it is appropriate to send roses to a lady the morning after a ball."

"An interesting observation," Charlotte said dryly. "One could certainly expect any gentleman, even one unaccustomed to the ways of Society, to know enough to send flowers to a lady following a particularly memorable evening." She paused deliberately. "Or even after a memorable *morning,* for that matter."

Baxter shot her a disconcerted glance. Charlotte could have sworn that a hint of ruddy color appeared high on his cheekbones. She favored him with her brightest smile.

Ariel was distraught. "Mr. St. Ives, surely you do not believe that your own brother conspired with Miss Post?"

He gave a dismissive shrug. "As I said, I intend to learn the truth of the matter. Once we know how Miss Post is involved in all of this, we shall have some notion of how to proceed."

Charlotte stepped quickly around the edge of the desk. "I wish to be present when you speak with your brother."

"Not bloody likely," Baxter said.

She gave him another smile, this one not quite so bright. "Let me put it this way, St. Ives. A bargain is a bargain. Either you take me with you when you confront Lord Esherton or I shall be forced to conclude that you wish us to pursue this investigation independently of each other. Our *partnership* will be at an end."

He regarded her with a thoughtful expression that did nothing to mask the banked flames in his eyes. "Blackmail is it now, Miss Arkendale? The range of your talents never ceases to amaze me."

The accusation hurt. She tried valiantly to conceal the pain behind a coolly amused look.

"In my business, Mr. St. Ives, one learns to use whatever tools happen to be at hand in order to complete the task."

"I see." He inclined his head and turned to walk toward the door. "Well, I trust you enjoyed the tool that you used so very effectively less than an hour ago in my laboratory, Miss Arkendale. I assure you, that particular length of iron has never been so well heated in such a small, warm crucible."

For an instant Charlotte could not believe she had heard right. And then outrage poured through her. "Of all the damnable nerve." She snatched up the nearest hefty object, a vase of pansies.

Ariel gave a small cry of alarm. "Wait, those are some of *my* flowers."

Her protest came too late. Charlotte had already hurled the vase. It struck the door, which Baxter had somehow managed to close very neatly behind himself as he stepped out into the hall.

A half hour after midnight, Baxter sat in the shadowed depths of the carriage and studied the front door of The Green Table from the opposite side of the street.

A light fog cloaked the scene. Carriages came and went, depositing raucous gentlemen in various stages of inebriation at the foot of the steps. Baxter saw Hamilton, Norris, and several laughing companions erupt from one vehicle. They bounded toward the entrance of the establishment.

"Well?" Charlotte demanded. "Did you see your brother go inside?"

"Yes. He has managed to avoid me all afternoon and evening, but I've finally cornered him." Baxter eased the curtain across the window and sat back in the seat. "I believe I recognize the premises. This house was once a popular brothel known as The Cloister."

"I recall hearing of The Cloister." There was sharp disapproval in Charlotte's tone. "Some of the so-called gentlemen I researched at the beginning of my career were rumored to favor the place. What would you know of it, sir?"

Baxter hoped that the darkness concealed his quick, amused grin. "I assure you, I am aware of it by reputation only."

"I see." Charlotte cleared her throat. "I do not believe that I have come across any reference to The Cloister for at least two years."

"It was closed some time ago. There has obviously been a change in management."

"Yes. It may be a rather raffish gaming hell now, but that is certainly a step up from a brothel, if you ask me."

Baxter smiled. In the deep darkness of the unlit cab he could barely make out Charlotte's face. The hood of her cloak shrouded her features.

He still was not quite certain how he had allowed himself to be convinced to bring her along tonight. Blackmail threats aside, she had a way of achieving her own ends, he thought. A strong, formidable woman, indeed. Perhaps that was one of the reasons on the growing list of why he was so attracted to her. She was definitely not the sort to succumb to a fit of the vapors or burst into tears whenever she wanted her own way. She stood toe-to-toe and insisted upon what she viewed as her rights.

As difficult as Charlotte was proving to be, there was something to be said for a strong-minded female, Baxter decided. With Charlotte, a man did not have to waste a great deal of unnecessary time and energy catering to a lot of damned delicate feminine sensibilities.

She had not complained of the fact that he had made love to her on a laboratory workbench, for example. He suspected that many women would have taken deep offense. He had to admit that the setting had lacked something in terms of romantic ambience.

On the other hand, she was the one who had labeled the passionate interlude an experiment, Baxter reminded himself. He supposed he should have been relieved that she had not placed too much importance on the event, but for some reason he could not stop brooding about it.

With each passing day, Charlotte was becoming increasingly adept at disrupting his calm, orderly existence.

"What will you do?" she asked.

"Go into The Green Table and drag Hamilton out here to the carriage, where I can speak to him in private." Baxter removed his

241

eyeglasses and placed them in the pocket of his greatcoat.

"Why are you taking off your spectacles?"

"Because I would prefer that no one take any notice of me. Those who know me are accustomed to seeing me in eyeglasses. I wish to keep this matter a private one between Hamilton and myself."

"I understand," Charlotte said gently. "It is a family thing, is it not?"

"Unfortunately, yes."

"But how will you be able to find Hamilton in the crowd without your eyeglasses?"

"A friend of mine, the Earl of Masters, is something of an inventor. He designed an interesting watch for me." He pushed open a window curtain far enough to allow a shaft of weak moonlight to enter the carriage. Then he removed his pocket watch and snapped it open. He held the watch close to his eyes as though trying to make out the time the way a man did in a shadowed room. He gazed at Charlotte through the glass watch cover, which was, in fact, a single lens.

"How very clever," Charlotte said. "A sort of quizzing glass."

"Masters is a clever man. He designed some of my chemical apparatus for me." Baxter closed the watch and put it back into his pocket. He reached for the door handle. "Don't suppose it's worth one more attempt to talk you out of being present when I question Hamilton?"

"Save your breath, sir. I was the one who

actually spoke to Miss Post, after all. If Hamilton is guilty of this mischief, which I doubt, I have some questions of my own for him."

"I feared as much." Baxter got out of the carriage. He turned back as a thought struck him. "I have a question of my own concerning Miss Post's visit to you."

"What is it?"

"What with one thing and another, I overlooked one very odd piece of this business."

"Yes?"

"Why was it that you did not believe Miss Post's tale? What made you think that she was not my cast-off paramour?"

Charlotte gave a ladylike snort. "Don't be ridiculous, Baxter. You would never abandon some poor woman who was pregnant with your child. Such a callous action would be completely out of character for you. Whoever sent Miss Post to me with that wild tale obviously did not know you well."

Baxter studied the line of her firm, straight nose, which was just barely visible beneath the hood of her cloak. "I think it far more likely," he said softly, "that whoever commissioned Miss Post to act her role did not know *you* well, Charlotte."

He closed the carriage door before she could respond.

He glanced back once as he went down the street toward The Green Table. She would be safe, he thought. The coachman from Severedges's would keep an eye on her.

In spite of the unpleasant scene that lay ahead, he found himself smiling a little as he walked through the light, swirling fog. Most ladies would have believed Juliana Post's outrageous story. It was an all too common tale. Women alone in the world very often fell prey to the cruel seductions of men who had few qualms about abandoning them once the liaisons became inconvenient.

In the course of her extremely unusual career, Charlotte had become better acquainted than most of her sex with the dark side of masculine nature. Her view of men was pragmatic to the point of cynicism. It would have been quite natural for her to have believed the worst that Miss Post had to tell her. Yet she had not given a moment's credence to the lie.

Baxter savored that thought as he approached the steps of The Green Table. For some reason that he did not want to examine, it was of vital importance to know that Charlotte had believed in him when faced with such damning evidence. Surely she had some spark of genuine affection for him that went beyond a mere desire for passionate experimentation.

A carriage rumbled to a halt in front of the gaming hell just as Baxter reached the steps. Loud laughter and coarse jokes sounded from the cab. The vehicle's door slammed open and five young, drunken dandies spilled out onto the pavement. One of them lost his balance on the wet ground and wound up planted on his rear. His friends found his predicament hilarious.

Baxter stood back in the shadows and waited as the newcomers righted themselves and paid the coachman. When they turned to stagger up the steps, he fell in behind them. They never noticed as he went through the door in their wake.

The dim, firelit interior of The Green Table was thronged. Without his spectacles, the scene had an unfocused quality that seemed remarkably appropriate. Baxter did not need his eyeglasses to conclude that there was little chance of anyone observing him in the crowd. It was still early by Town standards, but the men who filled the overheated room were already sunk deep in heavy play at the green baize-covered tables. No one paid him any attention.

A roaring fire on the large hearth threw a hellish red glow over the scene. The air was thick with the smell of ale, sweat, and smoke.

Baxter found a secluded corner protected by a large, well-endowed stone figure of a nude female. He removed his pocket watch and held it up as though to get a closer look at the face. He studied the crowd through the single lens. The faces of the hell's patrons sharpened abruptly.

There was no sign of Hamilton or Norris.

Frowning, Baxter started to close the watch. Movement on the stairs at the rear of the large room made him hesitate. He raised the lens again and took a quick look.

Several young men, including Hamilton and Norris, were on their way to one of the upper floors. Baxter wondered if there were private dining parlors above or if the new owner of the premises had elected to continue offering the services of a brothel in a more discreet fashion.

Then he recalled something Hamilton had said about the management providing a special meeting place for the members of his exclusive club.

Baxter shut the watch case and dropped it into his pocket. He did not need the single eyeglass to make his way across the room.

But when he got closer to the bottom of the staircase, he saw a large, somewhat blurred figure lounging against the banister.

While the crowd milled around him, Baxter took out his watch and risked another survey. One glance at the thick features of the heavy-set man on the stairs was all that was necessary. He was looking at a guard. The man had obviously been posted to protect the elite club members privileged to partake of the pleasures that were offered on the upper floors.

Curiosity and a strong sense of foreboding descended on him in equal proportions. The ground-floor gaming room of The Green Table was bad enough. It was the sort of place in which a careless young man could lose a great deal in a night's deep play. Whatever lay overhead was probably a good deal more unpleasant.

What sort of devilish nonsense had Hamilton gotten himself involved in? Baxter wondered.

He could almost hear his father's voice telling him to keep an eye on his younger half brother.

Stifling a resigned groan, Baxter eased his way back through the crowd to the front door. He waited until a group of patrons chose to leave and quietly attached himself to their number.

Outside on the pavement he made his way to the corner of the street. He paused to fish his eyeglasses out of his pocket and put them on. Then he turned and went down an alley that looked as though it would take him to the rear of The Green Table.

Most of the nearby buildings were dark at this hour but there was enough light from the windows and the kitchens of The Green Table to guide Baxter. The establishment was three stories high. From the alley he could see that the windows on the top floor were dark. But on the floor below, a tiny sliver of light escaped from one window.

Years ago, The Cloister had been notorious, Baxter reminded himself as he prowled through the shadows of the garden. In its heyday, it had been the sort of place that had traded in a variety of illicit activities and exotic tastes. It was an establishment that had needed clandestine entrances and exits, not to mention peepholes and hidden staircases.

It was the sort of place that had attracted his father.

A privy stood in the unkempt garden. As Baxter watched, a drunken man staggered out of the necessary and made his way back into the club through a rear door. A moment or two later, Baxter followed him. He found himself in a small servants' hall. It was empty. A flight of narrow, twisting steps led to the upper floors.

He took the steps with caution. Fortunately, they were all in sound condition. He paused on the first landing. The door that opened onto the hall was locked. He had not thought to bring his lock picks, so he was obliged to pause long enough to correct the problem with the wire earpiece of his eyeglasses.

A moment later he was inside the darkened corridor.

He was about to make his way down the hall toward the room where he thought he had seen a light when he heard the scrape of a shoe on a wooden stair tread.

The sound was too light and too tentative to have been made by the guard.

He waited in the shadows. A figure swathed in a voluminous cloak entered the narrow hall.

He stepped quickly away from the wall and locked one arm around his pursuer's throat.

"Do not move. Not one word. Not one sound," he warned very quietly.

The trapped figure froze and then nodded quickly, silently. Baxter caught a whiff of a familiar scent, part herbal soap, part female, absolutely unmistakable. The particular fragrance was forever registered on his senses. He would go to his grave able to recognize it.

It would no doubt be his grim fate that even on his deathbed, he would still suffer the sweet, aching tug of desire whenever he inhaled it.

"Bloody hell, Charlotte. What are you doing here?"

Twelve ❧

"I saw you leave the club and go down the street. But you went off in the wrong direction. I did not know what to think." Charlotte was breathless, not only from the anxiety that had impelled her to leave the carriage, but also from the mad dash along the alley and the climb up the rear stairs.

The shock that she had just received upon finding herself pinned in the dark by a man's unyielding arm had only made matters worse. The realization that the man who held her was none other than Baxter was a tremendous relief but it was not doing much to slow her racing pulse.

Baxter sounded angry. *Very* angry. There was an ice-and-steel edge to his voice that she had never before heard.

"I told you to wait in the carriage."

Charlotte struggled to take several deep, fortifying breaths. "I was concerned. I did not know what was going on. I thought you might need my help."

"If I had needed your assistance, I would have asked for it."

"Really, Baxter, there is no call to lose your temper with me. We are in this together, as I keep reminding you."

"How could I possibly forget?" Baxter released her and gave her a small push toward the door. "We shall go back the way we came. Quickly."

"But why did you come up here in the first place?"

"To find Hamilton. But that matter must wait. The first order of business is to get you out of here."

"There is no reason why we cannot go ahead with whatever plan you had in mind."

"There is every reason why we cannot."

A burst of muffled masculine laughter echoed from the chamber at the far end of the hall. Baxter stilled. Charlotte felt him turn to glance down the corridor. She followed his gaze.

There was a small, undraped window in the wall at the end of the narrow hall. It provided just enough illumination to reveal the two rows of closed doors that lined the passage. A tiny ray of light winked from beneath the last door on the left.

"Hamilton is in that chamber?" Charlotte asked very softly.

"I suspect that is where the club members meet."

She was intrigued. "You intended to spy on him?"

"Let's just say that I was curious." Baxter reached past her to open the staircase door.

Footsteps thudded on the lower stairs. A fresh

dose of alarm went through Charlotte. Someone was coming up the rear staircase. Baxter did not swear aloud but she could almost hear his silent *bloody hell.*

He closed the door as quietly as he had opened it.

He seized her arm and pulled her down the passageway. She noticed that he did not bother to try the first three doors. Instead, he chose the next one. She breathed a sigh of relief when it opened at his touch. She did not relish the prospect of being caught in the hall by whoever was tromping up the stairs.

It would be not only awkward and embarrassing, but quite scandalous if she and Baxter were discovered there tonight. The fashionable young gentlemen of the club were likely to be incensed at being spied upon by Baxter St. Ives and his fiancée. Word would spread through the ton with the speed of a fire in the stews.

Baxter eased her through the doorway of the small chamber. Charlotte wrinkled her nose at the stale, musty smell that greeted her. It was obvious that the room had not been aired in some time. She moved with great caution, unable to see anything in the dense darkness.

Another distant rumble of laughter sounded from the room at the end of the hall. Baxter quickly closed the door. Charlotte felt him move and realized that he had put his ear to the panel. She knew that he was listening to the footsteps of the person who had climbed the back stairs.

She took a cautious step back and came up hard against another door. She realized it must open into the adjoining room, the one that separated this chamber from the one being used by Hamilton and his friends.

Outside in the hall, floorboards creaked as someone walked steadily past the room in which she and Baxter hid. Whoever it was did not pause. A servant going about his duties, no doubt, she concluded. Perhaps taking claret to the members of the club. She and Baxter would be trapped there until the man went back downstairs.

She touched Baxter's arm.

"What is it?" he asked in her ear.

"Another door. Leads to the next room. You might be able to overhear what is being said."

"I've got to get you out of here."

"You keep saying that but we can do nothing until the servant leaves again. And as we are already in the neighborhood, it seems a pity to waste the opportunity."

She felt him hesitate. She took his hand and guided it to the doorknob behind her.

"Bloody hell."

But she could feel him wavering. She wondered if Baxter considered her a bad influence. After a few seconds' pause, he apparently reached a decision. He stepped around her and slowly, carefully opened the connecting door.

Another wave of stale, long-closed-in air wafted out of the adjoining chamber. Charlotte leaned forward to peer around the corner.

252

There was just enough light from a partially draped window to see something of the interior. A sagging bed, the looming shape of a wardrobe, and a washstand stood on the threadbare carpet. A framed picture hung askew on the wall.

Baxter touched his fingertips to Charlotte's lips. She did not need the warning to remain silent. Only a single wall separated them from Hamilton and his friends.

There was another burst of laughter from the next chamber. Then it faded. Voices, less raucous now, could be heard through the wall.

Charlotte watched, mystified, as Baxter crossed the room to the wardrobe. He opened it cautiously and quickly examined the interior as though he expected to discover something of interest inside.

Plainly dissatisfied, he stepped back, gently closed the wardrobe door, and went to stand in front of the framed picture. After a moment's close study, he lifted it down from the wall.

A small circle of light appeared. Charlotte stared in astonishment at the hole in the wall. It would, she realized, provide a view into the chamber where Hamilton and his friends were gathered. She made a note to ask Baxter how he had known to look for the peephole.

He put his eye to the opening. She went forward, eager for a peek, and caught a faint whiff of a sweet, smoky, herbal vapor. It reminded her a bit of the incense Juliana Post used. But this was stronger, more intense. She saw Baxter pull back far enough to take a deep breath of the stale air in the room before he turned back to the peephole.

The voices of the club members could be heard more clearly now but they sounded blurred and subdued, as if the men were not only intoxicated, but a bit drowsy.

"Begone, man," someone said to the servant.

The door opened and closed. Footsteps sounded in the hall.

"It's time to summon our magician," one of the men announced in a dreamy voice. "Let us see what demonstrations of the powers of the metaphysical plane he has prepared for us tonight."

"A test," another man said in singsong tone. "He promised us a test. Let the great magician show us his skills tonight."

"Excellent notion," someone chortled weakly. "Let's see how clever our mage is. Let him put Norris, here, in a real trance. You'll volunteer, won't you, Norrie?"

"Why not?" Norris sounded languid but willing. "Always glad to conduct an experiment on the metaphysical plane. Summon the bloody sorcerer."

There was a shuffling sound next door, as though the furnishings were being shifted. Baxter took a step back from the peephole to get another breath of air. Charlotte saw the light coming through the small opening abruptly dim to a weak glow. Someone had turned down the lamp in the next chamber. The club members began to chant in an eerie, dreamlike cadence.

> *"Lead and silver, electrum and gold,*
> *Degrees of power, ancient and old.*
> *When the emerald laws reveal the sign,*
> *Mercury, sulphur, and salt combine.*
> *Pure knowledge exists for all to see*
> *But few will ever know the key..."*

The men repeated the chant, their voices thickening. Tongues got tangled. Someone giggled.

Charlotte tugged on Baxter's sleeve. He hesitated. She gave him a small push and he moved reluctantly aside to allow her a peek.

She took a breath, stood on tiptoe, and put her eye to the hole. She found herself gazing into a dimly lit chamber that was clouded with smoky incense. There was a large wardrobe against the far wall. She recognized Hamilton and Norris. They and the other club members lounged on large Turkish pillows around a brazier. Each had a glass of claret in one hand, but they all seemed more interested in the fragrance of the burning herbs than in the wine.

> *"That which the heirs of Hermes desire*
> *Is revealed to the laborers in the fire."*

The words were almost unintelligible now. The men nodded over their glasses. The incense that drifted through the tiny peephole was irksome. It made Charlotte's eyes water and blurred her vision. She turned her head away to take a breath of fresher air.

"Behold, the magician," one of the men announced with a small giggle. "He appears before us."

Charlotte quickly put her eye to the peephole again. She was startled to see that there was a new figure inside the secret chamber. She was quite certain that the door had not been opened. It was as if he had simply materialized out of the wardrobe.

The magician walked slowly across the room to stand amid the languidly sprawled men. He was cloaked from head to foot in flowing black robes. A heavy hood was pulled down very low over his face. Charlotte could not make out his features—because of the shadows cast by the hood, she thought. Then the newcomer turned his head slightly. Light glinted on a gleaming black silk mask that concealed his entire face.

It is only a gentlemen's game, she thought. *An entertainment Hamilton and his friends have invented to amuse themselves.* But she could not stop the shiver of dread that feathered her nerves.

"Let us see how strong this power of yours really is," Norris said with an air of bravado that sounded false.

The shrouded figure raised his hand. An object dangled from his fingers, a glittering pendant. The club members stared at it with undisguised fascination.

Frozen fingers traced Charlotte's spine. The

incense had become almost overpowering. She tried to get a closer look at the pendant but it was impossible to make it out from this distance.

She flinched when Baxter's hand clamped around her shoulder. Without a word she stepped back.

Baxter took a turn at the peephole. Charlotte put her ear to the wall.

"I've got it," one of the club members said. "Put him into a trance that can be tested at some later time."

"Make Norrie cluck like a chicken tomorrow night in the midst of the Clapham soiree."

"Have him bare his arse in Pall Mall at the height of the shopping hour."

"Persuade him to dance with Lady Buelton's horse-faced chit."

"There is no power," Norris declared in ringing accents, "neither in this world nor on the metaphysical plane, that could make me dance with Buelton's daughter."

Weak laughter greeted this announcement. And then a hush fell in the chamber.

Charlotte pressed closer to the wall but she heard nothing. She prodded Baxter again. He hesitated and then stepped aside.

She peeked through the hole and was startled to see that the chamber had been further darkened. Someone had put out the lamp. The coals on the small brazier still glowed but the red-gold glare did not illuminate the faces of the men.

The magician lit a single candle and placed it directly in front of Norris.

As Charlotte watched, the cloaked figure moved in the shadows. The edges of his robes swirled around him, flapping gently in the manner of great, black wings. The pendant in his hand swayed slowly, catching and reflecting the light of the candle.

The club members began to chant again, this time in a heavy, throbbing rhythm that echoed the beat of the blood in Charlotte's veins.

"Lead and silver, electrum and gold,
Degrees of power, ancient and old."

Charlotte strained to watch the proceedings, heedless of the strong scent of the incense. She thought she heard the magician speak but his voice was pitched below the rising level of the chant. Another chill lanced through her but she could not pull back.

She had to get closer, she realized. She wanted to see the pendant. She *needed* to see the pendant. Nothing had ever been quite so important.

Baxter gripped her wrist and tugged her away from the peephole. Charlotte tried to wriggle free of his grasp. He put a hand over her mouth and forcibly pulled her from her observation point. She started to struggle. He held her more securely. His palm tightened over her mouth. He locked her against his chest so that she could not move.

Angrily she tried to pry at his fingers. Baxter tightened his hold. Charlotte realized her head was spinning. She took several breaths that were not laced with incense. Suddenly the small, moonlit chamber in which she stood came back into focus. She relaxed abruptly against Baxter.

What on earth had happened? she wondered, chagrined by her own odd behavior. His hand still covering her mouth, Baxter tugged her toward the connecting door. She understood. It was time to leave. He was absolutely correct, she thought. Best to remove themselves from the premises now while the club members and their pet magician were involved in their curious ritual.

She touched Baxter's hand to let him know that she was ready to accompany him. He hesitated briefly and then slowly removed his palm from her mouth. Charlotte said nothing.

Baxter took her hand and guided her back through the connecting door. They emerged into the chamber where they had first taken refuge.

Baxter went to the hall door, opened it, and peered out into the corridor. Then he pulled Charlotte into the passageway.

They went carefully down the corridor to the door that guarded the back stairs. Baxter opened it, glanced down, and then nodded.

"There is no one on the staircase. I'll go first. We must hurry."

Charlotte did not argue. She followed him quickly down the cramped, twisted stairs. Baxter paused again, briefly, in the small servants' hall at the bottom. There was no one about.

The noise of the gaming room at the front of the house was a dull roar in the distance.

A moment later they were safely outside. Charlotte saw that the fog had grown far more dense during the time that she and Baxter had been inside the club. It shrouded the garden, glowing weirdly with the reflected lights from the windows.

As they passed the mist-shrouded privy, a man's guttural voice, lifted in bawdy, off-key song, boomed from the interior.

"So I showed her me prick,
and said, 'Take yer pick.'
The fair lady blushed and stammered and
*   sighed.*
'Tis impossible to choose,
so I'll take both," she cried...."

Charlotte allowed Baxter to haul her out into the alley, where it was almost impossible to see anything at all. The toe of her half boot struck a hard, solid object. She winced and stifled a groan.

"Are you all right?" Baxter asked without slowing the pace.

"Yes. Just a discarded crate, I believe."

He did not reply. Together they rounded a corner and emerged into the street. Carriages came and went in the fog, their lights gleaming with an unnatural, faerie quality in the mist. Shouts and drunken laughter echoed from the steps of The Green Table.

Charlotte tugged the hood of her cloak

more securely around her face. Beside her, Baxter removed his eyeglasses, tilted the brim of his hat, and pulled up the high collar of his greatcoat. The simple adjustments made a remarkable change in his appearance. He led Charlotte across the street.

A moment or two later they were safely seated inside the carriage. Charlotte exhaled deeply and fell against the cushions as the vehicle clattered into motion. She watched Baxter light the carriage lamp.

"What was that all about?" she demanded.

"I believe Hamilton and his friends were about to observe a demonstration of mesmerism." Baxter finished his task and lounged into the corner.

Charlotte studied him intently. The fiery glow of the lamp created a fierce mask out of his hard features. It glittered on the gold frames of his spectacles and flashed on the lenses. She could almost see him sinking into the vast depths of his own thoughts. Cold intelligence replaced any hint of emotion in his eyes.

"Animal magnetism, do you mean?" she asked.

"Yes. The effects of which were supplemented with some sort of drug in this instance."

"Of course. The incense." Charlotte frowned. "I may have inhaled a bit too much of it myself there at the end. It was the oddest thing, but I was overcome with a sudden desire to get a closer look at the pendant the magician used. It was as though I simply *had* to see it."

"I know," Baxter said dryly. "You were most insistent."

She flushed. "Rest assured, it was only a temporary effect. I feel quite restored to my usual self now."

"Charlotte, my dear, the word *usual* can never be applied to you."

She did not know how to take that remark, so she allowed it to pass. "About this mesmerism nonsense. I have read accounts of Dr. Mesmer's work and I've studied descriptions of those who claim to use similar techniques to achieve remarkable medical effects. But I have always assumed the whole business to be nothing but the worst sort of quackery."

"So have I, but the poets are quite taken with it. And so is my butler, Lambert, for that matter. He is receiving treatments for his aching joints from a Dr. Flatt."

"But what we witnessed tonight had nothing to do with medical treatments."

"No." Baxter contemplated the mist-shrouded street through a gap in the curtain. "But there are those, including some followers of a man named de Mainauduc, who are said to experiment with mesmerism as a means of investigating occult matters."

"Occult?"

"Alchemy, for example."

"The chanting," Charlotte whispered. "I thought I caught some alchemical references in that strange poem the club members used to summon their magician. 'Mercury, sulphur, salt.' "

"You are correct." Baxter did not look at her. He seemed to be absorbed by the darkness outside the carriage. "Mercury, sulphur, and salt were once held by the ancient alchemists to be the basis of all things, including gold. There was a theory that if one could separate the supernatural essence of those substances from the material form in which they are found, one would possess, among other things, the secret of transmuting any metal into gold."

Something in his voice riveted Charlotte's attention. "Among other things? What more could any alchemist want beyond the ability to turn lead into gold?"

Baxter looked at her then. The dangerous fires burned behind the lenses of his glasses. "For a true alchemist, the secret of transmuting base metal into gold was no more than a sign that one was on the right track."

"I don't understand. What was the real objective of such experiments?"

"The alchemists sought the Philosopher's Stone, the secret, fundamental knowledge of the world that would unlock unlimited power."

Another of the strange chills went through Charlotte. It was not unlike that which she had experienced earlier when she had watched the magician. She studied Baxter's face, transfixed as she so often was by the cold fire that burned in his eyes.

This was different. Baxter was different. He had nothing in common with the black-robed magician she had just seen.

263

But a powerful intellect coupled with an unshakable will was always a dangerous combination. And Baxter possessed both.

The sounds of the streets receded into the distance. The fog and the night seemed to absorb everything until the interior of the carriage was the only solid place left in the world. All else was composed of insubstantial mist.

She was trapped in this moving sphere of lamplight with her lover, a man whose own unacknowledged hungers rivaled those of the ancient alchemists. A shattering realization struck her in that frozen moment. If Baxter did not discover that love was the true name of the Philosopher's Stone he sought, they might both be consumed by the flames of their passion.

"What is it, Charlotte? You have an odd expression."

The sharp question broke the small spell. She blinked and then looked away from Baxter's intense gaze.

"It is nothing," she said. "I was merely contemplating the other alchemical references in the chant. What does the phrase 'laborers in the fire' mean?"

"That was an old term for alchemists. It came about because all of their work was done in a crucible heated with fire."

"And the reference to Hermes?"

"Hermes Trismegistos. Many believed that he was the source for the laws of alchemy that were supposedly inscribed on an emerald tablet."

"The Green Table," she whispered.

Baxter's smile was devoid of any humor. "Yes. The name of the hell itself. It would seem that Hamilton and his friends have made mesmerism and alchemy the cornerstones of their secret club. They have added some rituals and herbs and found themselves a suitably dramatic magician to amuse them."

"Perhaps he found them," Charlotte suggested.

"Quite possibly. An amazing number of charlatans have become extremely wealthy after attracting patrons from the higher social circles. Most of those who move in the ton claim to be stricken with perpetual ennui. Their never-ending boredom leads them to seek out the strange and the exotic for entertainment."

"I suppose there is no great harm in Hamilton's choice of amusements," Charlotte said slowly. "His secret club appears to be less recklessly inclined than some. At least he is not out risking his life in neck-or-nothing phaeton races conducted at midnight. Nor does he descend into the worst sections of the stews in search of novelty. The Green Table is not a noble establishment, but there are worse."

"True." Baxter gave his attention back to the foggy scene outside. The silence swirled around him.

"What disturbs you, Baxter?"

"Connections."

"What do you mean?"

When he turned his head to meet her eyes,

265

Charlotte once more felt the icy touch on her spine.

"Drusilla Heskett's little sketch."

"What of it?"

"I know now why it appeared vaguely familiar. I'm almost certain that I saw it a long time ago in one of the ancient alchemical texts in my library."

Charlotte stared at him. "You believe it is related to alchemy?"

"I cannot yet say for certain. I have not been able to locate it yet. It may take some time. It has been years since I noticed such a design and I do not recall which book contained it."

"Dear God." Charlotte let the news skitter around in her brain while she struggled with the implications. "That would mean that there's a connection between The Green Table club and the murder of Mrs. Heskett."

"It's only a possibility," Baxter emphasized quietly. "An unlikely one at that. But I will grant that it should be researched."

"Why do you say unlikely?" Charlotte felt almost feverish with the excitement of the discovery. "It is a direct link. Do not forget that Mrs. Heskett was involved in a liaison with Lord Lennox, whose son, Norris, is a member of the club. He was the one undergoing the mesmerism experiment tonight."

"Yes, but it was Lord Lennox, not his son, who was Drusilla's lover." Baxter smiled briefly. "I think I can state unequivocally that Lennox has nothing to do with The Green Table. Not his kind of thing at all. In any event, only young men of Hamilton's age appear to be members."

"Perhaps, but it's possible that poor Drusilla came across some information about one of the members of the club while she was involved with Norris's father." Charlotte frowned. "I cannot think what sort of information would get her killed, however."

"That, of course, is the great mystery here. What could she have learned that would be worth her life? The club members appear to be dabbling in mesmerism but so are a good many other people."

"I do not like the feel of this, Baxter."

"Nor do I."

"If there is a murderer in The Green Table club, your brother could be at risk."

He met her eyes again. "We will take this step by step, just as one does any well-constructed experiment. First, I shall confirm my suspicions about the drawing. Then we shall see if we can discover the name of the owner of The Green Table. Whoever he is, he must know something about this business."

Charlotte regarded him with an admiration that she did not trouble to conceal. "I believe, sir, that you are going to prove to be an extremely useful man-of-affairs."

Thirteen ❧

The small book was old, one of the most ancient in Baxter's library. He had not had occasion to examine it in a long while. It was one of a number of alchemical texts that he had acquired over the years. He was not certain why.

Alchemy was a subject that properly belonged to the past, not the modern age. It was chemistry's dark side, a devil's brew of occult studies, metaphysical speculation, and supernatural secrets. It was rubbish.

But there was a sense of deep mystery about alchemy that had always intrigued him, especially in his younger days. The endless, obsessive quest for the Philosopher's Stone, the search for the basic laws that governed nature, drew him in some deep, elemental fashion that he could not explain.

And so he had collected books such as this one.

The leather binding was cracked, but the thick pages were in remarkably good condition. If he had not been so exhausted from the long, sleepless night, he would have been briefly amused by the title page. In the long tradition of alchemists who chose to write treatises on their subject, the author had assigned himself a flamboyant pseudonym. Aristotle Augustus.

Almost as riveting as Basil Valentine, Baxter thought, the name he had used for *Conversations on Chemistry*. But, then, he'd been only twenty when he had authored the book, just down from Oxford. He'd felt the need of a pseudonym that carried some weight.

Basil Valentine had been a legendary alchemist, a man of mystery. He had delved deeply into the arcane arts of the fire. He was said to have discovered great secrets and learned the nature of raw power.

In short, the name had sounded a good deal more exciting and romantic than Baxter St. Ives.

Baxter liked to think that he had matured a lot since Oxford.

He braced himself with both hands spread wide on the polished ebony desk and studied the slim volume that lay open in front of him. The Latin title translated into English as *A True History of the Secrets of the Fire*.

The drawing, a crude picture of a triangle inside a circle, was located near the center of the slender volume. Unlike Drusilla Heskett's sketch, this was more easily comprehended. The squiggles were not worms, but various mythical beasts. The dots were tiny symbols that Baxter recognized as having alchemical references.

The drawing was the usual mixture of metaphors and cryptic designs so beloved by the alchemists. The ancients had reveled in the obscure and had gone to great lengths to conceal their secrets from the uninitiated. Baxter knew that he was looking at a diagram that was meant to be an alchemical key, a pictorial description of a secret experiment that, if conducted perfectly, would lead to the discovery of the Philosopher's Stone.

There was no doubt but that it represented a direct link with The Green Table. But the questions still remained. Why had Drusilla Heskett copied the diagram into her watercolor sketchbook? Why had someone felt the need to steal the book from Charlotte and why was Drusilla dead?

Baxter closed *A True History of the Secrets of the Fire* and glanced at the tall clock. It was five-thirty in the morning. After taking Charlotte home, he had been unable to sleep. Driven by a need for answers, he had spent what had been left of the night there in the library. He was in his shirtsleeves. The coat and cravat he had worn that evening lay draped across a nearby chair.

Wearily he removed his eyeglasses and rubbed the bridge of his nose. Foreboding sat on his shoulder, a great dark bird of prey. He could sense the gathering danger. A plan of action was required. He would have to formulate one as quickly as possible. The most important goal was to protect Charlotte while the matter got sorted out. But first he needed some sleep.

A thump and a loud voice out in the front hall interrupted his thoughts.

"Get out of me way, you clumsy oaf. Ye cannot stop me. Move, damn yer bloody hide."

Baxter sighed. The new housekeeper had a mouth on her that would have done justice to a dock laborer. On the positive side, at least she was an early riser. The last one had often slept through breakfast.

Another thud sounded from the hall.

"I ain't hanging about another moment. I'd have left yesterday if me sister had been able to give me a bed for the night."

"If you would perhaps give it another fortnight, Mrs. Pearson." Lambert's pleading tones were muffled by the wall. "It is so difficult to find staff. And Mr. St. Ives does pay well, you know."

"I don't care how much that madman is willing to pay his staff. All those strange goings-on in that laboratory of his. And right in the middle of the day, too. A lady shrieking as if she was bein' fiendishly tortured. I won't tolerate that sort of thing. Get away from the door, ye doddering old fool."

There was another short murmur of protest from Lambert, a loud exclamation, and a very final-sounding thump. The front door slammed with sufficient force to shake the wall.

Silence fell.

A soft knock on the library door a moment later made Baxter close his eyes in bleak anticipation.

"What is it, Lambert?" He turned slowly to face the door.

Lambert hovered anxiously in the opening. Apparently he had been roused from his bed and had not had time to finish dressing. His sparse gray hair stood straight out from his head. His jacket was unbuttoned and he was wearing only one shoe. He managed to clear his throat with great dignity.

"Begging your pardon, sir, the new housekeeper just gave notice."

"Bloody hell. There have been no untimely explosions, no flashes of light, no electricity experiments. What went wrong this time?"

"Among other things, Mrs. Pearson was apparently overset by the, uh, incident in the laboratory yesterday."

"What incident? I was not performing any experiments yesterday." Baxter broke off abruptly as he recalled just what he had been doing in the laboratory. Fiendishly torturing a lady. He felt a curious sensation of heat in his face. Good God. He was turning red.

"The lady's scream," he muttered.

"Aye, sir." Lambert shifted awkwardly. "The lady's scream."

Baxter scowled. "I was merely demonstrating the most effective technique for the operation of the blowpipe. My fiancée is interested in scientific matters. She became quite enthusiastic when she witnessed the lively fire that was produced."

"Indeed, sir." Lambert looked wistful. "It must be rather pleasant to be able to operate one's blowpipe effectively. My own has been giving me trouble for some years now."

"Yes, well, why are you standing about, Lambert? Get yourself some breakfast and then take yourself off to the agencies as soon as they open for business. We must find ourselves a new housekeeper."

"Aye, sir." Lambert bowed his head. "Shall I prepare some eggs and toast for you, Mr. St. Ives?"

"Not necessary." Baxter idly massaged the back of his neck. "I'm going to sleep for a few hours. I had a long night."

"Very well."

"Oh, one more thing." Baxter went around behind his desk and opened a drawer. He removed a sheet of foolscap, picked up a quill, and scrawled quickly. "Please have this message carried to Esherton's house as soon as possible."

"Of course, sir." Lambert frowned as if a thought had struck him. "Speaking of messages, sir, did you see the one I left in the salver on the hall table? It arrived last evening while you were out."

"No, I did not get it."

"From your aunt, I believe." Lambert hobbled across the hall to the table and plucked a folded note from the silver tray. He carried it slowly into the library.

Baxter glanced at the note from Rosalind while he waited for the ink on his own message to dry.

Dear Baxter:
Is there any news? I am most anxious to hear from you. Surely you have uncovered some information by now.

Sincerely,
Lady T.

P.S. Lady G. is already inquiring as to the wedding date. I have put her off for a while but I cannot do so forever. You know what an inveterate gossip she is. Perhaps we should simply announce a day sometime in the distant future? Next Christmas?

As if he did not have enough problems, Baxter thought. On top of everything else, Rosalind wanted to set a fictitious wedding date to crown his fictitious engagement to Charlotte.

"Begging your pardon, sir." Lambert appeared even more dithery than usual. "I shall, of course, attend to the matter of acquiring a new housekeeper and I shall see that the message is sent. But this is the day of my regular appointment with Dr. Flatt. If you do not mind, sir, I would very much like to keep it. My joints are quite sore this morning."

"Of course, of course. Do not miss your appointment." A thought occurred to Baxter. "Does Dr. Flatt utilize any herbs or incense in his therapies?"

"No, sir. He uses the power of the gaze and certain movements of the hands to focus the animal magnetism. Works wonders, he does."

"I see." Baxter yawned as he folded the note for Esherton. "I vow, I do not know what I would do without you, Lambert."

"I try to give satisfaction, sir." Lambert took the note, turned, and moved slowly, painfully down the hall toward the kitchens.

Baxter eyed the staircase through the open doorway. His bedchamber seemed very far away at the moment. The sofa was closer and much more convenient.

He closed the door of the library and walked back across the room to set his eyeglasses down on the table that held the brandy decanter. Then he sprawled on the cushions.

For a moment he gazed at the ceiling. Above all, Charlotte had to be kept safe.

Sleep claimed him.

❧

The heavy dark wings of the cloak swirled around the monster in the hall. She was relieved that she could not see his face in the shadows. A part of her did not want to know anything more than she already did about the creature. It was as though some innate sense of decency deep within her resisted the necessity to look upon evil and see its face in human form.

But her intellect warned her that evil that could not be identified and named was all the more dangerous in its anonymity. She steadied the unloaded pistol in her hand.

"Leave this house at once," she whispered.

The monster's beautiful laugh sent ripples of dread through the darkness. The small waves moved out beyond the past, out into the future where he knew that the pistol was not loaded.

"Do you believe in destiny, my little avenging angel?" the monster asked pleasantly.

The door of the bedchamber flew open.

"Charlotte. Charlotte, wake up."

Charlotte opened her eyes. She saw Ariel rushing toward the bed. The skirts of her nightgown and a hastily donned wrapper whipped about her bare feet.

"Ariel?"

"You cried out. You must have been dreaming. A nightmare, I collect. Are you all right?"

275

"Yes." Charlotte struggled to a sitting position against the pillows. Her heart still pounded in her chest. Her skin was damp. "Yes, I'm all right. A bad dream. Nothing more."

"Brought on by this business of investigating Drusilla Heskett's death, no doubt." Ariel paused to light the taper in the stand beside the bed. The flame illuminated her worried face. "Was it one of the old dreams? The sort you had after the night Winterbourne was murdered?"

"Yes." Charlotte drew her knees up under the quilt and wrapped her arms around them. "It was one of those. I have not been troubled by them in a long while. I thought they had disappeared forever."

Ariel sank down on the edge of the bed. "What precisely did you do with Mr. St. Ives this evening? You came home so late. I did not see you after you left the Hatrich soiree. Where did you go?"

"It is a long story. I will tell you the whole of it in the morning. Suffice it to say that Baxter attempted to locate Hamilton at his club but we were not able to speak to him."

"I see."

Charlotte hesitated. "Has Hamilton ever spoken to you about mesmerism?"

"Animal magnetism, do you mean?" Ariel's fine brows drew together in a slight frown. "He mentioned it when we went out onto the terrace at the Clydes' ball. I believe he has an interest in the subject. He seemed to know a great deal about it. He claimed that its potential has been overlooked by most modern scientists such as, ah…"

"Such as his brother?"

"Well, yes." Ariel sighed. "He seemed rather scornful of Mr. St. Ives's interest in chemistry."

"I see." Charlotte pushed back the quilt and got out of bed. She went to stand at the window. "Baxter and I learned tonight that Hamilton and his friends are experimenting with mesmerism at their club."

"What of it? Many people form clubs and societies in order to investigate scientific matters that interest them."

"Yes, I know." Charlotte touched the cold window glass with her fingertips. She did not know how to explain the strange fear and the unwilling fascination she had experienced earlier that night while observing the activities of The Green Table club. What she had seen had not been good. It had agitated her imagination to the point of bringing on the old nightmares. "But I fear Hamilton's club may be somewhat unusual."

"Charlotte, I do not mind telling you that I am becoming more and more concerned about this situation."

"So am I." It was a relief to say it aloud. Charlotte turned. "Baxter and I feel there may be a link between The Green Table and Drusilla Heskett's death."

"No." Ariel got to her feet. "You cannot mean to imply that Hamilton had anything to do with Mrs. Heskett's murder. I will not believe it."

"I'm not implying anything of the kind. But perhaps someone else in his club had a hand in it."

"But the club members are all friends of his. Surely none of them would be involved in murder."

"Does Hamilton know all of the club members well? There are several of them, you know. I counted a half dozen, at least, this evening. Perhaps one or two are not particularly close cronies of Hamilton's."

"Perhaps." Ariel nibbled thoughtfully on her lower lip. "I could no doubt determine if that is true. Would it help, do you think, if I asked him about his friends?"

Charlotte hesitated. "No. Let St. Ives handle it. They are brothers, after all."

"Yes, but I fear there is very little affection between them."

"Baxter was charged with responsibility for Hamilton. He will fulfill his obligations."

"You sound very certain of that."

Charlotte smiled wearily. "I am."

Ariel watched her closely. "When I said a moment ago that I was becoming increasingly concerned about this matter, I was not referring only to the Heskett murder."

"What did you mean, then?"

"Do not mistake me. I do worry about the investigation, but there is something else that alarms me just as much, if not more."

"What on earth are you talking about?"

"Are you falling in love with Mr. St. Ives?"

The question stole Charlotte's breath.

Several seconds ticked past before she recovered from the impact.

"Charlotte?"

"Yes," Charlotte said softly.

"I feared as much," Ariel whispered. "It seems that you had the right of it after all when you said that he was dangerous."

Time moved with the thick, oozing quality of honey leaking from a broken pot. Baxter could see the flask of acid arcing toward him through the fiery shadows. He tried to get out of its path, but it was impossible to swim quickly through the flowing amber. All he could do was turn away and raise his arm to shield his eyes.

The flask struck his shoulder. The acid ate quickly through the thin linen of his shirt. And then it was on his skin, burning with the flames of hell itself.

He managed to reach the window. Below, the sea waited for him. He leaped into the darkness.

Explosions roared through the laboratory, turning it into an inferno. An instant before the cold seas closed over his head, he heard Morgan's voice.

"Do you believe in destiny, St. Ives?"

And then there was only the crashing of the sea against the rocks.

Baxter came fully awake in an instant, his pulse pounding in his veins. He felt the dampness on his back and for a horrifying instant he thought it was the acid.

279

He levered himself up, off the sofa, clawing at his shirt. And then he realized that it was his own sweat that had plastered the linen to his skin. He sank back down onto the cushions and rested his elbows on his knees.

He leaned forward, exhausted, and took several deep, shuddering breaths. He sought the center of himself, searching for the sense of control he needed.

The crashing waves still echoed in his head.

"Bloody hell, St. Ives. Get a grip on yourself." Baxter exhaled slowly, deliberately, willing himself into the calm, detached state that served him so well.

The loud smashing noise sounded again. Not the nightmarish memory of seawater against rocks. A fist against the front door.

Baxter rose slowly to his feet, shoved his hands through his hair, and straightened his shirt. Anger coursed through him. He had not had the dream for a long while. He had hoped it had disappeared into the void forever.

"Open this door."

Hamilton.

Baxter remembered that Lambert had left the house to run various errands. He crossed the library, went out into the hall, and opened the front door.

Hamilton stood on the front step. His jaw was rigid. His eyes were narrowed to mere slits. He lifted his expensively gloved hand and revealed the crumpled sheet of foolscap that he held. "What is the meaning of this outrageous message?"

"I wanted to get your attention."

"How dare you threaten to cut off my quarterly allowance if I do not dance attendance on you?" Hamilton slapped his stylish riding crop against his boot as he stalked into the hall. He snatched off his high-crowned hat and tossed it onto the table. "You have no right to restrict my income. Father told you to handle my investments until I turned twenty-five. He did not tell you to steal my inheritance."

"Calm yourself. I have no intention of depriving you of your fortune." Baxter waved a hand toward the library. "I simply need some information from you and I need it rather quickly. Sit down. The sooner we have this conversation, the sooner you will be on your way."

Hamilton threw him a suspicious glare and then he strode into the library and flung himself down onto a chair.

"Well?" he asked. "What is it you must know?"

"First, I should show you something that I discovered in a book." Baxter went to the desk and picked up the small volume he had left lying there. He turned to the picture of the alchemical key. "Have you ever seen this drawing or its like?"

Hamilton glanced impatiently at the picture. He opened his mouth, obviously intending to dismiss it out of hand. But his eyes widened in shock. "Where the devil did you get this?"

"So you do recognize it." Baxter closed

the book. He leaned back against the edge of the desk and studied Hamilton's angry face. "Something to do with your club, I presume?"

Hamilton tightened his fist around the riding crop. "What do you know of my club?"

"I am aware that you conduct experiments with animal magnetism. Mesmerism, some call it. And that you use ancient alchemical references and a drugging incense to set the stage, so to speak."

Hamilton leaped to his feet. "How did you discover all this?"

Baxter shrugged. "I have my sources."

"You have no right to spy on me. I have told you that what I choose to do in my club is none of your affair."

"It may surprise you to know that I agree with you."

"Then why the devil are we having this conversation?"

Baxter turned the book in his hands. "Because a picture very similar to the one I just showed you appeared in a watercolor sketchbook belonging to Drusilla Heskett."

Hamilton looked baffled. "Are you speaking of the Mrs. Heskett who was murdered recently?"

"Yes. I will be blunt, Hamilton. It's possible that there is some connection between one of the members of your club and Drusilla Heskett's death."

"You cannot possibly know such a thing," Hamilton exploded. "How dare you make accusations of that sort?"

"I'm not making accusations. I'm attempting to alert you to the possibility that there may be a connection here. That's all."

"I have had enough of this outrage." Hamilton started for the door. "I will not tolerate your interference in my affairs. I may not possess my rightful fortune, but I am the Earl of Esherton, by God. I do not bow to the whims of a bastard."

Baxter held himself motionless. With the skills he had honed over a lifetime, he concealed even the smallest flicker of a reaction. "There is one other small matter, *my lord.*"

Hamilton reddened in response to the icy politeness in Baxter's voice. "I do not intend to answer any more of your blasted questions."

"This is a simple one," Baxter said very softly. "How well do you know Juliana Post?"

"Post?" Hamilton scowled. "I know of no one by that name." He leveled the riding crop at Baxter. "I am warning you, St. Ives, stay out of my affairs. Is that quite clear?"

"I understand you very well. So did Father." Baxter smiled wryly. "He always claimed that there was a great deal of himself in you."

Hamilton's mouth tightened. He looked briefly confused, as if he had not expected such a mild response. Baxter had the impression that he was about to say something else. Instead, he swung around and made for the door.

Baxter remembered what Charlotte had said last night. *If there is a murderer in The Green Table club, your brother could be at risk.*

Another voice, his father's this time, also echoed in his brain. *You will look after your brother after I'm gone. He'll need some guidance for a while. Boy's the very image of myself when I was his age. Hot-blooded and reckless. Make sure he doesn't break his neck, Baxter.*

"Hamilton."

"What is it now?" Hamilton glowered from the doorway.

"You are correct when you say that I have no right to interfere with your pursuits." Baxter hesitated, choosing his words with care. "But for your mother's sake and for the sake of the title that Father bequeathed to you, I trust you will exercise some degree of caution. It would be a pity if you got yourself killed before you could produce an heir."

"I assure you, there is no danger for me at The Green Table. You are merely attempting to alarm me. You wish to make me uneasy in my friendships. It's quite petty of you."

"Do you think so?"

"You surely cannot expect me to believe that you're genuinely concerned with my welfare."

"Why not?" Baxter smiled thinly. "At least when you deal with me, you have the assurance of knowing that I have no reason to plot against you. After all, if you get yourself killed, the earldom doesn't come to me. It goes to our very distant, extremely obnoxious cousin in Northumberland."

"I suspect you would somehow contrive to keep your hands on the money, though." Hamilton stormed out into the hall, seized his hat, and reached for the front-door knob. "Where the devil is your butler, for God's sake? Did you lose him, too? I don't know why you cannot keep staff—" He broke off abruptly as he yanked open the door. "I beg your pardon, Miss Arkendale."

"Lord Esherton," Charlotte murmured.

Baxter frowned at the sound of her voice. He crossed the library and reached the doorway in time to see her rising from one of her graceful curtsies.

The familiar jolt of aching awareness sang through him at the sight of her. She was dressed in a green and white pelisse and a gown trimmed with green velvet ribbon. The wide brim of her matching straw bonnet framed her vivid eyes. Little corkscrew curls of dark redbrown hair bobbed in front of her small ears.

"Charlotte." He started toward her. Then he saw the hackney coach that was standing in the street. "What the devil are you doing here at this hour? And why are you alone? You should have brought your housekeeper or your sister with you. I do not want you dashing about on your own like this anymore."

Hamilton rolled his eyes in derision. "Ever the gracious host, St. Ives. One would think that you could come up with a more hospitable greeting for your fiancée."

Baxter set his teeth. It occurred to him that Hamilton no doubt had a point.

Hamilton gave him a superior, sarcastic smile and then inclined his head over Charlotte's gloved hand.

"I must tell you that if I were in your shoes, Miss Arkendale, I would definitely reconsider this engagement. Baxter's poor manners are hardly likely to improve after the marriage."

Charlotte grinned as she stepped into the hall. "I shall bear your warning in mind, Lord Esherton. I hope I am not interrupting."

"Not at all." Hamilton shot Baxter another angry glare. "We have just finished our discussion."

"Already?" Charlotte shot Baxter a quelling glance. But she was all smiles for Hamilton as she casually untied her bonnet strings. "Did he ask you about Juliana Post?"

"What is all this nonsense about some woman named Post?" Hamilton moved out onto the front step. "I have never heard of her."

"I was certain that would be your answer." Charlotte's eyes glinted with satisfaction. "But Baxter felt he had to ask."

"I see." Hamilton's lip curled. "My dear half brother seems intent on amusing himself by interfering in my personal affairs these days. One would have thought that his forthcoming marriage would hold more interest for him. Good day to you, Miss Arkendale." He pulled the door shut behind him.

Charlotte whirled to confront Baxter. "I told you that I wished to be present when you spoke to him about Miss Post's visit. Now look what you have done. I suspect you did not employ any tact at all. He's obviously quite overset by whatever it was that you said to him."

"Tact is not my strong suit."

"I've noticed. At least you got your answer. I told you that he was not responsible for Miss Post's visit."

"So you did."

"Which means that she may, indeed, be connected to this business, after all," Charlotte said. "The murderer must have employed her to break up our association because he knew that together we were a threat to him."

"I do not see how he could have known that. The only thing we had done at that point was search Mrs. Heskett's house and then got ourselves engaged. Damnation, Charlotte, why did you come here alone?"

She frowned. "Never say that you are truly angry with me simply because I came here without a companion?"

"Yes." He whipped off his glasses and began polishing them with his handkerchief. "Yes, I am bloody furious with you. All the more so now that I know Hamilton was not the one who sent Miss Post to see you."

"But, Baxter, it is broad daylight. There was no danger."

"Bloody hell, woman, we are investigating a murder." He shoved the glasses back onto his nose. He had lost his temper again. The knowledge appalled him. "The least you could do is display some common sense in the process."

"There is no need to rail at me, sir. I must point out yet again that I do not take orders from you."

If he possessed any common sense of his own,

he would shut his mouth right now, Baxter thought. Hamilton was right; when it came to handling women and their damned delicate sensibilities, he was clumsy, ungracious, and ham-fisted.

He looked into Charlotte's beautiful eyes and he knew again the powerful sense of dread that had descended on him earlier. *She might be at risk*. The dark wings of the recent nightmare stirred and fluttered at the edge of his mind. Anger was the only emotion strong enough to keep the fear at bay.

"Very well, Miss Arkendale," he said, "we are agreed that you do not take orders from me. If you have no concerns about your own safety, however, you might at least show some regard for my peace of mind."

Her eyes widened with comprehension. "Yes, of course," she murmured.

For some obscure reason, her sudden, calm, polite agreement did nothing to pacify him. Instead, he felt obliged to defend his foul mood. "It is not as though I don't have enough to worry about as it is. My aunt is insisting upon answers that I do not have. Maryann expects me to keep out of trouble my wretched half brother, who will pay me no heed. I have not had any time for my chemical experiments since this whole affair began and I have just lost the fourth housekeeper in five months."

"I quite understand, Baxter." Charlotte gave him a brisk, bright smile. "I regret that your life has been so disrupted of late. But never fear. This will all soon be over and you will be free to return to your customary routine. Just think, when we have finished this affair, you need never set eyes on me again."

Baxter had a sudden vision of himself hurtling toward the crashing waves far below the castle window. The old acid scars burned with cold fire. He fought an inexplicable surge of panic with all the powers of logic and reason at his command.

"Yes, I am well aware of that," he said very quietly.

A terrible silence descended.

He turned and led the way back into the library. "So long as you are here, I may as well tell you that I think we must change the focus of our researches. Rather than investigate Drusilla Heskett's other suitors, I believe we should look more closely at the members of Hamilton's club."

"Excellent notion. I quite agree with you." She followed him into the library.

"We cannot overlook the fact that there is a connection to Lennox's heir, young Norris."

"Indeed. Mrs. Heskett was having an affair with his father. But I cannot envision Norris as a murderer."

"Neither can I," Baxter admitted. "But it is a place to start. I shall enlist my aunt's assistance. We require an invitation that will get us inside the Lennox mansion as soon as possible."

"That should not be difficult," Charlotte said.

"Ariel tells me that Norris's eldest sister is giving a masquerade ball at the family home in two days' time."

Fourteen ᔑ

Charlotte watched proudly as Ariel, costumed as a water sprite, was led out onto the dance floor by another in a long string of partners.

"Isn't she spectacular?" Charlotte smiled fondly as she watched the dancers whirl beneath the jeweled lights of the colored lanterns that had replaced the chandeliers for the evening. "I vow, she has danced every dance since we arrived."

"She's just a blur to me," Baxter said gruffly. "Especially in this dim light. Not wearing my spectacles, remember? They're in the pocket of this damned domino cape."

"Oh, yes, I forgot. You can hardly wear your spectacles with your mask, can you?" She glanced at him and felt a curious dread that had nothing to do with their plans for the evening.

The long, black, hooded cape and half mask of Baxter's austere domino was indistinguishable from several other similar costumes in the crowd. She knew he had chosen the black domino because he thought that it would make him virtually anonymous in the thronged ballroom and he had been correct.

But she feared that the unrelieved darkness of the flowing cape and mask suited Baxter all too well. She had a sudden vision of Baxter disappearing forever into a dark cavern with his alchemical fire and crucible.

In a moment of whimsy, she had chosen to attend the masquerade as Diana the Huntress. As she had explained to Ariel, the costume seemed appropriate for a lady who was hunting a murderer.

"I detest masquerade balls," Baxter grumbled. "Grown people running about in masks and costumes. Utter nonsense."

"You must admit, this particular ball will be quite useful to us."

"Indeed. I shall rely on you to tell me when Ariel takes the floor with young Norris," Baxter said.

"She advised me a few minutes ago that she has made certain that Norris would have the next dance."

The plans had been formulated that afternoon. It was Ariel who had suggested that she could provide an extra measure of insurance for Baxter. She had pointed out that it would be simple enough to make certain that Norris was occupied for at least some of the time Baxter needed to locate and search his bedchamber.

"We appear to have a few minutes to wait." Baxter abruptly set his champagne glass down on a nearby tray. "May as well spend them on the dance floor."

Charlotte blinked. "Are you asking me to dance, Baxter?"

"Why not? Supposed to be engaged, aren't

we? Engaged people do that sort of thing. I assume you can manage a waltz with that silly bow and arrow you've got dangling from your wrist."

"They're part of my costume. And, yes, I think I can manage the waltz." She raised her brows behind her feathery mask. "I did not realize that you danced, sir."

"It's been some time. Several years, in fact." He took her hand without waiting for a formal acceptance of his offer. "Expect it's rather like riding a horse. Doubt that one forgets how to do the thing."

She hid a smile as she allowed him to lead her toward the dance floor. "Let's hope that is the case, because other than that gallop around the floor with Lennox the other evening, I have not had any practice in an age."

He stopped at the edge of the crowd and took her into his arms. "We won't try anything fancy."

She chuckled. "We shall likely resemble a pair of rusty barges sloshing about on a lake filled with sleek sailing yachts."

"Don't be ridiculous." Behind the openings in his black mask, Baxter's eyes were intense. "You are the most graceful barge in the room."

The awkward compliment should have amused her but instead warmed her to her soul. "Thank you, sir. That is the most charming thing anyone has said to me in a long while."

Without another word, he tightened his arms around her and swept her out among the brilliant sails.

Just as she had anticipated, Baxter's dancing was all power and control. But there was an underlying sensuality in his movements that reminded her of the way he made love. She gave herself up to the moment. There would not be many such, she reminded herself. She must seize each one that came along, drain it of its memories, and store them up against the possibility of a long, lonely future.

As the strains of the waltz swelled around her, Charlotte briefly forgot the reason she was there with Baxter in the first place. She only knew that she was in the arms of her lover, the man whose face she would see in her dreams for the rest of her life.

The jeweled lanterns created a spangled pattern of lights on the dancers. The ballroom was transformed into a shadowy faerie land populated by costumed legends and masked myths. Gods and goddesses from ancient Greece mingled with the old deities of Rome and Egypt and Zamar. Highwaymen and pirates conversed with queens and elves. And on the surface of the bejeweled lake that was the dance floor, Diana the Huntress whirled in the arms of an alchemist.

When the music ended at last, Charlotte felt an inexplicable urge to burst into tears. Her affair with Baxter might not last any longer than this perfect dance, she thought. A moment out of time that she would cherish forever.

"Charlotte?" Baxter came to a halt and stood looking down at her. "Good God, what is it? Did I tread on your toes?"

She shook off the gloomy mood with an

act of will. "No, of course not." She managed a smile. "I thought we did rather well, sir. We did not disgrace ourselves by sinking to the bottom out here among the pretty yachts."

His hand clenched fiercely around hers. "No, we did not. We managed to stay afloat."

"That bodes well, don't you think?" She heard the ill-concealed hope in her own voice. And then she caught sight of Ariel's blond head, unmistakable with its garland of delicate sea fronds. "Baxter, Norris has just gone over to Ariel to claim his dance. You had best be on your way."

"Yes." Baxter turned abruptly and hauled her quickly to a shadowed corner near the terrace. "Wait here. I shall not be long."

"Be careful."

He did not respond. He surreptitiously removed his pocket watch, glanced briefly through the glass cover to orient himself, and then turned and walked out onto the darkened terrace.

Charlotte watched him go, amazed at how easily he appeared to vanish into the night. She knew that he was headed toward the conservatory at the rear of the great house but she lost sight of the black domino before he had got as far as the stone steps. One moment she was aware of the outline of the black cape against the hedge and the next she could not see it.

A liveried servant appeared with a tray of glasses. Charlotte took some lemonade and then turned to watch Ariel and her new partner.

Norris was dressed as an ancient Roman. He looked quite dashing in his toga but she noticed that he did not seem to be conversing with his usual enthusiasm.

The minutes ticked past. Charlotte grew restless. She should have accompanied Baxter, she thought. She should not have allowed him to convince her to stay down there.

She silently counted the seconds as she listened to the music and watched the dancers. Her uneasiness increased. She could only hope that Baxter had been able to locate Norris's bedchamber quickly and that it would not take long to conduct the search.

She was attempting to follow Ariel and Norris as they swung into a long, whirling turn when a sudden whisper of night air from the terrace stirred the flounces of her forest green gown.

Startled, she turned quickly and saw a familiar figure in a black domino standing in the shadows on the other side of the open French doors. In the darkness, it was difficult to see him clearly. The hood of his black cape was pulled down low over his masked face. The edges of the cape were closed, concealing his hands. The folds swirled around his black boots.

"Baxter," Charlotte whispered.

She ought to be vastly relieved by the sight of him, she thought as she hurried through the French doors. He had obviously accomplished his goal quite quickly. She could not explain why little frissons of ice were jangling her nerves. Perhaps it was because the night air seemed several degrees colder than it had a few minutes ago. She was only steps away from the man in the black domino when she realized that something was wrong. She had made a mistake. It was not Baxter who stood there.

The figure in the cape and mask was too tall, too lean, too elegant. He lacked Baxter's powerful shoulders and aura of solid strength. Intuitively, she sensed that this stranger was not someone she wished to meet.

"I beg your pardon, sir." She came to an awkward halt. "I thought you were an acquaintance."

The man said nothing. Beneath the edge of the half mask, full, sensual lips curved. The folds of the dark cape parted to reveal a single red rose gripped in a black-gloved hand. Silently he held out the blood-red blossom.

Charlotte took a step back. She glanced at the rose and then at the masked face beneath the hood. "I fear you have confused me with someone else, sir."

"No." The voice was a raw rasp of sound that lacked any trace of warmth. "There is no mistake."

She shivered. There was something in the ragged words that called up old terrors. Impossible, she thought. She had never heard this voice. No one could forget such an unnatural sound.

She struggled to suppress her wholly irrational reaction. The poor man had no doubt suffered an injury to his vocal cords, she told herself.

Perhaps he had been born with a deformity of the throat or mouth.

She managed a weak smile. "I do not believe that we have met, sir. Please excuse me, I must go back inside. Someone is waiting for me." She turned to flee.

No, she was not running from him, she thought, irritated. She was merely chilled and anxious to return to the warmth of the ballroom.

"In all your researches into the lives of men, have you ever given consideration to the subject of destiny?"

Charlotte stumbled and nearly fell. She caught herself on the terrace wall.

No, it could not be the monster. The voice was not the same.

She would never forget that other voice. It had been a dark, oily thing that had slithered through the night. This voice was harsh and broken.

She turned slowly to confront the figure. She must not allow her imagination to run riot. Logic and reason, not old fears, were the tools needed to deal with this.

"I beg your pardon. What did you say?" she asked with a calm she did not feel.

"It's not important." The masked figure held out the rose. "This is for you. Take it."

"I do not want it."

"You must take the rose." The rasping voice lowered until it was no more than a whisper. "It is for you and no other."

There was a strange, compelling quality about the ruined voice. It beckoned and fascinated.

"Come. Take the rose."

The lights and music from the ballroom receded into the distance. She was alone out there in the night with this man. "We do not know each other. Why do you want to give me a flower?"

"Take the rose and see." The words were slivers of frost on a grave.

She hesitated, but she knew that she could not turn and run. Danger did not disappear when one turned one's back on it. She had to know what this was all about.

Reluctantly, she took one step forward and then another. The figure in the flowing black domino waited with seemingly infinite patience.

When she was within reach, the black-gloved fist opened in a disturbingly graceful gesture. Only then did she see that a folded piece of paper was impaled on one of the thorns.

She seized the flower. The stranger bowed exquisitely, turned, and swirled away into the night.

She hurried back toward the jeweled lights, pausing just inside the ballroom to unfold the note. She read the message beneath an emerald-colored lantern. Eerie green light dappled the words.

Your alchemist lover seeks the Philosopher's Stone of vengeance. He is obsessed with destroying his brother. He will use whatever means he believes will transmute the past, including your affections. But he will never succeed in his goal to turn the base metal of his bastard status into the gold of true nobility.

The bastard once betrayed one who trusted him. He will not hesitate to betray again. Take heed before it is too late. Do not become his victim.

Charlotte drew in a sharp breath and crumpled the note in her hand. She turned quickly to search the shadows, but the stranger in the black domino had disappeared.

Baxter removed his eyeglasses, stuffed them into his cape pocket, and quickly retied the mask. He stepped out into the corridor, closed the door of Norris's bedchamber, and headed quickly down the hall to the rear stairs.

He did not use his spectacles or the watch glass to make his way down the steps. The wall sconces were unlit and it was too dark to see in any event. He relied on his sense of touch and the memory of the even spacing of the treads.

He did not know whether to be relieved or disappointed in the results of his hasty search. He had found nothing that proved helpful. The most obvious connection between Drusilla Heskett's death and The Green Table was through Lennox's heir. But perhaps in this case the obvious link was not the right one.

He could hear the muffled strains of the waltz from the ballroom as he descended the stairs. At least his timing was good, he thought. The dance was just ending. He was anxious to return to Charlotte.

He recalled the waltz they had shared before he had set off on his fruitless task. She had been warm and graceful and full of feminine vitality in his arms, just as she was when he made love to her. The scent of her had aroused the hunger that always seemed to seethe just beneath the surface of his awareness these days. It was becoming increasingly difficult to envision his life without her in it.

Her words of the previous afternoon echoed in his brain as he slipped through the shadowed conservatory. *Just think, when we have finished this affair, you need never set eyes on me again.*

Moonlight filtering through the glass panes lit Baxter's path. The rich smells of earth and growing plants assailed him. It occurred to him that Lennox might be interested in participating in some agricultural chemistry experiments. He made a mental note to inquire. Then he recalled the barren sweet pea pots sitting on his laboratory windowsill. Perhaps there was no point in such experiments.

He used the eyeglass in his watch to make certain that he did not trip over a pot or a stray hoe as he headed to the far door.

A moment later he was safely back in the gardens. He made his way toward the blurred glow of colored lights that was the ballroom.

When he reached the terrace a familiar, slightly unfocused, figure loomed in his path.

"I thought I told you to wait inside, Charlotte."

"Baxter, is that you?"

"Of course it is. Who the devil did you think it was?"

"Never mind, it's a long story. I'll tell you later. Something more important has come up. Hamilton is desperate to find you."

"Hamilton?" He frowned as she moved closer. The concerned expression on her face sharpened as she came into focus. "What does he want?"

"Baxter? Is that you?" Hamilton's voice came from the far side of the terrace. "I've been searching for you." He hurried forward. "I must speak to you at once."

"Well, you have found me. What is it?"

"This is a…a personal matter." He glanced uneasily at Charlotte. "I beg your pardon, Miss Arkendale. I must be private with Baxter."

"Whatever you have to say can be said in front of Charlotte," Baxter muttered.

"Do not concern yourselves," Charlotte said quickly. "I'll wait inside the ballroom while you have your conversation."

"Bloody hell." Baxter had had enough of trying to peer through the mask. He untied it and dropped the black cloth into his pocket. Then he located his spectacles, put them on, and glared at Charlotte's retreating figure. The light glinted on her little golden bow and arrow. It also revealed the rose she carried in one hand.

He started to ask her where the rose had come from and then closed his mouth when he realized that she had moved out of earshot.

"Baxter, this is important." Hamilton stepped in front of him. Baxter reluctantly focused on him. He saw that Hamilton was not attired in a costume. He wore an elegantly tied cravat, a perfectly cut evening coat, and fashionably pleated trousers. His unmasked face was set in grim lines.

"I'm somewhat occupied at the moment, Hamilton. What is this all about?"

"The day before yesterday—" Hamilton swallowed heavily and tried again. "The day before yesterday, you advised me to be careful. You warned me that there might be some danger connected to my club."

Baxter gave Hamilton his full, undivided attention. "Has something happened?"

"Not to me," Hamilton said quickly. "But I am worried about Norris. We conducted an experiment in mesmerism the other night."

"Yes, I know. Young Norris was the subject."

Hamilton searched his face. "How is it that you are aware of that?"

"Never mind. What of it? Did Norris make an ass out of himself in someone's ballroom earlier this evening? I doubt that Lennox will be pleased, but I hardly think that whatever happened will prove to be a disaster. The

Lennox fortune is capable of overcoming the ill effects of virtually any outrage, including Norris's bared arse."

Hamilton stared. "I do not know how you could possibly have learned the details of our experiment but that is not important now. The thing is, in the end the magician"

"Magician?—"

Hamilton's mouth thinned impatiently. "The person we employ to conduct the experiments. We call him our magician. It was all very amusing, you see. At any rate, the magician did not instruct Norris to cluck like a chicken or lower his trousers in a ballroom. It is much worse than that."

"What did he do?"

"He used mesmerism to persuade Norris to call out Anthony Tiles."

"Norris challenged Tiles to a duel? I don't believe it."

"It's true," Hamilton whispered. "Tiles has been involved in at least three duels during the last two years. He has an astonishing temper. And he is a brilliant marksman. He always draws blood."

"Yes, I know."

"At least one of his opponents is said to have died from his wound. Another took the bullet in his shoulder and can no longer use his left arm. And the third simply disappeared. No one knows what happened to him but some say that he was so badly injured he must continually dose himself with laudanum to kill the incessant pain."

"I agree that Tiles has carved out a formidable reputation for himself."

"They say he practices daily at Manton's. A deadly shot. No sane man would challenge him."

"Precisely. It makes no sense that Norris would do so."

Hamilton's expression twisted. "But that is just what he has done. It is all so unlike him, Baxter. Norris is the most good-natured of all my acquaintances. He has never been quick to anger. He is my best friend and I fear that he has signed his own death warrant."

"Instruct your magician to undo the effects of his experiment."

"We cannot locate him." Hamilton's air of desperation increased. "We do not know where he lives or how to reach him."

Baxter frowned. "How did you first encounter him?"

"He contacted us. Offered to instruct us in special techniques that would enable us to make direct contact with the forces of the metaphysical world. It was all very interesting and great fun. But now something has gone wrong."

"Indeed," Baxter said softly.

"Things have got out of hand. I fear Norris will likely get himself killed at dawn."

"Are we talking about this coming dawn?" Baxter asked warily.

"Yes. Tomorrow morning. Everything is moving so quickly."

"Have Norris make an apology to Tiles. I suspect it will be accepted."

"I tried to convince Norris to make an apology but he will not hear of it. He is not himself, Baxter. A few minutes ago he danced with Miss Ariel as if he had not a care in the world. Yet at dawn he will be facing Tiles. It's madness."

Baxter contemplated the lights of the ballroom.

"Baxter?" Hamilton scowled. "Did you hear what I said? Norris is going to risk his neck at dawn. We have got to stop him."

"Whom did Norris name as his seconds?"

"He said that, as I am his best friend, I must be one of them. He instructed me to choose the other. He says he cannot be bothered."

"And have you selected the other second?"

"No. For God's sake, the last thing I want to do is plan this damned duel. I came directly here to find you. You've got to help me, Baxter."

"Well, if you haven't got another second yet, that simplifies the situation," Baxter said calmly. "I shall assist you."

Hamilton looked horrified. "But I want to stop the duel before it takes place."

"That may not be possible. The mesmerism practiced by your magician appears to be quite powerful."

"What will we do? We cannot allow Norris to get himself killed."

"There may be a way to control the results of this experiment."

The knock on the front door came at three-thirty in the morning. Charlotte was alone in her study, busily scribbling notes to calm herself. Ariel was not home yet and Mrs. Witty was sound asleep in her bedchamber at the top of the stairs.

Charlotte had been unable to rest. She had been restless since she had returned home from the masquerade ball. She did not know whether it was the encounter with the stranger in the black domino or Hamilton's desperate expression that worried her the most. Perhaps it was a combination of both.

At the sound of the knock, she got to her feet and hurried out into the hall. When she peered through the glass she saw Baxter standing in the shadows on the front step.

She wrenched open the door and smiled tremulously up at him. "I was hoping that you would find time to stop by before you went home. I have been most anxious to speak to you."

"I did not know if you would still be awake."

Charlotte stood back and watched as he tossed his hat onto the side table with an absent movement of his hand. There was an abstracted, preoccupied air about him. She knew that his keen intellect was focused on whatever problem Hamilton had brought to him.

"Is it serious?" She closed the door.

Baxter walked toward the study. "At dawn this morning, Norris is scheduled to meet one of the most infamous duelists in all of London."

"Oh, *no*." She hurried after him. "How on earth did poor Norris get into such a terrible situation? He seems so mild-mannered and friendly and likable. Not at all the type to get involved in a duel."

"He isn't." Baxter went to the brandy tray and picked up the decanter. "He had a little help."

"What do you mean?"

"Remember the magician who was entertaining Hamilton and his friends at The Green Table?"

"Of course. What has he got to do with this?"

"After we took our leave, he apparently used mesmerism to persuade Norris to go out and challenge a man named Anthony Tiles."

"How dreadful."

"Hamilton and the others were unable to stop Norris. After the deed was done, they were unable to make him offer an apology. They tried to locate the magician so that he could break the trance but they do not know his whereabouts."

"Dear God." Charlotte sank slowly into a chair in front of the fireplace. "So Hamilton came to you for help."

"Yes." Baxter's eyes gleamed briefly over the top of the brandy glass. "Strong evidence that he was at the end of his tether and did not know where else to turn. Hamilton has never come to me for help in the past."

"What will you do?"

Baxter shrugged. "I have concocted a plan that, if it is successful, will end the thing without bloodshed."

"And if it's not?"

"Someone may get killed."

Charlotte folded her hands very tightly together. "Your plan will work."

"Thank you for the vote of confidence. Hamilton certainly entertains doubts."

"Precisely what is your plan, Baxter?"

He smiled wryly. "Nothing very bold or exciting. It is based on my knowledge of chemistry."

"Then I'm certain that it will prove very bold and exciting. Indeed, it will be quite brilliant." She paused. "It would be interesting to witness the results."

He raised one hand in a gesture that was both a warning and an appeal. "Don't even consider the possibility of attending the duel. I will have enough to worry about as it is."

"I suppose that is true. What sort of man is this Anthony Tiles?"

Baxter sipped his brandy. "He's a bastard."

She smiled wryly. "Which sort? Born or made?"

"Both. His father was a viscount. Heir to the Coltrane fortune. Anthony was born on the wrong side of the blanket, as they say. The result of his father's affair with the family governess.

There were no legitimate sons. A nephew got the title and the estates. The knowledge of all that could have been his has eaten at Tony for years."

"You sound as if you know him."

"We were acquainted at Oxford."

"If he was a friend once, can you speak to him?"

"It wouldn't do any good." Baxter went to stand at the window. "Tony clings to an extremely rigid code of honor. He will tolerate no slight of any kind."

"I see."

"He spends his time in the gaming hells and stews looking for trouble. He encounters it with amazing frequency. He has at least three duels under his belt. Probably more."

"No wonder Hamilton is terrified for his friend." She tightened her hands. "This Anthony Tiles started life in much the same way you did."

Baxter braced one fist against the mantel and gazed into the fire. "We are both bastards, if that is what you mean."

"But he has become a bastard by deed as well as by birth," she said quietly. "You, on the other hand, have made yourself into a true gentleman."

He looked up swiftly. Firelight glinted on the lenses of his eyeglasses. "What the devil does that mean?"

"Anthony Tiles has obviously allowed the facts of his birth to set him on a path that is almost certain to destroy him. Thank God, you have carved out a different destiny for yourself."

"Hmm."

"Your father knew that you had become a man of integrity. He realized that he could entrust the family fortune and the safety of his younger son to you. He must have been exceedingly proud of you, Baxter."

Baxter said nothing. He watched her for a long while and then, without a word, he turned away from the fire and dropped down onto the sofa. He kept one booted foot on the floor and angled his other leg across the cushions. Wearily he shoved his fingers through his hair.

"When this business at dawn is behind us, I intend to find that bloody quack who calls himself a magician. I do not like these experiments of his."

Charlotte closed her eyes and leaned her head against the back of the chair. "Baxter, you will be careful tomorrow, won't you?"

"I'm not the one who must face Tiles's pistol if things do not work out as I have planned."

"I know you too well to believe that if something goes wrong, you will simply stand back and allow Hamilton's best friend to be shot down in cold blood." She opened her eyes and looked at him. "Promise me that you will not do anything that might cause this Anthony Tiles to turn against you and perhaps challenge you."

A fleeting trace of amusement hovered at the edge of Baxter's mouth. "Don't concern yourself. I vowed years ago never to get myself killed in anything so stupid as a duel."

"I am pleased to hear that." She smiled in spite of her uneasy mood. "Poor Baxter. All you asked was to be left alone in your laboratory but you've been forced to emerge from it in order to deal with all of these vexing problems."

He raised his brows. "There are problems and there are problems."

"What does that mean?"

He put down his unfinished brandy and got to his feet. He went to where she sat in front of the fire and gently drew her up out of the chair. "Some problems are vastly more interesting than others."

"Am I a problem for you, then, Mr. St. Ives?" she asked softly.

"Yes." He bent his head and crushed her mouth beneath his own.

Fifteen

His need for her swept through him in a wave. He cradled the back of her head in one hand and kissed first her lips and then her throat.

Would she always have this effect on him? he wondered. One moment his thoughts were focused on the problems of murder and a duel, the next he could think of nothing but the bone-deep satisfaction of having Charlotte in his arms.

He was slowly growing accustomed to the

unsettling effects of passion, Baxter thought, but he was no closer to understanding it tonight than he had been at the start of this affair. The mystery of the thing was as strange and compelling as any alchemist's quest for the Stone.

"Baxter?" Charlotte grasped the lapels of his coat. "Is there time?"

He raised his head just long enough to lose himself for an instant in the fathomless green promise of her eyes. "Not as much as I would wish." The truth of his own words struck him in a searing flash of understanding. "Bloody hell, there is never enough time."

"It's all right." She brushed her lips across his chin.

"And there is always the possibility that someone may walk in on us." He cast a baleful glance around the small study. "What's more, there is never a bed in the vicinity."

"Baxter—"

"How the devil is one supposed to conduct a proper affair when one does not even have a bedchamber at one's disposal?"

She pressed her face into his shirt and began to make soft, muffled sounds. Her shoulders quivered.

Alarmed, he pulled her closer and patted her awkwardly. "Good God, Charlotte, don't cry. I shall think of something."

"I'm sure you will. You always do."

The muffled sounds against his chest grew louder. Her whole body shook beneath his hands. He realized that she was giggling.

He put his thumbs beneath her delicate jaw and raised her head. The warm laughter danced in her eyes.

He did not require Hamilton to point out the obvious. No man who possessed even a spark of romantic sensibility would have wasted time complaining about the inconveniences of the situation at a moment such as this.

"I'm delighted that you find it so amusing," he muttered.

"I find it fascinating. Thrilling. Unbearably exciting." She stood on tiptoe, wrapped her arms around his neck, and kissed him. Hard and very enthusiastically.

He silently consigned his own glaring lack of a romantic soul and the assorted inconveniences of the situation to the devil.

The feverish need returned in a tidal wave that flooded his senses. "Why is it," he said against her mouth, "that I cannot seem to get enough of you?"

Charlotte did not respond. She was too busy unknotting his cravat and peeling off his shirt and coat. In a moment he was bare to the waist.

Her fingers brushed against the old acid scars. She pressed her lips to his savaged shoulder and kissed him gently. Baxter had to close his eyes against the deep longing that welled up within him.

He drew a breath, steadied himself, and then unfastened the tapes of her gown. Slowly he lowered the bodice and watched as the firelight turned her elegant breasts to gold.

She touched the corner of his mouth. "When you look at me in that manner, you make me feel quite beautiful."

He shook his head, dazed by the storm of emotion that pounded through him. Reverently, he brushed his thumbs across her nipples. "You are beautiful."

"And you, sir," she said in a soft, husky voice, "are quite wonderful."

He groaned and lowered his head to kiss the high curve of one rounded breast. She gripped his shoulders very tightly. Her head fell back. Clinging to him with both hands, she slid the sole of her slippered foot slowly up along the length of his calf. When she started to move it back down to the floor, he closed one hand around her thigh and held her pressed warmly against him. The skirts of her gown swirled around his breeches.

He could not wait another moment. He lifted her into his arms and settled her on the sofa. He stood back long enough to unfasten the front of his breeches and then he leaned down to push her skirts up to her waist.

Very deliberately he parted her thighs until her left foot was on the floor. She gasped when she realized how completely open she was to his gaze. Belatedly she tried to close her legs.

"No. Please. I want to see you." He went down on one knee beside the sofa. He felt her leg tremble against his ribs.

He put his palm against the warm, pink flesh of her sex. She shivered. On the floor beside him, her foot arched in response to the caress.

"Baxter?" The tip of her tongue appeared at the corner of her parted lips. It disappeared again when she moaned softly.

He leaned forward to inhale the exotic perfume of her body. She glistened in the firelight. He parted the soft folds of skin to reveal the tiny bud.

He bent his head and kissed her intimately with exquisite appreciation.

"Baxter." Her fingers tightened in his hair. "Good heavens, what are you doing?"

He ignored her breathless query and all the disjointed demands for an explanation that followed. He used his tongue to arouse the small nubbin until it was taut and full. He did not pause until she was speechless.

When she screamed softly and dug her nails into his scalp he rose quickly and settled himself on top of her. He licked the taste of her from his lips as he plunged into the tight, hot core of her body.

She convulsed around him, drawing him so deeply inside that he thought he might somehow become a part of her. In the alchemy of that union he was no longer alone.

Everything within him went rigid. In the next moment his climax roared through him, a searing, cleansing fire that somehow left him free in a way that he had never known.

The incense smoldered on the brazier.

He inhaled slowly, deeply, savoring the heightened level of awareness. The power would soon be his to command.

He was ready.

"Read the cards, my love," he whispered.

The fortune-teller turned over three cards. She studied them for a long moment.

"The golden griffin draws closer to the phoenix," she said at last.

"This grows more fascinating by the hour."

"And more dangerous," the fortune-teller cautioned.

"True. But the danger adds a certain element of interest to the thing."

The fortune-teller placed another card on the table. "The griffin's connection to the lady with the crystal eyes grows stronger."

"We must conclude that she is not a random thread in this tapestry, after all." He was pleased.

Baxter?" Charlotte stirred languidly. She threaded her fingers through the hair on his chest. "It is getting late."

"I know." Reluctantly he shifted position to untangle himself from the froth of her skirts. He got to his feet, adjusted his breeches, and glanced at the clock. "Less than an hour until dawn. Must be on my way. Hamilton will be anxious."

Charlotte sat up quickly and fumbled with the bodice of her gown. "What about poor Norris? I should think he would be the nervous one."

"Haven't seen him yet." Baxter reached for his eyeglasses, shoved them on his nose, and then grabbed his shirt. "Hamilton says he's very calm about the whole thing."

"Perhaps the fact that he's in a trance accounts for his unnatural calm."

"Bloody magician. Got a lot to answer for." Baxter scooped up his coat and swung around to say farewell. The sight of Charlotte looking deliciously disheveled made him wish very badly that he did not have such a pressing appointment. "I shall send word when the thing is finished."

"Be careful, Baxter." The last of the sweet sensuality disappeared from her eyes as she rose from the sofa. "I do not like this. It has been a strange night. There is something that I did not get a chance to tell you."

"I shall call on you later this afternoon." Baxter broke off as he caught sight of a wilted red rose lying on the desk. "There's that damned flower I saw you carrying earlier at the ball. Meant to ask you about it. Got distracted. Who gave it to you?"

"It's a long story. It can wait until you've resolved Hamilton's problem."

He did not care for the troubled expression in her eyes. He crossed the room and plucked the rose off the desk. Then he saw a folded piece of paper beneath it. A chill crawled across the nape of his neck.

"What's this? A note, too?"

"I assure you, there is no call for jealousy."

"I'm not jealous. I do not possess the hot-blooded nature required for such a ludicrous emotion."

"Indeed." She looked pensive. "I do, you know."

"What the devil are you talking about?" he asked as he unfolded the note.

"I would hate it if some woman sent you flowers or gave you letters."

He glanced up, startled by the vehemence in her voice. For an instant the expression in her eyes distracted him from the note in his hand. He cleared his throat. "I doubt that any female would send me a posy."

"Hah. Don't place any wagers on that, St. Ives. It is a wonder that I do not have to fend off my competitors with a stick. I suspect that the reason is that you have kept yourself out of Society for so long that no one knows you very well. It's fortunate for me that you prefer to spend your time in your laboratory."

Baxter felt the heat rise in his face. *Bloody hell, now she's put me to the blush. Is there no limit to her power over me?* "You need not concern yourself with competitors. There aren't any."

"Excellent."

He forced his attention back to the note in his hand. He read it quickly and then read it through a second time in growing disbelief. *Your alchemist lover seeks the Philosopher's Stone of vengeance....He will use whatever means...including your affections....Do not become his victim.*

"Bloody hell."

"It is not important now, Baxter. You must deal with the duel first. Then I will tell you about the note and the rose."

He crushed the paper in one hand and met Charlotte's eyes across the room. "Who gave you this?"

"I do not know who he was. He wore a black domino. When I saw him, I assumed it was you. But his voice..." She hesitated, as though searching for the words. "It was all wrong. Broken." She glanced at the clock. "You must go. I promise to tell you everything later."

"This is the second time that someone has attempted to turn you against me."

"A useless exercise." She shook out her skirts as she went to open the study door. "Hurry, Baxter. Hamilton will be waiting. He is depending upon you to save his friend's life."

She was right. There was no time now to get the full story from her. First things first, Baxter reminded himself.

"Damnation." He went out into the hall, picked up his hat, and opened the front door. He looked back at her as she watched anxiously from the entrance of the study. "You have been up all night. Go to bed. I shall call upon you this afternoon. We shall discuss this matter of the note at that time."

"Very well, but you will send word about the outcome of the duel?"

"Yes."

"And you will be careful?"

"As I keep reminding you"—he turned to go down the steps—"I'm not the one who is scheduled to meet Anthony Tiles at dawn."

"I know. And as I keep reminding you, Baxter, I comprehend your true nature too well to believe that you will be as careful as I could wish."

"I don't know where you gained the notion that I'm the reckless, neck-or-nothing type. Not only do I lack the temperament for that sort of dashing behavior, I also lack the proper tailor. Good night, Charlotte."

❧

Dawn arrived with a light, drifting fog that cloaked Brent's Field in a swirling gray shroud. An appropriate atmosphere for such a grim and stupid affair, Baxter thought.

He stood with Hamilton and watched as the paces were counted off by a young man with an air of dissipation that would have done credit to a confirmed rake twice his age.

"One, two, three…"

Pistols pointed toward the sky, the blank-faced Norris and the feral-eyed Tiles paced away from each other.

"...eight, nine, ten..."

"Are you sure this will work?" Hamilton asked in a low voice.

"That is the twentieth time you have asked me that question," Baxter muttered. "And for the twentieth time, all I can tell you is that it ought to work."

"But if it doesn't—"

"Be quiet," Baxter ordered very softly. "It is too late to alter the plans."

Hamilton subsided into nervous silence.

Baxter cast him a swift glance as the deadly cadence was called. Hamilton was a good deal more anxious about this business than his friend on the field. Norris was definitely not his usual self. Baxter had studied him covertly as he had gone through the preliminaries.

Norris had the air of an automaton. He answered direct questions but he would not discuss the situation in any detail. He seemed oblivious to most of what was going on around him. When Hamilton had pleaded with him one last time to give Tiles the apology that would halt the duel, Norris had appeared not to have heard him.

"...fourteen, fifteen, sixteen..."

Hamilton shifted and gave Baxter another quick, searching glance. Baxter shook his head once, silently warning him not to speak.

He had done his best to give Norris the best possible odds in the event that his plans were unsuccessful. He had negotiated with Tiles's seconds for a distance of twenty paces rather than the fifteen that had been suggested. The additional space between the opponents would make accuracy more difficult, even for a man of Tiles's skill.

"...seventeen, eighteen, nineteen, twenty." The dissipated young man grinned with unpleasant anticipation. "Make ready. *Fire*."

Baxter heard Hamilton catch his breath. On the field, both men turned. Norris made no attempt to aim carefully. He simply pointed the pistol in Tiles's general direction and pulled the trigger.

The explosion boomed loudly in the fog.

Tiles did not even flinch. He smiled coldly and raised his pistol.

Norris lowered his weapon very slowly. A perplexed expression passed over his face. He stared at Tiles, who was taking careful aim, and then he looked at Hamilton. Baxter could see the gathering shock and horror in his eyes. He turned back to Tiles. His mouth worked but no words came. A mouse confronting a snake.

With chilling calculation, Tiles fired his pistol.

A second explosion echoed in the fog.

Norris blinked several times and then looked down at himself as though expecting to see his own blood.

He was not the only one who looked surprised. All of the men gathered to witness the duel gazed at the still-upright, uninjured Norris in astonishment.

"Damnation, Tony missed his man," someone finally said.

The doctor who had been paid to attend the duel emerged from one of the carriages with an expectant, businesslike expression. He came to a halt when he saw that Norris was still standing.

Baxter stepped forward. "One shot each. That was the agreement. It's finished." He watched Tiles, who was examining his pistol with great attention. "Honor has been satisfied. You know how quickly rumors of this sort of thing spread. Let's all go home before the authorities get word of this meeting."

There was a general murmur of agreement. The prospect of being arrested for participating in a duel was enough to add a lively spring to everyone's step. The men headed for the various carriages parked beneath the trees on the side of the field.

Baxter frowned at Norris, who still looked scared and confused. The glazed expression was gone from his eyes, however. He was once again fully aware of his surroundings.

"I'll take Norris to the carriage." Hamilton started toward his friend.

Baxter touched his arm briefly. "I want to speak to both of you later. This morning. Before you take Norris home."

Hamilton hesitated. Then he nodded. "I don't know what we can tell you, but we owe you some answers. Norris and I shall accompany you back to your house."

Baxter started toward his carriage. Anthony Tiles stepped into his path.

"St. Ives, a word, if you don't mind."

Baxter stopped, removed his spectacles, and began to polish them with his handkerchief. He did not need his eyeglasses to see the penetrating inquiry in Tiles's gray eyes.

For all his notoriety, Tiles was not yet as dissipated or as debauched as his companions. Baxter sensed that the festering rage that was eating him from the inside out still provided a sense of purpose. When it had devoured too much, Tiles would be destroyed. Charlotte was right. Anthony was crafting his own bad end.

"What is it, Tony?"

"It has been a long time since Oxford, has it not?"

"Yes."

"I have not seen much of you in recent years. I have missed your companionship."

"Our interests have diverged."

Anthony nodded pensively. "Indeed. You always did have a peculiar penchant for your laboratory. And I have always preferred the hells. But we still have one thing in common, do we not?"

"Yes." That both of them had been born bastards had drawn them together for a time at Oxford, Baxter knew. Perhaps some remnants of that friendship still survived.

"I confess that I was surprised to see you here this morning. I would not have thought that this was your sort of sport."

"It isn't." Baxter replaced his spectacles. "And if you had any sense, Tony, you'd find something more useful to do with your time than engage in dawn meetings. One of these days you'll find yourself facing someone whose aim is more deadly than your own."

"And perhaps one whose powder has not been tampered with?"

Baxter smiled faintly. "I trust you are not making any accusations of fraud. After all, your own seconds witnessed the loading of the powder."

"Yes, but neither of my seconds is a chemist." Anthony's expression was surprisingly wry. "They would not have known if a very clever scientist substituted altered gunpowder."

"Come now, Tony, everyone heard the powder explode when you pulled the trigger."

"There was certainly a great deal of sound and fury," Anthony agreed. "But it signified nothing. The ball is still in my pistol."

"You don't need the blood of young Norris on your hands. We both know he's not your customary quarry. He was not himself when he challenged you."

"I will grant that it was out of character for him." Anthony looked thoughtful. "And I will agree that there would have been no great satisfaction in lodging a bullet in him."

"I am pleased to hear that." Baxter made to move toward the carriage.

"One more thing, St. Ives."

"Yes?"

Anthony eyed him from beneath half-closed lids. "You are here this morning, I suspect, because the new Earl of Esherton asked you for help in saving his friend's life."

"What of it?"

"Rumor has it that the old Earl left you in charge of his fortune and told you to keep an eye on young Hamilton."

"Your point, Tiles?"

"Your half brother got what should have been yours. You are in an ideal position to destroy the inheritance that was denied to you." Anthony's hand tightened into a fist. "Why have you not done so?"

Charlotte's words echoed in Baxter's head. *Anthony Tiles has obviously allowed the facts of his birth to set him on a path that is almost certain to destroy him. Thank God you have carved out a different destiny for yourself.*

He looked at the man who had once been his companion, perhaps even a friend, and sensed a truth that he had never before confronted. His father had not bequeathed him the title but he had given his bastard son something of himself. Anthony had not been so fortunate.

"I will not say that I have not reflected on the past at times," Baxter said slowly. "But perhaps I have avoided the temptation to dabble in serious vengeance because I discovered a more absorbing interest."

"Ah, yes, your passion for chemistry." Anthony's mouth curved derisively. "But to my mind there is nothing so interesting as revenge."

"Take some advice from an old acquaintance. See if you cannot find something more amusing than the gaming hells and dueling field.

You grow too old for this kind of thing, Tony."

"I pray you will not lecture me. It is bad enough that you have interfered with this morning's entertainment."

"No need to play the complete cynic." Baxter glanced toward the carriage, where Hamilton and Norris waited. "I'm well aware that you took the noble path in this fiasco. I doubt that you are concerned with my thanks, but you have them."

"Excellent." Anthony's smile was distinctly wolfish. "I may find a use for your gratitude. But I assure you that it is misplaced. I never trouble myself with noble behavior. No profit in it for a bastard."

"Then perhaps you have simply grown more weary of your current pursuits than you know."

"What the hell does that mean?"

"From where I stood it was possible to see that you aimed slightly high and to the left. Had your pistol not failed you, the bullet would likely have gone past Norris's ear, not through his chest." Baxter raised his brows. "I do believe that my involvement in this affair was unnecessary."

Anthony gave him an odd look. Then, without a word, he turned and walked back toward his phaeton and his self-imposed loneliness.

Baxter watched the other man mount the stylish vehicle and drive off into the fog. He had a sudden image of Anthony gradually becoming a ghost.

Baxter's insides clenched. *That could be me.*

On the surface he and Anthony seemed very different. Tiles filled his life with feverish excitement and risk. Baxter preferred the orderly, self-contained world of his laboratory. But they had each in their own way built walls to seal out the emotions that could make them vulnerable.

Those same walls ensured that they would be alone the whole of their lives.

Always in the past Baxter had resented and resisted those who had dragged him temporarily out of his laboratory to undertake some irksome family obligation. When his tasks in the outside world had been accomplished, he been relieved to retreat back into the predictable, well-regulated gloom of his personal realm.

But this time he was not so eager to return to the comfort of his flasks and crucibles and blowpipes. He no longer wanted to be entirely alone.

Charlotte studied the plump, rosy-cheeked, gray-haired woman seated at the planked table in front of the kitchen fire. "It was very good of you to come here today, Mrs. Gatler."

"Mrs. Witty promised me that it would be worth my while." Mrs. Gatler narrowed her robin's egg blue eyes. "She also promised that you'd never tell a soul that I talked to you about what happened that night."

"You have my word on it. I have a reputation for confidentiality."

"That's what Mrs. Witty said." Mrs. Gatler slanted a sidelong glance at Mrs. Witty, who was busying herself with bread dough on the other side of the room.

"You can tell 'er anything, Maggy." Mrs. Witty gave her a reassuring wink. "Knows how to keep a secret, she does."

"Another cup, Mrs. Gatler?" Charlotte picked up the teapot.

The arrival of Drusilla Heskett's former housekeeper had taken her by surprise. Ariel had left the house less than half an hour earlier on a shopping expedition with Rosalind. Baxter had sent a message around assuring her that the duel had ended safely but he had not yet come to call.

She had been writing down notes about the investigation, trying to make some connections in her mind, when Mrs. Witty had triumphantly announced the arrival of Drusilla Heskett's housekeeper.

"Took me some doing to find her," Mrs. Witty had confided en route to the kitchens. "She didn't particularly want to be found."

"I believe I will have some more tea," Mrs. Gatler said. "Bit of a novelty, y'know, havin' the lady of the house pourin' tea for me."

Charlotte smiled blandly. "My pleasure." She did not tell her guest that she would have been equally happy to pour gin if it would have loosened her tongue. "Now, then, about the murder."

329

Mrs. Gatler darted one last glance at Mrs. Witty and then she leaned forward. "He didn't know I was there, y'see."

"Who didn't know?"

"The one who shot her dead. Mrs. Heskett had given the staff the night off. She often did that when she was expectin' Lord Lennox to call." Mrs. Gatler chuckled. "Those two liked havin' the freedom of the whole house when they went at it. Kitchen, cellar, drawing room, you name it. All over the place, they was."

"Stamina," Charlotte murmured.

"You can say that again. Well, I was supposed to go to my sister's that night but at the last minute I changed me mind. Wasn't feeling up to it. Decided I'd stay home and take a tonic for the pains. I was in my room behind the kitchens when I heard him in the hall."

Charlotte frowned. "Whom did you hear? Lord Lennox?"

"No, no, not him. Always knew when Lennox was in the house." Mrs. Gatler shook her head in admiration. "Those two made a lot of noise. It was amazing, it was."

"Please continue, Mrs. Gatler. Did the man in the hall make a commotion?"

"No. That's what was so odd. Arrived silent as the dead. Only reason I knew he was there was because I heard Mrs. Heskett speak to him."

Charlotte stilled. "She knew him, then?"

"Don't think so. She seemed startled to see him. Demanded to know what he was doing in her house."

"You say you heard him in the hall. Didn't he knock on the front door?"

"No." Mrs. Gatler's brows furrowed. "I would have heard him. I figured he must have had a key."

"A key?"

"Mrs. Heskett was in the habit of giving keys to her favorite gentlemen friends." Mrs. Gatler shrugged. "Lennox had one."

Charlotte exchanged a look with Mrs. Witty. Then she turned back to her visitor. "What happened next?"

"Well, I heard the two of 'em talk for a while there in the hall. Leastways, I heard Mrs. Heskett. Couldn't rightly hear him. His voice was pitched real low. But I knew that he was saying something because every so often Mrs. Heskett answered."

"Did you go out into the hall to see if your mistress needed anything for her guest?"

"No, I certainly did not. It was supposed to be my night off. If Madam had known that I was around, she'd likely have sent me to the kitchens to prepare a cold collation for her gentleman friend." Mrs. Gatler grimaced. "The quality never remembers staff's night off when they've got something they want done. Isn't that right, Mrs. Witty?"

Mrs. Witty made a commiserating noise and went back to kneading the bread dough.

Charlotte poured more tea. "Please continue with your story, Mrs. Gatler."

"Well, let me see. Where was I?" Mrs. Gatler frowned. "Not much more to tell.

After a while Mrs. Heskett and the gentleman went upstairs. A few minutes later I heard the shot. Sent me into a panic, it did. I swear, I couldn't even move for the longest time. Then I heard him on the stairs."

"You heard the killer's footsteps?"

"I heard his voice." Mrs. Gatler gave a visible shudder. "Mrs. Heskett's spaniel must have got in his path. He swore at the little beast. Told it to get out of his way."

"Tell me everything you heard, Mrs. Gatler."

"I think he must have kicked the poor dog. I heard it yelp. Next thing I know, there's footsteps coming down belowstairs into the back hall. Went right past my room. I just held my breath and prayed. Never been so terrified in my life."

"Did the man pause?"

"No, thank the good Lord. He went straight on out through the kitchens. I didn't leave my room until I was sure he'd gone. Then the dog started to howl. After a while I went upstairs. That's when I found Mrs. Heskett. She was just lying there in a pool of blood. It was terrible. I don't believe that she died instantly."

"Why do you say that?" Charlotte asked quickly.

Mrs. Gatler looked uncomfortable. "She'd sort of dragged herself across the carpet. Got as far as the wardrobe. She'd opened a drawer. There was blood all over the wood. Probably tried to haul herself to her feet. It was dreadful."

No, Charlotte thought. Drusilla Heskett

was not trying to stand. She used her last ounce of life to hide the sketchbook. She knew it held the only clue that could point to her killer.

"Why didn't you summon the magistrate immediately?" Charlotte asked. "Why did you not come forth to tell what had happened?"

Mrs. Gatler looked at her as though she was not very bright. "D'you think I'm mad? I was the only one in the house that night. The authorities would have assumed that I was the murderer. Staff always gets the blame in a situation such as that, y'know. I'd likely have been arrested. They'd have said I was caught trying to steal the silver or some such thing."

Charlotte drummed her fingers on the table. "What, precisely, did the killer say when he stumbled over the dog?"

"What? Oh, yes. On the stairs." Mrs. Gatler swallowed the remains of her tea and looked up with a troubled expression. "I think he said, 'Get out of my way, you bloody cur.' Or something similar. But to tell you the truth, it wasn't the words that stuck in my head. It was the voice."

Charlotte froze. "The voice?"

"Real rough and hoarse." Mrs. Gatler shuddered again. "Made me think of rocks rolling around inside a coffin."

"Dear God." Charlotte very nearly stopped breathing. The man who had given her the rose and the note was the same one who had murdered Drusilla Heskett. She had actually stood face-to-face with Drusilla's killer.

No, not quite face-to-face, she reminded herself. The man in the black domino had worn a mask. There was only one person who might be able to put that graveled, broken voice together with a face.

"What's wrong, Miss Charlotte?" Mrs. Witty brushed the flour from her hands and frowned in concern. "You look as though you've been hit by a thunderbolt."

"The man who employed Juliana Post to tell me those falsehoods about Mr. St. Ives was likely the same man who gave me a note last night." Charlotte rubbed her temples as she tried to reason out the logic of the situation. "It has to be the same man."

"How can you know that?" Mrs. Witty demanded.

"The stratagem was the same in both instances. In each case an attempt was made to make me believe the worst of St. Ives." Charlotte flattened her palms on the table and pushed herself to her feet. "And that man is very likely the murderer. Oh, my God, I must hurry."

"Where do you think you're going?" Mrs. Witty called as Charlotte dashed across the kitchen.

"To see Juliana Post." Charlotte paused briefly in the doorway. "I fear that she is in grave danger. I must warn her."

"But, Miss Charlotte—"

"Mr. St. Ives will be calling soon. When he arrives, kindly tell him where I have gone."

Mrs. Witty scowled. "Why ever would Miss Post be in danger?"

"Because she is the only one who may be able to identify the killer. I can only hope that he has not yet realized that she is a threat to him."

Sixteen 🖋

"While you spoke with Tiles, Norris confided to me that he can recall nothing connected directly to the duel." Hamilton turned to pace back across the library. "He doesn't remember the instructions he received when the magician put him into a trance. He does not even recollect the experiment."

"Did he give you any reason for calling Tiles out?"

"No. None. He does not remember the act. He claims that it was not until he fired his pistol that he suddenly realized that he was confronting the most dangerous duelist in all of London. And he did not even know why."

"Does he recall that you and the other club members attempted to dissuade him from going forward with the duel?"

"No." Hamilton came to a halt in front of a wall of books. He grasped the rail of the library steps. "As you saw, he was obviously badly shaken by the whole incident."

One glance at Norris's bewildered, utterly exhausted expression had convinced Baxter that a serious interrogation of the young man would be useless. He had reluctantly instructed the coachman to set Norris down in front of the large Lennox mansion. Hamilton had seen his friend indoors and then returned to the carriage to accompany Baxter home. Neither had said a word until they walked into the library.

"When Norris recovers, he will discover that he has acquired himself an enviable reputation," Baxter said. "He is, after all, one of very few men who has had the audacity to call out Anthony Tiles and survive unharmed."

"True." Hamilton's mouth quirked in spite of his obviously somber mood. "It's rather ironic, is it not? Norris is the most even-tempered, good-natured man I have ever met and now he will be known as a bold and dashing man of the world, a reckless, neck-or-nothing out-and-outer."

"Should do wonders for his social life. I trust his new image will not go to his head."

"Unlikely." Hamilton's smile faded. "He is grateful to be alive. The last thing he wants to do is risk his neck anytime soon."

"As he appears to have no memory of the affair, I must rely upon you for information. Will you help me discover the identity of this quack you call a magician?"

Hamilton turned to face him. His eyes were bleak, his mouth grim. He looked a good deal older than he had yesterday, Baxter thought.

"Yes, I'll do whatever I can," Hamilton said. "I'm well aware that I'm in your debt, Baxter."

"You owe me nothing."

"What the devil do you mean by that? You

saved my friend's life. I cannot begin to repay you. Neither can Norris."

"You were the one who took steps to save Norris's neck. You put aside your personal feelings and came to me for assistance. That took courage, will, and resourcefulness."

Hamilton flushed. For a moment he looked as confused as Norris had after the duel. "I did not know where else to turn. I had tried logic and reason on Norris. He did not respond to my pleas or my arguments. We could not find the magician. I was desperate."

"I know. You did what you believed necessary to save a friend's life, even though it meant asking my help. I know how difficult that must have been. If Norris is grateful to anyone, he should be grateful to you."

"I was not the one who knew how to alter the chemicals in the gunpowder."

Baxter shrugged. "If it's any consolation, I don't believe that Tiles would have shot Norris in cold blood."

"Everyone knows Tiles is utterly ruthless."

"That is certainly his reputation. But he had nothing against Norris."

"The lack of a reason would not have stopped a man of Tiles's nature." Hamilton frowned. "Do you think he suspects that something was wrong with the gunpowder?"

"He's not stupid."

Alarm flashed in Hamilton's eyes. "You mean he knows what happened today?"

"He has a fairly accurate notion of what went wrong with his pistol, yes. And he is well aware that I am a chemist. It did not require a great deal of reasoning for him to put the facts together and come up with a theory."

"Hell's teeth, Baxter. If he knows about the gunpowder, he may well blame you. He might call you out. You could be his next victim."

"Don't tell me that you're worried about my neck?"

"It would not be right if Tiles tried to take revenge against you because you helped me save Norris."

"Rest assured, there will be no duel between Tiles and me. We were friends once at Oxford. Although we have gone our separate ways, there is an old bond between us that cannot be easily broken."

Hamilton stared at him. "What bond is that?"

"We are both bastards."

"I don't understand. What has that to do with anything?"

"The circumstances of one's birth have an amazing influence on one's circle of friends in later years. Consider your acquaintance with Norris. The basic element that you have in common is that you're both heirs to old titles and old fortunes. That factor will provide a link between the two of you that will last the whole of your lives. You will likely have sons who may well marry his daughters and so on. It's the way of the world."

"I see what you mean." Hamilton shifted uncomfortably. "Nevertheless, in spite of your opinions, I am very glad that Norris's safety this morning did not depend upon Tiles's whim."

"Tiles can be somewhat unpredictable, I'll grant you that much. But I think enough has been said on the subject of the duel." Baxter sat forward and folded his hands on top of the desk. "Let's get down to more pressing matters. We must find that damnable magician before he puts anyone else at risk with one of his mesmerism experiments."

"I have agreed to help you, but I still cannot bring myself to believe that he intended Norris to die." Hamilton rubbed the back of his neck. "The experiment went awry, that's all."

"I'm not so certain that it was a failure."

Hamilton looked up quickly. "What do you mean?"

"I suspect that the results of the affair may have been entirely satisfactory so far as the magician was concerned."

"What are you talking about? Why would the magician have wanted to get Norris killed?"

"That's one of the many questions I wish to ask him. Now tell me everything you can."

Hamilton sighed. "That won't be easy. I have never actually seen his face. He always wore his costume when he appeared among us. It was part of the game, you see."

"I take it that he performed his act several times in front of you and your friends. There must have been some distinguishing characteristic that you can recall."

"Well, he does possess a rather strange voice," Hamilton said.

❧

Charlotte lifted the heavy brass knocker on Juliana Post's front door and banged it loudly for the third time. Still, no housekeeper arrived in response to the summons.

The sense of anxious dread grew stronger. Something was wrong. Charlotte knew it in the same way that she sometimes knew other things, such as the fact that Baxter was not the dull, bland man that the rest of the world believed him to be and that the harsh-voiced figure in the black domino was deadly.

She slammed the knocker once more. Perhaps she was too late. The man with the broken voice might have already paid a visit to Juliana.

Calm yourself, she thought. Juliana might simply be away from home for a few hours. Perhaps she had gone shopping.

But where was the housekeeper?

There was no point pounding again on the front door. It was obvious now that no one would respond. Charlotte glanced down into the front area below the street. There was no sign of anyone about in the kitchens.

She had to get inside the house. She would not be able to rest if she simply left this place and returned home.

With a quick glance at the street to make certain that no one was watching, she opened the small gate and hurried down the steps into the front area of the house. Down here she was safely out of sight of anyone who chanced to pass by on the street.

All was quiet in the small, paved space that served the kitchens. Charlotte peered through the windows. There was no one about down there, either. She tapped sharply on a pane.

When there was no response, she tried the door.

Locked.

The decision to break one of the window-panes was difficult but she could not come up with any other way to get into the house. It was too bad that Baxter was not with her, she thought. He was good at this sort of thing.

She took off her bonnet, held the brim so that it covered one of the small windowpanes, and then waited until a large carriage rumbled past. When the clatter of hooves and wheels was at its height, she swung her heavy reticule at the bonnet-covered glass.

The small pane shattered. The shards dropped to the kitchen floor. Charlotte waited a moment but no one came running to investigate.

She eased her arm through the broken win-dowpane and groped for the door lock.

She was inside in a matter of seconds. Housebreaking was a surprisingly uncom-plicated business.

She went through the kitchens to the stairs that led to the ground floor.

"Is anyone home?" she called loudly. "Miss Post?"

An eerie silence was the only answer.

Her sense of foreboding increased as she slowly climbed the stairs. An unwholesome scent greeted her in the front hall.

"Juliana? It's Charlotte Arkendale."

No response.

She sniffed cautiously. The smoky smell was familiar. She recalled that Juliana used an exotic blend of incense to provide atmosphere for her fortune-telling sessions.

This is different, Charlotte thought. *Not the same fragrance as last time. But I know it. From where?*

And then it struck her. This odor was very similar to the unwholesome incense that Hamilton and his friends had used in their private chamber at The Green Table. But there was a subtle difference. This time the vapor seemed darker, more acrid.

"Juliana?"

The door to the small parlor that Juliana used for her fortune-telling sessions was closed. Charlotte could see tendrils of scented smoke wafting out from beneath it.

A terrible sense of urgency washed through her. She rushed down the hall to the door, grabbed the knob, and twisted frantically.

The door was locked.

Shocked, she glanced down at the unyielding lock and saw the key. Someone had deliberately locked the room from this side.

"Juliana."

Frantic now, Charlotte unlocked the door and yanked it open.

Great billowing clouds of incense curled out into the hall and swirled around her. It stung her eyes and made her head swim.

She stepped back quickly and grabbed her handkerchief from her reticule. Taking a deep breath, she folded the cloth once and held it over her nose and mouth.

She dashed into the exotic black and crimson room. The incense was so heavy in there that it appeared as though a fog had settled inside the parlor. Her eyes watered. She could take only a moment to search for Juliana. She knew that she would not be able to stay in this room any longer than she could hold her breath.

She almost stumbled over the low fortune-telling table. She looked down and saw several cards lying faceup. One of them had fallen to the floor. It depicted a shrouded figure holding a scythe. An unmistakable image of death.

She stepped around the table and looked toward the hearth. A bundle of crimson satin robes was tumbled on the floor next to the scarlet sofa.

Juliana.

Lungs burning, Charlotte rushed toward the prone figure on the carpet. She could not tell if Juliana was dead or alive. There was no time to check.

Holding the handkerchief with one hand, she grabbed one of Juliana's ankles and started to drag her toward the door. Fortunately, Juliana's satin robes slid easily along the carpet.

But the door was very far away. She knew

she would not make it if she did not take a breath. She was already dizzy.

She inhaled cautiously through the handkerchief.

The linen reduced the intensity of the incense but it could not filter out all of it. At first Charlotte thought that it had had no effect. Then she watched in horror as the black and scarlet room began to melt and dissolve before her eyes.

The incense, she thought. It was doing this to her. She must keep moving toward the door.

The weight of Juliana grew heavier. The parlor was a sea of blood. The door was the entrance to hell. A monster waited on the other side of the threshold.

It's the incense. The incense. I must keep going forward.

One more step. Just one more little step, she promised herself. Then she could take a breath.

She pulled Juliana through the doorway to Hades...

...and found herself on a cool tile floor.

She tore the handkerchief away from her face and sucked in the less tainted air of the hall. A violent fit of coughing overcame her.

"Bloody hell. Charlotte."

"Baxter. Baxter, I'm here."

The sound of his voice was more invigorating than any tonic. She took another gasping breath and wiped her tearing eyes. She blinked several times and saw Baxter striding toward her through the light haze. He had entered the house via the kitchens, just as she had.

"What has happened here?" he demanded in a soft and terrible voice.

"Thank God, you came. I am so glad to see you. It's Juliana. I do not know if she is still alive."

She could not focus properly on Baxter. As he came toward her he appeared to shift and re-form in some subtle fashion. It was as if he were transmuting back and forth between two different states of being, one human and one...something else. Something dangerous. His alchemist's eyes burned too brightly in the incense-tainted haze.

Baxter searched her face. "Get out of here. Quickly. I shall attend to Miss Post."

"There is so much of this strange vapor." Charlotte frowned. The hall did not look quite right. The staircase had slid several feet to one side. "I fear there is a fire in the parlor."

"I'll check after I get you and Miss Post into the carriage. Move, woman. No, not the kitchen stairs. For God's sake, use the front door. It's closer."

"Yes, of course." She could not think clearly. Everything was wavering, turning different colors, changing shape. She felt as though she were moving through a dream, a nightmare.

She swung around and lunged for the doorknob, which was floating in the fog. She barely managed to grab hold of it before it took flight. She struggled with it.

"Open it," Baxter ordered in a voice that cut through the crimson haze.

Summoning all of the willpower she possessed, she wrenched at the doorknob. To her infinite relief, it turned in her fingers. The door opened.

Fresh, crisp air rushed into the incense-laced hall. She breathed deeply as she staggered down the steps. The world steadied a little. She saw Baxter's carriage on the street in front of the house.

She tried to move toward the cab door but it seemed to shift position and size when she reached for the handle.

"Here, now, Miss Arkendale, I'll handle that for ye." The coachman jumped down from his box and grabbed the door from her fumbling fingers. "There ye go."

He put a firm hand under her elbow and propelled her into the carriage. Charlotte fell onto the seat. She glanced through the window and saw that Baxter was right behind her. He had tossed Juliana over one shoulder.

"What's happenin' in there?" the coachman asked. "House fire? Shall I summon aid, sir?"

"I don't think there's a fire." Baxter dropped Juliana onto the floor of the carriage. "Hold a moment. I'll go back and take a closer look."

Charlotte's head was beginning to clear. She leaned out of the carriage window. "Baxter, be careful. That incense is most unwholesome."

346

He did not respond. She saw him jerk a handkerchief out of his pocket as he went back through the front door of the house. She waited anxiously until he reappeared a moment later.

"No fire. Just a brazier heaped with incense. Nasty stuff. It will soon burn itself out." Baxter glanced at the coachman as he vaulted into the carriage. "Miss Arkendale's house. Kindly do not waste any time. I don't want to loiter about in this neighborhood."

"Aye, sir." The coachman slammed the cab door and leaped up onto the box.

The vehicle set off down the street at a brisk clip.

Baxter settled himself on the seat across from Charlotte. His eyes were very fierce behind the lenses of his spectacles. "Are you all right?"

"Yes." She looked down at Juliana sprawled on the floor of the carriage. "And Miss Post is alive, thank heavens."

Baxter leaned down to touch the side of Juliana's throat. "So she is."

"She must have been overcome by the incense. I'm almost certain that it was not the same mixture of herbs she used the last time I visited her. This vapor reminded me of the noxious smoke Hamilton and his friends used the other night. But this was stronger."

"Yes." Baxter studied Juliana. His face was set in hard, bleak lines. "I do not believe that Miss Post was accidentally overcome by that incense."

Charlotte met Baxter's eyes across Juliana's motionless form. "The magician tried to murder her."

"Yes."

His name is Malcolm Janner. I loved him and he tried to kill me." Juliana, freshly bathed and garbed in one of Ariel's wrappers, huddled on the sofa in front of the parlor fire. Her voice was still hoarse from the smoky incense. Her eyes were reddened and damp with tears. "I thought he loved me."

Charlotte paused in the act of pouring another cup of tea. She touched Juliana's hand. "He is a monster. Monsters do not respond to love."

Baxter stirred slightly near the mantel. Charlotte felt his gaze on her. When she glanced at him, she saw that he was watching her closely. But he made no comment.

She turned back to Juliana. "What happened today?"

"He asked me to read the cards for him. He does that quite often. It was one of the things I never comprehended about him."

"What do you mean?"

"Malcolm is a man of keen intellect but he is obsessed with metaphysical and occult science. He believes that I really can tell fortunes. Indeed, I think that was the reason why he pretended to love me. I never dared to let him know that my fortune-telling skills were nothing more than an act I had created in order to make my living."

"Why the incense?" Baxter asked.

Juliana glanced at him. "He is forever experimenting with it. He has created a special mixture that he says heightens the faculties and elevates one's sense of awareness. He feels it helps him contact the forces of the metaphysical plane."

"Was that what was burning in the brazier?" Charlotte asked.

"Yes. But the incense is very potent. It must be used carefully. A small amount of it has the effect of altering the way one perceives things. But too much can kill."

"There was certainly far too much of it in your parlor today," Charlotte said.

"After I read the cards for him this morning, he put more incense on the brazier." Juliana closed her eyes in mute anguish. "When I told him that it frightened me, he said that he would make certain that I was safe. He put on his mask, the one he dons whenever he wishes to remain unaffected by the incense. I grew very dazed and disoriented."

"Go on," Charlotte said gently.

Juliana opened her eyes. Tears streamed down her face. "He picked me up. Placed me on the sofa. I thought he was going to make love to me as he often does after I read the cards for him. I could no longer see him clearly but I shall never forget his voice when he told me that he did not need me anymore. That

I had become a problem. He promised that I would feel no pain. I would simply go to sleep and never awaken."

"Dear God," Charlotte whispered. "You were on the floor when I found you. You must have fallen from the sofa."

Baxter frowned. "That is no doubt what allowed you to live long enough for Charlotte to discover you and pull you to safety, Miss Post."

Juliana glanced at him in wan surprise. "What do you mean?"

"In the course of my experiments I have frequently observed that smoky vapors tend to be lighter than other airs. In a sense, they seek to rise and float above them. The air that was closest to the floor in your parlor therefore remained less tainted with the incense."

Charlotte was impressed. "A very clever analysis of the situation, Baxter."

He gave her a wry look. "Thank you. I like to think that not all of my time in my laboratory is wasted."

Juliana shuddered. "Whatever the case, I owe my life to you, Miss Arkendale. If you had not come to see me when you did, I would have expired from the effects of that ghastly incense. What stroke of fortune made you decide to visit me today?"

"It was not fortune," Charlotte said briskly. "It was logic. And, well, perhaps a bit of luck. Let us say that I had obtained some information that caused me to conclude that the voice of this man of mystery was the key to the whole affair. You were the one person I knew who could quite possibly put a face to that voice."

Juliana gripped the lapels of her wrapper. She stared into the flames. "Malcolm hated his voice. He said it was an outrage that he had been stricken in that manner."

Baxter watched Juliana for a moment. "I spoke with my brother today. He confirmed that the so-called magician who amuses the members of the Green Table club possesses a voice that is unusually harsh."

Charlotte looked at him. "According to the person I interviewed this morning, so did the man who killed Drusilla Heskett. And the man in the black domino who spoke to me last night at the masquerade ball also had a strange, rough voice."

"Bloody hell," Baxter muttered. "Why did you not tell me all this?"

"There has been no opportunity."

"It must be Malcolm," Juliana whispered. "He established The Green Table club and lured young men of important families into it. It was all part of his plan."

"What is this grand scheme?" Baxter asked. "Is he out to destroy the gentlemen of the club?"

"Destroy them?" Juliana appeared genuinely startled. "Of course not. Why on earth would he do such a thing?"

Light glinted on the lenses of Baxter's spectacles. "Some people will go to great lengths to gain revenge. If this magician harbors some grudge against the young men he enticed into the club, he might have thought to arrange their deaths through the use of mesmerism. This morning I witnessed how such a murder could take place."

"You are correct on one count," Juliana admitted. "Malcolm has no love for high-ranking gentlemen of the ton. He scorns the lot. But I do not believe he intended to kill any of them. If I had thought that murder was his goal, I would never have agreed to help him."

"What, precisely, is his goal?" Charlotte asked gently.

"He seeks wealth and power. He claims that by rights he should have possessed both at birth. The fact that he was denied his heritage is a source of great anguish and rage to him." Juliana hesitated. "Because of my own circumstances, I understood the depth of his feelings on the subject."

"Yes, of course." Baxter's hand clamped around the mantelpiece. "It all becomes clear now. He thought to control the new generation of young, powerful lords through the use of mesmerism and the drugging incense."

Juliana nodded and dabbed at her eyes with the edge of her wrapper. "He has studied Dr. Mesmer's work and that of many others who have experimented with animal magnetism. He has perfected the techniques of inducing a trance. He uses the incense to facilitate the operation."

Charlotte's palms were suddenly damp. "Baxter, what happened at dawn this morning was indeed a test, was it not?"

"Yes, the ultimate test of the magician's

control over his subjects." Baxter removed his eyeglasses and shook out his handkerchief. "No wonder Hamilton and the others could not locate him when they sought to make him break the trance. He had no intention of calling off his experiment before he got the results."

Charlotte was awed by the implications. "If he proved that he could use his techniques to send a young man to his death, he would know that he had achieved the degree of power he sought."

"I do not know what you witnessed this morning," Juliana said with an air of desperation. "But I am certain that Malcolm does not intend to murder all the young bloods of the ton."

"I believe you." Baxter methodically polished his eyeglasses. "This morning's work was simply an experiment, as I said. I suspect that his ultimate goal is to control the gentlemen of The Green Table after they come into their titles and estates. He was obviously willing to sacrifice one of his subjects in order to prove that he had accomplished his objectives."

"Just think of what he might be able to do if he could put a number of wealthy, powerful gentlemen into such strong trances," Charlotte said. "He could use his skills to make them do anything he wished. He could control their investments, their political opinions, their very lives."

"Indeed." Baxter slipped his spectacles back into place. The gold flames in his eyes flared. "And in so doing, his own power would be almost unlimited."

Juliana's mouth trembled. "Malcolm was born a bastard. He could not abide the whims of a cruel fate that had left a man of his intellect and strength of will forever barred from his fortune and society's most powerful inner circles."

"So he sought to shape his own destiny," Charlotte said slowly.

Baxter frowned. "What is this about destiny?"

"On the night of the masquerade ball Malcolm Janner asked me if I believed in destiny." In spite of the fire, Charlotte found the parlor cold. "I recall his words quite clearly because someone else once said something very similar to me."

Juliana dried her eyes. "Malcolm often spoke of destiny. He felt he had a great one, you see. That was one of the things he wished to have verified whenever I read the cards. I was always careful to make certain that he got the fortune he wanted. I feared the effect on his spirits if the cards predicted an ill outcome."

"Bloody hell." Baxter's voice was so soft that Charlotte barely heard him. "It's not possible. The man is dead."

"Who is dead?" Charlotte asked quickly.

Baxter closed one hand into a fist on top of the cold marble mantel. "I will explain later."

Charlotte hesitated, wanting to pursue the matter. But she could tell from the shuttered look in Baxter's eyes that he did not intend to say anything more in front of Juliana.

"When I entered the parlor today," Charlotte said to Juliana, "I noticed that one of the cards lying faceup on the floor was an image of death."

Juliana shook her head. "I gave him the same reading that I always do. I made certain that all the signs indicated a positive outcome for his plans. He seemed very satisfied."

Charlotte summoned up the scene in her mind. "Perhaps when he picked you up to carry you to the sofa the hem of your robes brushed against that particular card and knocked it to the carpet."

"I suppose so," Juliana said listlessly.

"Odd that the card fell faceup and that it was the one card in the deck that the magician would not have wished to see," Charlotte said very quietly.

Baxter pinned Juliana with his intent gaze. "Where does this man who calls himself Malcolm Janner reside?"

Juliana flushed. "I know you will not credit this, but the truth is, I do not have his direction. He said it was best that way. He claimed he wished to protect me in the event that his plans failed. All I can tell you is that he spent a great deal of time at The Green Table. I believe he kept a sort of office there."

Charlotte glanced at Baxter. "We did not investigate the top floor of the establishment."

"I doubt that he lives there," Baxter said. "Too obvious. But he would require access to the upper floor in order to stage his magical act. Perhaps it would be worthwhile to have another look around the premises."

"Excellent notion," Charlotte said.

Baxter glanced at her. The full force of his implacable will gleamed in his eyes. "This time, I shall go alone."

"But I can be of assistance."

"Don't even consider the notion."

Charlotte raised her brows at his coldly decisive tone. "We shall discuss the matter later, sir."

"No," he said in the very even, very neutral voice that he used whenever he was at his most inflexible. "We will not."

Charlotte abandoned the argument for the moment. She had a more pressing concern. "We must make arrangements to protect Miss Post. If Malcolm Janner discovers that she is not dead, he may well make another attempt on her life."

Baxter's mouth curved slightly in a humorless smile. "Then we shall make certain that he is convinced that she is no longer among the living."

"How will you manage that?" Juliana asked.

"We shall do what everyone in Town does when it is deemed necessary to make an important announcement to Society," Baxter said. "We shall send a notice to the newspapers."

Seventeen

Two hours later, Baxter prowled restlessly around Charlotte's parlor. A damp-eyed Juliana Post had been safely packed off for the north in a hired carriage from Severedges Stables. Notice of 'a fatal occurrence due to a small house fire' had been sent to the newspapers. With luck it would appear in the morning. Plans for an investigation of the third story of The Green Table were simmering in the back of his mind.

He was making progress on the list of tasks he had assigned himself, but he took little satisfaction from the orderly progression of events. He was in control of the situation, yet he could not escape the sense of a gathering darkness that had nothing to do with the fall of night.

Morgan Judd was alive. It was impossible, but the facts could no longer be denied. The one thing that did not fit was the description of his voice.

"Thank you for all that you did for Miss Post." Seated in a corner of the yellow sofa, Charlotte watched as he paced past on his way to the opposite end of the room. "You were most kind, Baxter."

"You were the one who went to warn her and thereby saved her life." Baxter paused in front of the window and clasped his hands behind his back. "Considering her record in this affair, it would be interesting to know just why you feel so protective of her."

"I suppose it's because she and I have so much in common," Charlotte said quietly.

"What in God's name can you possibly have in common with that woman?"

"I would have thought it obvious. We are

both descended from families whose fortunes had, to put it delicately, declined. We had both been left to deal with callous, dishonorable men who had control over our lives and our incomes. We both found a way to create careers for ourselves that enabled us to escape the usual fates of women in our situations."

Baxter threw her an enigmatic glance. "Your careers also allowed you to avoid the risks of marriage, did they not?"

"Indeed. Although poor Juliana managed to get involved with a man who appears to be more deadly than the average husband. Which only goes to prove that an affair can be just as dangerous as a marriage, I suppose."

Baxter adjusted his spectacles. "I hardly think Miss Post's case is typical."

"Perhaps not." Charlotte grew thoughtful. "Nevertheless, I wonder if it would be worth my while to offer my services to ladies who are contemplating a romantic liaison as well as to those who are considering marriage."

She's serious, Baxter thought. He suddenly became aware of the fact that his jaw was locked in place. He swallowed to release some of the tension. "I doubt that there would be much call for that sort of thing."

"You may be correct. It is passion that usually governs one's decision to become involved in an affair, and when one is consumed by such a strong emotion, one is not terribly interested in facts."

"Indeed."

"And everyone knows that passion is a

fleeting, short-lived sensation. When it has run its course, one can simply end the affair. Not at all like marriage, which requires more discretion and sound logic because one is, after all, stuck with one's husband for life."

Stuck. He sighed inwardly. "Indeed."

"Yes, I do believe you have the right of it, Baxter. There would likely be few clients who would employ me to investigate a potential lover."

"You appear to have sufficient demand for your services as it is."

"Yes, well, enough of business. I saw the look on your face when Miss Post spoke of Malcolm Janner. You know him, do you not? Who is he, Baxter? And how on earth did you make his acquaintance?"

He forced himself back to the matter at hand. "If my suspicions are correct, his real name is Morgan Judd."

"Judd?"

"I am sorry to say it, but we were friends at Oxford."

"Friends?" Her voice sharpened in disbelief. "Did you share the same bond with this Morgan Judd that you did with Anthony Tiles?"

"Yes. Morgan was also a bastard. He was the offspring of the heir to an earldom and the daughter of country gentry. His mother died in childbirth. His father ignored his existence but his mother's family saw to it that he was educated as a gentleman. I do not think that Morgan ever forgave either of his parents."

"He blamed them for depriving him of his proper station in life?"

"Yes."

"Was it only the bond of your mutual lack of legitimacy that connected you to Morgan Judd?"

"At first, yes." Baxter watched a carriage pass in the street. "But Morgan and I shared something else as well. Something that was even more binding. An interest in chemistry."

"I believe I begin to understand."

"At Oxford, they called us the Two Alchemists. We spent every waking moment in the study of chemistry. We set up a laboratory in our lodgings and used our clothing allowances to purchase glassware and equipment. When the others met to drink coffee and read poetry in the evenings, Morgan and I conducted experiments. We lived and breathed science."

"What happened?" Charlotte asked.

"We drifted apart after Oxford. We corresponded for a time. Exchanged news of the results of our chemical work. But after a while we simply lost contact. Morgan lived in London for a while but we rarely encountered each other."

"There is more to that part of the story than you have told me," Charlotte said gently.

"You are perceptive. The truth is that, in addition to chemistry, Morgan had...other interests, which I did not share. Those interests became increasingly important to him after Oxford. He grew obsessive where they were concerned."

"What sort of interests?"

"He was drawn to the worst hells and the most unpleasant brothels. As time went on, his tastes in such things grew more jaded and debauched. There was something in him that fed on the darker side of life."

"No wonder your friendship failed."

"He also became keenly interested in the metaphysical and the occult sciences. At first those subjects were a game to him. He toyed with them in the manner of the Romantic poets. But by the time he left Oxford, it was all much more than an amusing diversion. He had begun to talk of fulfilling his true destiny."

"Destiny." Charlotte repeated the word in a soft, troubled voice. "I vow, the word haunts me."

Baxter turned slowly around to face her. "I saw him briefly on the street once several years ago. He told me that I was a fool because I had not used my knowledge of chemistry to forge a grand destiny for myself."

"You said that you thought he was dead. What happened to him?"

"Do you recall my small adventure on behalf of the Crown?"

"Baxter, are you telling me that was connected to Morgan Judd?"

"Yes. He was working for Napoleon. Creating lethal chemical vapors intended to be used against our people. I used our past friendship to convince him that I wished to work with him. I told him that I had changed my mind about forging a great destiny."

"I see."

"I betrayed him," Baxter said. "I told him that I wanted to share the wealth and power that Napoleon had promised. But once I had verified what he was about, I destroyed his laboratory and notes. There was a terrible explosion. I barely escaped with my life."

"The acid," she whispered.

"He threw it at me in the course of the struggle."

"Dear heaven. He could have blinded you."

"Yes, well, I was trying to ruin him at the time."

"He deserved it." Charlotte paused. "You believed him dead in the explosion?"

"I was certain of it. A body was found two days later. Burned beyond recognition. But Morgan's rings were on the fingers of the corpse. There was no reason not to think that it was Judd who had perished."

"It is very strange." Charlotte's voice was so low that it was barely audible. "But I am almost convinced that I once encountered Morgan Judd myself."

He turned to look at her. "The monster in the hall outside Ariel's door?"

"Yes." She shuddered and hugged herself very tightly as though she had suddenly become very chilled. "That night he asked me if I believed in destiny. The man in the black domino who gave me the rose asked the same question."

"Bloody hell."

"But the speech of the two men was so

vastly different." Charlotte searched his face. "The monster I met five years ago had a voice that could have lured one down into hell."

"That is the thing that makes no sense." Baxter took off his eyeglasses and plucked the handkerchief from his pocket. "Morgan Judd's voice was a well-tuned instrument. There is no other way to describe it. When he read poetry aloud, his listeners were enthralled. When he spoke, heads turned to listen. He could have given Kean competition on the stage had he chosen to tread the boards."

"But the magician's voice is just the opposite. It makes me think of shattered glass." Charlotte frowned. "Although it is strangely fascinating in a bizarre fashion."

"If I am right and we are dealing with Morgan Judd, then there are two possible explanations for the change in his voice."

"What are they?"

"The first is that he is deliberately manipulating it so that he won't be recognized."

Charlotte shook her head. "I don't think that is the case. You would have to hear him to understand. His is a voice that has been damaged."

"Then we must consider the second possibility."

"What is that?"

"I did not escape that explosion and fire unscathed." Baxter finished polishing his eyeglasses. "I was marked for life. Perhaps Morgan was also."

"I don't understand. Miss Post said nothing about scars or injuries when she described him to us. She said that he was as handsome as Lucifer himself. Except for his voice."

"There were many unusual and dangerous chemicals in Morgan's laboratory that night," Baxter said. "Who knows what caustic vapors were released during the explosion and fire?"

"Do you think that some of them might have been powerful enough to affect a man's throat if he inhaled them?"

"It's possible." Baxter pushed his eyeglasses back onto his nose. "Whatever the case, we know that the magician is dangerous. He killed Drusilla Heskett and he tried to murder Miss Post and young Norris."

"Baxter, he knows that we are investigating him."

"Yes. On two occasions he tried to discourage our alliance by attacking your trust in me. By now he must know that he has failed."

"He most certainly has."

Baxter smiled faintly. "You do me a great honor, Charlotte."

"Nonsense. I deal in fact."

What had he expected? he wondered. Had he really thought that she would tell him she believed in him because her passion for him was so deep? He was turning into an idiot.

He cleared his throat. "Yes, well, I appreciate your support, nonetheless. We must hope that Morgan will assume he is safe for the moment."

"Because he will believe that the only person who can identify him is dead?"

"Yes, but there is no way to know how long we can continue to make him think that Juliana Post expired from the effects of the incense."

Charlotte drummed her fingers on the back of the sofa. "We must act quickly."

"I shall arrange to take a look around the upper floor of The Green Table tonight. In the meantime, we must continue to behave as if nothing out of the ordinary has occurred. It is imperative that we give no sign to indicate that we are any closer to identifying the killer now than we were yesterday."

"I assume that means we must attend the usual number of levees and soirees this evening."

"Yes. And your sister and my aunt must also continue with their customary routine. But I am going to take steps to make certain that all of you are well guarded."

Charlotte glanced at him in surprise. "What do you mean?"

"I shall hire a pair of Bow Street Runners. One to keep an eye on you, Ariel, and Aunt Rosalind while the three of you are out this evening. The other to keep watch on this house."

She gave him a wan smile. "I will not argue with you."

"I cannot tell you how relieved I am to hear that."

"But," she added quickly, "I really do believe that I can be of assistance to you tonight when you search the premises of The Green Table."

"No. I forbid you to accompany me and that is final."

"But, Baxter, you must take someone with you. I won't hear of you going in there alone."

Anger, fueled by fears for her safety, swept through him. "Charlotte, this is a deadly affair. You will do as I tell you. There will be no further discussion of the matter."

"Really, Baxter, you are behaving abominably. You have no right to make every decision. I am the one who launched the investigation and I will not tolerate your high-handed, arrogant manner. You are not my husband, you know."

Baxter sucked in his breath. "I am very well aware of that, Miss Arkendale. I am only your lover, am I not?"

Someone moved in the parlor doorway. Baxter turned quickly and saw Hamilton standing there.

"I beg your pardon," Hamilton said. He looked embarrassed. "I told your housekeeper I could announce myself. Am I interrupting?"

"Not at all," Charlotte said. "Do come in, Hamilton. Ariel is out at the moment but I expect her very shortly."

Hamilton moved hesitantly into the parlor. "Actually, I came in search of Baxter. His butler told me that he might be here."

"What do you want?" Baxter asked. "I'm busy."

"I understand." Hamilton's mouth tightened. "I came to offer my assistance."

"Baxter is making plans to search the top

floor of The Green Table tonight," Charlotte said.

Hamilton glanced at her and then looked directly at Baxter. "Perhaps I can help. I know my way around the premises, at least as far as the floor where the club members gather."

"I do not require your assistance," Baxter said swiftly.

Hamilton's expression tightened.

"Baxter, pray consider his offer," Charlotte said. "Your brother's knowledge of the club premises would be extremely useful."

Baxter flexed his hands. "You don't understand."

"Of course I do," she said crisply. "You feel bound by your oath to your father. You promised to look after Hamilton, not put him in harm's way."

"Hell's teeth, I'm not a child," Hamilton snapped. "I don't need a nanny."

"Quite right," Charlotte said. She turned to Baxter. "I'm certain that your father did not intend for you to protect Hamilton all of his life. He wanted his heir to mature into manhood."

Hamilton threw her a grateful look. Then he glared at Baxter. "For God's sake, I'm two-and-twenty. When is someone going to notice that I am already a man?"

Baxter gazed at him for a long moment. His father's dying words rang in his head. *I know I can trust you to look after Hamilton.*

"Your knowledge of the club might prove

useful," he conceded reluctantly. "But the situation is not free of risk."

"That bloody magician very nearly got my best friend killed this morning," Hamilton said fiercely. "Who knows what he will do next? I have a right to help expose him."

Baxter glanced at Charlotte. To his surprise, she had nothing to say. She inclined her head a fraction of an inch in silent encouragement.

When did a boy become a man? Baxter wondered. He did not know the answer because he could not recall ever having been a child. It seemed to him that he had been obliged to uphold the responsibilities of an adult all of his life.

"Very well," he said quietly. "We shall make our plans. For God's sake, don't tell your mother."

Hamilton's tense features relaxed into the fabled Esherton grin. "Never. You have my oath on it."

I hope I do not regret this," Baxter said later that night.

He stood beside Charlotte at the edge of the dance floor. The Hawkmore affair was a crush. It would be the talk of the ton tomorrow. Tonight, it offered perfect cover.

If Morgan Judd employed spies, they would find it difficult to keep track of anyone in this throng. With luck, no one would even notice when he and Hamilton slipped away to depart for The Green Table.

"I know it was not easy for you to accept Hamilton's offer of assistance," Charlotte said. "But this is a perfect opportunity for you to show him that you have faith in him."

"He still seems so damnably young in so many ways. The very fact that he got involved in The Green Table club is proof that he's hardly mature."

"I suspect that Hamilton has learned much from this experience. It's obvious that Norris's brush with death had a very sobering effect on him."

"I cannot deny that. Nevertheless—"

"Look at the bright side, Baxter. Taking Hamilton with you tonight gives you the ideal excuse for refusing my assistance in the venture."

Baxter smiled in spite of his uneasy mood. "You have a succinct way of summing up a situation, my dear. I wondered why you dropped your demands to accompany me. Now I see that you simply could not pass up the opportunity to help forge a brotherly bond between Hamilton and myself."

"The bond already exists. You have honored it even as you have denied it." She fixed him with very serious eyes. "Have a care tonight, Baxter."

"I've told you often enough, it's not my nature to take foolish risks."

"No, indeed, you prefer to take calculated

risks. To my mind, they are far more dangerous." She touched the sleeve of his coat. "I shall wait up for you."

"There is no need. I'll call upon you in the morning to tell you what we discovered, if anything."

"No. Please come to see me tonight when you've accomplished your task. I do not care how late it is. I will not sleep until I know that you and Hamilton are safely away from The Green Table."

"Very well." He looked down at her gloved hand resting on the black fabric of his coat. A flash of intense sensation went through him.

She cares.

For all her wariness of the male sex, Charlotte seemed to trust him. And for all his years of self-imposed solitude, he suddenly knew that he would be very lonely when Charlotte went out of his life.

Whatever this emotion was that had so disrupted his orderly, peaceful existence, it was more than fleeting passion.

An overwhelming sense of urgency gripped him. It had nothing to do with The Green Table. He closed his own hand tightly over Charlotte's.

"Baxter?" She gave him a quizzical glance. "Is something wrong?"

"No. Yes." He struggled to find the words he needed to argue his point in a logical fashion. "When this is finished, I wish to speak to you about the future of our liaison."

She blinked. "The future?"

"Bloody hell, Charlotte, we cannot go on like this. Surely you can comprehend that."

"I thought everything was going quite smoothly."

"An affair is all very well for a few weeks."

"A few weeks?"

"Perhaps even a few months," he conceded. "But in the end the whole thing becomes quite tedious."

A great stillness came over her. "Yes, of course. Tedious."

Relieved that she had grasped the point so quickly, Baxter plunged on. "There is the enormous inconvenience, for one thing."

"Inconvenience."

"All that damned scurrying about to find a suitable place to, uh, display our mutual feelings," he explained. "I mean, it's all very well to use a laboratory bench, or the carriage, or the library sofa on occasion, but over the long term, I suspect it will prove extremely tiresome."

"I see. Tiresome."

"A man of my years prefers the comfort of his own bed." He had a sudden, extremely vivid recollection of how little a bed had mattered on the few occasions when he had made love to Charlotte. "In the main."

"Baxter, you're only thirty-two."

"Age has nothing to do with it. I was never inclined toward a career as an acrobat."

She lowered her eyes. "I have always found you to be quite agile, sir."

He decided to ignore that. "And then there is the constant threat of gossip. It can be quite unpleasant. As we discussed, it might well have an ill effect on your business."

She pursed her lips. "Yes, I suppose so."

He cudgeled his brain for other arguments. The most obvious one hit him with a force that twisted his insides. He drew a breath to steady himself. "And you must consider the possibility of pregnancy."

"I understand that there are devices that a gentleman can wear that will prevent that sort of thing."

"It may very well be entirely too late," he said grimly. "That is the great difficulty with an affair, you see. One cannot always control the situation. Charlotte, there are any number of reasons why our liaison cannot go on indefinitely."

She gazed at him and said not a word. At that moment Baxter would have bargained away the secret of the Philosopher's Stone to be able to read the expression in her eyes. And then she glanced past his shoulder and smiled.

Hamilton coughed discreetly. "Baxter? According to our plans, it's time for us to leave."

"Bloody hell." Baxter glanced over his shoulder. Hamilton and Ariel stood just behind him. He could only hope they had not overheard the conversation. "Time. Yes. We must be off."

"Baxter." Charlotte touched his arm again.

"You will remember your promise to call upon me later this evening."

"Yes, yes, I'll stop by on the way home to give you a full account." He nodded brusquely to Ariel and turned to make his way through the crowd toward the entrance.

Hamilton raised one faintly derisive brow and then paused to bend gallantly over both Charlotte's and Ariel's hands. They curtsied gracefully.

Baxter stifled a groan. He would only make himself look ridiculous if he turned back now to attempt a more charming leave-taking, he thought.

Hamilton leaned against the green velvet squabs of his sleek, well-sprung carriage and eyed Baxter with amused eyes. "Why don't you just come straight out and ask her to marry you?"

"What the devil are you talking about?" Baxter muttered.

"I heard enough of the conversation to conclude that you were trying to convince Charlotte to consider a proposal of marriage rather than a liaison. Why beat about the bush?"

"The nature of my association with Miss Arkendale is none of your concern."

Hamilton idly examined his ebony walking stick. "As you wish."

"Furthermore, if you dare to mention the word *liaison* in connection with her name again, I can guarantee that not only will you never take possession of your fortune, you will find yourself lacking several front teeth the next time you try to use your smile to charm a lady."

"That serious, is it?"

"I suggest we change the subject."

Hamilton shook his head. "You may be a man of science, brother, but you are hopelessly inept when it comes to dealing with the ladies. You should spend more time reading Shelley and Byron and less studying chemistry."

"It's a bit late to try to reshape my entire character. Not much point, in any event."

"Why do you say that? It's obvious Charlotte has a *tendre* for you."

Baxter was annoyed by the spark of hope that flickered within him. "Do you think so?"

"No question about it."

"She may care for me but I don't believe that she cares for the notion of marriage."

"Well, then, it's up to you to convince her that marriage to you would be a sound decision."

Baxter scowled. "That is precisely what I was trying to do when you interrupted me a few minutes ago."

Hamilton gave him a knowing smile. "Father believed that I had a great deal to learn from you. But perhaps there are a few things that you could learn from me. Feel free to ask for my advice any time you require it."

"We have a rather more pressing matter on our hands at the moment, in case it has slipped your mind."

"It has not."

"Did you bring your pistol?"

"Yes, of course." Hamilton patted the pocket of his greatcoat. "Two of them, in fact. What about you?"

"I've never practiced enough to become a decent shot. I depend upon other tools."

"What do you mean?"

Baxter removed one of the glass vials from his pocket. He held it out on his palm. "Items such as this."

Hamilton looked intrigued. "What is it?"

"A sort of instantaneous light. Break the glass and there is a small, very bright explosion. It can light one's way for two or three minutes or temporarily blind an opponent. If it is held next to combustible material such as kindling, it will ignite a fire."

"Damned clever. Where did you get these?"

"I make them in my laboratory."

Hamilton gave him an odd smile. "Perhaps I should have paid a bit more attention to *Conversations on Chemistry*. When this is over, do you think you might have time to show me how to perform some of your more interesting experiments?"

"If you like." Baxter hesitated. "It has been a long while since I had a colleague to assist me."

Hamilton grinned. "Lately I have begun to wonder if I got some of Father's passion for science, after all."

Baxter glumly considered his bleak future. "I have begun to suspect that I may have got a bit more of his passion for other things than I had previously believed."

Eighteen

Charlotte sipped lemonade and surveyed the crowded ballroom floor, where Ariel was engaged in the waltz with yet another distinguished and rather besotted-looking young gentleman. Pleased with the glow of pleasure on Ariel's face, she smiled at Rosalind, who had come to stand beside her.

"Lady Trengloss, I wish to thank you for what you have done for Ariel. My mother would have been so pleased to know that my sister had a taste of a London Season."

"It has been my pleasure. Haven't had an opportunity to fire a young lady off into the ton since my last niece came out. Forgotten how much fun it all is." Rosalind wielded her elegantly painted silk fan with enthusiasm. "Ariel is a charming young woman. She has attracted any number of admirers."

Charlotte sighed. "I fear that all of them will swiftly disappear once it becomes known that my engagement to your nephew has been called off. I confess, I worried about that a great deal at the start of this business, but Ariel insists that she does not care a fig if her admirers vanish when they learn the truth."

"She is very levelheaded for her tender

years." Rosalind gave Charlotte a sidelong glance. "For which you must take the credit, I believe, my dear."

"Not at all. She has always been inclined in a practical direction. Ariel quite rightly declares the Season to be a fine source of entertainment, rather like the theater. She tells me that when the curtain falls, she will be content to go back to her usual pursuits."

Charlotte prayed that would be the case. Ariel was still so young. No matter how much common sense one possessed at nineteen, life was bound to seem a bit dull when the invitations and the posies ceased arriving at the door. The important thing was that Ariel did not get her heart broken during her brief experience of Society.

As for her own heart, Charlotte thought, her only hope was to immerse herself in her work until it mended. But she knew that no matter how many new clients she took on or how many interesting inquiries and researches she made into the backgrounds of gentlemen, she would never be able to forget her lover with the alchemist's eyes. There could never be another Baxter.

Rosalind gave her a considering look. "As long as we are discussing such matters, I feel that I should tell you that I am as grateful to you as you say you are to me."

"If you refer to my investigations, I assure you I entered into them for my own purposes."

"I was not speaking of the murder inquiries."

Rosalind folded her fan with a snap. "I may as well be blunt. I have been concerned about Baxter ever since he returned from Italy three years ago. He had always been far too somber for his years. Even as a child, he possessed an unnerving degree of self-mastery and restraint. He always kept a certain distance between himself and others."

"As though he were observing and measuring you the way he would examine one of his chemical experiments?"

"Indeed." Rosalind shuddered delicately. "Quite disconcerting at times. But after the dreadful accident in Italy, he disappeared from Society altogether. He almost never emerged from that cave he calls a laboratory. I feared he was developing a distinct tendency toward melancholia."

"Melancholia?"

"There is a strain of it in the blood, you know."

Charlotte frowned. "I was not aware of that. Everyone says that his parents were an outrageously charming, exciting pair who were the talk of Society. I understood them to be full of the liveliest spirits."

"A bit too lively at times," Rosalind said quietly. "There was a price to be paid for such strong passions. And I do not speak of reputations."

"I understand. It has been my observation that people of strong passions often have both a dark and a light side to their temperaments. It is as if nature sought to forge some sort of balance in their humors but in the process created extremes."

"Very observant, my dear. That is precisely how it was with Baxter's parents. Esherton, for all his intellect and delight in life, had a dangerous temper and a tendency toward great recklessness. It's a miracle he survived to enjoy old age. As for my sister..."

"What about her?" Charlotte prompted.

"She was beautiful, intelligent, and gloriously effervescent. Most of the time. She indulged her independence and her eccentricities. Everyone who knew her was enthralled by her, even when she behaved outrageously. Only her family and her most intimate friends knew that on occasion she would sink into the depths of melancholia."

"It would seem that Baxter became an alchemist out of sheer necessity," Charlotte said.

"Alchemist? Whatever do you mean by that?"

"I believe he sees himself as the product of a mix of extremely volatile chemicals. He felt he had no choice but to learn to control the fires that might ignite dangerous explosions."

Rosalind's brows rose. "An interesting analogy. What I wished to say, my dear, is that I believe you to be the best thing that has happened to Baxter in years."

Charlotte was so startled, she nearly dropped her lemonade. "Lady Trengloss. That is very kind of you but surely you overstate the case."

"It's no less than the truth. You appear to

understand him and deal with him in a way that no one else can quite manage."

"Come now, he is not all that mysterious."

"Actually, he is, but that is beside the point. Pardon my curiosity, but I must ask you a very personal question."

Charlotte eyed her warily. "Yes?"

"There is no delicate way to phrase this so I shall come straight out with it. Has Baxter by any chance mentioned the possibility of a real marriage between the two of you?"

"No." Charlotte took a deep breath. "He has not." *And a short while ago he as much as told me that there was no possibility of any other sort of long-standing connection, either.*

Their passionate liaison had become inconvenient. It seemed to Charlotte that the brilliant glow of the chandelier dimmed for a moment.

But she had more pressing concerns, she thought. She would not rest easily tonight until she knew for certain that Baxter was safe.

❧

Baxter raised his candle to view the empty chamber in which he and Hamilton stood. He studied the unmarked layer of dust on the floor. "No signs of anyone having been in this room for years."

It was as though they walked through an abandoned house, he thought. The thick walls and heavy floor timbers muffled even the noisy reverberations of the crowded gaming room on the ground floor.

The upper story of The Green Table was another realm, a gray, spectral world where only a magician would feel at home.

"This makes the fourth chamber we've investigated up here," Hamilton said. "I vow, I'm expecting to see a specter at any moment."

"Only someone inclined toward Romantic poetry or Gothic novels would see ghosts in these rooms."

"As it happens, I'm inclined toward both the poetry and the novels," Hamilton said cheerfully.

Baxter shot him a speculative glance. "I do believe that you're enjoying yourself."

"This is the most exciting thing I've done in months." Hamilton grinned. "Who would have thought that I'd be in your company when I did it?"

"I'm aware that you find me hopelessly boring, Esherton. But bear in mind that I hold the purse strings of your fortune for another few years."

"You certainly know how to ruin the mood."

Baxter turned to leave the dusty chamber. "Come. Time grows short and there's still one more room on this floor." With a last glance at the undisturbed chamber, he walked back out into the hall.

"I'm right behind you, brother." Hamilton followed quietly.

Baxter went toward the closed door located at the end of the corridor. An old, tattered carpet that stretched the length of the hall silenced his footsteps.

"This one should prove more interesting than the others." Baxter came to a halt in front of the central door.

"Why do you say that?"

"This chamber is located almost directly over the one you and your friends use for the meetings of your secret club."

Hamilton studied the door with interest. "What of it?"

"You say your magician appears without warning. One moment he is not in the room, the next, he is standing in your midst."

"You believe he descends into our meeting chamber from this room?"

"As I told Charlotte, this mansion was once a brothel. Such establishments are commonly equipped with peepholes and hidden staircases."

"Good God." Hamilton gazed at him in frank astonishment. "Are you saying that you actually discuss such things with Miss Arkendale?"

"Charlotte is a lady of many varied and unusual interests." Baxter surveyed the doorknob. There was no film of dust to mar the metal. It gleamed dully in the flickering light. Someone had recently entered this chamber.

"If a discussion of brothels constitutes your notion of polite conversation, it's little wonder that you've never experienced much luck with the ladies, Baxter." Hamilton reached out to open the door. "I really must remember to give you some pointers." He grinned over his shoulder as he pushed the door open and walked into the room.

Baxter felt rather than heard the rumble of hidden gears. "Hamilton, wait."

"What's the matter?" Hamilton took the candle from him and strode into the center of the chamber. He glanced at Baxter, who hesitated on the threshold. "The place is empty, just like the others. Is something...*Baxter, the door.*"

Baxter sensed the movement overhead. He looked up and saw a solid gate fashioned of iron. With a sound like that of a sword being drawn from a scabbard, it descended swiftly downward out of the lintel. He realized that when it was in place it would seal the chamber.

He only had a second to make a decision. He could either retreat back out into the hall or join Hamilton inside the treacherous chamber.

"Bloody hell." He crouched and threw himself swiftly across the threshold.

With a soft, sighing scream, the iron door slammed into the floor.

"Christ." Hamilton stared at the metal wall that now occupied the space where the door had been. "We're trapped."

A sudden, acute silence descended.

Baxter straightened. He saw that Hamilton was correct. The single window was covered with an iron shutter.

"Opening the door and crossing the threshold obviously triggers the mechanism that activates the gate," Baxter mused. "Quite clever. Presumably the owner of this place knows how to prevent that guillotine from carving him up like a leg of mutton every time he enters this chamber. Must be a hidden switch somewhere on the outside wall."

Hamilton whirled to face him. "Baxter, this is not an interesting little problem to be solved with scientific deduction. We're trapped."

"Perhaps." Baxter continued to study the chamber.

Unlike the other rooms on the top floor, this one was sumptuously furnished. There was a heavily draped bed, a large wardrobe, a massive desk, and a Chinese screen. A stone fireplace occupied one wall.

He began to prowl the room. "Perhaps not."

"What the devil does that mean? I must tell you, Baxter, this is no time to become cryptic and inscrutable."

"Give me a moment to think."

"You should have stayed out in the corridor," Hamilton muttered. "Why did you enter this chamber when you saw that the gate was closing? Now we are both locked inside this place. If you had remained outside, at least you would have been free."

"Whoever designed this room will have been clever enough to ensure that he had an escape route for himself," Baxter said absently.

He took the candle and held it aloft. He saw the note on the wide desk immediately. The sheet of foolscap was folded and sealed.

"Even if there is a means of escape, how are we to find it?" Hamilton demanded. "Baxter, we could be trapped in here until we die of thirst or hunger. No one will hear us through these walls."

Baxter did not respond. His entire attention was riveted on the note. He walked toward the desk.

"Baxter? What is it?"

"A message." Baxter set down the candle. He picked up the note and looked at the seal. The wax was embossed with the same alchemical image that Drusilla Heskett had drawn in her watercolor sketchbook. A triangle within a circle. "From the magician, I believe."

Hamilton hurried toward him. "What does it say?"

Baxter broke the seal and unfolded the crisp foolscap. There was only a single line on the page.

A man who is born without a destiny must fashion one for himself.

"What does it mean?" Hamilton asked.

"It means that we were expected." Baxter crushed the note in his fist. "Come. There is no time to delay."

"I'm quite willing to leave this chamber." Hamilton narrowed his eyes. "How, precisely, do you suggest we accomplish that feat? Neither of us is small enough to get up that chimney."

Baxter started to tell him that the wardrobe

was the most likely place to conceal the entrance to a hidden staircase. But a familiar odor stopped him cold.

"Incense," he muttered. "Bloody hell."

Hamilton frowned. "Yes. I can smell it." He glanced around the room in consternation. "But how is it entering this chamber? There is no brazier in here."

Baxter turned toward the fireplace and held the candle aloft. Great puffs of pale, smoky vapor billowed silently out of the cold stone hearth. "Someone on the roof is using a large bellows to force the incense down into this room."

"It is not quite the same fragrance as the incense that we use in our meetings. Stronger. Not as pleasant." Hamilton coughed. "And there is far too much of it. Good God, what are they trying to do to us?"

"Use your cravat to shield your nose and mouth." Baxter pulled his own neckcloth free and quickly fashioned a mask for the lower half of his face.

Hamilton did the same.

Baxter turned back to the wardrobe and yanked open the doors. "There has to be a mechanism here somewhere. Your magician appeared out of the wardrobe in the chamber downstairs."

He touched one of the panels at the back with questing fingertips. Then he prodded the bottom.

"The incense is too heavy." Hamilton's voice was muffled by his cravat. "It will choke us to death."

Baxter glanced at him. Hamilton was staring, transfixed, at the ugly clouds that roiled forth from the fireplace.

"I could use some assistance here, Esherton." Baxter deliberately put an icy, authoritative edge on his words. He needed to get Hamilton's full attention.

Hamilton swung around with an odd, jerky movement. Above the edge of his makeshift mask, his eyes were slightly glazed. "What... what do you want me to do?"

Baxter's fingers brushed against two small indentations in the corner of the wardrobe. "I believe I've found our escape route." He tugged hard. The back panel of the wardrobe swung open with a well-oiled squeak. A shadowed opening appeared.

"A staircase." Hamilton gazed at the narrow flight of steps that led down into the darkness. "How did you know it would be here?"

"I saw how your magician materialized in the chamber below the other night. There had to be a staircase in this wall. It was the only solution."

"You saw him? Baxter, you never cease to amaze me these days. Discovering this staircase was a damned brilliant deduction."

"Simple logic." Baxter picked up the candle and stepped into the wardrobe. "As I said, the brothel that previously occupied these premises catered to exotic tastes. Patrons paid extra to use staircases and peepholes in order to watch the activities taking place in various rooms."

Hamilton stepped into the wardrobe behind him. "For a chemist, you seem to know a great deal about this sort of thing."

"I cannot take the credit." Baxter started down the small staircase. "Father mentioned this particular brothel to me on one or two occasions. He was something of an expert on such establishments. Close the wardrobe door. It will block some of the incense."

"Father had a wife, by God." Hamilton shut the wardrobe door. "And a mistress, too, come to that. Why in blazes did he frequent brothels?"

"An excellent question." Baxter inhaled and caught the tang of incense through the linen neckcloth. "Damn. The incense is seeping through the wardrobe doors. Hurry."

"I feel a little odd." Hamilton's boots thudded softly on the steps. "My head is spinning."

"It cannot be far." Baxter sucked in his breath as the flame of his candle suddenly blossomed into a blinding, golden ball of fire. He nearly dropped the taper. "Bloody hell."

This batch of incense was very powerful, indeed. It was already affecting his senses, even in a limited dose.

"Baxter?"

"Don't stop."

It seemed to take forever to negotiate the cramped staircase. Invisible tendrils of the vapor followed them. Baxter realized he was staring too intently at the candle flame. He had a sudden, overwhelming urge to throw himself headfirst into it.

Hamilton's hand clamped unsteadily on his shoulder. "Everything is so strange. This incense is foul stuff."

Loud footsteps echoed from the chamber above just as Baxter stumbled into a wooden panel set into the wall.

"There's someone up there," Hamilton whispered. "Looking for us."

Baxter listened to the voices as he fumbled with the panel.

"Where are they?" a man growled. "I won't stay in this room long, I tell ye. Not even with these masks."

"They're in here somewhere. They tripped the snare, didn't they? Must have fainted by now. Collapsed on the other side of that desk or behind the screen, most likely."

"Hurry. The magician said that too much of this damned smoke can kill. He wants 'em alive."

Baxter found a handle. He shoved hard. The wooden panel moved silently aside. The candlelight revealed the inside of another wardrobe. For some reason it required an enormous effort to open the doors.

The room beyond was empty and unlit.

He staggered out of the wardrobe.

"I recognize this place," Hamilton whispered as he followed Baxter. He jerked off his cravat and drew a deep breath. "This is the room where the members of my club gather for our experiments. Always wondered how the magician managed the trick of appearing when we summoned him."

Voices from the chamber above echoed eerily down the staircase.

"Hell's teeth, they're not here," one of the men shouted. He sounded on the edge of panic.

"They've got to be here." There was sharp desperation in the other rough voice. "We heard 'em when we were on the roof."

"Look behind the screen."

"Smoke is so damned thick in here, it's hard to see. Got to find 'em. Pete and Long Hank will have the Arkendale female by now. If we don't bring St. Ives to him, the magician will murder us with one of his bloody tricks."

Baxter shoved Hamilton toward the door. "Go. Find Charlotte. Maybe it's not too late."

"You hired Runners to protect her."

"I cannot rely on them."

"But what about you?" Hamilton demanded softly.

"I must let them take me."

"No."

Baxter met his eyes. "Don't you understand? If they've already got Charlotte, then it's the only way I'll find her."

"But what if they don't have her yet? You'll be risking your neck for naught."

"I know how to look after myself. Just go. You must try to protect Charlotte."

Hamilton's eyes, still watering from the effects of the incense, were eloquent with reluctant understanding. He nodded once, abruptly, and then, without a word, whirled and ran to the door.

Baxter took a deep breath of the relatively fresh air in the room and stepped back inside the hidden staircase. He slid the panel shut and started up the steps.

"The bed," one of the men in the room above said hoarsely. "Look beneath the bed."

Baxter made it to the top of the steps. The vapor was not so strong as it had been a few minutes earlier. The men had opened the iron gate and allowed fresh air into the chamber. Nevertheless, there was enough of the incense left to unsettle his concentration. He had to work very hard to make his way quietly into the wardrobe.

"There ain't anyone under the bed. This is bloody strange, if you ask me. Maybe we're dealing with another magician."

"Don't be a fool. Look inside the wardrobe."

Baxter got the secret panel at the back of the wardrobe closed. He collapsed on the bottom of the heavy wooden closet in what he hoped was a realistic faint.

The wardrobe doors slammed open.

"One of 'em's in here." The voice was thick with relief. "He's wearing spectacles. Must be St. Ives. No sign of the other one, though."

"Then we bloody well don't tell the magician that there was a second cove with him," the other man said decisively. "It'll be our necks, if he finds out one got away."

"Agreed. But where did the other one go?"

"Must have got out before the trap closed. Don't matter none. St. Ives is the important one. And from the looks of things he'll be sound asleep for a good long while."

Rough hands reached for Baxter. He forced himself to remain limp and unresponsive as he was dragged from the wardrobe.

His eyes were already closed in order to add credence to his role, so he decided that he might as well say a prayer. *Let Hamilton get to Charlotte before the magician's men do.*

Nineteen

An hour later Baxter lay on a cold stone floor and listened to the voices of the two guards.

"St. Ives don't look so bloody dangerous. Waste of time foolin' about with that damned incense, if ye ask me. Would have been a lot simpler to just use a pistol."

"You heard what the magician said." There was a defensive note in the second voice. "St. Ives is trickier than he appears."

"Far as I'm concerned, you and Virgil got the easy one. The Arkendale female nearly scratched me eyes out, she did. Brained poor Long Hank with that reticule of hers. He's still got a headache. Got a tongue like a fishwife on her, too."

So much for his faint hope that Hamilton would get to Charlotte before Morgan Judd's men did, Baxter thought.

"We must have used a mite too much of the incense on St. Ives," the second man said uneasily. "Still sound asleep."

"Good thing you didn't accidentally kill him with that damned vapor. The magician wouldn't have been pleased. He wants to handle that part of the business himself."

There was a short silence. The second man lowered his voice. "Does it strike ye that the man's becoming bloody odd?"

"Who? St. Ives? From what I've heard, he's always been a bit odd."

"Not St. Ives, ye fool, the magician."

The first man cackled softly. "I'll wager that he's always been odd, too. But he pays well." Boots sounded on the stone as he made for the door. "I'm going down to the kitchens to get something to eat. Give that damned bell pull a yank when St. Ives opens his eyes."

"The magician said I was to signal him first. Ye know what he's like if we don't do exactly what he tells us."

"Bloody magician and his bloody signal device."

"Bring back a slice of that ham pie for me." The man who had been left to guard Baxter raised his voice. "And some ale. From the looks of this cove, I'm going to be here awhile."

There was a muffled response, footsteps receded down a stone hall, and then silence fell.

Baxter considered the situation. It was not unlike a laboratory experiment. A mix of volatile substances had been brought together in a crucible and set over a fire. But in this case he was not the detached observer who stood back and made notes. He was one of the chemicals in the mixture.

They had searched his clothing before

bundling him into the carriage. One of the men had taken his knife. He was relieved to discover that he still had his eyeglasses. He could feel the wire frames curved around his ears. He had feared losing them once or twice during the hectic hourlong carriage ride.

Fortunately he'd had the cab of the darkened vehicle to himself during the journey. His captors, apparently certain that their bound and drugged victim would not cause any problems, had elected to share the driver's box and a pint of gin.

Baxter had occupied himself with the task of slicing through his bindings. He had been obliged to break the lens of his watch case in order to create a sharp edge. But the makeshift knife had proven effective. The men who had carried him up the staircase a few minutes ago had not noticed that only some shreds of fiber held the rope in place around his wrists.

He remained quiet a moment longer, mulling over possibilities, contingencies, and probabilities.

As in the case of any good experiment, chemical or alchemical, it all came down to fire. And as in any interesting experiment, there was always the risk of an explosion.

Baxter stirred, groaned, and opened his eyes.

A short, squat, heavily built man, who had been lounging on a stool several feet away, surged to his feet. A large pistol was stuck into his belt. He gave Baxter a relieved, gap-toothed grin.

"Here now. Decided to wake up, did ye?" The guard came to stand over him. "About time. The magician's been waitin' for ye. Said I was to send him the signal when ye opened yer eyes. Reckon I'd better get to it."

"A moment, if you please." Baxter smashed his booted foot into the guard's leg.

The heavy man muttered a choked yelp, staggered back, and clawed at the pistol in his belt. "Ye stupid cove. That won't do ye any good."

Baxter snapped the remaining threads of rope around his wrists and rolled up off the floor in a single motion.

The guard's eyes widened at the sight of Baxter's untied hands. He reeled to the side but his injured leg gave way. Baxter was on him in an instant. He slammed a fist into the guard's jaw.

The pistol clattered on the floor. Baxter scooped it up, cocked it, and got to his feet. He aimed the weapon at the man's broad midsection.

"I'm not accounted a good shot, but this is a very large target."

The guard blinked several times and looked quite baffled. "The magician said ye'd be right muddleheaded and slow when the effects of the incense wore off."

"The magician was wrong," Baxter said softly. "Now, tell me about the bloody signal device."

Charlotte tugged desperately on the length of rope that tethered her wrists to the post of the vast crimson bed. She had been struggling with the knot ever since the kidnappers had left her alone in the chamber.

She had some range of movement because of the extension of the rope, but the knot itself was still tight. If she sat straight up, she could raise her hands as high as the velvet fringe of the hangings but that was as far as she could go.

The bed was massive. Its four heavily carved posts were adorned with images of strange, mythical creatures. Snakes, dragons, and phoenixes were so finely wrought that they appeared to writhe in the wood.

She surveyed the stone chamber and concluded that the bed suited the room. A thick crimson and black carpet covered the stone floor. The mantelpiece was fashioned of black granite. Heavy scarlet drapes trimmed with black silk fringe hung from the windows and pooled on the floor.

Everything in the chamber was trimmed in hues of blood red and black. Charlotte recalled Juliana's choice of hues for her fortune-telling parlor. Black and red were obviously the magician's colors.

She glanced at the bedside table. It held only a single candle. One of the ruffians who had abducted her had snatched her reticule after she had used it to give his companion a sharp blow to the skull. She did not know what had become of it or the small pistol inside.

She eyed the taper that stood in a black iron stand and wondered how long it would take for the dainty flame to burn through the thick rope that bound her. It was the sort of scientific question that Baxter could no doubt have answered immediately.

The door opened.

Charlotte turned her head quickly, hoping against hope that Baxter would magically appear. From the snippets of conversation that she had overheard during the wild carriage ride to this strange mansion, she had concluded that he had also been kidnapped.

Her stomach clenched when she saw the man in the doorway.

He was not wearing a black domino, nor were his features concealed by the shadows that had masked him the first time she had seen him five years ago. But the searing cold that seemed to emanate from him was unmistakable. She wondered that she had not recognized it instantly the night of the masquerade ball.

She was face-to-face with the monster in the hall.

She saw at once that his true nature was hidden behind a face of extraordinary masculine beauty. Black hair curled over a broad forehead. A fine, straight nose and arrogant cheekbones lent an air of aristocratic breeding. He was dressed in the first stare of fashion. His snow-white cravat was intricately tied. His coat, trousers, and boots were expensively tailored and fitted his tall, lean form to perfection. He wore the garments with an elegant ease, as if he had been born for such style.

He was well camouflaged, Charlotte thought. One had to look closely to see the icy, reptilian intelligence that glittered in his dark eyes.

She sat very still on the crimson quilt and took a steadying breath. Her pulse pounded in her veins. Panic would resolve nothing, she thought. One had to confront evil or all was lost.

She raised her chin a fraction higher and straightened her shoulders. "Morgan Judd, I presume?"

"So we are properly introduced at last, my little avenging angel." The shattered-glass voice conveyed icy amusement with remarkable clarity. Morgan inclined his head in a gesture of mocking grace. "I have looked forward to this meeting for some time."

"Where is Baxter?"

"My staff will signal me when St. Ives awakens." Morgan produced a pistol from the pocket of his pleated trousers. He held it rather carelessly in one hand as he walked across the crimson and black carpet to the brandy table. "I fear he got a rather heavy dose of the incense. My men are not skilled in its use."

"Dear God." Another layer of fear unfolded inside Charlotte. What if Baxter never awakened? She could not forget how near Juliana had come to death.

A small frown marred Morgan's brow. "I really must experiment a bit more with the mixture. It is still much too unpredictable."

She would not think about all the terrible possibilities, Charlotte told herself. She would concentrate on the matter at hand. Baxter would be all right. He had to be all right.

She schooled her voice to a tone that dripped with scorn. "I hardly think you need to brandish your pistol, Mr. Judd." She indicated her tethered wrists. "Or do you gain some sort of pleasure from waving it about?"

"Forgive me, Miss Arkendale." Morgan poured a measure of brandy and turned to her with a faint smile. "It is not because of you that I prefer to keep my pistol at the ready."

Comprehension dawned. "You fear St. Ives so much, then?"

A flicker of annoyance lit the reptilian eyes. "I do not fear him, but I have learned the hard way to take precautions. He is a deceptive man. Much more dangerous than he appears."

"I quite agree." Charlotte fixed him with what she hoped was a commanding stare. "Why have you brought us here?"

Morgan sipped his brandy. "I would have thought it obvious to a woman of your admirable intellect. I am weaving a destiny for myself, and for some inexplicable reason, you and St. Ives are apparently fated to appear in the pattern. I tried to work you both out of the design, but when that failed, I concluded I must reweave that portion."

There was a movement in the doorway.

"Still working on your grand destiny, Judd?" Baxter asked dryly.

Morgan smiled slowly. "St. Ives."

"*Baxter*." Charlotte's heart leaped at the sight of him.

He was there, looking just as he had when he left the ballroom several hours earlier. Just as Baxter was supposed to look, she thought. A little out of fashion, slightly rumpled, and much too staid for a man of thirty-two. But the disguise he had adopted was no more effective than Morgan Judd's. She could see the true nature of both men quite clearly.

Baxter walked into the chamber with a pistol in his hand. His greatcoat was draped over one arm as if he had just returned from a ride in the park. But the firelight glinted on the lenses of his spectacles and his eyes burned with ruthless promise.

Morgan aimed his pistol at Charlotte as he set down his brandy glass. "My staff has failed me, I see. Really, it is so bloody difficult to get reliable help. I was supposed to receive a signal when you awakened, St. Ives."

"Don't blame your staff," Baxter said. "I cut the bell pull on my way here. In fact, I located the closet where all of the signal bell pulls connect and severed the lot. None of your people will hear a thing if you try to use the mechanism. An ingenious design, by the bye. But quite useless now. Amazing how one small weakness can destroy the most clever scheme."

Morgan's jaw hardened but he merely

shrugged. "Do not be so certain of yourself, St. Ives. I survived Italy and I shall triumph tonight." He motioned slightly with his hand. "Put the pistol down, or I will blow your lady's brains across the wall. We both know the damn thing won't do you any good from that distance. You were never a decent shot."

"Quite true." Baxter set his pistol on a nearby table. Then he looked at Charlotte. "Are you all right, my dear?"

His voice was as calm and emotionless as ever but his eyes blazed hotter than the flames of the pit. Charlotte had to swallow twice before she could answer.

"Yes," she whispered. "I'm unhurt. What about you, Baxter?"

"Perfectly fit, as you see." He turned his attention back to Morgan. "What the devil is this all about?"

Morgan sighed. "Your interference in my affairs was a nuisance at first but then I began to view it as a most intriguing challenge. One can hardly ignore the workings of one's own destiny, after all."

"Indeed." Carrying his coat over his arm, Baxter walked slowly across the carpet to the nearest window. He stood gazing out into the night with a thoughtful expression. "Interesting subject, destiny. The ancient philosophers believed that one's character is the key to one's fate."

"Indeed," Morgan murmured. "I am in complete agreement."

Charlotte watched him with tense antici-

401

pation. Although he kept the pistol aimed in her general direction, his attention was entirely upon Baxter.

Baxter turned his head at that moment and glanced at her over his shoulder. His face was unreadable but there was an intensity in his gaze that riveted her. He was trying to convey some message. She sensed that he wished her to do something.

But what could he expect from her? she wondered. There was little she could do in her present circumstances.

Except talk.

Of course. If Baxter had a plan, and she was certain he would not have entered this chamber without one, then he no doubt wished her to distract Morgan Judd while he implemented his scheme.

"Why have you gone to the trouble to bring us here tonight, Mr. Judd?" she demanded in her sharpest tones.

Morgan looked briefly at her. "It is not often that one has the opportunity to engage in conversation with people who can appreciate one's abilities."

"Rubbish. Surely you are not so vain that you felt you must drag us here merely to boast."

"You misjudge him, my dear," Baxter said. "Morgan's vanity knows no bounds. But that is not why he kidnapped us, is it, Morgan?"

"As pleasant as it is to be among those who have the intellect to grasp the greatness of my plans," Morgan said, "I must confess, there was another reason why I went to the trouble of bringing you here tonight."

"We got too close, too quickly, did we not?" Baxter's smile was fleeting. "You want to know how we managed the trick."

"Very succinctly put, St. Ives. I thought that getting rid of the Heskett woman would most likely be the end of it. But as one can never be positive about such things, I set someone to watch her house. I knew from my man's description that it was you who searched the premises that night. And when I learned that you had become intimately involved with Miss Arkendale, I realized that she must have been the woman who accompanied you."

Baxter nodded. "Your man told you that we had taken something from Drusilla Heskett's house."

"A book of some sort, he said. He told me that the lady was the one who had carried it away and that she appeared to be very much in command of the situation." Morgan made a rasping sound that was no doubt meant to be a laugh. "I could not believe he had got it right but I decided to search her house in any case."

"You took the sketchbook," Charlotte accused.

"When I saw that there was nothing incriminating in it, I again dared to hope that that would be the end of things." Morgan shook his head. "But the two of you continued your alliance."

"Which you tried to destroy first by sending Juliana Post to Charlotte with a pack of lies and then by giving her the note warning her that I could not be trusted."

Morgan shrugged. "Obviously neither attempt shook her trust in you. I must congratulate you, St. Ives. I would never have guessed that you could summon up the degree of charm that it requires to induce such touching loyalty in a woman. Who would have thought you the romantic sort?"

Baxter ignored him. "Why in God's name did you find it necessary to murder Drusilla Heskett?"

"I'm afraid that Mrs. Heskett was quite indiscriminate in her choice of paramours. She formed a very short liaison with a man in whom I had been obliged to place a certain amount of trust. I do try to avoid telling anyone my most closely kept secrets, but sometimes it cannot be helped. One cannot do everything for oneself, after all. One needs one's man-of-affairs."

Charlotte was astonished. "Mrs. Heskett had a liaison with your man-of-affairs?"

"From all accounts, she tended to be quite democratic in such matters. In any event, my man apparently got drunk one evening and showed her one of my medallions. He told her that he knew a great deal about me and that he was biding his time. When I had acquired the power and wealth I sought, he intended to blackmail me. I believe he went so far as to assure her that he was an excellent candidate for marriage because his future expectations were very favorable."

"Mr. Charles Dill," Charlotte whispered. "He was one of her suitors."

"Indeed."

"I did not recommend him," Charlotte said. "My own man-of-affairs said that Mr. Dill was inclined toward unscrupulous dealings."

"He was correct," Morgan said dryly. "But, then, I require that in a man-of-affairs."

"How did you learn that Mr. Dill had confided in Mrs. Heskett?" Charlotte asked.

Morgan arched one black brow. "I make it a habit to periodically place those who are closest to me into a trance. I question them regarding their loyalty. They recall nothing of the interrogation afterward, of course."

"When you discovered that Mr. Dill intended to betray you and had said something of his plans to Mrs. Heskett, you decided to murder both of them," Baxter said from the windows.

"It was the only logical course of action," Morgan explained. "Getting rid of Dill was a simple matter. I added more potent incense to the brazier after I had finished questioning him. He never came out of the trance. When his body was discovered two days later, it was assumed he'd had a heart seizure."

"Then you set out to murder Mrs. Heskett," Charlotte said. "You made two attempts on her life and when those failed, you went to her house and shot her in cold blood."

"It's not always convenient to use the incense and the mesmerism," Morgan said. "And I do feel it's prudent to change one's methods from time to time. Predictability is not a virtue."

Charlotte narrowed her eyes. "I doubt that you need to worry overmuch about being burdened with too many virtues."

"I do so enjoy that sharp tongue." Morgan looked at Baxter. "What did you discover in Mrs. Heskett's sketchbook?"

"Why should he answer?" Charlotte shifted position on the bed, curious to see if she could draw Morgan's attention with movement. "You will murder us as soon as you have learned what you wish to know."

"I shall indeed have to kill St. Ives," Morgan agreed. "He is aware that I cannot possibly allow him to live. Now that he knows I am alive and on the brink of fulfilling my destiny, he would not rest until he had destroyed my plans. St. Ives is nothing if not tenacious."

"You can hardly expect him to tell you what you want to know, then," Charlotte said in a loud voice.

Morgan did not look at her. His attention remained focused on Baxter. "He will tell me because I am willing to bargain with him for your life, my dear."

Charlotte went cold. "Do not expect me to believe that. I am as much of a threat to your schemes as Baxter is. I know the same things he does. And I, too, will not rest until you have been brought down."

Morgan spared her a dismissive glance. "You are merely a woman and not a particularly charming one at that. But you do have a few marketable qualities with which to attract a man in my position. Your bloodlines are quite respectable. Not excellent, mind you, but good enough for my purposes."

"My bloodlines." Charlotte was stunned.

"Even more important, you have demonstrated superior intellect for a woman and a degree of boldness and courage that I wish to breed into my own offspring."

"Good God, sir, are you mad?" Charlotte whispered.

"As my wife, you will be in no position to testify against me." Morgan gave her a thin, cruel smile. "And every position to supply me with an heir."

"Your *wife*. Impossible." She got to her knees on the bed and regarded Morgan with scathing fury. "There is nothing on this earth that could induce me to marry you, sir."

"Ah, but there is." Morgan's cold eyes met hers for a brief, terrifying moment. "Mesmerism."

"Your techniques would never work with me."

"Do not be so certain of that. I perfect them daily. The right dose of incense together with the proper application of my scientific method of inducing a trance will turn you into the perfect wife, my sweet."

Charlotte's mouth was suddenly very dry. "I do not believe that any amount of incense or mesmerism can overcome my hatred of you. But even if it's true, the effects would only be temporary. Sooner or later I will come out of the trance and when I do, I shall find a way to kill you."

"That prospect should lend a certain fillip to our married life, eh?" Morgan gave a short croak of laughter. "Perhaps it will stave off the inevitable boredom that comes with a too-willing woman."

"Even if it were possible, and I assure you it is not, why would you wish to marry a woman who despises you so completely?"

Morgan's smile should have been a thing of beauty, but it turned Charlotte's blood to ice.

But it was Baxter who answered. His voice was soft, utterly devoid of emotion. The voice of the detached scientist making an observation. "Because you have belonged to me, of course."

Charlotte could scarcely breathe. She stared at Baxter's broad shoulders and could not find a single word to say.

"Precisely," Morgan said with husky satisfaction. "Every time I spread your thighs, Charlotte, I shall revel in my victory over the only man who ever came close to being my equal."

"You truly are quite mad," she whispered.

Anger flashed in Morgan's eyes. He looked at Charlotte with contempt. "Come now, my love, you owe me a great deal. You are an honest woman. I should think you would want to repay me."

"What do you mean?"

"It was I who arranged for your stepfather

to end up floating in the Thames the morning after you and I met. I altered your destiny that night. What would you have done if I had not got rid of Winterbourne for you?"

"You certainly did not murder him for my sake," she flung back. "You must have done it because he could not pay the gaming debt he owed to you."

Morgan raised one shoulder in another graceful shrug. "I admit you have me there. You're right, I did not do it for your sake."

Baxter turned casually away from the window and walked toward the brandy table. "Tell me, how did you manage to escape the castle that night in Italy?"

Morgan's head snapped around very quickly. "That is far enough, St. Ives. Not another step."

Baxter halted. "Very well. But be so good as to satisfy my curiosity."

"There was a hidden tunnel that led out of the laboratory." Morgan's mouth twisted. "I managed to get into it in time to escape the flames but I could not outrun the gases that were formed when the chemicals caught fire. I nearly choked to death on those foul vapors."

"Your voice was ruined by those gases, was it not?"

Fury, a dark shadow cast by a thunderous cloud, passed over Morgan's face. "You did this to me," he rasped. "And tonight you will finally pay for it."

"How dare you?" Charlotte shouted. "You tried to murder Baxter that night."

"Silence." Morgan flicked her another annoyed glance before he turned back to Baxter. "I think we've had quite enough reminiscing for the moment."

"I agree," Baxter said.

"Tell me what you found in Drusilla Heskett's watercolor sketchbook that pointed in my direction," Morgan said. "Tell me now, St. Ives, or I will kill your mouthy Charlotte."

"We found a very interesting sketch."

"Baxter, no," Charlotte said. "Do not tell him anything. He will kill you."

"Shut your mouth, Miss Arkendale," Morgan snarled, "or I shall do it for you."

Charlotte promptly opened her mouth again to tell him what she thought of him but she never got the chance.

With a sudden, terrifying rush of unseen wind and a sharp crack of sound, the heavy drapes at the window where Baxter had been standing a moment earlier, erupted into flames.

Morgan froze for an instant. Pure terror etched his handsome face. "No," he whispered. "No, god damn you, *no*."

"Bring back a few memories?" Baxter asked evenly. "Certainly does for me."

Morgan shuddered and then made an obvious effort to collect himself. He aimed the pistol at Baxter with shaking hands. "I'm going to kill you now. I shall get the information I need from your woman. And I will take great pleasure in doing so. Think of me between her legs as you die."

Charlotte saw Morgan's fist tighten around the pistol.

She opened her mouth and gave a blood-curdling scream.

Morgan flinched at the earsplitting sound.

Then, with a roar, the small fire on the hearth suddenly exploded into a great blaze. The tongues of flame shot past the fire screen, the talons of a great beast seeking prey.

"No." Morgan took a faltering step back and came up against the edge of the large bed.

Flanked by pillars of fire, Baxter walked slowly and deliberately toward Morgan. "There is no time," he said. "You must flee." The flames soared behind him as he went steadily toward Morgan.

Charlotte knew that he was counting upon Morgan's fear to supersede his deadly intent but she did not trust that factor. Another distraction was needed.

Crouched on her knees, she reached up and seized the silk fringe of the scarlet bed drapes. She pulled downward with all of her might.

The heavy hangings fell, an avalanche of crimson fabric. Some of it landed across Morgan's head and shoulders.

The rest of it crashed down on Charlotte. She was buried in a mass of dusty red velvet.

Morgan's shout of rage echoed on the stone walls. The roar of his pistol exploded across the chamber.

"*Baxter.*" Charlotte surfaced from the tumbled red drapes, choking from the dust and the smoke that filled the room.

The flames were spreading swiftly. Against the fiery backdrop, Baxter and Morgan were locked in a violent embrace. They fell to the carpet and rolled wildly. Firelight glinted on steel as they struggled for possession of the other pistol, the one Baxter had brought with him into the room.

Another shot reverberated off the walls.

For a timeless instant, neither man moved.

"*Baxter*. Oh, my God." Frantic, Charlotte scrambled to the edge of the bed. The rope brought her up short. "*Baxter*."

Morgan stared at Baxter with wide, stunned eyes. Blood soaked the snow-white front of his pleated shirt. "No. It cannot end in this way. I must fulfill my destiny."

Baxter started to get to his feet. Morgan clutched at his arm.

"I am fated to triumph over the golden griffin," Morgan whispered in his shattered voice. "Something has gone wrong." He broke off, coughing. "All wrong. I am a magician." Blood welled in his mouth.

He started to say something else but the words were drowned in the crimson tide. His hand slid away from Baxter's arm. He fell back on the carpet and lay still.

Baxter surged to his feet and turned toward Charlotte. She saw that he had lost his spectacles in the struggle.

"We've got to get out of here." He moved toward her.

"I cannot untie these ropes." For the first time Charlotte felt real fear of the fire. It occurred to her that she might not escape the dreadful chamber. Panic struck with dizzying force. "I have a knife in my reticule but I don't know where it is. They took it away from me. Dear God, Baxter." She stared at him, unable to speak her terror.

"My greatcoat. I dropped it." Baxter glanced around. "Quick. Where is it?"

"On the floor behind you. Not more than three paces. Straight back."

He turned and followed her instructions. "Ah, yes. You give excellent directions, my dear." He rummaged in his pockets and withdrew a blade.

He hurried back to the bed. "I retrieved this from the man who took it away from me earlier."

Working by touch, he fumbled briefly with the rope, got a grip on it, stretched it taut, and slashed downward with the knife.

She was free. Charlotte nearly collapsed with relief.

"Come. There is no time to lose." He seized her hand and yanked her off the bed. "You will have to lead the way, Charlotte. Everything in the distance is unfocused and indistinct for me."

"Yes, of course." She nearly tripped over Morgan's still form as she headed toward the door. She looked down and saw that a great quantity of blood stained the front of his shirt and coat. "What if he escapes again?"

"He won't escape this time," Baxter said in an emotionless voice. "He's dead."

"But how can you be sure?" she demanded as they raced toward the doorway.

"Even I cannot miss at such close range."

Charlotte was almost to the door when she caught the glint of gold out of the corner of her eye. "Your spectacles." She scooped them up and put them in his hand. "One of the lenses is broken but the other appears to be whole."

"Thank you, my dear." Baxter held the good lens to his eye. "It will do nicely."

They ran through the door and down the corridor toward the massive stone staircase. Smoke snaked after them.

The black and crimson room exploded into an inferno.

Baxter estimated that nearly a third of the top floor of the mansion was ablaze by the time he and Charlotte reached the main hall.

He heard shouts in the distance. Panicked servants and assorted ruffians fleeing the fire, he concluded. The confusion was a godsend. It would make escape much simpler. But there was still a risk that one of the villains, unaware that his master was dead, might attempt to halt them.

"Do you see anyone about?" He held the unbroken lens to his eye and searched for signs of movement in the shadows.

"No." Charlotte was panting but she did not slow her pace. "I think everyone is too busy attempting to escape."

"Excellent." He felt the chill wind blowing down the length of the hall and saw darkness at the far end. "The door is open."

"It would appear that most of the staff has already fled to safety. We passed no one on the staircase, so I think it's safe to assume that none of the servants feels inclined to rescue the master of the house."

"As Morgan observed, it's very difficult to get dependable staff these days."

They reached the front door and stepped out onto the steps.

"There's no one around." Charlotte peered into the shadows. "Which way shall we go? I have no idea where we are."

"Neither do I, but the flames are certain to draw someone's attention soon. There must be farmers and tenants in the district. Let's make for the road." He took Charlotte's hand and started down the steps.

"Baxter."

The alarm in her voice brought him up short. He whirled, the small penknife in his hand.

A dark figure loomed in the doorway.

"Here now, where d'ye think you're goin'?"

The man raised his hand. Even without the aid of his single eyeglass, Baxter had no difficulty recognizing the shape of a pistol.

"Good heavens," Charlotte said. "You're the villain who tried to stop us outside Mrs. Heskett's house."

"Aye, and there'll be none of yer tricks this time."

"We're of no use to you now," Baxter said.

"If the magician went to all that trouble to get hold of ye, I expect yer valuable. Reckon I'll take ye with me until I see what's what."

"Your master is dead in one of those chambers at the top of the house," Baxter said calmly. "There is no profit in this night's work. Be off with you before the mansion burns down around your ears."

"Must be some money in it somewhere," the villain whined.

Baxter sighed. "If it's merely money you're after, we may be able to come to an agreement."

The villain brightened. "A bargain, sir."

Before Baxter could offer him a sum of money to seal the deal, a pistol cracked in the darkness behind him.

With a cry of surprise and pain, the villain clutched at his shoulder and reeled back into the hall.

"Baxter. Miss Charlotte." Hamilton's voice rang through the night. "Are you all right?"

Baxter turned and raised his broken spectacles to his eye. Hamilton and Ariel rushed toward them from the shelter of a small grove of trees.

Hamilton held a pistol in each hand. His cravat fluttered around his throat in an extremely rakish manner. His boots gleamed. His curls were ruffled from the night breeze. There was an air of exuberant excitement about him that was unmistakable. Baxter had seen that same look in his father.

"Charlotte." Ariel flew to her. "Oh, thank God, I've been so frightened. Hamilton arrived just after those terrible men overpowered the Runners and kidnapped you. We managed to follow you in his new carriage. It is amazingly swift, you know."

"How clever of you." Charlotte wrapped her arms very tightly around Ariel. "Clever and brave."

Hamilton shoved his pistols into his belt. "Sorry to be so late in arriving, brother. Lost the trail a few miles back. Took forever to locate a farmer who remembered hearing a carriage go past his house. He told us about this place and said no one was allowed near it except the servants. Very mysterious, he said. Figured it had to be the magician's haunt."

"Brilliant deduction." Baxter grinned at the dashing image his brother presented. "I do believe that what they say about the earls of Esherton is true."

Some of Hamilton's excitement faded. "What's that?"

"They do everything with style."

Hamilton blinked in surprise and then he burst into laughter. "It's in the blood, brother. All of the St. Ives men have style. It just took me a while to notice yours. Quite unique."

Charlotte raised her head from Ariel's shoulder. She fixed Baxter with a brilliant, blinding smile that he could see quite clearly even without his broken eyeglasses.

"His style is one of the many things that I have always admired in him," she said.

Twenty

Two days later Hamilton lounged against one of the long workbenches in the laboratory. He watched with interest as Baxter busied himself arranging and rearranging the chemicals and apparatus that littered every surface.

"How did you cause the curtains to go up in flames and how did you create the explosion in the fireplace?" Hamilton asked.

"I told you I had a box of my new instantaneous lights with me." Baxter carefully polished a small Wedgwood crucible. "Charlotte distracted Judd long enough for me to break a couple of them in the folds of the curtains. I threw another one into the fire."

"Very clever. So Morgan Judd murdered his man-of-affairs and Drusilla Heskett and assumed that would be the end of it," Hamilton said.

"He had not counted on the fact that Mrs. Heskett had told someone that she feared one of her rejected suitors was trying to murder her." Baxter concentrated on arranging two rows of green glass bottles containing alkaline and metallic salts. "Nor had he made allowances for the possibility that Aunt Rosalind would insist upon investigating the death of her friend. Morgan had a great disdain for the female sex. He always did tend to underestimate them."

"And in the end he was done in by the ladies." Hamilton grinned. "Served him right."

"Indeed."

"Why do you suppose Mrs. Heskett made the little drawing of Judd's emblem?"

Baxter shrugged. "We can only speculate. Charlotte believes that it was Judd's man-of-affairs who actually drew the design in Mrs. Heskett's sketchbook. He may have been trying to explain the principles behind Judd's mesmerism techniques."

Hamilton nodded. "So he drew a picture to help with the task?"

"Perhaps. We'll never know for certain."

"You know, Baxter, it's the oddest thing, but I realize now that I often promised myself I would look inside the wardrobe in our meeting chamber at The Green Table. I knew the magician had to have a secret entrance but somehow I never got around to investigating."

"I suspect he made certain that none of the club members were inclined to look too closely into his affairs."

Hamilton's mouth thinned. "You mean he used his mesmerism tricks on us to convince us not to explore the chamber?"

"It seems likely." Baxter set down a glass bottle.

He was weary of answering questions. He had retreated to his laboratory in order to devote himself to the task of setting it to rights. Tidying up this chamber was something he did whenever he wished to ponder a subject. He found it soothing to clean retorts, polish instruments, and inventory his collection of flasks and jars while he did his thinking.

Unfortunately, his plans for extended contemplation had gone awry when Hamilton had bounded into the house twenty minutes earlier, eager to discuss the events of the past several days.

"Hard to believe that Drusilla Heskett was having an affair with a man-of-affairs," Hamilton said. "Baxter, do you think that most of the ladies of the ton are engaged in illicit liaisons with everyone from the footman to their husband's best friend?"

"I expect the number of women involved in such affairs is no greater than the number of gentlemen who are engaged in similar liaisons with the children's governess or their best friend's wife."

Hamilton winced. "Not a pleasant thought." His expression grew abruptly serious. "I don't think that I would like to find myself wed to a lady who took paramours."

"That is definitely something we have in common." Baxter examined a cracked flask. "I wonder if my glassmaker can mend this."

"Miss Ariel would never betray her wedding vows," Hamilton said softly. "She is a virtuous, extremely noble-minded lady."

Baxter raised one brow. "If you're thinking of making an offer of marriage in that direction, I had better give you a warning."

Hamilton held up one hand. "No lectures, please. I am well aware that I will not come into my inheritance for a few more years. But I would like to remind you that there is nothing in Father's will that says I cannot marry in the meantime."

"Father's will is not the problem. I don't give a damn whether or not you choose to wed. As it happens, I believe Miss Ariel would make you an excellent countess."

Hamilton brightened. "Do you?"

"Indeed. But I had better tell you that if you expect to offer for her, you must be prepared to have your reputation and personal affairs thoroughly investigated by Charlotte. I can promise you that she won't allow her sister to marry a man who has the inclinations of a rake."

Hamilton smiled slightly. "In other words, our dear, departed father is not a good recommendation for me?"

"No, he is not."

Hamilton exhaled heavily. "Then perhaps it's just as well that I don't take after him in every particular. Between you and me, I have no interest in pursuing little opera dancers or hanging about in brothels. I want a marriage of true love and affection."

Baxter peered at him. "Good lord. You're serious about this, aren't you?"

"About making an offer to Miss Ariel? Yes. I have never met a more charming, more intelligent woman. Nor one so brave. Do you know, Baxter, she absolutely insisted upon accompanying me the other night when we chased after Miss Charlotte and her kidnappers. Nothing I said could induce her to stay behind. She even made me instruct her in the use of a pistol on the way, just in case. She is a lady of great spirit."

"Runs in the family, apparently," Baxter muttered.

Footsteps sounded in the hall. Rosalind, dressed in a pale pink gown, a raspberry-colored pelisse, and a massive pink satin hat, appeared in the doorway. "There you are, Baxter. I've been looking for you."

Hamilton straightened. "Lady Trengloss."

"Hamilton." She turned back to Baxter. "Why have you not answered my messages? I sent at least two yesterday and another one this morning."

Baxter wondered if he would ever get his laboratory to himself. "Good day, Aunt. Lambert did not tell me that you had come to call."

"Your butler barely managed to open the door a moment ago," she retorted. "I lacked the patience to wait for him to shuffle the length of the hall to announce me. Really, Baxter, you must pension Lambert off one of these days. How on earth can you run this household with him?"

"He is the only member of the staff who has stayed longer than two months. If I got rid of him, I would have no one at all to run the bloody household." Baxter dropped the cracked flask into a bin. "Was there something you wanted?"

She shot Hamilton an impatient glance and then gave Baxter a considering look. "I came to thank you for solving the mystery of my dear friend's murder."

"You did that the morning after the events." Baxter picked up a feather duster and began wielding it over the jars of chemicals. "I'm rather busy at the moment, so if there's nothing else—"

"Very well, that is not the only reason I came to see you." Rosalind narrowed her gaze. "I have some family business I wish to discuss."

"Hamilton is family," Baxter said.

Hamilton glanced at him with surprise and then smiled. "Indeed."

"As you wish." Rosalind glared at Baxter. "I shall come straight out with it. Do you still intend to end your engagement to Miss Arkendale now that the Heskett business is finished?"

The feather duster froze in midair. Baxter turned slowly to confront his aunt. "That is a personal matter that concerns only Miss Arkendale and myself."

Something in his voice clearly took her aback. Rosalind blinked. Her mouth worked once or twice and then she sputtered in an uncharacteristic fashion. "Well. Well. I only meant to say that"

"He's afraid to ask her for her hand," Hamilton explained in a confidential tone. "He thinks she'll turn him down flat."

"Do shut up, Hamilton," Baxter said through his teeth.

Hamilton grinned, unabashed.

"Why on earth would she turn him down?" Rosalind demanded. "She's five-and-twenty. A spinster with no fortune to recommend her. She must realize that under the circumstances she's highly unlikely to do any better than Baxter."

"Thank you, Aunt Rosalind," Baxter muttered. "Always nice to have one's relatives offer such strong support."

"She appears to be quite fond of Baxter," Hamilton said. "The problem is that she's not at all keen on marriage. Ariel told me that her sister believes marriage to be a terrible risk for a woman."

"What rubbish. We're talking about marriage to Baxter." Rosalind gave an unladylike snort. "Hardly a risk. I vow, I do not know of a more mild-mannered, placid, sober-minded, even-tempered man in all of London."

"I quite agree." Hamilton's eyes glinted with unholy glee. "One would have to say that our Baxter is the most unflappable, the most steady, the most reliable, the most dependable of men."

All the qualities of a good spaniel, Baxter thought. He returned to his dusting with a savage vengeance.

"What's this about steadiness and dependability?" Maryann demanded from the doorway. "What on earth are you talking about, Hamilton?"

Baxter groaned. "Bloody hell." If he were the sort who actually believed in destiny, he thought, he would have been tempted to think that he was the victim of a very malign fate today. Was he never to have any peace in his own laboratory?

"Hello, Mother," Hamilton said. "What are you doing here?"

"I came to call on Baxter."

Rosalind nodded toward Maryann with a minimum of civility. "Lady Esherton."

Maryann's expression congealed. "Lady Trengloss. I did not realize you were here." She turned her back on Rosalind and looked at her son. "I trust you were supplying Baxter with a list of the characteristics that are most desirable in a good servant. He certainly requires a new butler. The one who opened the door for me just now did not even bother to announce me. Merely waved me down the hall to this door."

"Actually, we were describing Baxter's many outstanding qualities," Hamilton said. "We have concluded that he has every characteristic required to recommend him to Miss Arkendale."

"Indeed," Maryann said vaguely. "I'm sure they will do very well together. Baxter, I wished to speak with you in private."

"I'm not giving private interviews today, Maryann." Baxter tightened his grip on the feather duster. "As you can see, I'm occupied with other matters at the moment."

Maryann frowned. "Whatever are you doing with that duster? Don't you have any maids about the house?"

"No, but it does not signify. I never allow anyone to set my laboratory to rights except myself. Maids have a way of dropping bottles of chemicals and breaking instruments." He planted his hands on his hips. "I would like to request that all of you take your leave."

Maryann bridled. "Really, there's no need to be rude, Baxter."

"Rudeness is part of his unique style," Hamilton murmured.

Maryann ignored him. She drew herself up with great dignity. "I came to express my appreciation for your actions on Hamilton's behalf."

Hamilton rolled his eyes toward the ceiling.

"There is no need to thank me," Baxter said gruffly. "Hamilton helped save himself and everyone else. He proved to be very cool in a crisis and if I am ever again in such unpleasant circumstances, I cannot think of any other man I would sooner have at my back."

Hamilton flushed a dark red. His eyes lit with an awkward gratitude. "Any time, Baxter."

"Having said that"—Baxter raised his duster as though it were a magic wand he could use to rid the laboratory of unwanted guests—"will you all please consider me thanked and take yourselves off? I have things to do here."

Before anyone could respond, a swirl of bright yellow muslin caught Baxter's eye. He turned to see Charlotte in the doorway. Ariel stood behind her.

"Miss Ariel," Hamilton exclaimed. "And

Miss Charlotte." He inclined his head in a graceful greeting and then went forward to take the women's hands. "Allow me to tell you that you are both in fine looks today."

Baxter watched Hamilton bend gallantly over each gloved hand. He should do the same, he told himself. There were, indeed, a few things he could learn from his younger half brother. But for some reason he seemed to be rooted to the floor at the moment.

He felt his very soul expand at the sight of Charlotte. She looked so breathtakingly vivid. The laboratory grew sunnier with the addition of her presence. No, not just the laboratory, he thought. His whole bloody life had brightened because of her. A future without her would be bleak beyond description.

She was his Philosopher's Stone. God help him if he lost her.

"Charlotte," he said softly. Hamilton slanted him a speaking glance. Baxter cleared his throat. "Miss Ariel. Good day to you, ladies."

"Good day to you." Charlotte smiled at everyone but her eyes went first to Baxter. "I see we have a crowd."

"They are all just about to take their leave," Baxter assured her brusquely. "I did not realize that you had arrived, Charlotte. Where the devil is Lambert? I shall have him bring in some tea or something."

"He appears to have stationed himself at the front door on a somewhat permanent basis," Charlotte said.

Ariel laughed. "He claimed that what with

all the comings and goings this morning, he could not possibly be expected to get anything else accomplished."

Hamilton grinned. "We are all attempting to thank Baxter but he insists upon showing us the door."

"I've got things to do," Baxter growled.

They all ignored him.

"Such an incredible chain of events," Ariel said. "Who could have imagined how it would end?"

"Indeed." Hamilton chuckled. "The magician must have been stunned when he realized that his machinations had drawn his old nemesis, Baxter, into his sphere."

"I'm not so sure about that." Charlotte hoisted her large reticule onto a workbench. "I rather think he viewed Baxter's part in the affair as yet another manifestation of his so-called destiny."

Hamilton raised his brows. "Perhaps it was."

Ariel looked intrigued by that notion. "Indeed. I have been thinking about something Charlotte mentioned the day she rescued Juliana Post. She said she noticed that the death card had fallen faceup on the floor. Miss Post claimed that she always gave the magician the fortune he wished to hear. But on that day, she unwittingly read him his true fate."

Rosalind's eyes widened. "I vow, it gives one shivers, does it not?"

Baxter scowled. "What bloody nonsense. Miss Post told us herself that she didn't draw that card. It must have got accidentally flipped over by the hem of her robes when he picked her up and carried her to the sofa."

Hamilton narrowed his eyes. "Perhaps it was not entirely an accident."

"It would seem a bit difficult to blame such an omen on mere coincidence," Rosalind agreed with relish.

"The entire affair positively reeks of a mysterious hand from the metaphysical realm," Ariel declared.

Maryann was clearly fascinated. "Quite odd, all of it."

"*Enough,*" Baxter roared. "The situation was no more than the result of a logical progression of events."

"What do you mean?" Ariel asked.

It was Charlotte who answered. "Baxter's right in one sense. There is a certain logical inevitability about events in the affair. After all, Morgan Judd must have realized that he was setting certain wheels in motion when he allowed Hamilton into The Green Table club."

Maryann frowned. "Why do you say that?"

Charlotte looked at her. "Judd must have known that when he involved Hamilton in his grand scheme, he was certain to attract Baxter's attention sooner or later. If you ask me, some part of his obsessive nature could not resist taking the risk. I suspect that, deep inside, he wanted Baxter to know that he had survived Italy. He wanted to gloat, to prove that he was the more clever of the Two

Alchemists. And he wanted to exact revenge."

"I see." Hamilton tipped his head slightly to the side as he considered that. "I can well comprehend that Judd may have wished to demonstrate his superiority. But why would he assume that Baxter would give a bloody damn about what happened to me?"

Charlotte smiled wryly. "Oh, I'm certain it never occurred to him that Baxter would try to extricate you from The Green Table club, let alone save your friend Norris. Judd assumed that Baxter had destroyed his own soul with resentment and anger just as he himself had done. But he knew that he could use you to get Baxter's attention and that was what he wanted."

"Even though Baxter was a possible threat to his plans?" Rosalind asked.

"He intended to kill Baxter after he had demonstrated his cleverness." Charlotte gave a small shrug. "Judd was his own worst enemy. His arrogance and bitterness and cruel nature created a devil's brew within him that was more virulent than any acid."

Rosalind grew thoughtful. "So, one way or another, Baxter would have wound up in the middle of the affair even had I not asked him to investigate Drusilla's death."

"Quite right," Charlotte said. "And I had no choice but to get involved because Mrs. Heskett had been a client. I had to determine if her death had, indeed, been at the hands of one of the suitors I had investigated." She grinned at Baxter. "The only part of this whole thing that could even remotely be termed a coincidence occurred at the very beginning when I suddenly found myself in need of a new man-of-affairs."

"And Baxter applied for the post," Rosalind concluded.

Baxter tossed aside his duster. "Even had she not been in the market for a man-of-affairs, I would have made contact with her one way or another. The trail from Mrs. Heskett's death led to her."

Hamilton waggled his brows and lowered his voice to a sepulchral tone. "Fate or a logical progression of events. Who can decide?"

"I can bloody well decide," Baxter said forcefully. "And I say there is not one event in this entire matter that cannot be accounted for by logic. And that is the end of the discussion. I want all of you out of this laboratory immediately. Begone."

"You heard him," Hamilton said cheerfully. "We are no longer wanted. Let us be off."

Baxter was briefly gratified. He watched the entire lot turn toward the door. Then he realized that Charlotte, too, was preparing to leave.

"Bloody hell, not you, Charlotte. I wish to have a word with you."

She paused to give him a polite, inquiring look.

Hamilton shook his head with an air of sad reproach as he shepherded everyone else through the door. "One of these days, Baxter, we really must have a chat about your lack of social polish."

Baxter felt his face turn unpleasantly warm. "On your way out, kindly instruct Lambert to bring a tray of tea to the laboratory," he said gruffly.

"And another discussion about your unfortunate problems with household staff," Hamilton added over his shoulder.

Baxter waited until he heard the front door open and close before he looked at Charlotte. She gave him a quizzical smile.

"What was it you wanted, Baxter?"

He cleared his throat. Then he removed his eyeglasses and began to polish them with his handkerchief. It was easier this way, he thought. He could not see her face quite so clearly now. Perhaps without the distraction of her wonderful eyes, he would be able to marshal his arguments in a coherent fashion.

He turned on his heel and began to pace. "You may recall that two nights ago we happened to be standing together on the front steps of Morgan Judd's mansion."

"I am hardly likely to forget the night in question."

"Yes, well, perhaps you do not recall precisely what you said that evening."

"I'm sure that I said a great many things. There was much to talk about, after all. We had both had a narrow escape."

Baxter concentrated on polishing his spectacles. "I refer to one particular sentence."

"I see. Which sentence was that?"

"You mentioned that one of the many things that you admired in me was my style."

There was a beat of silence.

"Yes," she said. "The innate style of the St. Ives men. Very impressive."

Baxter came to a halt in front of the window and put on his eyeglasses. "I wondered if, perhaps, there was anything else that you felt you could admire—" He broke off as he caught sight of the three pots on the sill. "Good God, Charlotte. The sweet peas."

"What about them?"

"They've sprouted." Euphoria rushed through him. He seized one of the small containers and turned to show her the tiny sprig of green. "Look. All three pots."

"That's wonderful." She smiled at him with warm, glowing eyes. "Congratulations."

He felt dazed. "Bloody hell. Maybe there are such things as omens and destiny. Charlotte, I may as well come straight out with it. I've fallen in love with you."

"Oh, Baxter."

"I must know if you think there's any chance that you could ever return my love?"

Her smile became glorious. Her green eyes held all the secrets of the Stone. "I think I fell in love with you the day we met."

He stared at her, afraid that he had not heard correctly. "You're certain?"

"I was so afraid that you did not love me."

He set down the sweet pea pot and caught her close. "I would have thought it bloody obvious."

"You said our liaison was inconvenient," she reminded him.

He frowned. "It is. Damnably inconvenient. Charlotte, I know that you have no great desire to wed. If you want to go on as we have been, I shall abide by your wishes. But I would far rather have you with me on a regular basis. I want to see your face when I sit down to breakfast every morning. I want to hold you in my arms when I fall asleep at night."

"Yes." She raised her head from his shoulder and lifted her hands to run her fingers through his hair.

"I want to be able to show you the results of my experiments," he continued. "I want to spend long, quiet evenings with you. I want to consult with you on your investigations. I thought I proved myself a very creditable man-of-affairs."

"You did, indeed."

"I am well aware that I am not the most romantical man in the world."

"You are wrong, sir. You are the most romantic man I have ever met."

He stared at her, transfixed. "I am?"

"Most definitely." She smiled again and stood on tiptoe to brush her mouth against his. "If you are trying to ask me to marry you, my answer is yes."

Epilogue

Midnight
London, one month later

It was her wedding night.

How very odd. She had never planned to have one.

Charlotte propped her elbows on the windowsill, rested her chin on her hands, and gazed out into the darkness. The day had been hectic, what with the wedding, the move into Baxter's house, and the general excitement that had pervaded all events. She should have been exhausted but she had never felt more intensely alive.

She turned away from the window when she heard the connecting door open. At the sight of Baxter, her spirits soared.

He was wearing a plain black dressing gown. The gold rims of his spectacles glinted in the candlelight. Behind the lenses, his eyes were brilliant with love and unveiled desire. He surveyed the room with deep satisfaction as he walked toward her.

"A warm chamber, a comfortable bed, and every amenity. I believe I told you that marriage would be considerably more convenient than an affair for a man of my nature," he said.

"I will admit that there is a great deal to be said for convenience." She smiled and put her arms around his neck. "Nevertheless, I trust I shall not discover that you married me simply to obtain the services of Mrs. Witty in your household."

He grinned and folded her close. "I confess that I always seem to be a bit pressed for staff, but I would not have gone so far as to marry merely to obtain a housekeeper, not even one as admirable as Mrs. Witty."

"I am relieved to hear that."

At the feel of his strong, solid body, a warm longing flowered in Charlotte. She leaned her head against his shoulder and savored the sensation of happiness that had descended upon her.

Some part of her had been searching for this man, she thought. He was her true soul mate. This sense of an indefinable connection to him had been there from the very start of this affair. Destiny? She would never know. And in the end, it did not matter. She and Baxter had found each other.

"Do you know," Baxter whispered against her throat, "I have come to believe that the science of chemistry may not be able to explain everything in the world, after all."

"Perhaps some mysteries are not meant to be revealed by the powers of science."

"That may be true." He swept her up into his arms and carried her toward the shadowed bed.

"I knew from the very start that you were

a man of strong passions and dangerous inclinations, sir."

He settled her against the pillows and leaned over her, his hands braced on the white sheets. His eyes were the color of molten gold in a hot crucible.

"What an odd coincidence," he said very softly. "I gave myself much the same warning about you. A lady of strong passions and dangerous inclinations, I said. Not at all my sort."

Charlotte reached up to pull him to her. "Obviously we were meant for each other."

"Obviously." Baxter took her into his arms.

His kiss held the secret of the enduring fire that created the alchemy of love.

If you have enjoyed reading this large print book and you would like more information on how to order a Wheeler Large Print Book, please write to:

 Wheeler Publishing, Inc.
P.O. Box 531
Accord, MA 02018-0531